THE
HALLOW
HUNT

Also by

MARGIE FUSTON

Vampires, Hearts & Other Dead Things
Cruel Illusions
The Revenant Games

THE
HALLOW
HUNT

MARGIE FUSTON

SIMON & SCHUSTER

London New York Amsterdam/Antwerp Sydney/Melbourne Toronto New Delhi

First published in Great Britain in 2025 by Simon & Schuster UK Ltd

First published in the USA in 2025 by Margaret K. McElderry Books,
an imprint of Simon & Schuster Children's Publishing Division,
1230 Avenue of the Americas, New York, New York 10020

1 3 5 7 9 10 8 6 4 2

Simon & Schuster UK Ltd
1st Floor, 222 Gray's Inn Road
London WC1X 8HB

www.simonandschuster.co.uk
www.simonandschuster.com.au
www.simonandschuster.co.in

The authorised representative in the EEA is Simon & Schuster Netherlands BV,
Herculesplein 96, 3584 AA Utrecht, Netherlands. info@simonandschuster.nl

A CIP catalogue record for this book is available from the British Library.

PB ISBN 978-1-3985-3467-4
eBook ISBN 978-1-3985-3468-1
eAudio ISBN 978-1-3985-3469-8

Printed and Bound in the UK using
100% Renewable Electricity at CPI Group (UK) Ltd

MIX
Paper from
responsible sources
FSC® C171272
FSC
www.fsc.org

For the ones who sacrifice everything for those they love.
And for Liam, the bravest boy I know.

ONE

BLY FROZE UNDER THE COLD STARE OF THE witch's eyes that burned a brighter blue against the backdrop of fresh snow glittering in the fading sunlight. In another life, she might have found the eyes pretty and the witch handsome with his curly dark brown hair that just brushed his square jaw.

Or not. He wrapped his hands around the iron bars of the cage he stood in, glaring down at Bly with disgust on his face. That was no way to look at someone who was supposed to be saving you.

Especially when you hadn't been freed yet.

"Bly."

She turned at the sound of her name. Hazel watched her with raised eyebrows. The other woman understood why she hesitated but wouldn't tolerate it.

Bly focused on Hazel. The older witch had kind eyes. The same blue as the witch in the cage. The same blue that still haunted Bly's nightmares. Sometimes Bly just needed to look at Hazel to remind herself that not all witches were the ones who stole Elise. Hazel had been kind to her during the witches' trials, and Bly had even caught her in the woods freeing humans during the Games. Plenty of witches were compassionate and good. Her mind understood that, but her heart still surged to cast blame in moments like these.

"Hurry up, human," said the caged witch in front of her.

Bly turned back to him, baring her teeth as if she were a vampire capable of taking a bite out of him. He gave her a snide grin. Maybe he *was* a bad witch. She could picture him laughing at Elise's head lolling to the side as he jostled her onto the stretcher.

She shook away the thought and forced herself to speak to him. "What are you here for?"

He continued to look at her as if she were a mouse scurrying over his boot.

"Answer or I'll walk away."

She hoped he'd remain silent. Then she could leave him. That was their rule. Everyone had a chance to explain why they were in one of these prisons tucked away in the woods. Both the vampires and witches built these hidden places full of people they weren't supposed to keep alive: vampires and witches who were turned over in the Games or taken away as punishment for harming a human in the market. The rules said they should be killed, a onetime prize of enemy blood. None of them were supposed to be kept indefinitely for the miserable existence of providing an endless supply.

And then there were the humans—most of whom had committed crimes of desperation while struggling to survive. Or people like Elise who'd done nothing more than touch a cursed mushroom and ended up being traded to the vampires by the witches.

She was starting to turn away when he spoke.

"I was turned over during the Games three years ago." Some of the snark had left his voice.

Bly eyed his worn clothes, the rusty stains on his shirt at the creases of his elbows.

Of course, he could've been lying just so she'd free him, but it was surprising how many of them told the truth. The witch in the cage next to him would not be freed. She'd admitted to death-cursing a human woman for accidently splashing mud on her skirts in one of the Gap's markets, allowing the vampire guards to seize her as punishment. She'd been proud of it.

Bly's hand clenched around the spell that would break the lock to his cage.

This witch could go on to hurt a human.

Hazel's shoulder lightly brushed Bly's as she came to stand beside her. "Would you like me to do the honors?" Hazel asked.

"Please," snapped the caged witch.

Hazel focused solely on Bly. "He's not the one."

"I know." But that was part of the problem she still had. Bly looked at every new witch like they were the one who had taken her sister.

Sighing, Bly spoke the spell in her hand and broke the lock. Before she could even step back, the witch shoved through the door, hitting Bly's shoulder with a metal bar and sending her stumbling back. Only Hazel's hand on her elbow kept her backside from hitting the snow.

Bly hissed, pulling an arrow from the quiver on her back on instinct. She didn't have a bow, though—she wasn't a good shot yet, but she'd tied binding spells to the arrowheads, giving her the ability to spell someone in a fight without getting as close. She took a step after the witch, then stopped. What was the point? Nothing she did would get her what she wanted. Shoulders slumping, she looked around at the empty cages.

This prison had been hidden deep in the woods that surrounded Vagaris in a thick ring of pine trees that vampire guards had rested their backs against before the rebels rendered them unconscious. A cluster of gleaming metal cages that were tall and too narrow to lie down in sat in a tight circle in the center of the clearing.

The guards had mostly gone down peacefully, spelled to sleep by rebels wearing invisibility. But those spells were rare, and the group had to use them sparingly, so there'd still been a fight. One guard had been decapitated after drawing blood from half their group.

Bly blinked as she took in the aftermath. Red marred the white landscape.

Blood and snow and no Elise. It had been almost a year and a half since her sister had touched the cursed mushroom and the witches had stolen what Bly believed was her dead body, and forty-six days since Bly had entered the Games to win the witches' prize and raise her sister from the dead, only to win and find out that Elise was not dead at all.

Her only lead on Elise had come from the most unlikely of sources—Donovan, the very vampire prince she'd handed over to the witches to win their prize in the first place. Before the witches had dragged him away, Donovan had told her that he knew where her sister was, but everything came at a price, and he'd only tell her if she could free him.

He'd given her hope, but after months with no other leads, it had become barely enough to keep her going.

Yet she'd gotten her hopes up again. She hadn't found Donovan at the Havenwhile prison they'd raided last week, but if Donovan knew where Elise was, it had to mean she was in a Vagaris prison, so when Bly had gotten the lead on this place, she'd let herself believe that this was it.

But Hazel said there were many prisons out in the woods— kept hidden and outside the walls of the city so the rulers could deny their existence, and kept small so that their whole blood supply couldn't be wiped out in an attack.

Bly just had to keep working with Hazel's group toward their goal: Free everyone who didn't deserve their fate, and eventually, Elise would be in one of the prisons they raided, but in the meantime, others deserved their help. It was just hard to care about others when the person you loved most was missing.

Hazel understood Bly's true motives though. Bly didn't think the older witch cared if her goal had never been to free everyone: Bly'd been the one to bring the group the location of this Vagaris prison. She'd risked her neck for it. Hazel surely didn't care if Bly'd done it for Elise and not the witch who'd almost knocked her to the ground seconds ago. Hazel saw the bigger picture.

Hazel squeezed Bly's elbow before letting it go. Bly hadn't realized she'd still been hanging on to her.

"Are you coming home with us?" Hazel asked.

Bly didn't understand why Hazel insisted on calling it *home*. The rebels moved to different locations at each new moon. With a group that was a mix of vampires, witches, and humans, there was no safe home in the vampire city of Vagaris or the witch city of Havenwhile, and nobody had ever really been safe in the poverty-stricken human villages that sat in the Gap between the warring cities.

Bly shook her head. She wasn't going, and it certainly wasn't a *home*. She didn't have one of those.

After the Games, she hadn't known what to do. Elise was somewhere with a death curse running through her veins. Bly had assumed Elise was trapped in Vagaris, but she wasn't sure.

She couldn't go back to her parents and tell them what they'd already guessed from the moment she'd entered the Games: She'd lost—even though she'd won—because she'd failed to retrieve Elise, and she hadn't even managed to get the money from either prize.

So no, she couldn't go home. Home was a place for rest and comfort. Her parents' place had never even been that for her before Elise was gone.

Elise wasn't a ghost anymore, but Bly had turned into one. All she did was haunt the living, searching for the things that had once made her alive.

In a moment of weakness, she let her thoughts stray to Kerrigan, the one person who'd made her *feel* again even when she didn't think it was possible—and now the one person whose memory she avoided at all costs. After all, it was useless to dwell on what she could never have again, not after what she had done to him. Kerrigan had willingly gone with her as a sacrifice to the witches, but when the idea of losing him became as unbearable as the idea of *not* saving her sister, Bly had betrayed him in the worst way by handing over his brother, Donovan, to the witches instead.

She'd stolen his sibling to save her own.

Better to stay a ghost.

That's how she'd ended up with the rebels. She'd sought out Hazel after the Games, mostly because she didn't know what else to do. Hazel didn't call herself a rebel though. The word held too much violence for her taste, which was why Bly preferred it. Hazel called her band of prison breakers "Healers." They were a group formed from witches, humans, and vampires who saw the evil at the very foundation of their world and fought to change it in any small way they could. They didn't just work to empty the illegal prisons held on both sides; they also stole supplies from wherever they could to pass to those in the Gap who needed it most.

They called themselves Healers because they wanted to save and not hurt . . . at least whenever possible.

Bly's gaze flicked over the headless vampire again.

They were slapping bandages on a wound that would never heal.

But Bly didn't need to heal the world, just find Elise.

And the Healers had need of ghosts—or at least people who didn't care if they were harmed while chasing their goals.

Bly shook herself. Hazel had drifted away to help some of the freed prisoners who hadn't run. The other rebels milled about doing the same and securing the vampire guards in the empty cages where they'd be found by next shift.

She should have helped, but instead, she pulled her cloak over her head and drifted into the woods.

"Bly." Hazel's voice caught up to her, but Bly didn't want to listen. She was done pretending to care about the cause for tonight.

"We have a new lead on Havenwhile prison," Hazel said. "It could be nothing, but they spotted a man with red hair."

That made her stop. A new lead on Donovan? Something in the pit of her chest stirred—the dying gasps of the hope she was trying to keep alive.

"Where?" Bly breathed, finally looking over her shoulder.

Hazel shook her head, too smart to trust her with the location when she was fresh with disappointment. "We leave for it at midnight in four nights."

"We can get there sooner than that," Bly snapped.

Hazel tsked. "And be at our best strength? We need to scout more. Make our plan. You're welcome to come back to camp with us and help with preparations. Keep yourself busy."

Bly sighed. She didn't like preparing. She wanted action. Hazel knew that.

"I'd rather locate another lead here." It helped to have something else once they'd raided a prison and found nothing. It helped if she stayed restless and searching. If she paused, she was afraid she might lose whatever was pushing her forward.

Hazel didn't press. Bly appreciated that about her. She might have thoughts about how Bly was going about this, but she understood that it was Bly's choice and still helped her.

"Stay safe," Hazel said.

Bly didn't say she would. She walked away and slipped through the trees with the same ease she'd always had, letting her palms scrape across the rough oak bark and her fingers comb the pine needles, knocking loose soft piles of snow. The horror of the Games had tried to strip her of her love for the forest, but it hadn't won. She'd refused to let it. The unknown hidden behind the densest brush had always held both danger and possibility, and that hadn't changed.

Although her heart sped a little more from fear than anticipation these days.

She'd gotten good at ignoring both feelings. They didn't bring her closer to finding her sister.

She reached the walls of Vagaris easily, slipping through one of the hidden cracks she'd learned to find, thanks to watching Demelza during the Games.

At least she had one thing to thank the witch for.

Two, actually. Demelza had chosen to break the rules and leave Donovan alive.

He was the tangible thread to getting Elise back. And Kerrigan. Though the latter seemed too much to hope for.

She slipped through the wall and slid down the dark streets like she belonged there. Once, her dreams had been bright and flowery, more like Havenwhile, but now she felt safer in Vagaris, not because it was closer to Kerrigan, but because it was farther from Demelza and Nova.

Before she'd found Hazel, Bly had gone back to Demelza. She wasn't sure why—she had nothing to barter for Donovan's release, but for some reason, she thought pity would prevail. It hadn't. Demelza had sent Nova after her. The witch had made Nova one of her personal guards, and Nova had been all too eager to accept the task of making sure Bly couldn't reach Demelza again. Nova clearly still held Bly responsible for Vincent's death. During the Games, Bly had worked with the siblings, agreeing that they would split the prize: They would keep the money while Bly claimed the resurrection spell. But after Nova died, Vincent had tried to claim the resurrection prize to bring his own sister back. To settle the fight, Demelza had made Bly and Vincent duel, and Bly had won.

Which left Vincent as the human sacrifice who would fuel the resurrection spell that ultimately brought Nova back from the dead.

Nova would never forgive Bly for that, and Bly didn't blame her.

So when Demelza had sent Nova after her, Bly had barely gotten out, and she hadn't been inside Havenwhile since.

Bly reached a house that was like so many of the others in Vagaris: solid stones overtaken by moss that let off a chill only a vampire wouldn't notice. She shivered, realizing for the first time that the cold had numbed her face. Clenching her stiff fingers, she knocked.

The door swung open as if he'd been standing behind it, waiting, and Emerson's stare slid over and behind her to the empty spot where he'd undoubtedly hoped to find Elise.

She shook her head, confirming what he'd already guessed.

His face fell as he stepped back, turning away from her for a moment.

It didn't hurt like it once would have. She knew too well that her feelings for Emerson had never really deepened beyond friendship—they'd been part of a childhood fantasy she'd misinterpreted as reality.

She'd found true passion and then had snuffed it out while trying to save it.

Emerson moved to the table, and she followed, sitting across from him. His home was no warmer than outside.

They stared at each other, two cold people hoping to find someone to bring them back to life.

But at least they had each other. The Games had put their friendship through fire with Emerson questioning her every step of the way, but the experience had forged them into a perfect blade, each of them a sharp and equal side with the singular goal of cutting down anyone who tried to stop them from finding Elise.

He'd apologized more than once for not believing in her. Elise was alive somewhere, and he'd be dead if Bly hadn't fought for him.

Bly had never noticed before the Games that their friendship had been strained—that he'd looked down on her dreaming as foolishness and that she'd resented his cautiousness in turn—but things were different now. They talked through all their ideas together. He appreciated her ability to make a reckless plan, and she appreciated his ability to help shape it into the safest option.

And they were always planning. Although, once in a while, they'd share a rare peaceful moment together when the plan was done, and there'd be nothing to do but wait. The solid absence of Elise would fade away, and it'd be just the two of them. Sometimes Bly would bake an apple tart, and they might even joke about how it wasn't nearly as good as what Elise could do. Sometimes Bly would bring Emerson a block of wood from the forest and watch as he began to carve a figure that he'd never finish. It was enough for them to hold on to some shreds of who they'd be together once they found Elise.

Today wasn't a day for that, though.

Bly spoke first. She felt like she had to give him something. "They have another lead on a Havenwhile prison." She left out the part about the man with red hair. A little hope could keep you going, but too much hope could kill. "Can you get away? We'd need to be at camp in four days' time."

"I'll try to get someone to cover." He hadn't been able to make tonight's raid. As a vampire prince, he'd taken over handling many of the vampires' forges. His own father worked for him now. And even though she knew Emerson was still as much a ghost as she was without Elise, she could tell that he actually liked the job. He'd already managed to improve working conditions for the humans. She'd been right about that at least: Emerson made a kind and good vampire.

Still, she wondered if he had regrets—if all the sadness on his face was the absence of Elise or if some of it was the loss of his human life.

She was afraid to ask him . . . afraid of how he'd feel if they didn't find Elise before the death curse stole her.

Emerson stood up from the table and lit the fire like he always did for her even if she never mentioned the chill. He rarely bothered for himself despite the fact that vampires loved fires even though they didn't really feel the cold. Emerson said the heat from a flame was enough to make their skin feel a tiny bit human.

Bly preferred the numbing cold, but she appreciated the gesture.

They sat for a while in the empty silence of people who shared a pain they didn't want to talk about.

Bly's fingers and toes began to ache as she thawed. She couldn't let herself get too comfortable. Her night was just beginning.

She rose from the table. "I'm going to change."

Emerson finally focused on her. His muted expression betrayed a flicker of worry, but he gave it no voice. This was a plan they'd both agreed on—both reckless and practical.

Bly kept trying to tell herself it'd work, but she'd burned up too much of her hope during the Games.

The goal in the Games had been clear: Win and get Elise. There were rules and outcomes.

Finding Elise now seemed even more like a dream, and Bly's dreams had a history of not panning out.

Her chair scraped as she pushed it back against the table, wanting a noise to fill the silence.

Emerson reached out a hand as she moved by him, grabbing onto her wrist for a moment. The gesture always gave her strength, but his hand was cold, and he let her go, still saying nothing.

She moved to the bedroom she had here, pulling open a wardrobe where she kept some of her clothes. Her fingers brushed against several silky gowns created by spelled spiderwebs. Hazel had given her the spells because Bly had told her she wasn't just looking for Elise at these parties, that she might also overhear key information about others that needed rescuing. And Bly had delivered. She'd been the one to find the prison they'd just freed— she'd followed Kerrigan to it three nights ago, but she'd been looking for Elise and Kerrigan was surely looking for Halfryta, the head of the witches, who they'd handed over in the Games to win Emerson his immortality.

Demelza had promised Kerrigan a fair trade for Donovan if he'd return her mother. Unfortunately, Donovan would only tell Bly where to find her sister if she freed him *before* Kerrigan traded the witch who killed their parents for him.

She was racing against Kerrigan, and he didn't even know it.

She selected a bright red dress that reminded her of blood in the snow. The neckline plunged almost to her navel, but the sleeves were warm and long. The skirts were cut high in front with a waterfall of material in the back, but she wore skintight black pants underneath. She'd be warm enough while still looking the part.

She laced up black boots to her knees.

Turning to the small mirror above the dresser, she undid her curls from her bun, letting them roll off her shoulders in soft waves. Most bleeders wore their hair up, showing off the vulnerable expanse of their neck, but Bly felt somehow safer with her hair down, like it was a shield.

Silly. If she drew the wrong attention, having her hair down wouldn't offer any protection.

She touched the choker at her throat—a fine gold chain magicked on with a red jewel shaped like a drop of blood in the center. It was the mark of a bleeder. She hadn't realized how coveted the job was until she'd needed something that would let her stay in the vampires' city. Emerson had reluctantly helped her secure the position with his new status as a prince.

She hid it when she didn't need it. She knew he hated her taking the risk, but tonight, she needed it on display.

Watching herself in the mirror, she picked at the fraying end of the blue ribbon around her wrist—the constant reminder of her own selfishness, which had destroyed so many lives. A token that never let her forget why she was doing this in the first place.

When she came out of the room, Emerson had gone.

She tried not to let his absence bother her. He did his own searching when he wasn't working, placing himself in bars where he could hear the gossip.

Vampires loved to brag.

Maybe they'd get lucky. Or maybe they were both searching for a girl who was dead by now. Each second they didn't find her could be the moment the death curse struck.

Her chest tightened and her breathing turned shallow before she forced herself to inhale and exhale. She needed to move without thinking or she'd end up curled into a ball, trying to avoid the crushing weight of worry.

Slipping out the door, she moved through the darkness. Vagaris was a raucous place under the moonlight once you'd drifted away from the side streets and onto the main ones filled with bars and vampires drinking blood and booze in equal measure. An occasional human joined the mix, laughing while unhealed wounds dripped, but bleeders were rare and strictly monitored and most would be in the fortress where the wealthiest vampires held their parties.

That was where she needed to be. She spent most of her nights there. She moved past the guards and walked through the long hallway with an ease she didn't feel. She was always keenly aware of how easy it would be to find herself with fangs in her neck that wouldn't release until she died. She'd hardly be the first bleeder to disappear.

Everyone's luck ran out eventually in this blood-soaked world.

Entering the ballroom, she paused, mouth gaping slightly as she took it in. She'd heard the vampires liked to change their décor on a whim, but she hadn't seen it before now.

Gone was the maze of golden berry bushes that surrounded the giant fountain. Instead, golden oak trees with red-tinted leaves overtook the room. Orbs of light hung from them, casting everything in the shadows of their clawing branches. Plush black-velvet sofas and chairs were strewn haphazardly beneath the canopy, and even though the night was young, they were filled with couples embracing or feeding.

Bly took a tentative step inside. She preferred the sharp golden maze where it was easier to hide. Even though she wore the jewelry of a bleeder, she'd yet to let another vampire feed on her. Only Kerrigan's fangs had punctured her skin.

In the past, she'd been able to drift around the room, brushing off anyone who asked her for a bite with the excuse that she'd already committed to someone else. It worked. Some of the wealthiest employed their own bleeders and did not like to share.

It'd be a harder lie without the winding maze.

She needed to find a good spot to blend into the shadows. Instead, she found herself searching. She hated the way her eyes always looked for him first. She told herself the only reason she found him so easily was because of his height and the copper shine of his hair. It was impossible to miss him even if she tried.

Though, she never tried.

Her throat always tightened when she spotted him, as if he'd reached out and slid his hands around her neck. But he'd never gotten close enough to touch her.

This time, she heard his laugh before she saw him. Not his real one—the fake one that made him sound like an asshole who only cared about having a good time.

Spinning on her heels, she faced him. His lips were curved into a flirtatious smirk, but his eyes weren't on her—they were on the pretty brunette vampire on his arm. He seemed so enamored with her that he wouldn't have even glanced at Bly as he passed if his shoulder hadn't bumped hers.

"Pardon," he said with a laugh that died a slow death as he actually turned and took her in. His face shifted to a blank expression with a swiftness that made her head spin.

This was the closest she'd been to him since that day he'd walked away from her in the woods. It wasn't that she hadn't tried to get close to him at these parties, to say how sorry she was one more time, but he'd always turned his back and disappeared the moment she tried. So she watched him flirt and laugh and waited for his eyes to land on her, but they never did—she didn't even catch him looking quickly away.

He truly wanted nothing to do with her.

There wasn't even hate in his expression as he looked down at her now. Just nothing.

"Kerrigan." His name came out tight and strangled from her throat.

He winced as if it were a barb, and she finally saw something flash across his face: disgust.

Her heart sped at the sight of it. At least he felt *something* toward her. She still existed to him, even if that look said he wished she'd disappear forever.

"Well, she's lovely," said the vampire on his arm. "Should she come with us?"

"No," Kerrigan snapped.

"Such a pretty neck, though," the vampire pressed.

Did Kerrigan's eyes flit to her neck for just a moment? She almost brushed her hair away from it, but that would be ridiculous. She wasn't actually trying to sell him her blood.

"She's not to my taste," he said coldly.

Bly winced.

He started to pull away, the brunette pouting slightly on his arm as she stared longingly at Bly.

"I'm—" Bly started.

"Don't." He snarled the word as he spun back around with viciousness that made Bly step back. Even the vampire on his arm looked startled before he twisted and pulled her away into the crowd.

Only a few minutes later, Kerrigan's fake laugh drifted through the crowd once more. His mask was back in place. She'd ripped it off for a moment, and she wasn't sure she should try again. Before, when he'd finally let her in, she'd seen a vulnerable boy who regretted his monstrous past. She wondered if that vulnerable boy had been swallowed by the monster once more.

She'd done that to him.

She tracked his movements, watching him lounge on a sofa with his arm around the brunette. Even though he'd be better off without Bly, she still needed him. He hadn't completely gone back to his party-boy ways. It was just a façade to hide his true goal: searching for Halfryta to trade for Donovan. And if he found the witch and made the trade, then the truth of Elise's whereabouts would stay with Donovan, and she was certain Donovan wouldn't help her then.

That's why she was here. Kerrigan was checking the Vagaris prisons for the witch, and if Donovan had seen her sister, then she was somewhere locked away *here*. Kerrigan could still help her get her sister back by leading her to the prisons he found—she just couldn't let him know that she was using him. Luckily, Hazel supplied her with spells to help her track him unnoticed.

But even Kerrigan didn't seem to know where the queens kept

all their secrets. Sometimes Bly followed him through the woods and down corridor after corridor only for him to end up slamming his fist into a tree or stone wall in frustration. Bly suspected that despite his high station, the queens' trust of Kerrigan only went so far.

He was still her best lead.

It was hard to watch him, though, to constantly want to reach out and grab him and yell at him that she knew his carelessness was an act. He was hurting underneath. She wanted to heal him even though she'd caused the wound.

And she was still causing it. He'd just confirmed that her presence was nothing but a knife cutting him again and again.

If she loved him, she'd let him go, but here she was, because at the end of the night, she was still going to fight for Elise. She'd already sacrificed too much to stop.

She would keep her distance, though. She could do that at least.

Bly clung to the shadows in the corners of the room. Twice, she told a vampire that she was already taken for the evening before drifting off like she had somewhere to be. Once, she caught the obnoxious vampire prince Benedict watching her with narrowed eyes as he often did. His attention made her uneasy. He'd tried to steal Halfryta from them at end of the Games. He was friends with Donovan, and he was Jade's brother, which made him her natural enemy.

Ignoring him, she focused on keeping Kerrigan in her line of sight.

After an unbearably long time, Kerrigan finally extracted himself from a tangle of people around him and slipped to the edge of the room, wobbling on his feet as if he were one drink shy of collapsing. He stayed in the corner for a moment, eyes darting around and then up to the balcony where the queens held their smaller court. The queens had been hanging over the railing earlier, Melvina laughing with some of the crowd, and Allena watching everything with cool eyes. They were gone now or hidden in the darker recesses.

Kerrigan stumbled to the door at the back of the room, which she knew led to the arena. She hadn't really wanted to see that particular place again, but she'd do what she must.

She reached into the pocket she'd carefully placed in the folds of her skirt, freezing as her fingers brushed nothing but silk. The spells she normally carried were still in the dress she wore last time: the wing of a dragonfly that would make her invisible and a tuft of fur from a wolf that softened the sounds of her movements. It was a careless mistake to come without them—she'd been too caught up in the crushing disappointment of not finding Elise again.

It'd be a bigger mistake to follow a vampire without any spells to mask her presence.

But she needed another lead to grasp onto if the Havenwhile prison turned up nothing in four days.

Ducking, she wove through the crowd, for once not being stopped by anyone asking for a taste.

Opening the door, she stuck her head out into the night. The full moon lit the arena like a spotlight, but at least she wasn't here to perform this time. It seemed like years since she'd fought for Kerrigan's attention on these blood-soaked stones, but in this moment, all she wanted was to be invisible to him.

She shut the door gently behind her. Kerrigan had already

reached where the arena touched the lake, and Bly held her breath as he looked from side to side, but he didn't glance back. Turning right, he crept along the edge of the water.

She waited until his dark shape bled into the forest that hugged the water before scurrying down the sloped arena. At least there were no obstacles to scale, no witch waiting for her gruesome fate. She paused just at the shoreline, searching the trunks of the trees for any shift of movement. Nothing. She'd waited too long, but it would have been worse to rush after him without her spells and be caught.

Hoping to guess his direction, she took a step into the woods before pausing. There. She twisted her head like a wolf catching the scent of a rabbit.

Kerrigan would smile if he could see her like this: her the wolf and him the rabbit.

She shook herself. Of course he wouldn't smile. It was a ridiculous thought.

Kerrigan crept along the side of the fortress. He'd doubled back. Did he already know she was trailing him? She should let him go. They had their lead on Donovan to follow, and Bly and Emerson would leave tomorrow night to make the three-day journey to where the rebels were currently camped.

But what if Elise was in *this* prison? She didn't want to miss any chance no matter the risk.

She couldn't follow him out in the open in the shadow of the fortress wall, so she headed deeper into the woods until she could barely keep track of him through the thick clusters of trees, and then she moved parallel to him, darting as quietly as possible from tree trunk to tree trunk, hoping he didn't turn and investigate the gentle crunch of snow beneath her boots or the occasional snap of a branch.

With any luck, she'd sound like nothing more than a wandering herd of deer. After all, it was the things in the forest that didn't make noise that you had to fear.

The stone walls ended, and Kerrigan strode on without hesitation. They continued until Bly couldn't feel her fingers or toes and the only warmth was the running of her nose. Finally, Kerrigan stopped in a patch of forest that looked the same as everything that had come before, but he moved to a particularly wide oak tree and ran his hand across the trunk before making a sharp left.

When a thread of laughter broke the night, Bly slid behind a pine. Kerrigan was ahead of her and to the right, and he paused, leaning his back against a tree as he slipped a hand inside his vest. He vanished.

Curses. He hadn't forgotten *his* spells, and she couldn't follow the air. There had to be guards just beyond her sight, but she had no way to pass them and see what they had hidden out here in the trees, so she waited.

And waited. She probably should've left as soon as Kerrigan disappeared. There was no way to know if he would come back the same way or if he'd be visible even if he did. Those spells were precarious things. The amount of time they worked was never quite the same, and he might have minutes or even hours before he reappeared. Kerrigan was taking a risk even using those to slip past the guards. He was as desperate and careless as she was. At least they had that in common.

Though she doubted he'd try to free Halfryta now. He was too smart for that. He'd be looking for weaknesses, planning to come back later. She needed to see him again and read his face. She was certain she'd be able to tell if he'd found what he was looking for or not.

That's why she lingered.

Shivering, she pulled the front of her dress closed.

Without a warmth spell, she wouldn't last much longer.

She needed to move—at least head back toward the fortress. She'd have a better chance of catching sight of Kerrigan again if she waited there.

The guards laughed again, their chatter rising and falling as they struck up another conversation.

She took a step. The crunch of her boot on a dried pinecone echoed through the night.

Her heart pounded, drowning out everything else. No . . . the guards had stopped talking, and the silence was worse than if she could hear them moving toward her, but she held her muscles in place even though they begged to run. She didn't have a speed spell, and she wasn't foolish enough to believe she'd outrun them without one.

A hand clamped over her mouth so hard that it muffled the scream that tried to rip from her. Another hand wrapped around her waist, trapping her arms at her sides before lifting her up and backward into a hard chest. Her feet began to kick until she looked down and saw nothing. She was invisible.

TWO

"SHH." KERRIGAN'S BREATH WAS A SOFT hiss behind her ear.

She stopped moving, let herself relax against him, feet dangling as he held her.

Guards dressed in red stepped beside them moments later, scanning the woods, their stares hopping over Bly and Kerrigan without so much as a pause before they strode on.

She expected him to drop her, but he held her until she was tempted to close her eyes and pretend like they were lying in a hammock, her against his chest, with the stars above them. The fantasy hurt, but she let herself linger in it until he shifted his grip on her, letting go of her mouth to scoop her up and cradle her to his chest before sprinting through the woods. She tried to tuck herself into him, but branches tugged at her loose hair, ripping it from the roots. She didn't cry out.

Once they'd reached the edge of the forest with the fortress and the arena looming in front of them, the shroud of invisibility fell as Kerrigan broke one spell with another.

He dropped her so quickly that she landed on one knee, barely stopping herself from toppling over.

As soon as she stood, she understood why he hadn't remained invisible.

He wanted her to see the fury on his face.

It made her step back. He moved in a blur after her, and before she knew what was happening, her back hit a tree. She tried to turn away and found his hands around her throat, fingers caging her neck with the slightest pressure, thumbs brushing against either side of her windpipe.

Her pulse thrummed, and it wasn't from fear. She'd been dreaming of his hands on her neck, his body pressed close, but then she looked up into his face.

The emotion from a moment ago had dissipated. At least she'd understood his fury—she deserved it, but now, his face was uncaring, his eyes cold and hard. For the first time, she could actually picture him in the arena as a child, beating his brother down again and again with ruthless detachment.

Bly had awoken a part of him that she'd never wanted to see.

She didn't try to break free. Sometimes you needed to fight, but other times it was better to play dead.

"I knew it." Kerrigan's voice was distant, as if he were speaking to himself and not to her.

His eyes finally narrowed in on her. "A prison was attacked earlier—one I visited last week." His hands tightened. One more squeeze and he'd be choking her. "You?" he asked.

She tried to nod, but the movement was uncomfortable.

"How?"

She'd attempted to tell him before, when she'd first joined the Healers, but anytime she got near him, he'd turn his back on her and walk away. And now she wasn't sure she should trust him— not the version of him standing in front of her.

He ran his thumbs up and down her windpipe. A movement clearly meant to be a threat.

She shivered despite herself.

Something broke through his stoic expression, his eyes pulsing as black as the night around them, but it was gone as quickly as it appeared.

"Speak," he ordered.

She coughed uncomfortably. She told herself that she didn't have any choice but to trust him.

"The witch we saw in the woods after . . ." After they'd spent an evening in each other's arms, pretending their kisses weren't real, that they weren't flirting with tragedy. That had been a mistake. Bly coughed again, and he eased the pressure on her neck ever so slightly. "The witch who was releasing those two humans tied to the tree trunks in the woods . . . she leads a group of rebels who search for the captives being held illegally by the vampires and witches."

Kerrigan shook his head. "A fool's mission. You won't make a difference. I would know."

He'd been a rebel once, trying to help humans escape a world that used them for their blood. It had ended with him losing his best friend and the respect of the vampires.

Pausing, he cocked his head as his eyes searched her face. He'd loosened his grip enough for her to turn away from his searching, and he gave a sharp, bitter laugh when she did. "But you don't care about that, do you? You only care about helping the person *you* love."

She wanted to care. An explanation was on her lips: Of course she wanted to save others besides Elise, but it seemed like too much to hold in her heart. Too much to worry about when she could barely hold on to the shred of hope that kept her looking for her sister.

"I'm searching for Donovan too," she whispered. It was true. Kerrigan didn't need to know Donovan held the key to finding Elise. Besides, she'd want him back anyway.

For Kerrigan.

Despite the fact that his hands were tightening around her neck again. "The last thing I want is your help."

He leaned back slightly as if he'd release her and go, but she wanted him to stay. This was the most he'd spoken to her since the Games. She wanted him near her even if he hated her. Even if it hurt.

"Wait . . . was Elise there?" Her voice sounded pained and desperate, and she swallowed at her own vulnerability. She didn't want him to see it.

"I wasn't looking for her," he snapped.

"I know . . . I just thought . . ." That he would still help her if he had the chance. But why would he? After she'd put him in the same torment as her? They were both trying to get their siblings back now.

His expression softened for the briefest moment before hardening again.

Or it was only a shift in the shadows.

But then he said, "I didn't see anyone who looked like her."

Her body sagged against the tree. His fingers were still around her neck, and her movement made them too tight until he pulled back, placing his hands against the trunk on either side of her head instead.

She missed his touch and hated herself for it.

"Halfryta?" she asked.

He didn't answer, and she couldn't read him.

"I could help you free her," she pressed. She meant it, and she didn't. She desperately wanted to be on his side again. If they freed Halfryta now, she could tell him about Donovan's bargain—that his brother would only tell her where to find Elise if she got to him before Kerrigan traded the witch who'd killed their parents.

Kerrigan might agree. They'd hold Halfryta themselves as a backup plan while Kerrigan helped the rebels search for Donovan.

But she knew that plan wasn't a dream. It was a delusion.

He'd free his brother and forget about her sister. Kerrigan was a vampire, and despite the soft sides he'd shown her, he'd been raised to put himself first—he'd fought against his nature before, but her betrayal would ensure he wouldn't this time.

"I don't," he said slowly, "want you anywhere near me or my brother ever again."

Her exhale of breath was sharp against the soft sounds of night.

His own breath rasped out of him. She thought he was close to wrapping his hands around her throat again.

Dropping his hands from the tree, he released her from her cage.

"Go," he growled.

Her instincts told her to run, and she had to remind herself that she still had the wolf in her that he'd seen that first day in the woods.

He growled again when she didn't move, low and threatening. He reached out a hand and grabbed her shoulder as if to force her away.

"The rebels have a lead on a Havenwhile prison," she rushed out. "The scouts have caught sight of a man there with red hair so bright it burns in the dark."

Kerrigan froze.

"Emerson and I leave tomorrow night to join the rebels to try and free him. You could come. We could always use an extra—"

"Stop."

The word *vampire* died on her lips.

"I don't want your help, Bly." His hand tightened to a bruising pressure on her shoulder. "For all I know, you've found your sister with the witches and brokered a trade to lure me out there."

"I wouldn't—"

"Save it for someone you didn't already betray." He shoved her away from him, and she stumbled, feet catching on her dress. She went down on her side, snow crunching under her weight. Kerrigan lurched slightly toward her, and she wasn't sure if he was planning to help her up or kick her. He seemed in the mood for the latter, but he stopped. All he did was stare down at her, his face half in the shadows and half in the moonlight.

Digging her already numb fingers into the biting snow, she pulled herself up, scooting back from him before standing. Her teeth chattered, the only sound between them.

Kerrigan glanced over his shoulder toward the prison. When he turned back, his teeth flashed with a confident smile. "I don't need your help." And then he strode by her, leaving her with the cold realization that he was closer to freeing Donovan than she was.

· ✦ ·

Bly stood in Emerson's forge, watching him hammer away at a sword held over the flames. Sweat beaded on her forehead. She used to love watching him work, but now all she felt was restless.

For all his new vampire senses, he hadn't noticed her.

She said his name, and he looked up. He hated being interrupted, even though he said he liked having her there, like old times. He scanned her face with sharp interest before he turned back to his work. She wondered what about her he expected would look different once she had saved her sister. Would her eyes be brighter? Would she be smiling? She tried to imagine what she'd look like when she'd finally found Elise but couldn't.

Finally, Emerson put down his tools and faced her as he wiped his hands on a soot-stained rag.

"I followed Kerrigan to another prison deep in the forest to the left of the lake." She thought back to Kerrigan's eyes, the way they shifted away from her toward those guards. His expression. "Kerrigan thinks Halfryta is there."

Emerson frowned. "You talked to him?"

"I asked him to come with us to Havenwhile for the next prison break. He said he didn't need to. He looked back at where the prison was . . . and I saw hope on his face." She desperately wanted to be happy for him, but Kerrigan's success would lead to her failure.

"Did he go back to the prison right then?"

Bly shook her head. "I don't think he was prepared to get her out yet. We still have time."

Emerson sucked in a breath. "He could beat us. If he gets to Halfryta, if he actually frees her within the next day, he could reach Havenwhile before we get to Donovan."

Bly swallowed. "We'll reach Donovan first."

"We can't risk that. We don't even know if Donovan is *there*, Bly."

She bit her lip, debating telling him about the report of someone with red hair, but other people had red hair, and she couldn't find it in herself to give Emerson a glimmer of hope that could so easily be crushed. She'd bear that on her own. "What are you suggesting?"

He went silent for a long moment, his expression calculating. "We tell the queens what Kerrigan is planning. Get them to move Halfryta and buy us more time."

"I can't do that," Bly whispered. What if the queens simply killed Halfryta instead? And they *never* found Donovan? She couldn't gamble like that.

"Don't grow a conscience on me now."

She winced.

Emerson ran a hand over his hair. "Sorry—I didn't mean . . ." He trailed off because he did mean it. She'd made the selfish choice before, trying to have everything, but she still had nothing. She at least had to learn from that.

"If Kerrigan frees Donovan before we do, then we just ask Donovan to tell us anyway," Bly said.

"Ask him to tell us from the goodness of his heart?"

"He might."

Emerson considered it, then shook his head. "Wishful think-ing even for you."

"I bet he'd tell Kerrigan."

"Do you honestly believe Kerrigan would even help you? After everything?"

The question stung.

Because she didn't know the answer. She desperately wanted to believe that Kerrigan would help her save Elise, despite every-thing, if she begged him.

Her side ached from her fall after he'd shoved her away from him, and she could still picture the chilly hate in his eyes as he stared down at her.

Emerson nodded at her silence.

"I can't do that," she said again. She'd put her sister over his brother once before, and even though Kerrigan had made it clear he'd never forgive her for it, doing the same thing again so bla-tantly . . . she'd be lucky if he didn't rip her throat out.

She thought of his hands around her neck. The threatening pressure that had been meant to scare her . . . and didn't.

Her cheeks grew hot.

Emerson had turned away.

"Let's leave now," Bly said. "We can get Hazel to strike the Havenwhile prison sooner. We'll have a better chance of beating him." She'd race Kerrigan, but she wasn't going to undermine him.

"The Healers don't change plans," Emerson said with his back still to her.

It took time to gather all the rebels for a large-scale attack. Not all of them lived in the woods in their roaming camp. Some held positions in the cities that were important for funding the group and stealing supplies.

Everything done right took time, and Hazel had always made it clear that Bly's goals would come second to what was best for the group. Bly respected that. It also made her want to scream.

Emerson took her wrist in his hand. She used to read the gesture as romantic, but now she saw it for what it had always been: one friend anchoring another when he sensed she was coming unmoored. She hadn't even seen him turn and approach her. She blinked away the blurriness in her eyes.

"Go rest," he said. "We'll leave tomorrow. Hazel might strike early if we reach her sooner than planned. It can't hurt to ask."

He was only telling her what she wanted to hear, but she nodded, taking the lie as the gift it was meant to be.

THREE

HAZEL, AS PREDICTED, WOULD NOT WAVER from her plan. Like most cautious people, she was smart and didn't back down when she was right.

And Bly had to admit that she was too tired to be of use at the moment. She and Emerson had made the three-day journey in two thanks to speed and energy spells, and Bly's refusal to rest. More than ever, she loved the feeling of her legs turning weak from exhaustion, the way it made her mind focus solely on taking one more step, the way her heart beat so hard from the strain of it that she didn't have to feel anything else at all.

Now, she sat by the fire with Emerson, her body so weak that she didn't care as much that they wouldn't make their move until the following night. The thought of even standing seemed exhausting.

In the dim light, she could imagine that Emerson's eyes were still the rich brown of before and not the storm cloud of a vampire. She missed the brown, even though she'd never tell him that, because whenever she looked into the gray, it reminded her that she still had him. Emerson was only alive because he was a vampire.

Elise would have to change too if Bly found her in time. She was still death cursed after all, and there was only one way out of that. Bly would look into her sister's brown eyes and finally be reminded of their exact shade just in time to make them gray. Then everyone she cared about most in the world would be immortal: Emerson, Elise . . . Kerrigan.

They'd live forever and Bly wouldn't.

She wondered how it'd feel to grow older and crawl slowly toward death all by herself. She felt lonely just thinking about it. But she was getting ahead of herself.

She had to find Elise first.

And then a way to make Elise a vampire. Bly'd probably have to play the Games again, and Emerson would sponsor her this time. The thought made her stomach sink. Her future unrolled in front of her as a series of bleak choices. Every time something went her way, she'd have another problem to deal with.

Her dreams of pretty dresses and a simple life living off the land with someone she loved seemed like the hopes of another person—a girl who had died that day in the forest when Elise collapsed. All she really had left was her will to take one more step.

That was enough.

"Bly." Emerson saying her name seemed like nothing more than a memory from her past until he said it again. "Bly? Are you okay?"

She blinked. She hadn't realized that she'd been staring

straight into his dark eyes still. Her mind had been torn in half between the past and the future.

Emerson was here. Alive. They'd managed to save him, and they'd do the same for Elise.

"I just wish we could've gone tonight," she said. When all her focus was on taking the next action to find Elise, the moments where she had to sit still were the worst: the days when she wasn't traveling from Vagaris to the rebels' camp or trailing Kerrigan, when she was left alone with nothing but her own thoughts, were too painful to bear.

"I hate waiting," she said more to herself than Emerson.

Someone scoffed to her left. She hadn't bothered to notice who else sat beside her at the fire, and now she turned to the hulking figure that leaned forward, holding his palms over the embers despite the fact that he didn't get cold.

Alexander was one of the vampires who worked with the rebels. He'd been rescued from a vampire prison where he'd been held for ten years for the crime of attempting to kill a fellow vampire who had murdered a bleeder. Alexander had been in love with the bleeder. Killing a bleeder was worthy of banishment in the world of vampires, but just attempting to kill a vampire was worthy of a harsher sentence: a cage too small to lie down in and an eternity of staring through bars.

People said that Alexander had remained silent for an entire year after he'd been freed. She'd also heard that he had a tendency toward violence and pushing Hazel's pacifist boundaries. It had been he who'd decapitated one of the vampire guards during the last prison break.

Bly would've thought that made them more allies than

anything else since it wasn't a secret that she also struggled with Hazel's rules.

But here he was, glowering at her, and it wasn't the first time she'd caught him looking at her like she was the enemy.

Bly matched his expression. "What's your problem?"

"You," he said. Even though he spoke now, he still wasn't known for long, eloquent speeches. He went back to glaring at the near-dead fire, and Bly should've let it go, but his annoyance gave her something else to focus on besides her worry.

"Care to elaborate?" she asked.

"Sure. I don't like you."

She waited for him to say more. Apparently that was his idea of specifics.

She really didn't need another vampire disliking her, but then again, what was one more?

Bly glanced at Emerson, who gave a small shake of his head. He wanted her to leave it alone.

"You don't even know me," she said to Alexander. "There are plenty of vampires that have reason to hate me. I don't recall you being one of them."

"Except I *do* know you." His voice was low and harsh. "You march in here with your own vendetta and see us as a personal army you can use to get what *you* want. I heard you asking Hazel to move our plans to tonight, despite the fact that not everyone is here yet and we'd be shorthanded. All because your sister is death cursed. You have a ticking clock, and you don't care about more dead bodies in your wake as long as they aren't the ones you love. Am I wrong?"

Bly bit the inside of her cheek hard enough to taste copper.

Alexander shifted on the log he sat on, leaning slightly in her direction as if he could smell the blood.

Emerson leaned forward too, but Bly knew it was only to intervene if he needed to, not because he lacked self-control. Emerson had the same relentless control as a vampire that he'd had as a human. Bly had never even seen his eyes go black with hunger.

Emerson having her back always made her braver, and she wanted to tell Alexander that he was wrong, that she cared about changing their world and fighting for this cause, because she'd once had a fantasy about being that person.

But he was right. She had begged Hazel to go tonight, knowing it was riskier for everyone. She'd been willing to gamble not just her life but everyone's in the group just to increase the odds of reaching Elise in time.

The blood in her mouth tasted like condemnation.

"That's what I thought," Alexander muttered.

"You're one to talk, Alexander." The voice that spoke was soft and lilting.

Marianna stepped out of the shadows, seating herself across from Alexander. Bly had no idea how long she'd been listening. The woman spoke like a ghost and moved like one too.

Marianna was Hazel's niece and one of the unlucky witches who'd failed to master spells as a child and was cast out from Havenwhile by the elders. Hazel said it was the moment that made her snap and decide to do something. She'd found her niece and started collecting anyone who didn't fit in their world, whether they were witch, human, or vampire.

Now Marianna was a master of glamour spells. She wore

her hair in braids that hugged her scalp before trailing down her back, and they were always spelled a different color. Tonight, they glowed silver like rays of moonlight dripping down Marianna's warm brown skin.

Marianna nodded her head in Alexander's direction. "When he first came, he'd disappear by himself all the time, trying to find the vampire that had killed his lover. What he found instead was himself in another cell." A faint smile flitted across Marianna's lips. "He's the only one who can boast that we had to rescue him twice."

Bly half expected Alexander to stand up and strangle the woman. He only grunted and ground his heel into the dirt.

Marianna turned to Bly, her smile gone. "I believe he only wants to warn you about heading down a path that leads to folly. We all come here with wounds, but if you're always running, they'll never have a chance to heal."

The words hit Bly in the gut. She understood. The moment Elise had crumpled to the forest floor with a cursed mushroom in her hand, a wound had ripped Bly almost in two, and she'd been fighting to staunch the bleeding ever since, but each step only ripped her open further.

Marianna nodded at her as if she knew exactly what Bly was thinking, but she frowned slightly like she already knew Bly's future was a bleak one. Her lips lifted as she turned back to Alexander. "Anyway, don't think we don't want you here. Alexander might speak now, but that doesn't mean he's good at communicating." Her voice took on a teasing tone.

Alexander looked up and met Marianna's eyes, and the scowl that Bly thought was a permanent fixture on his face softened.

Oh. He loved her. Bly hadn't noticed before. Even though Hazel's group was composed of those who'd been wounded by their world enough to see the unfairness at its core, prejudices you were raised on didn't disappear overnight, and often Bly noticed rebels congregating together with their own kind even in the woods outside the cities.

But Marianna and Alexander, a witch and a vampire, were clearly two people from different worlds who were healing their wounds together.

Bly had had a brief glimpse of what that felt like.

Before she'd torn herself more.

She was happy for them, but she couldn't take the hurt of watching a togetherness that felt out of reach for her. She rose from her seat, pausing to meet both Alexander's and Marianna's eyes. "Thank you," she said.

She meant it, even though Marianna's advice would do her no good.

✦ ✦ ✦

Bly knelt in the snow, bracing her palms against the rough bark of the tree that hid her. Her body shook, but not from the cold that seeped through the wool of her trousers. It was the anticipation.

With any luck, she'd fix her heartache *and* Kerrigan's tonight, and she wouldn't need someone to slowly heal with her like Alexander and Marianna had.

It'd be like it never happened.

An owl hooted, followed by soft thuds echoing in the night.

Bly was in the second group of rebels. Emerson was in the

first group that had used the last precious stash of invisibility spells to sneak up on the witch guards who surrounded the camp. Their scouts had already mapped where each one would be, and rebels had crept close to them and struck at the sound of the owl hooting, which was really Peter, one of the rebel witches who had the uncanny ability to mimic every bird under the sun.

There were no sounds of alarm. All the witches' guards were down.

A sharp whistle split the night, and that was Bly's cue. The darkness lit with spells as Bly cast her own as well.

She sped forward as she scanned the trees above her. The witches' prisons were different from vampire ones. Trickier. The cages weren't clustered on the ground and easy to release once the guards were taken care of. The witches hung their prisoners from the trees.

Bly's speed faltered as she reached the first one. A cage made from a tangle of branches woven together hung from an ancient oak. A woman sat in it, dressed in a white gown, gleaming like a captured dove.

The plan was to free whoever you reached first. The old oak had low branches that would be easy to scramble onto. She could release her in a mere moment. The woman's pale hands wound around the branches that caged her as she noticed Bly.

Bly kept running. Someone else would help her.

She ran to the next tree and the next until she stopped in front of a tall pine with a cage halfway up impaled by the branches that held it in the air. Bloodred hair shown through the bars.

Her hands clasped the lowest branch, and she hoisted herself toward whoever was in that cage, trying to stop the excitement bubbling through her. It'd hurt too much if it wasn't him.

Her legs burned and her arms ached by the time she pulled herself up to a branch that jutted out beside his cage.

"Well, aren't you the clever little rabbit?" Donovan's fangs flashed white against the night.

Her heart thrummed, but it wasn't a rabbit's skittish beat. It was a hunter who'd cornered her prey.

"Tell me where to find my sister."

"No time for that." Donovan looked up into the branches above them. The moon was dark tonight, leaving them with nothing but the slim light of Bly's spell. Donovan glanced back down at her. "Someone was cleverer than you. Now let me out." She didn't get a chance to ask what he meant. His arm darted through the bars, snatching the collar of her vest, yanking her so quickly toward the cage that her cheek scratched against the rough bars.

Holding the spell behind her back, she fought his grip.

They both froze when the night exploded around them. More lights blazed to life in the trees and across slender bridges that connected them, illuminating a horde of silhouettes.

Witches. They'd been hiding in the darkness above them this whole time.

Donovan had been bait.

"You could have said something," Bly hissed as she tried again to break from Donovan's grip. The only advantage she had were the bars between them.

"And risk you bolting without freeing me first? Not a chance."

A witch dropped onto the same branch Bly stood on. He thrust a knife toward her side.

Donovan let go of her just in time to grab the witch's wrist, snapping it with a crunch. The witch howled as Donovan plucked the knife from his useless hand and plunged it in and out of his heart. He fell, hitting the branch Bly stood on so hard that she barely kept her footing.

Donovan grinned at the bloody knife in his hand and then back at Bly, but before she could imagine what he intended to do with it, another witch descended from above. She landed on the opposite side of the cage and straddled a branch as she pulled a bow from her back.

Donovan flung the knife, planting it dead center in the witch's throat. Somehow the witch kept her balance on the branch for a horribly long moment, her mouth opening and closing as blood leaked out of the corners. Finally she slid off.

Turning back to Bly, Donovan brushed his hands together. "Where were we? Yes. Time to free me."

Bly gulped. She'd scooted back on her branch just out of his reach and glanced at the chaos below. The fight looked vicious. She'd bet that some of the prisoners they'd freed had been planted by the witches, but their group was large too. She couldn't tell who was who, but the fight below appeared too close to call. She was keenly aware that if they'd attacked a day earlier, they would have lost.

She couldn't let this change her plan. The upper hand had to stay hers until she got what she needed. "My sister's location," she demanded again.

"I believe the deal was you had to free me first." Donovan reached out a hand and shook the door of his cage. A vampire would have been able to break through wood, so it had to be spelled.

"Except I have no guarantee that you'll tell me once you're

free. What's going to stop you from knocking me out of this tree or snapping my neck?"

"My brother," he answered. He sounded uncharacteristically sincere.

Bly glanced down, thinking for a moment that Kerrigan had come. That he was in the fight below, but then she realized what Donovan meant. He wouldn't kill her, and he'd uphold his bargain *for Kerrigan*. Not because Donovan was noble, and it was the honorable thing to do, but because he knew Kerrigan would be upset with him if he hurt Bly. Bly wasn't so sure that was true anymore, but the thought warmed her regardless.

Still, she'd be a fool to trust him. He was playing with her emotions. It had almost worked. "I'll free you as soon as you tell me what I want and not a second before."

Donovan laughed. "You, my dear, were never meant to be human . . . which is exactly why I don't trust you. What's to stop *you* from leaving me trapped here once you get what you want."

"Your brother," she whispered, the words barely audible over the sounds of battle below.

They held each other's stare for a long moment, both of them acknowledging that they were two people willing to go to extreme lengths to get what they wanted and that they were two people who shared someone they loved.

Donovan nodded, deciding. "She's with Benedict."

"What?" Bly pictured the pretty vampire with the seductive grin. She couldn't imagine him holding someone captive but looks were deceiving. "Where's he keeping her?"

"I'm afraid that's all you're going to get at the moment." He stared pointedly at the lock.

"Break," she said, activating the spell in the stone in her hand. She was reaching toward the lock when a blow sent her feet sliding on the branch. Pain exploded in her arm, and she slipped, tumbling off the branch before her body jerked again, and she found herself dangling by her wrist, caught in Donovan's outstretched hand.

"Pull me up." Her teeth clenched, clipping her words.

"Toss me the spell."

She tried, but her arm screamed in pain. She was pretty sure that she could no longer move it.

Donovan's eyes narrowed.

"Please."

Miraculously, he started to pull her up. Her feet swung, trying to find purchase.

"Hold still. You're making this more difficult than it needs to be," he grunted.

She willed her body to go limp, despite her desperation to find something to hold her besides a vampire who didn't even like her, but her efforts didn't matter.

An arrow impaled Donovan's wrist.

He hissed as his grip loosened. His blood dripped onto her face.

And then she was falling. Branches slapped her, tearing her clothes and ripping her skin. Her fingers clawed for anything at all to save her until her back hit the ground. She couldn't breathe, her lungs lost somewhere in the fall. Her vision blurred in and out until finally she managed to suck in a sliver of air that stung her throat. Her eyes cleared just in time to see a girl looming over her. She wore the clothes of a witch, but her form was gaunt from years of human hunger and her eyes were dead with human pain.

Nova held a bow in her hand, no doubt notched with the same type of arrows that had just ripped into Bly's arm and Donovan's wrist.

Bly coughed. Her chest still didn't want to hold air. "I thought you preferred an ax," she wheezed.

"I do." Nova slung the bow across her back and pulled a small ax from her waist. Her eyes traveled over Bly as if deciding where to strike first.

Bly was certain that Nova didn't intend to give her a clean or quick death. "Nova—"

"Don't," she said. "This is for my brother."

Bly tried to use her working arm to scramble back, but Nova's foot came down on her chest, pushing out the precious air that Bly had managed to regain while pinning her to the ground.

Bly didn't close her eyes. She felt like she owed it to Nova to watch. After all, she couldn't really blame the girl for wanting her dead. Bly had stolen too many siblings in her fight to save her own. Kerrigan was making her pay with his coldness, and now Nova would make her pay with her life. Both seemed fair.

Nova raised the ax over her head. The blade glistened in all the light from spells that had turned this chunk of forest into a garish stage surrounded by darkness. For a moment, Nova just stood there, holding Bly's life in her hands, staring down at Bly with a blank look on her face. She wished Nova's face gave away some of her thoughts: What would Bly's death buy her? Happiness? Probably not, since it wouldn't bring Vincent back. Satisfaction then? Or just a single moment of relief?

She wanted to know, but Nova gave her nothing.

"Nova! I said to bring her to me, not chop her in half!" The command rang across the battle, and Nova and Bly both turned toward the woman who'd yelled.

Demelza stood above them on one of the bridges that hung between two pines. Her red hair had been braided over one shoulder, and it glared like an open wound against the night. Behind her, another flash of red caught Bly's attention. Donovan's head drooped against his chest, no doubt spelled to sleep, and two large witches carried his limp body between them.

Bly should have freed him. Donovan would have gone home to Kerrigan and told him how Bly had saved him before falling to Nova's ax, and at least the memory of Bly could have been a heroic one instead of a selfish one. Instead, when Kerrigan finally got him back, Donovan would have another story about the girl who'd tossed aside his life for her sister's.

She couldn't die like this. She tried to push up on her elbows, forgetting her arm wasn't working and Nova's boot was still firmly planted on her chest. Shifting her head to the side, she looked at her injury for the first time, and her head swam. An arrow protruded from her bicep, the shaft broken from the fall into a jagged few inches of wood. Reaching across her chest and Nova's boot, she attempted to get ahold of it. All she did was end up panting from the pain as the movement tore more flesh.

"Let me help you with that." Nova bent down and yanked the arrow free.

Bly screamed as her vision blurred. When she could see again, Nova stood over her with her ax raised above her head once more, waiting. She wanted Bly to see the blade coming. She didn't care about Demelza's orders.

The ax swung down halfway to splitting Bly's skull in two

before another blade darted in front of Bly's face to stop the blow.

Nova turned her ax in the direction of Bly's rescuer.

Kerrigan held the sword that had saved her.

He sidestepped Nova's attack easily, and Nova's powerful swing carried her into a spin.

Kerrigan struck the back of Nova's head with the hilt of his sword, and she collapsed onto Bly, her ax falling from her hands toward Bly's face again.

Kerrigan caught it by the handle, twisting it in his grip.

He'd saved her. More importantly, she'd asked him to come tonight, and he had.

But then he stepped over Bly pinned under the unconscious Nova with barely a glance down at his feet.

He wasn't here for her. He was here to make sure that she didn't lose his brother. Regret pierced her chest, and it hurt worse than the wound in her arm. She'd let him down again. She'd had time to save Donovan and hadn't.

Kerrigan took a couple steps away before turning around. He strode back and kicked Nova's limp body off to the side before reaching down, grabbing Bly by the front of her shirt, and yanking her to her feet.

She cried out at the way the movement jostled her arm, and Kerrigan's eyes widened as he looked over her body, clearly just realizing she was hurt.

"Kerrigan!" Past Kerrigan's shoulder, Jade spun and slashed with daggers in each fist. He'd trusted Jade to help him when he hadn't trusted Bly.

Her eyes stung.

He held her just long enough for her to find her feet.

"Get out of here," he said as he released her and spun away.

She wanted to follow him and make sure he stayed safe, but she worried she'd just get in his way.

Pain lanced her arm again, and she thought another arrow had found her, but it was Marianna at her side, ripping away Bly's bloody sleeve before winding a tight cloth over the leaking hole.

"I'm sorry, but we're low on healing spells and vampire blood at the moment." Marianna glanced around at the battle around them. "All our vampires are a little too busy to give more."

Worry coated her voice. As far as Bly knew, the Healers had never been in such an all-out battle. There were scuffles when things didn't go as planned, but Hazel's careful attention to details had kept them from this.

It was a mess.

Kerrigan and Jade were a blur, witches falling in their wake as they stepped over bodies in pursuit of Donovan.

Hazel and Demelza both yelled for their people to retreat.

Nothing would stop Kerrigan though. He moved as if he were untouchable with Jade a white-haired demon at his side. They were outnumbered. Most of the rebels had heeded Hazel's orders and pulled back into the woods, leaving Kerrigan and Jade to chase the witches alone.

Pure rage could make a person twice as formidable, but in the end, numbers would always win, and finally, a witch broke through Kerrigan's flurry of movements, spelling him. He hit the ground, unconscious. Jade fell to a sleeping spell a second behind him. The witches surged over their bodies like ants as Bly darted forward.

She halted as Demelza's firm voice rang out. "Leave them. I need him free."

Kerrigan was Demelza's best chance at getting her mother back.

Demelza's eyes slid to Bly, standing too close to the cluster of witches. "I'd heard you were spotted running around with these pests. You're the one I wanted tonight." Her stare shifted to Bly's back, and Bly half turned, ready to tell Emerson to leave her behind, but it wasn't just Emerson behind her. All the rebels stood in a silent line at her back.

There was no upper hand for either side. The witches had set the trap and taken them by surprise, but none of them had counted on Kerrigan and Jade, stronger than everyone with their royal blood, tipping the scales, and some of the freed prisoners who hadn't fled now stood with the rebels.

Demelza focused on Bly again. "Next time." She gave a sharp, birdlike whistle, and the witches fell back instantly, dragging the unconscious Donovan with them.

Bly took a step after them. Kerrigan would still be trying to reach Donovan if he could. He'd still be fighting, and Bly should fight in his place. She owed him.

Emerson's hand on her arm stopped her.

She started to shrug him off but stopped herself. She didn't have Donovan, but she had a name. Benedict.

She couldn't be reckless when Elise still needed her. Afterward . . . maybe she could trade herself for Donovan if Demelza wanted her so badly.

The thought soothed her.

Kerrigan had been willing to lay down his life for Elise

once, and Bly could do the same for his brother . . . after Elise was safe.

He'd have to understand what she felt for him then.

A few of the rebels gathered up Kerrigan and Jade and began heading back into the woods. Bly turned, coming face-to-face with Alexander standing just behind her.

"Thanks for having my back," she said.

He looked her up and down. "Hazel's orders. I would have let the witch have you." He turned and walked away.

Bly sighed. What happened when the cost of Bly in the group started to outweigh the benefits? Would Hazel help her the next time or cut her losses?

"He's just an ass," Emerson said as they took up the tail end of their retreat.

Bly nodded, but she understood where Alexander was coming from. He was right to hate her. She was using them the same way she used everyone. Would she really keep helping once she found Elise?

She decided not to think that far ahead.

✦ ✦ ✦

Kerrigan was soft when he slept. The moonlight lit his face, leaving it kissed by shadows. It reminded her of the person he'd been before she betrayed him.

She fought the urge to reach out a finger and brush it across his lips. Instead, she glanced over her shoulder toward the bustling camp. They were packing to relocate just in case anyone had followed them back from the fight. They usually moved in a pattern with rotating locations at each new moon so that their people could still find them. This would be messy. It would take time to spread the word of a new place outside their pattern, but they hadn't lasted this long without getting caught by being careless.

Bly and Emerson wouldn't be leaving with them, though.

They had a name. New plans and a hope that no longer seemed out of reach.

"Bly," Emerson said. "Let's go." For once, he was the one who wanted to rush forward without thinking, storm Vagaris, strangle Benedict until he surrendered Elise. Bly was forced to take his role: the cautious one. They couldn't tip their hand. Whatever Benedict's purpose in keeping her sister, there was no guarantee that he wouldn't just kill her if he knew they were coming for him.

It was illegal to hold a human captive. They'd talked about going to the queens, but that seemed risky as well. If Benedict found out, he might destroy the evidence.

Bly had played through so many scenarios that ended with Elise's death.

She'd been reckless once before, but she needed to be patient.

Emerson said her name again. She didn't look away from Kerrigan.

"He might know where we can find Benedict." She'd already given Emerson the flimsy excuse for waiting.

Kerrigan had saved her. Maybe he'd help.

At least, she wanted to thank him.

Emerson stomped away. He came back a moment later and held a vial he must have asked Hazel for under Kerrigan's nose. "Wake."

Kerrigan's eyes flew open, and he was on his feet in a blur, his hand gripping the hilt of his sword as he spun. "Donovan." His brother's name was a hoarse shout.

Some of the rebels stopped packing, hands drifting to pockets with spells or blades on their belt.

"He's gone," Bly said. "The witches still have him."

Kerrigan spun toward her. "You . . . ," he breathed. The word sounded soft, and for a second, she thought there was relief in it. He stepped toward her, and she reached out a hand before his face twisted into a snarl. "I should kill you. I'd have a better chance saving my brother if you were in the ground."

He said the words with such vitriol that Bly believed them. She dropped her reaching hand and stepped back.

He followed her, hands clenching and unclenching at his sides, and she wondered for the briefest moment if he would do it. After all, she'd once thought she could murder a witch in cold blood for what they'd done to Elise, and hadn't Bly done the exact same thing to Kerrigan's brother? *She* was his villain. He had every right to want her dead. The only question was whether he'd follow through or not. Kerrigan was a vampire. He had a bloodlust in him that had been nurtured and fed since before he had even been turned. Only the good in him kept him in check, but perhaps she'd pushed him too far.

She had no doubt that he *could* do it. At least in the heat of the moment—though she hoped he'd regret it later. He closed the remaining gap between them, and this time she didn't flinch away. She held her ground, not because she thought he wouldn't hurt her but because she couldn't bear the thought of running away from him.

Kerrigan glowered down at her. She stared up into his eyes, waiting for that sliver of control to snap. She wondered how he'd do it. Ripping into her throat with his fangs? A quick neck break? The dagger at his waist? No. She was pretty sure he wouldn't use a weapon. It'd be personal. He owed her that much.

A hand flattened against Kerrigan's chest, but it wasn't Bly's.

"Back up." Emerson's voice was low and firm.

Kerrigan's chest heaved under his palm. Emerson didn't push him. It'd do no good anyway; even as a vampire, Emerson's strength wouldn't rival Kerrigan's.

But some of the rebels had crept closer to them. Bly met Hazel's narrowed eyes over Kerrigan's shoulder. Emerson might not be able to stop Kerrigan, but the entire rebel group? Blood would spill. The only question was whose.

Bly gave her head a tiny shake, and Hazel frowned but nodded. If someone was bleeding here, it would be Bly and Bly alone.

Emerson's other hand found Bly's shoulder and pushed her back with enough force to make her lose her footing for a second. He wasn't quite used to his vampire strength yet.

Emerson wedged himself between them, facing Kerrigan, but Kerrigan's stare remained locked on Bly like Emerson wasn't even there. "You told the queens I'd found Halfryta, didn't you? Jade and I went back at dawn, and the whole damn prison had disappeared. You were the only one who knew besides Jade, and she's in love with my brother. That leaves you." His voice held barely contained fury, but then it cracked, letting in a brokenness that almost brought her to her knees. "But why?"

His face hardened against his vulnerability. He looked like

he'd walk right through Emerson to destroy her.

He hadn't come because she'd asked. She hadn't even told him where they were going. They must have found the prison empty and followed her and Emerson to the rebel camp and then bided their time until the rebels led them here.

"I d-didn't . . . ," she stuttered.

"Don't lie." His words were cold. He wouldn't believe any defense.

Because he was right. She was the logical culprit . . . except Emerson had known. She tried to step around Emerson's broad back as she realized who the guilty one actually was. He held out an arm to block her.

"Bly's not the one who told the queens you knew where Halfryta was," Emerson said.

"Emerson . . . ," Bly warned.

"I did."

Kerrigan finally turned his focus from Bly and zeroed in on Emerson. Despite the confession, Kerrigan seemed to regain a little of his control once he wasn't looking at Bly. That hurt. Emerson had just confessed, but the weight of Kerrigan's anger was still for Bly.

After all, Emerson wasn't the one who'd handed over Donovan. All he'd done was go along with the plan.

"I will ask you then," Kerrigan said. "Why?"

"Your brother swore he would only tell us where Elise is if we freed him before you could trade the witch for him."

Kerrigan's face went slack, and then his eyes pinched in thought as he shook his head. "Bastard," he muttered. But the curse wasn't directed at Emerson. Kerrigan seemed to understand that Donovan was quite capable of thwarting his own release if it meant still having revenge on Halfryta.

"You could've told me." Kerrigan's eyes were back on Bly.

"When?" she asked him. "When your face was buried in someone else's neck? When your back was turning on me?" She was keenly aware of everyone listening around them and how much this sounded like a lovers' quarrel.

Kerrigan sighed. "You had your chance a few nights ago."

She glared at him. He shifted, glancing briefly at his feet and back again, and she wondered if he was remembering his hands around her throat.

He couldn't blame her for not telling him then. All it would've done was make him act quicker to free the witch.

"It doesn't explain what just happened," Kerrigan said. "You hesitated. You had time to free him. I saw it."

Bly's face went numb because he was right. If she'd been thinking of Kerrigan, she would've freed Donovan without hesitating and trusted that the vampire would follow through on his word. But she hadn't. All she'd been thinking about was the thread of power that she had over him in that moment and how she couldn't let go of it until she'd secured what she'd wanted.

Their world wasn't one built on trust, and she definitely didn't trust Donovan. And even if she wanted to trust that Kerrigan would have her back and demand that his brother hold up his end of their bargain, she no longer did.

She lifted her chin. Part of her was ashamed, but most of her felt like she'd only done what was logical. "I wasn't going to let him out until he held up his end of the deal."

Kerrigan ground his teeth. "And did he?"

"Yes," Bly whispered, "but I got shot down before I could free him."

"Don't pretend you're sad about it."

"I wanted him free." Kerrigan couldn't really believe she'd leave his brother trapped on purpose.

"You hate him."

"I'll find him again," she promised.

"Even now that you know where your own sister is?" He hesitated. His voice softened a fraction. "Where is she?"

"He didn't tell me *where*, actually." She flicked a look at Jade. Emerson had not woken her, but Bly didn't want to utter her brother's name. "He told me who."

Kerrigan seemed about to ask for more information, but he stopped. He seemed to be shutting down whatever bit of compassion had made him ask if she'd gotten what she needed.

"Then no," he said, "I don't believe you'll keep searching for my brother, will you? Not when you have your own sister to find."

She wanted to tell him that he was wrong. But of course, he wasn't. All she wanted to do was get back to Vagaris to find Elise.

"I'll help you," she said again.

He shook his head. "You go your way, and I'll go mine. Your help only hurts, Bly." He bent down and roughly scooped Jade up before hanging her over one shoulder. He started to turn away before pausing and glancing back. His stare dropped pointedly to the ribbon on her wrist before he threw one last dagger. "Have you considered the possibility that your sister is better off wherever she's at? How much longer until you are the cause of her downfall once more?"

He turned, not even waiting to see if his blow had hurt her.

The words did exactly what he intended them to, hitting a fear that was already a gaping wound in her chest. Nobody Bly loved was safe with her.

FOUR

KERRIGAN COULD EASILY BE DESCRIBED AS pretty with his sharp cheekbones that contrasted his soft lips and his full-lashed eyes. Benedict possessed an entirely different type of beauty. Everything about him was harsh and angled, even the slant of his lips when he smiled. He was a jewel-encrusted dagger sparkling in the sun—a beautiful thing you might reach for only to get cut on an edge that was sharper than it appeared.

He'd be the one cut and bleeding by the end of the night if she had anything to say about it.

Bly glanced around the room. Benedict never failed to appear at these parties, and Bly always had to work particularly hard to dodge him. She knew he'd want her once she became a bleeder. His eyes always tracked her at some point in the night, but even though he'd drifted in her direction many times before, he'd never been relentless in his pursuit or he certainly would have caught her, and she might have had to take her charade to a new level.

Tonight, she would, though.

She and Emerson had already found and broken into his rooms in the fortress. No Elise. The rooms had been bare and empty and didn't seem like a place Benedict would spend time, which meant he stayed somewhere else. They had tried to follow him through the night more than once, but they'd always lost him. He'd be there one moment and gone the next, and she was certain that he used invisibility spells.

She finally spotted him beneath the canopy of red with a drink in his hand, laughing with a group of vampires she didn't recognize. It took all her effort not to run straight toward him, grab hold of his sapphire blue shirt, and shake him until his mouth popped open and the location of her sister tumbled out.

No, that wouldn't do. She had to be clever about this, and she couldn't be too eager.

Drifting around the edge of the room, she let her eyes wander as usual, her attention skimming over vampires and humans locking lips and locking fangs with flesh. Perhaps it was only her nerves, but the party seemed more sinister than usual. The smell of blood and alcohol pressed in on her like a warning despite the fact that she'd grown used to the scent.

Her skin prickled with unease as if someone had breathed on her neck. She turned but found nothing. Her heart throbbed a little too hard, and she tried to breathe deep as she assessed the room again.

Her breath caught in her throat as she met his stare. Not Benedict . . . Kerrigan. She'd never caught him looking at her in all this time, and she expected him to glance away or turn his back like he'd done so many times in the past month to make it clear that she was nothing but another warm body in a sea of willing arteries.

But this time he held her stare. She couldn't read his expression, and she took a faltering step toward him as if he'd called her name before stopping herself. Despite her desire to understand what was behind his look, she could not go to him. He'd said all he needed to say in those final moments before he'd left her last time. His words were a hole in her gut.

Whatever lurked behind his expression, it wasn't good. She turned her back on him.

She grabbed a bubbling drink the color of reluctant morning sun from one of the ornate gold trays passing by in the hands of a server. Pressing the cool glass to her lips, she gulped a quick swallow, savoring the assault of bubbles on her tongue and the way the alcohol made her head swim.

Still, she felt him watching as if he were right behind her.

She spun, and her drink smashed into the chest of a vampire whose hand reached out and closed over her fist that held the drink, steadying it and saving the last swallow of sloshing liquid.

"Kerrigan." His name came soft and startled from her lips. She tried to pull her hand away from him, but his grip held firm even if it wasn't harsh. She glanced down at his hand over hers and then back up at his face. "What are you . . ." She stopped herself. She didn't need to know what he was doing. Whatever it was, it wasn't meant to help.

"Your ruse is growing tired," he said. "You wear the mark of a bleeder, but people are noticing that you never seem to bleed at these things." He cocked his head as he examined her neck as if looking for evidence to the contrary.

"What do you care?" She tried to extract her hand from his again and failed. She was trapped until he decided she wasn't.

His brows furrowed for a moment as if she'd caught him, but then his expression shifted into something she knew well: that mask he'd worn so easily before their time together had slowly stripped it from him. His lips quirked into an easy, charming smile, and his eyes glinted with a dangerous mirth. "I'm going to help you, love." He leaned down until his lips almost touched the curve of her ear. "If you want to be a bleeder, then I'm going to make sure you bleed."

She was keenly aware of the parting of her lips and her too shallow breaths. She couldn't see his face, but she knew he was smiling. Whether for show or because he was actually delighted in her reaction, she didn't know. She hated that he could still wake up desire in her even when he was being cruel. It'd be so much easier if she felt nothing.

He pulled back with a satisfied smirk on his lips, and he finally released her hand before reaching up and winding a lock of her hair around his fingers until he held it tight like a leash.

"There are whispers," he said slowly, "that you're exclusive with someone, but nobody can figure out who." He sighed dramatically. "Unfortunately for you, you're much too pretty to slink around the shadows without multiple sets of fangs salivating for you." His tongue flicked across his bottom lip.

"Again, what do you care?" she repeated, more slowly, careful to keep her voice steady.

He shrugged. "I don't, if we're being completely honest, and the one thing I'm not is a liar." He put a bit of bite into the last word, and he gave her hair a tug that was just shy of being painful. "But I saw an opportunity for some fun."

"You said we should go our separate ways."

"I changed my mind. You've made yourself a thorn in my side. I intend to make myself a fang in your neck." His eyes traveled down her dress. It was a waterfall of gold that dipped between her breasts and left her back completely bare. The fabric cinched tightly at her hips before cascading to her ankles, and a slit went up one side, flashing her leg anytime she walked. "You should have worn something else if you wanted to hide. Did you know that I love my drinks wrapped in gold?"

Her cheeks went hot, but her words grew bold. "So you do still want me."

Something flashed in his eyes . . . a sliver of something real behind his mask. Whatever game he played, it was a precarious one for both of them.

"I may hate you, Bly, but a vampire has needs, and you've been flashing that beautiful skin of yours for the past month. Maybe we can have some fun now that you know exactly where we stand."

"Why would I want that?"

He raised an eyebrow. His stare drifted down to her almost naked chest and the very visible evidence of her heart beating way too fast. They both knew it wasn't from fear.

He was toying with her, and she liked it.

She hated how desperately she yearned for him to lean in and press his soft lips against her neck before feeling the prick of his fangs. She wanted that, but she wanted it the way it was before when she trusted him. This was not the Kerrigan who'd promised to help her get back everything she'd lost, who'd held her in his arms and told her to believe in him, who'd imagined eternity with her even as he was willing to die to save her from her guilt.

He was offering none of that. He wanted to use her, but he was also making it clear that she would be using him too. She tore her eyes away from him for the first time since he'd approached her. They were the center of attention. Was it true what he'd said? Were people suspicious of her? She couldn't have that.

She focused on him once more, trying to decipher what this was really about. Was it simply him having a good time or was he actually worried for her? Did he still care underneath the mask he'd slipped back in place?

It shouldn't matter, but it didn't stop her from wondering.

"Fine." She swallowed. "Let's get this over with."

He grinned, leaning back on his heels as his gaze traveled over her once more. "And how would you like it?" His smile faded for a moment, and he reached out a hand to a passing tray, grabbing his own drink. His fingers relinquished her hair before resting on the dagger at his waist. He cleared his throat. "I'm in the mood for a little blood in my drink."

He was giving her an easy out. Blood in alcohol was a popular request. Apparently, vampires loved the surge of lightheadedness along with the boost in their power that blood gave them. It made them feel both invincible and weightless at the same time.

She felt a rush of gratefulness. It'd prove she was giving her blood to someone without making the act intimate.

But she didn't want to look weak.

"No." She stretched her chin up and to the side. "Take my neck."

His eyes went black in an instant. She wasn't the only one who still felt something. It was her turn to smirk.

His mask vanished, and she saw all the raw truth underneath: rage and hurt and . . . longing. Her chest swelled at the sight of it because, despite everything that she had done and all the hurt she'd caused, he still felt something for her. At least a glimmer of it. This moment wasn't just a game. But as quickly as the mask had fallen, he snapped it back in place and morphed into that cold, smiling monster once more.

"Brave girl," he said, and then he added in a whisper, "but I'd expect nothing less."

He brushed the back of his hand across her jaw before sliding her hair away from her shoulders and cupping the back of her head. Without shifting his attention from her, he held out the drink in his hand, and a servant rushed to take it.

Kerrigan snaked his arm around her back, fingers spreading across her bare skin, softly pressuring her to close the gap between them, and she did. Her legs shook. His gentleness felt like a trap.

His hand at her nape curled into her hair and tugged, drawing her chin up as he bent down until his mouth hovered over her exposed neck.

He held the position for an excruciatingly long time, until she felt like a statue cast forever in a moment of longing with no release.

When he finally bit, it was different from before, when his lips teased her first until she was so fevered that the sharpness felt like nothing but a harsher kiss.

This time, she was overly aware of her skin ripping and the intrusion of his fangs.

She jerked in surprise at the pain, and Kerrigan pulled back slightly, fangs slipping out. His mouth should have been closed over the wound, drinking, but he was hesitating, and she didn't know why. It didn't fit either of the roles they were playing. They'd been good at pretending before. They could do it again.

"Come on," she hissed quietly, and that was all it took.

His lips closed over the wound as his fingers curled against her back, scraping against her skin as he pulled her closer. She went willingly. Her free hand gripped the sleeve of his shirt. Her other hand still clenched the stem of her glass, and she was amazed that the force of her grip hadn't shattered it.

And then it was over. His fingers trailed across her back as his hand dropped away and her scalp tingled as he released the grip on her hair. She hadn't realized how tightly he'd held her until she was free.

His mouth was still parted when he pulled away, her blood staining his lips, and she stared up at his vulnerable expression, catching the need in it before he buried it once more.

He raised an eyebrow and stared pointedly at where she still held his arm. "Was that not enough for you?"

No. She wanted more. She wanted everything he'd given her before.

But she didn't say any of that; she forced herself to release him.

His tongue ran across the tips of his fangs, wiping away the blood there. *Her* blood.

She realized her own lips were still parted, and her breathing too audible.

His smirk returned.

She snapped her mouth closed.

After running his thumb across his own fang to draw blood, he reached toward her broken skin, but she twisted away.

"Let me heal you," he grumbled, moving again toward her.

The wound throbbed as she shook her head. "No, thank you."

"No need to keep the scar as a memory of me, love. You can always come back for more . . . as long as we both know what this is."

She glared at him. "You said my ruse was weak, and now one look at me says otherwise."

She moved to brush past him, and he stepped aside to let her go, but not before grabbing her arm and holding her near him for one second longer. "Careful walking around like that," he said. His voice had lost its fake charm.

He meant the words.

She was glad for them.

It was a good thing she was done hiding in the shadows because every eye was on her as she strode across the room. Subtleness didn't suit her anymore . . . it wasn't the right lure for what she wanted to catch.

Benedict watched her approach with his head cocked to the side, the smile on his lips spreading into a dazzling grin as she stopped in front of him.

"My dear Bly. You're looking particularly gorgeous this evening." His eyes drifted down, but unlike Kerrigan, who had taken in the whole of her, Benedict focused entirely on her neck.

The heat of her blood trickling out became scalding.

When he met her eyes again, his were black.

Her stomach rolled. Had he looked at Elise with that hunger?

He must have. What other purpose could he have for keeping her sister captive?

This was a monster.

Not all vampires were evil, but Benedict certainly had to be. Kerrigan hid his kind heart behind a similar playboy charm, but Benedict hid an evil one.

It took every bit of Bly's own acting skills to force a smile onto her face.

Benedict gave her a playful frown. "But you've been avoiding me, haven't you, dear?"

"I—"

"Don't bother." He waved a hand. "I'm sure you thought I'd retaliate over the whole Donovan fiasco. My lovely sister would sure like to. Lucky for you, she hasn't been to one of these shindigs since you tossed her lover to the witches."

He was right. That had been her second greatest fear in coming to Vagaris after the Games and masquerading as a bleeder. She worried that Kerrigan would tell everyone that she was the girl who'd handed over their prince, but all anyone seemed to know was that Donovan had been captured in the woods, fair and square. But Kerrigan had clearly told Benedict along with Jade. There could be others.

She supposed it didn't matter.

She'd already faced her greatest fear in coming here: seeing the hate for her on Kerrigan's face.

"Also lucky for you," Benedict continued, "I am not the vindictive sort. Life's too long for that. You and Donovan both played a game, and you"—he reached out and bopped her nose like someone joking with a small child—"won."

Her desire to break his finger was overwhelming.

He didn't notice what was surely on her face because he was looking at her neck again.

She held still, saying nothing at all until his eyes met hers again.

"The question is," he mused, "what changed? Every time I've gotten close to you in the past month, you've flitted away."

Before she thought he was just a nuisance, and now she wanted to murder him. That's what had changed.

The truth seemed like a bad answer.

"I've been . . . shy," she said. "But I think I've gotten over that, and you've been watching me. Wanting me," she stated boldly.

She expected him to grin at her bluntness, but his expression had grown uncharacteristically shrewd as he examined her.

"More like you were trying to lure a very specific vampire whom you loved so much that you betrayed him in the worst possible way. I'm sure you had some wild hope that if he just tasted you again, he'd forget about all that." He reached out and ran a finger through the trail of blood on her neck. "But he didn't even heal you. You felt what it was like to be drunk from by someone who doesn't care if you live or die."

She flinched. Kerrigan *had* offered to heal her—wanted to, even—but that last part still rang a little too true.

Benedict licked her blood slowly off his finger.

"You came to the wrong vampire if you think I'll make you feel any different."

"What if I just want more pain?"

His eyes were black again, and his smile sharpened. "In that case, you came to the right place."

He reached for her, but she shook her head. "Not here."

She forced herself to look back to where she'd left Kerrigan. He was there, watching with dark eyes. She couldn't tell if they were black or not.

Benedict followed her attention and sighed. "Just let go of him. *That* is a vampire who knows how to hold a grudge."

"Not here," she said again.

Benedict grumbled, but he took her hand and began tugging her through the crowd until they were in the hallway, turning not toward the exit but toward the maze of passageways that she knew led to his rooms. Rooms that definitely didn't have Elise in them.

She planted her feet and almost toppled over from him pulling her along.

He stopped, turning back to her. "Don't tell me you've had a change of heart?"

"No . . . I just . . . bad memories." His rooms were near Kerrigan's, so it wasn't too much of a stretch to suggest she didn't want to go there. "Can we go somewhere outside of here . . . in town?"

The black retracted slightly in his eyes, revealing the outer ring of blue. The contrast was unsettling. So was the expression that slid briefly onto his face: suspicion.

She'd overplayed.

But the suspicion slid away as he flashed his teeth in a smile probably meant to make any neck curve willingly in his direction. "Are you expecting me to wine and dine you? Take you to bed and devour you in more ways than one? I hate to break your heart, but I'm not Kerrigan. All I want is blood."

His stare shifted to behind her, and then his hands were

on her shoulders, pushing her backward into one of the many alcoves that lined this hallway. Her shoulders hit a life-size statue of a woman with a man embracing her from behind. The statue's naked breasts jabbed into Bly's back as Benedict pushed close enough that his chest would touch Bly's if she breathed too deeply.

"This will do just fine," he said. It felt like he loomed over her despite the fact that he was only a couple inches taller at most. "You do want this, right? I love a quick bite from just about any neck, but only when it's offered. Are you still offering?"

What about Elise? She wanted to spit at him. Unless Donovan had lied, Benedict had her somewhere ... doing what to her exactly if he refused to drink from Bly without permission? He had to be holding Elise prisoner until she gave in.

Despite his reassurances, he seemed capable of such a thing.

His eyes were full black again, and he drew in a long breath. He squeezed her shoulders he still gripped. "Answer me. I'll double whatever you normally charge."

"I'll triple it." Bly jerked at the sound of Kerrigan's voice. For a moment, she felt the familiar rush of relief to have him near her, but it faded. She needed to say yes to Benedict. That was her best play, even if he didn't take her to his hideaway. This could still be her way to get closer to him.

Benedict blew out an exasperated sigh before looking over his shoulder. "I thought you'd had your fill, Kerrigan."

Kerrigan replied with a wolfish grin. "You know me—I'm always hungry for seconds."

"Well, at least your brother would be pleased you have your appetite back." He turned back and winked at Bly. "Although he might find your tastes a bit questionable."

"And yours, apparently," Kerrigan said.

Benedict shrugged. "He wouldn't be surprised. He knows and loves me for the terrible vampire I am. But I'm afraid I cannot release the girl to you unless that's what she wants."

Kerrigan glowered. Both vampires turned to Bly. She swallowed, making her bloody throat bob, and they both followed the movement.

"I'll go with Kerrigan." She blurted the words without thinking. It wasn't the plan, but there he was, asking for her, wanting her with his dark eyes exactly the way she'd dreamed. If the moment between them had stirred something in him, she wanted to chase it. Maybe he'd give her a chance to plead for forgiveness, and they could work together again. Taking down Benedict would be safer with Kerrigan behind her.

Benedict shook his head as he let go of her and stepped away. "You're playing a fool's game," he said, looking between them, and then he was gone, striding down the hallway and leaving them alone.

Bly let out a breath of relief. She *was* playing a fool's game, just not the one Benedict imagined.

She looked expectantly at Kerrigan. She wanted him to close the gap between them, but he didn't.

"What do you think you're doing?" His words were harsher than she expected.

She'd chosen him—shouldn't that have softened him just a little bit?

"What I need to." Taking a step away from the statue, she closed some of the space between them.

"Benedict might not kill you on purpose, but he's careless."

He shifted to look after where Benedict had gone and nodded as if he'd just confirmed something. "He's the name Donovan gave you."

Bly chewed her lip. She wanted to trust him too badly. "Yes," she answered. "Can you help me? She's not in his fortress rooms. Do you know another place he might be? You were friends once, weren't you?"

He chuckled, shaking his head, looking at her like she was a sad, wounded animal who needed to be put out of its misery, a wolf with its leg broken in a trap. "You still think I'm trying to help you, but I just ruined your plan." He smiled. "Payback."

Her stomach sank. "I didn't . . . I told Emerson not to get in your way."

"You're telling me that you didn't think he'd do anything?"

She shook her head, doubting herself. Had she thought that? "No," she said.

"I don't believe you."

"I don't believe you, either," she said.

He raised his eyebrows in question.

"You didn't come here to break up me and Benedict to foil a plan you didn't even know I had. You were worried about me." She said each word slowly, like an accusation.

She took a bold step toward him, and he took a step back as if she would hurt him. She smiled despite the way her stomach clenched. He cared about her, but it scared him. He was afraid to be close to her.

"I wasn't," he said, but it was there in his voice: the lie.

She moved to go past him before he could collect himself enough to find the right words to shatter her heart again, but he grabbed her arm and pushed her back into the alcove against the statue once more.

"You're not going back out there like that," he growled.

For a moment, she didn't know what he meant, but then he bit his thumb, drawing blood and pressing it into the still-dripping holes in her neck before she could even utter a word of protest. As her skin healed itself, he fumbled with the scarf at his neck, releasing the white silk before wiping it across her bloody skin with a roughness that contrasted the airy material. When he pulled it back, it was streaked crimson.

He stared down at it and back up at her before striding away with the scarf clenched in his fist.

FIVE

BLY HAD A NEW, BETTER PLAN FOR GETTING Benedict's attention. One that would ensure that he'd actually take her to his home and not just his rooms in the fortress, but it wasn't something that she could put into action until five nights from now. The wait seemed impossibly long.

She needed a distraction, and the memory of Kerrigan pressing his scarf into her neck and wiping away her blood, even if his movements had been harsh and cold, idled in her mind.

He kept saying that he didn't care about her, but there were small moments that told her he *was* a liar even if he was lying to himself. She understood what he was doing. She'd hurt him, but he kept drawing her back to him with actions he couldn't seem to fight. So he used words to hurt her, hoping they'd be enough to keep her away. But she'd stolen his brother—harsh words wouldn't make them even. She'd already forgiven him for it.

He might hate her but hate and love could exist together. She was fairly certain that wasn't unusual. She might never be able to unbury the love from the hate, but the least that she could do was show him that she cared about getting Donovan back, because her actions so far said that she didn't.

So she'd gone to the nightly party again, avoided Benedict's searching eyes, and slipped out into the night after Kerrigan. She didn't bother with invisibility spells. She wanted him to know that she would follow him into the dark again and again to make up for what she'd done.

His light copper hair glowed in the moonlight as he kept a clipped pace that wove between the trees. He had to know that she was behind him, but he hadn't turned. His pace increased until she thought she'd have to use a speed spell just to keep up. A cold sweat broke out on her face, but she didn't think he was actually trying to lose her until he shifted around a particularly dense patch of saplings and brush, and when she followed, she found the night still and empty.

She stopped short, her breath coming too heavy and loud in the dark and her heart racing forward without her. Unease slithered up her spine.

"Caught you." The words brushed the back of her neck, an echo of what Donovan had spoken to her that first time she'd met them in the clearing. Kerrigan meant them now as a threat, no doubt. He was trying to recreate an unpleasant memory, except this time, Kerrigan was playing a different role. He wasn't the savior. He was the hunter cornering his prey.

But she was different now too. Her pulse still skittered, but she wasn't going to spin around in fear and put up a desperate fight. If he wanted to bite her, she'd welcome it.

She craved it.

She hadn't even noticed that her neck had arched, her head tilting to one side for him until she felt him lean over her, his breath brushing against the spot where her pulse throbbed just below the curve of her jaw.

"So hungry," he murmured, and she wasn't sure if he was talking about her or him or the both of them, but then his voice grew hard. "Pathetic."

She still wasn't sure which of them he meant, but she felt the cold night air creep back in between them as his body shifted away from her, and finally, she turned.

His face was painfully empty. "What do you want, Bly? There's no reason for you to follow me. You know where your sister is."

"But I don't."

"I doubt Benedict has her hidden in the woods."

"I don't expect to find her here."

"Then why are you bothering me? Looking for other ways to hurt me? You should know better than most that you already hurt me in the only way that was left." His voice cracked and so did his stoic expression. He seemed surprised by the emotion.

The raw devastation on his face felt like it was ripping Bly's throat out. She was bleeding for him, hurting for him, but anytime she felt pain for what Kerrigan was going through, she felt even more guilt. She didn't deserve to hurt for him when she'd been the cause of it. She didn't know what to feel. She didn't think she deserved to feel anything at all.

"I'm sorry," she said. The two words seemed so ridiculous. Meaningless in the face of what she'd done. Words meant to heal her guilt and not his pain.

He clearly felt the same. His face hardened.

"I know you don't want to hear that," she said. "I'm sorry . . . for saying it."

He glared at her. "You're sorry for saying you're sorry?"

If the moment wasn't so horrible, she might've laughed. Instead, she shook her head. "I don't want to say anything else because I know you don't want to hear it. I just want to help you. Show you that I'm . . ." She stopped herself from saying *sorry* again.

"I don't know what I have to do to convince you that I don't want your help. Playing with you yesterday was . . . a moment of weakness. All I really want, Bly, is to never have to look at you again. I didn't think there was anything left in this world that could cause me pain, but you . . ." He shook his head. "You proved me wrong." He was silent for a long moment, letting his words suffocate her. "You made me feel again. You made me feel . . . happy in a way I didn't think was possible for me anymore, and then you made me feel pain in a way I didn't think was possible for me anymore." His words grew horribly soft. "Now all I want is to go back to feeling nothing."

She hadn't meant to do any of that, but her intentions didn't matter. She'd taken a sad vampire and turned him into a wounded monster.

A tiny sob broke through her lips.

The sound of her crying didn't soften him. Instead, rage broke through his melancholy. He took two quick steps toward her, stopping just short of touching her. "What do I have to do to make you stop following me?" he ground out. Even in the dark, she could see that his eyes were burning black with a stare that seemed to have the power to strip her skin from her flesh. "Do I need to break your legs? Put you in the ground?" He gave a harsh laugh. "I'm not sure you realize exactly who you are dealing with."

She didn't. All she knew were the parts of his past that he'd told her. Nobody revealed the worst parts of themselves, but he was now.

She didn't flinch from it. "Do it," she said, "because that's the only way you're going to stop me from coming after you. I *am* going to help you get your brother back, and not because I'm trying to earn your forgiveness or win you back. I don't expect that, but you once asked me to watch you die in exchange for my sister's life because you needed to atone for your past. I'm begging you to let me atone for mine."

"But you *didn't* let me!" he snarled so close to her face that she could feel the heat of his breath.

"You're better than me," she said softly.

He took a quick step back as if the words had slapped him.

"Let me help you," she begged.

His shoulders slumped as if her pleading had punctured him and released some of his rage.

She expected something harsh. New words meant to break her and send her scurrying into the dark.

"Fine," he said. The word sounded like surrender. She wondered if the harsh things he'd said had broken something in him and not just her.

She wanted to reach for him but knew that her touch would only do more damage, so she buried her hands inside the pockets of her cloak and nodded. "I'll follow you then," she said.

He brushed by her.

She trailed him for hours through the night with only the sound of branches and leaves crushing beneath their feet. They found nothing, and when Kerrigan led them back to the fortress, he left her behind without a word.

✦ ✦ ✦

When she followed him the next night, he didn't acknowledge her presence at all. This time, he didn't leave the fortress, and they crept through hallways and hidden passageways that branched off from alcoves and seemed like dead ends. They came out into other hallways through pictures that opened like doors. Bly was in awe of the intricacies of the fortress. She savored the secrets Kerrigan showed her as she remained his silent shadow. Still, they found nothing.

And nothing around the edges of the lake on the next night.

On the fourth night, he sighed when he glanced behind him and saw her.

"Still here." It was more of a resignation than a question, but she answered anyways.

"Always," she said, which was perhaps a little bit dramatic.

He shook his head, seeming to think so as well. "I've actually got a lead tonight."

She expected him to tell her to leave him alone because he didn't actually trust her when something was on the line, but instead he said, "Stay close. If we get shot at, I want you near enough to take an arrow for me. You owe me." His voice was dry. She couldn't tell if it was a joke or not.

"Of course," she said, but he had already turned, heading into the woods. Bly kept one step behind him, relishing the closeness even though he didn't bother glancing back to make sure that she followed.

Eventually, he stopped at the base of a tall pine and rested his back against it, turning to her with a finger to his lips while motioning for her to step closer to him. She could smell the faint scent of cinnamon mingling with the sweetness of the pine, and she drew in deeper breaths, savoring the moment even though she knew it meant nothing to him. His head tilted away from her, listening to something she couldn't hear with her human ears.

"Ahead and to the left," he whispered. "You wait here."

He started to slip away from her, and she reached out a hand to stop him but thought better of it. "Let me help," she said.

He paused, looking back at her. His expression, as usual, gave her nothing.

"Invisibility?" he asked. "I only brought one."

"I have one." Her last one. Hazel had run out for now.

"Good." He thought for a minute. "Fine. You'll go into the camp and check the prisoners, and I'll skirt the perimeter and count the guards."

She hesitated. He was letting her take the greatest risk.

"Problem?" he asked. "You know you're free to leave if you'd like. I don't need you."

In answer, she slipped a hand into the pocket of her coat and pulled out a slender little box no bigger than her pinkie. She opened it and plucked out the dragonfly wing before crushing it in her fingers and whispering the spell.

She moved away from Kerrigan in the direction he'd told her as she reached into her other pocket and cast a stealth spell as well. When she looked over her shoulder, Kerrigan had disappeared. She didn't have time to worry about him.

With the stealth spell masking her movements, her main concern was being fast enough. The only thing that could go wrong was her invisibility spell not lasting long enough for her to get in and out. Popping into existence in a secret prison surrounded by vampire guards was not how she wanted to die.

She didn't have to go far before she reached the wall of guards that formed a red-clad circle around a wide clearing behind them. Half the guards faced outward while the others faced inward toward the cluster of jail cells that rose eerily out of place in the forest.

She held her breath as she stepped out into the guard's line of sight. But nobody so much as blinked in her direction. Invisibility always made her feel vulnerable. It was frightening to walk up to danger while it couldn't see you, knowing you'd be dead if that changed, but she swallowed her discomfort and reached the edge of their ring.

With the last prison, the guards had been spaced out, leaning against the trees in a more casual perimeter. These guards stood almost shoulder to shoulder, creating a wall of red.

Halfryta was there. Bly could practically feel it.

She imagined herself slipping through their defenses, finding the witch, and then telling Kerrigan the news. He'd cradle her face in his hands in his excitement and press his lips to hers before he thought twice about it, and even though it would still take more time to fix what she had broken between them, they'd look back on this moment as the start of a new future for them.

She shook herself. She wasn't doing this to earn his forgiveness, but sometimes she still fantasized it was possible. After all, she had very little in her current reality to keep her going.

The problem was getting through the guards. They may not be able to see her, but they'd certainly be able to feel her if she brushed up against them. It had to be why they stood like this.

She scanned the tree line around them, but of course Kerrigan had likely used his own invisibility spell by now. She wished she could see him. Would he be worried for her? He probably hadn't expected so many guards.

Stalking around the edges of their wall, she looked for a crack. There. A guard with shaggy brown hair and an animated, soft face had turned to whisper to the woman beside him, who smiled at whatever the other vampire said even though her eyes stayed glued to the forest.

Bly approached them. The vampire grinned as he spoke. "I'm telling you, it's the best place to get a drink. Sure . . ."

The vampire was close enough for the breath of his words to hit Bly's face as she turned sideways and shifted her body slowly between them.

". . . they mix their drinks like everyone else with blood sold in the market . . ."

Bly shuffled her feet side to side clutching her cloak to her body so no part of her touched them.

". . . but they have a bleeder on staff who adds a couple of drops of her fresh blood into each glass, and I swear it makes all the difference."

Almost there.

"Formation," barked a voice on the other side of the circle, and the grinning vampire's face fell as he snapped back to attention, forcing Bly to dodge his shoulder.

She stumbled into the clearing and fell, landing hard on her side. She held her breath, waiting for snarling faces to turn on her. But nobody moved. Her spells were still working. She got up and turned to the cages: one large square divided into four sections.

Her heart sunk immediately, but she still got up and circled them as if a different angle would change what she saw. One held a man with a thick beard and long, scraggly hair curled up into a ball on his side. His eyes were closed, so Bly couldn't tell if he was human or witch or vampire, but he looked like he'd been there for some time. The next cage held a witch with his blue eyes open and staring aimlessly into the dark. The third cage was empty, and the fourth held a hulking vampire with pale skin and dark brown hair shaved close to his scalp. His dark gray eyes glared out at the backs of his fellow vampires, and his hands gripped the bars so tightly his knuckles were white.

She spun, taking in the wall of guards that she'd thought had to have been meant for the head witch. Her eyes flicked back to the vampire. He seemed like someone who might warrant such security.

The imprisoned vampire's stare landed on Bly, and her breath caught in her throat. She held up a hand in front of her face and saw nothing. Darting to the left, she waited for the vampire's eyes to shift with her. He didn't register the movement. Her limbs tingled with relief.

She needed to get out of here before she *did* snap into view.

Sliding around the perimeter, she paused at the vampire who'd been chatting earlier. He faced inside now, his face glum and bored, his broad shoulders almost touching the vampires next to him.

Curses.

She glanced around, searching for a crack to slide through. One vampire stood with his legs a little too wide and another slouched a little to the right, leaving a larger gap open, but both would be tight. One wrong move and they'd feel her. They'd swing their swords down and, invisible or not, she'd bleed and possibly die, and then when the spell wore off, they'd find a human girl's broken corpse at their feet.

She needed help, but she couldn't ask for it. Kerrigan had probably already done his part and left.

She walked the perimeter again, feeling the eyes of every vampire on her even though they didn't see her.

Getting down on her hands and knees, she eyed the gap between the legs of the vampire with the widest stance. It was her best shot.

Something crashed in the forest. The vampire formation shifted, and Bly darted to her feet.

"Hold," said the captain. "It sounded like a tree."

Another snap of wood breaking against its will followed the crash. And then another.

Kerrigan. He must have guessed her problem. He wouldn't leave her . . . even if it was only because he needed to know who was behind the guards.

Bly shifted, so she stood behind the captain. Finally, he moved, stepping toward the tree line. "Harold and Angelica, with me. Close the gaps," he barked.

But Bly stepped forward, practically hugging the captain's back as the rest of the guards tightened their trap. She let out a soft sigh of relief, and the captain spun, looking directly at her without seeing her.

She held her breath as he pulled his sword a couple of inches from its sheath. She was tempted to run with the stealth spell masking the sound of her movements, but she had a feeling he was waiting to feel the barest stir in the air. He was smart, and if he swung his sword in a sweeping arc in front of him, he'd cut her in two.

Another crash sounded in the woods.

"Captain," said the vampire behind him.

He turned, glancing back in Bly's direction once more before jogging away.

Bly bolted, running until the night fell silent around her. Pausing, she pulled out the compass Emerson had given her. Even though she had a good sense of direction, and she always felt a pull toward exactly where she was heading, it never hurt to double-check. Especially when wandering far enough in the wrong direction might put her in the path of a banished vampire.

She tugged her cloak tighter across her chest. The winter cold turned violent at night and ate away at you until you couldn't feel whole pieces of yourself, but Bly barely noticed. Her own mind ate at her with the same violence.

She couldn't bear the thought of telling Kerrigan that Halfryta wasn't there.

Trying to pull herself out of the disappointment, she breathed in the smells of the forest that deepened at night as she moved: fresh pine, leaves turning to mulch, and frozen ground. It calmed her, if only for a moment.

The night was haunting—everything stripped to just a black outline of itself. A person might be standing in the cluster of trees, and unless the moonlight granted you a peek of their face, you might never know someone had been watching you. She missed Kerrigan's back walking ahead of her like a beacon, because however he felt about her, she had a feeling that her scream would bring him.

Or that could be wishful thinking.

Eventually a chorus of frogs leaked through the darkness, and the sound stole away some of her unease. She was almost there, and she imagined Kerrigan's relief at seeing that she'd got out safely. After all, he'd made sure she escaped.

She bit her lip, trying to stop her mind from wandering where it didn't deserve. He needed her. It didn't mean he cared.

She was trying to be more like Emerson these days and be practical with her thoughts. It didn't come easily.

Especially when she looked at Kerrigan.

He was a tall silhouette on the edge of the lake with the toes of his boots just shy of where the water met the stone of the arena. She wished they'd picked a different meeting place.

His arms were loose at his side, and he stared out at water that seemed endless in the darkness.

"Kerrigan."

He spun at the sound of her voice, eyes searching.

His invisibility spell had faded, but hers had not.

"I'm right here," she said.

He stepped toward her, arms out as if longing to hold her, and for a second, she stood there relishing the sight of him reaching for her, but his face held a terrified eagerness, and she knew it wasn't because he wanted to pull her to his chest. She had the information that he wanted.

"I'm here," she said again as she stopped in front of him. His searching hands brushed her shoulders before running up the sides of her neck and resting against her cheeks, and the touch wasn't hard or hate-filled like before.

"Tell me," he said. "I can't see you. Tell me."

His fingers brushed over her skin as if he could read the answer there, and a desperate part of her wanted to stay quiet, to let him keep searching her body. The second she spoke, he'd release her.

If they'd found Halfryta, then he would've pulled her to him and squeezed her with relief, but she'd taken his brother from him, and now she had to tell him that she hadn't found the witch that would bring him back.

"Bly." His hands pressed her face. "Speak."

"She wasn't there."

He didn't release her like she'd feared he would, but his fingers curled into claws against her cheeks, and she felt the tension in the touch as if he had to fight to stop himself from tearing her to pieces. One hand released her and the other shifted to grip her chin.

"That makes no sense. I saw the guards. We'd never station that many for a normal prisoner. Who was in there?"

"A vampire, a different witch, and a man . . . I think . . . I couldn't tell. And one empty cage. The vampire looked threatening enough to warrant the guards, but the extra guards could just be because the rebels freed a prison a few nights ago."

He shook his head.

"We'll find her. We'll go out again and again until we do." She reached out a hand and laid it across his chest.

He glanced down at the invisible pressure of her touch. When he looked back up, his eyes were fevered, but not in the way that haunted her thoughts, not black with passion and hunger. Dark with hate.

"You want to be close to me." He said the words as if they were a horrible curse, and she wanted to snatch her hand away from his chest, but she couldn't. "If I actually find my brother, I will have no use for you anymore. I'd be free of you."

Her hand trembled against the wool of his coat, but she still held it there.

"*That's* why I can't believe you. Because you're selfish enough to leave my brother rotting with the witches if it helps you."

"I wouldn't," she said, but the words sounded weak even to her own ears. They were a lie, and not because Kerrigan was right, but because she'd already done the thing he was accusing her of.

The invisibility spell dissipated, and they both looked down at her hand spread against his chest.

Kerrigan looked back up at her face. She wanted the spell back. She didn't want him to see her guilt. Or maybe she did.

She needed him to understand how sorry she was.

Even if she wouldn't take it back. Yes, she'd done it because she wanted to have everything: her sister back and Kerrigan alive. She hadn't thought beyond that. She hadn't let herself consider the way that choice would twist her dream into a nightmare.

But Kerrigan was alive in front of her. She'd do it again even if it hurt her . . . just to keep him safe.

His lips twisted into disgust. "Who are your tears for, Bly? Donovan? Or for yourself." He said it like a statement, like he wouldn't accept another answer.

"For you," she whispered. It wasn't the fact that Kerrigan hated her that killed her. At least, that wasn't all of it. It was because she'd changed the boy who wanted to die for her into one who wanted to kill her. She'd undone the steps he'd taken to get his humanity back after this world had tried to strip him of it. She'd turned him into a vampire in the truest sense of the word.

He took a step back, and her fingers trailed down his chest before her hand fell back to her side.

"Leave me alone, Bly," he said. "I thought I could trust you enough to help me now that you know who has your sister, but I don't think I can." He turned his back on her and strode into the night.

SIX

BLY WORE WHITE FOR THE FIRST TIME IN her life. White wasn't a color you wore in the Gap or in the woods where mud clung to the hem of every garment. Even during the trials for the Games, the vampires had been smart enough not to dress the humans in the color that would highlight the brutality of what they did. No, they wore red and purple as camouflage to hide the truth. But there were no such illusions here tonight.

All the bleeders stood next to high golden tables sprinkled around the room, wearing white silk dresses in various designs, looking like blank canvases waiting to be splattered with red. They didn't need to hide the truth. Each of them wanted to bleed for one reason or another.

Bly understood what it was like to *want* to bleed, even if that desire was reserved for Kerrigan, but she *would* bleed for anyone if it meant getting her sister back.

That's what she was doing here tonight.

Many bleeders chose to frequent the vampire parties or the streets of Vagaris, selling their blood to whoever struck their fancy, but there were others who craved more stability, and wealthy vampires could employ a bleeder to work exclusively for them. Stories of those vampires falling in love with the bleeders were often whispered in the Gap. Before she knew any better, Bly had always thought those tales were spread by the vampires themselves to lure people into the job, but now she had no doubt that it happened. She knew how easy it was to go from being disgusted by getting your blood drawn to craving it. She knew the way it felt to be a life source for someone you cared about. It was addicting.

Her pulse strummed a little too fast just thinking about it.

The bleeders here tonight wanted money and security, but some surely hoped for a pairing that ended in more.

These parties were hosted by the Blood Matcher: the vampire responsible for connecting bleeders who wanted to work exclusively with the vampires who wanted to pay them.

A vampire stopped in front of Bly, but not the one she was looking for. This one had muted brown hair pulled back into a tight bun at the nape of his neck, making his already sharp features appear cruel. Or maybe that was the coldness in his eyes as he appraised her.

She fought the urge to swallow. She didn't want to highlight her neck, but the vampires who had dressed her earlier had also piled her hair into a loose bun on the top of her head that let some of her curls spring free and brush her cheeks as well as her nape. Her throat was already on full display.

She didn't know whether to stare at the vampire or look away, so she glanced at her gold sandals and the thin ribbons that wound halfway up her calves where they ended in tiny bows.

It was probably a mistake to look timid. Like a rabbit. She steeled herself and glanced back up, but thankfully the vampire had already lost interest and moved on to a very attractive young man a few bleeders down.

None of the vampires perusing the room were Benedict. Emerson had been talking to other vampires in the bars, and while nobody knew exactly where Benedict hid himself away when he wasn't at the fortress, there were rumors that he kept a well-staffed house full of personal bleeders. Like Kerrigan, Benedict was a favorite of the queens and led gold mining expeditions that went deep into the forest beyond Vagaris. Bly had a hard time picturing him—the same vampire who'd yielded so willingly during their standoff in the Games—being cunning enough to take a team of vampires through banished territory, but clearly, he was good at it. Benedict was said to be one of the richest among the royal children, and Jade was his right hand. That had to be his secret to success. Bly had no problem imagining his sister tearing her way through any obstacle.

Whatever his secret, he had the funds to keep multiple bleeders on staff. This fact seemed to irritate quite a few of the town vampires who thought he was being selfish and hoarding them when the rules drawn between the vampires and witches only allowed each city to employ so many humans for the purpose of fresh blood.

Benedict had to come. They said he loved to browse even if he didn't buy.

Bly knew she'd catch his attention after the way things had

ended last time. But as the night wore on, more and vampires stopped in front of her. Some smiled with their fangs. Some looked at her like she was an object. Others said a friendly hello and wanted to chat.

But none of them were Benedict, and she began to worry.

If someone else chose her, she'd have to go. A bleeder could decide to leave and go back to the Gap at any time, but if Bly lost her job, she'd lose the access she had to Vagaris.

She'd be abandoning Emerson, and Emerson already wanted to just corner Benedict in a dark alley and try to overpower him and force him to give up Elise's location.

Benedict was older and stronger than Emerson, and even if they did catch him unaware, there was no guarantee he'd give them what they wanted, and then what would be left for them? They couldn't hold him forever when he'd trapped Elise somewhere. Benedict struck Bly as a vampire who would be smart enough to know that.

Emerson listened, but Bly had never seen him so close to acting rashly.

Standing here with no Benedict in sight made her doubt herself though.

Panic started to spread along her chest, and she tried to breathe slowly in through her nose and out her mouth. The last thing she wanted was her chest heaving or her skin flushing. If Benedict wasn't coming, then she didn't need to look more appealing.

Not everyone got matched, and maybe that was the best she could hope for tonight. But the next matching would be a month away. Too many days of wondering if each second was the one where Elise's death curse would yank the life from her.

Bly's chest tightened again.

But then she spotted his shock of white-blond hair and his chiseled face, which stood out even in a room packed full of pretty people and vampires.

The Blood Matcher was on him in a second, offering him a gleaming glass filled to the brim with a burgundy liquid that Bly had come to recognize as an equal mixture of blood and red wine. He took a deep swallow as his eyes wandered around the room and the Blood Matcher chattered next to him. Her chestnut curls bobbed with excitement, and her smile was gleaming and wide. Clearly, she thought Benedict would choose someone.

And then the Blood Matcher pointed at Bly. If Benedict came to every single one of these, then of course he was one of the vampires who would be excited by fresh prospects.

Benedict's eyes drifted from Bly's toes upward. When he reached her face, his drink lowered slowly from his lips. He raised his eyebrows as he lifted his glass back up in a cheers motion to her.

He spoke to the Blood Matcher for a moment longer before heading her way.

"Darling," he said when he reached her. "Your dearest love, Kerrigan, does not frequent these things. I could be wrong, but I don't believe he employs any bleeders. Such a bore." His focus shifted from her to scan the room as he lifted his glass to his lips once more.

"Who says I'm here for Kerrigan?"

His eyes snapped back to her.

"Well, it's him, not I, whose every move you've been tracking for the past few weeks. Not to mention the fact that he seems rather protective of you." He took another slow drink as he appraised her. "Despite what you did to his brother. Or did that turn him on?" He shrugged. "To each their own."

She winced. "I don't belong to Kerrigan."

"Then you're looking to belong to someone else?"

"I'm standing here, aren't I?"

The slight smirk that was always on his lips faded for a moment, and his expression grew more serious than she thought him capable of. "I don't know who you're trying to fool . . . me . . . or yourself."

A chill ran through her. She and Elise didn't look that much alike. There was no way a self-centered vampire like Benedict would notice whatever slight similarities there were between them, like the shape of their eyes or the roundness of their lips. But she couldn't risk any suspicion from him.

"I just want to forget about Kerrigan. If I have to fool myself for a while to get there, then so be it."

"I'm a big fan of fooling oneself if it makes you happy." He sighed. "Best of luck to you." He was no longer looking at her like she was hiding something, but his focus had left her altogether, and he drifted away.

She wasn't sure how to recapture his attention.

Maybe he didn't want to get between her and Kerrigan. She wasn't exactly sure why he'd care though. If anything, it seemed like Benedict would want her just to spite Kerrigan given that Kerrigan had killed his brother all those years ago, but he had said he didn't hold grudges.

She couldn't quite figure him out. She wouldn't want to if not for Elise, but now that she was trying, there seemed to be more to him than met the eye—a lurking sadness behind his charm that reminded her of Kerrigan.

But what she didn't want to do was sympathize with him. Unless Donovan had simply lied to her, behind Benedict's pretty face was a monster who kept humans against their will despite the fact he had plenty of money for bleeders.

She wanted to stomp after him, smash his glass against his head, and demand answers.

Instead, she placed a placid smile on her face and tried not to look overly appealing to anyone else.

"You're popular."

Bly jumped at the voice so close to her ear, shifting away on instinct from the thought of fangs one strike away from her neck. But the teeth that flashed a smile at her had no sharpness even though the curve of the man's lips did.

"I'm jealous." The man sighed, hooking his thumbs into the top of his white trousers in a way that pulled them past the angle of his hips. He wore no shirt over his smooth, tanned chest. A bleeder just like her.

"I don't think you need to be," Bly said.

He laughed before it trailed into another sigh. "I appreciate that, although I haven't gotten even a nibble. But you're new. Brand new, it seems. Bleeders talk. Did your sponsor tire of you already? Or did you tire of them? If you used someone just to get in and try to get a better match, you might not live to regret that. Vampires hold grudges."

"I . . ." Bly wasn't sure how much to tell about herself, but in all her time here, she'd been so busy tailing Kerrigan that she'd never bothered to get to know another bleeder. But she wanted to. She wondered how they had even gotten here when you needed a vampire to sponsor you. She'd had Emerson. Not many humans had a vampire friend. "I know the guy who won the last Games. He sponsored me, but he doesn't drink blood . . . from the source."

"That won't last," he said with a laugh.

Bly wondered if that were true—if living in this world would slowly cut Emerson into something sharper. She hoped not.

"What about you?" she asked, genuinely curious.

"Same old story as most. A vampire saw me in the market and fancied me and told me I could live a life of pure luxury in exchange for blood. What she didn't tell me was that vampires grow bored quickly." He shrugged.

"Have you thought about going home?"

"To the Gap? That's not a home, it's a prison. I like it here. I like giving blood. It's easy. I just like it best when it's one vampire and I get luxurious accommodations. I'm hoping for a royal," he said wistfully.

"I hope you find the right match."

"And you. I'd better go back to looking delectable," he said with a wink, pulling away.

As the night wore on, Bly's legs began to ache with tiredness, but it wasn't long before the Blood Matcher began beckoning bleeders from their tables. All of the humans smiled when they were tapped, and then they met the vampire who wanted to employ them. The Blood Matcher made sure that they had a fair agreement in place before they were allowed to leave.

Bly had a sneaking suspicion that the care about a bleeder's well-being was only for show. For every story that gave a romantic happy ending for a bleeder, there was another that ended in death.

Like the girl Alexander had been in love with.

When the Blood Matcher finally stood in front of Bly, her smile was wide, and her fangs brushed her red-painted lower lip as she spoke. "I knew I'd find the perfect match for a gorgeous girl like yourself. Come." She held out her hand, and Bly took it even though her body had suddenly gone numb, and she couldn't quite feel the woman's hand in hers as she stepped into the crowd. Bly's head swiveled, looking for Benedict. This had been a horrible plan. She was surprised Emerson hadn't talked her out of it.

The Blood Matcher stopped walking, and Bly blinked. She closed her eyes a second time and opened them, somehow believing that the world would right itself if she only stopped seeing for a moment.

The wrong vampire stood in front of her. The vampire with the sharp face and the hair wound in a tight bun. The one with mean eyes without a trace of charm.

Not Benedict.

"This is Prince Callum," the Blood Matcher said, and she kept chattering without once losing the wide smile on her face, but Bly's ears were roaring, and she didn't catch anything until the Blood Matcher's smile slipped slightly as she reached out and grabbed Bly's arm, her long nails just a little too sharp. "I said, does that sound fair to you?"

Bly's lips felt heavy.

Annoyance leaked into the Blood Matcher's chipper voice. "A hundred coins a month for a two-year contract." The Blood

Matcher smiled back at Callum. "All of Prince Callum's bleeders retire after two years and go back to the Gap set for the rest of their lives. Doesn't that sound more than generous to you?"

The nails on Bly's arm dug in just a little bit more.

A hundred coins a month sounded like more money than Bly would ever see if she went home to the Gap and took on either her mother's or father's profession or something else entirely. If she never found Elise, then this could be the job for her. After all, she certainly didn't hate it when Kerrigan bit her. How much different could another vampire be? At worst, it'd be like giving blood in the market. She could do that.

But something nagged at her. The Blood Matcher had said that Prince Callum employed his bleeders for two years and then they went back to the Gap. Why? Why give up a profession they enjoyed to go back to the very world they had tried to escape?

What did he do to them to make them take their money and run?

Bly swallowed. The prince's eyes didn't track the movement. He stared at her blankly.

"Does she not speak?" he asked. "I don't care if she doesn't, but let's move this along, shall we? I'm parched," he said, even though he held a drink in his hand.

"Yes," Bly said. The word came out faint and scratchy as if it had been choked on the way out.

"Good choice," said the Blood Matcher, her voice cheerful and light again as if she couldn't read any of Bly's discomfort. "Run along now with Prince Callum, and if you need anything or even if you want to break the agreement, you come see me," she added, but she'd already turned away, giving no weight to the promise before disappearing into the crowd, clearly eager to make her next match.

"Follow," Callum said before turning crisply on his heel and stalking toward the door.

Bly's feet moved after him without hesitation because she didn't know what else to do. Saying no would mean her position would be revoked, the choker around her neck that gave her access to Vagaris cut off, and the only way in would be through the witches' secret passageways, but even if she got onto the streets, she'd never be allowed into the parties the royal children frequented. She'd never get close to Benedict again.

Or Kerrigan.

She turned slightly just before stepping through the door that led to the streets, looking for the vampire she'd come for.

She found Benedict watching her with no trace of the signature smirk on his lips and his eyebrows drawn into an expression that looked almost like worry. But he had no reason to care about her, and if he wanted her, he'd had his chance.

She turned away and stepped into the night. She was supposed to be leaving here and heading to her sister, but now she was even further away.

A shadow stirred down the first side street they passed, and Emerson took a step out toward them. He was supposed to be there to trail Bly and Benedict back to his home, and things clearly weren't going as planned.

Bly desperately wanted to run to him, let him intervene, but Callum gave off the air of someone old and deadly.

She shook her head.

The best thing she could do was play the part she'd thrown

herself into. She could at least gossip with the other humans employed in Callum's household. He'd almost certainly have a housekeeper. Bly would make friends with other humans who lived and worked in Vagaris. They'd have their own whisper network. This could still get her closer.

She sensed Emerson following.

His presence made her feel a little bit braver.

So did the morning light that had started to chase away some of the darkness of Vagaris's tight streets, turning everything a muted gray. Surely people weren't drained of blood with the sun alive to witness it. Those types of horrors only happened in the shadows of the moon.

She was being naïve, of course, but sometimes a lie was better than fear.

They turned a corner onto a street that looked like any other with rows of stone houses with purple and red shutters that were slowly closing to the daylight.

The house they stopped in front of had three stories of deep burgundy shudders that were already latched tight against the incoming morning and a wooden door stained cherry.

Callum didn't bother looking behind him to see if Bly was still following as he opened the door and stepped inside. In fact, he hadn't glanced back at her once the whole way here.

She could have disappeared with the shadows.

But he must have been used to bleeders following without question, either out of excitement or desperation for the money he was offering.

Bly was desperate too, just in a different way.

Stepping inside, she blinked, trying to adjust her eyes as the door clicked shut behind her. The rising sun didn't exist in here. The stone floors with matching walls and the midnight curtains drawn across the windows on either side of the entryway turned the house into a dungeon.

An older woman with pale skin and salt-and-pepper hair stood in the center of the room, and Callum nodded his head at her once in greeting. "Change her," he ordered, and then brushed by, taking stone steps up to the floor above.

Panic flared in Bly's chest. Her fingers fumbled under the neckline of the dress the Blood Matcher had put her in to her own chemise she wore underneath where she'd stitched a tiny pocket. She pulled out a sliver of spelled mushroom then hid it pinched between two fingers. She'd never planned to go with Benedict without a weapon, and she wasn't going to relinquish that weapon now.

The woman opened one of the doors off the entryway and ushered Bly inside a room that was nothing but a cold stone box. She hadn't noticed Bly's frantic scramble.

She tsked as she looked Bly up and down. "They dress you in less and less every time he brings one of you home," she said.

Bly hated the condemnation in her voice. Even if Bly was only doing this to get her sister back, in another life, it might have ended up being a career she'd chosen and enjoyed. Kerrigan had opened that part of her, but she could have ended up finding it on her own.

Although . . . perhaps not here. It seemed particularly dangerous to be matched with a vampire you didn't know and then follow him into a house that felt like a prison all while hoping for the best.

The woman pulled open the closet and removed a long, draping white gown and waved at Bly to disrobe. When Bly didn't move, she said, "Hurry up, girl. I'm eager to be done with this." She made no move to turn around and give Bly an ounce of privacy, so Bly gritted her teeth and pushed the straps of her dress from her shoulders, letting it pool around her ankles.

"Shoes too," the woman said.

Bly unlaced the delicate strings that held them to her calves and stepped free of them.

The housekeeper gruffly pulled the new dress over Bly before letting it pool all around her ankles. The long sleeves cinched around her wrists and a high collar went all the way to her chin.

Bly frowned. She expected something that was cut low around the neck. Something that would make it easy to take blood from the source. This didn't seem like the type of clothes you'd want to dress a bleeder in. The only skin showing was her face and her hands. A vague unease rolled in her stomach.

Her mind still danced around the fact that in coming here, she was choosing to get bitten by someone. She'd made that choice before, of course, but this was different. With Kerrigan, she'd craved it. This time it was a calculated decision that had nothing to do with desire.

She wondered if she'd like it as she tugged at the high collar around her neck, but she decided it didn't matter.

"Come along." The housekeeper beckoned her out the door, and Bly followed down the hallway and up the stone steps. The floor against her feet was rough and cold. She hadn't been given other shoes.

At the top of the stairs, the woman opened a heavy door and

waited silently for Bly to pass through. Bly hesitated. It wasn't too late to change her mind, pull up the strange gown, and bolt out of this house, but she swallowed and stepped inside the pitch-black room. She jumped as a bolt slid into place behind her.

SEVEN

HER HEART THUDDED WITH EACH PASSING moment, but she didn't say anything at all. She could feel him in here, and he intended to scare her with the dark and silence.

If he meant for her to break first and say something, she wouldn't.

"Now, you're an interesting one." His voice spoke from behind her, and she spun even though she could see nothing but the faintest shadow that was there and then gone.

A second later, the room glowed to life, and she twisted back around, blinking and vulnerable.

Callum sat behind a desk of gleaming dark wood topped with sleek white marble. He leaned back in his chair, his arms draped casually over the edges with a passive expression on his face as if he hadn't just been behind her trying to toy with her fear. He had the look of someone who enjoyed nothing, but she knew he *was* enjoying this.

"Much better." His voice was dull, bored even, as he looked her up and down. "Some of my kind are quite backward in their proclivities. It's not about your body. It's about your blood." His stare was intense, as if he could see straight through her clothes to map each vein and artery underneath. His words should have been a comfort—that he wasn't interested in her besides the thing she proclaimed she wanted to sell: her blood.

But a chill crept down the back of her neck.

She forced herself to look away from him. There were windows in the room, but they were shut tight against the morning. The only light was from an ornate lamp with a gilded base and a red glass globe that cast the room in bloody light. A massive fireplace took up one wall, but it sat empty without even a pinch of ash. Bly bet this place had never felt a shred of warmth. But the thing that really caught her attention was the shelves to her right that took up the entire side of the room from floor to ceiling. She hadn't noticed at first that it wasn't books that lined them. They were objects.

She took a few steps closer to the shelves, tracking Callum out of the corner of her eye as she went. She had the distinct sense that he might pounce on her, though he didn't even lean forward in his seat.

"Spells," she whispered as she got closer. Each one was lovingly placed on its own little carved wooden pedestal: a dried white mushroom laced with sky blue just like the one held carefully between her fingers, an iridescent dragonfly wing, even a vampire's fang, the root still crusted in blood. She'd never really turned her back on Callum as she looked, but she turned to face him fully now.

"You like witches?" Bly asked. All vampires bought and used

spells, but a display was something else entirely.

"I like power."

"You're brave to leave them out in the open." She wanted to say something to unsettle him even though it was foolish. She wanted to play instead of being played with.

His eyes narrowed before he gave a shrug. "Humans are never bold enough to try for them."

She swallowed every retort that burned her tongue.

Her best option was still to play the long game, find Elise, then disappear from Vagaris forever.

She pushed thoughts of Kerrigan away.

"Let's begin, shall we?" Callum waved two fingers in a gesture for her to come, and she moved to stand opposite him at the desk as he pulled open a drawer and removed two items: a clear glass goblet and a small dagger with a gold-dipped hilt set with five rubies cut into glittering drops of blood.

He pushed the cup across the desk so it sat evenly between them and then picked up his knife, running his thumb across the jewels as he did. "Ready to bleed for me?"

She said nothing, and he held out his hand, beckoning her to do the same. She did, giving him the hand without her hidden spell, pleased that her arm didn't shake. He held her hand palm up between them before placing the knife against her skin.

She tried not to squirm. She'd rather be bitten.

Her eyes closed.

"Watch," he said.

She hated him in that moment, but she listened. The blade bit into her skin by her pinkie, and her arm jerked in response. Only his grip on her kept her from yanking back. For a moment, she thought that was it, but then the knife began a slow crawl, splitting the skin all the way to the base of her palm on the opposite side.

She hissed at the slow, excruciating pain and finally looked up to find Callum focused on her face and not her hand. She resented the tears that gathered in her eyes, but she refused to allow their escape. She wanted to give him as little as possible.

He tipped her hand, and her blood dripped into the cup before he released her and grabbed the glass stem. He swirled it in front of his nose, still staring at her as her blood swished and coated the sides.

He drank it slowly. His expression held no seduction—just the thrill of power that came from consuming a part of her while she watched.

Her stomach rolled, and it took everything in her not to bend over with the nausea.

Eventually, he sat the cup down, the remnants of her blood pooling in the center.

She still held her hand over the desk, and it dripped garishly onto the white top. That's why it was the one bright thing in the room.

"That's enough for one night." Callum gave her a dismissive nod as he took a key from his pocket and tossed it onto the desk. It landed in her blood. "Let yourself out. Leave the key."

Bly didn't move. Her hand burned. A cut like that wasn't going to scab over by itself anytime soon. The housekeeper didn't seem like the type to bother with healing spells for bleeders.

"Aren't you going to heal it?" she managed to get out.

"Seems like a waste when I'll just open it tomorrow."

She ground her teeth.

"In fact, I'm still a bit famished. Give me your other hand."

His eyes gleamed, but there wasn't a trace of black in the steel gray. He wasn't hungry for anything besides her pain.

This was why the bleeders stayed for two years and then didn't come near the vampires again. He tortured them. They weren't paid for their blood; they were paid to endure abuse. It was sick. But they probably stayed because of the obscene amount of money he was offering.

Nothing in this world ever worked out in favor of a human.

He thought he could buy her pain, but she had too much of that without his help.

"I want to leave." Her clenched hand dripped blood down the length of her white skirt.

"No."

"The Blood Matcher said—"

"Silly girl, do you think a single person in this city cares about those rules? The doors and windows are already locked, and only I have the key for the outside."

Bly's eyes flickered to the collection of spells.

"Try it." There was the barest hint of excitement in his voice. That's why he kept them out in the open . . . as bait for desperate people. She wondered how many of them actually had tried to escape and how many had resigned themselves to this fate for the money.

"This room will be locked anytime I'm not in it, so if you want to take your shot, now is as good a time as any."

She didn't budge.

He sighed after a moment. "I must say, I'm a little disappointed.

There was something about you that made me think you might fight."

She stared at him, understanding exactly what game he played. If one of the bleeders *did* try to pick up a spell and use it against him, he'd be able to punish them in any way he saw fit. Nobody would blink an eye if that bleeder came forward about the abuse if Callum claimed that they had raised a hand against him first.

Everything in her wanted to spit in his face.

His eyes narrowed as he watched her. "Give. Me. Your. Hand."

"No. Give me the knife. At least let me do it to myself."

He paused for a moment before offering the hilt to her. She grabbed it and pressed the sharp blade against the palm of her hand until she could feel her skin just on the edge of splitting.

Callum slid his glass across the desk and held it there, waiting for her to bleed into it. She looked up and met his eyes.

He smiled knowingly.

She slammed the knife through the back of his hand. Her wrist ached with the force of the blade hitting the marble on the other side of it.

Callum didn't even flinch. He stared at the knife and the blood gathering on the table for a moment before yanking it from his flesh. He sat the blade gently on the desk. "I was hoping you might do something like that." He grinned, and it was the most emotion she'd seen on his face.

He stood, and she took a stumbling step back as his chair scraped across the floor.

She was darting for the wall of spells, pretending like she needed one, when his hand wrapped around the back of her neck.

He flung her, and she landed hard, catching herself on her

elbows. Scrambling backward, her hands scraped against the unpolished stone until her back hit the wall, and he was on her again, grabbing her by the high collar of her dress and pulling her to her feet.

He pressed the tip of the knife below one eye and then the other. "I'll make you cry tears of blood every day for the next two years as punishment."

"Those are the only tears you're going to get," she ground out. Her voice sounded fiercer than it should have, facing a vampire with a knife hovering close to her eye, but whatever fear she felt was drowned out by pure rage turning her insides to fire.

A rage for every single human who'd found themselves stuck here or in another vampire's awful trap because the rules of this world were nothing but a façade meant to make them think that they had some semblance of safety.

Only power guaranteed safety, and humans had no means to secure it. That was the reason the stories of vampires falling in love with bleeders were so popular in the Gap. It wasn't about love. It was about finding someone powerful enough to keep you safe.

But most people ended up with someone like Callum, who was scratching his knife across the tender skin underneath each of her eyes. His eyes were still blank without a trace of hunger, just an emptiness that was much more terrifying.

He didn't want her to bleed because of his nature, his need to consume. He wanted her to bleed because he liked it.

"You might not cry tonight," he said with a distanced voice that matched his stare, "but eventually, you will."

She'd stopped fighting and started acting as if she were nothing but the prey he saw her as. Her hands were at her sides, and she pressed them into the wall to stop from flailing as the tip of the blade split the skin just beneath her eye. It took everything in her not to jerk her head to the side and drag the knife across more of her skin.

Blood leaked down her cheek like tears.

Callum smiled at the sight as he moved to the next eye and sliced again, and still, she didn't fight. She needed him to believe she'd surrendered. She'd only have one chance to land her strike.

He pulled the blade away from her to admire his handiwork.

Lifting her hand, she slapped him across the face, but as much as she wanted him to feel pain, it wasn't about delivering a blow. It was about casting the spell in the sliver of mushroom pinched between her fingers.

"Sleep," she said.

His eyes widened for the briefest moment before he collapsed at her feet. His knife clattered onto the floor beside him, and she knelt down, picked it up, and held it clenched in her hand, staring at her blood on it.

She thought about carving into him, leaving her own mark the way that he'd left his. Even if he healed while he was sleeping, he'd wake up with the remnants of what she'd done to him and have to wash his own blood from his body.

Her fingers trembled around the hilt of the blade. Making him bleed was the darkest dream she'd ever had, but she didn't want to be a person who dreamed of violence. She missed the dreams she'd had before of sunsets and pretty dresses and peacefulness outside the world she existed in.

She'd never have lovely dreams again if she became like this monster.

Her hand opened, and the knife clattered against the stones at her feet.

She snatched it back up when she heard footsteps pounding up the staircase outside the door. She wasn't going to draw blood on a sleeping vampire, but she wouldn't hesitate to defend herself.

The handle of the door rattled violently, and then the wood shuddered as someone threw themselves into it. Muffled voices cursed. Did the housekeeper somehow know what she'd done? Were the guards already here for her? She searched the room and found no way out. She raced to the shelves, scanning the spells and grabbing another sleeping one along with a binding spell. The door shook again before cracking and swinging open, banging against the wall.

Bly stood, feet apart with her arm holding the knife in front of her just the way Kerrigan had taught her.

All she could make out in the darkness of the hallway were broad shoulders before Emerson stepped inside.

Her knees went weak with relief, but she locked them in place. They weren't safe yet. "Were you followed?" She peered into the dark behind him. "We need to go."

Bly had a feeling that despite being human, the housekeeper was loyal to Callum and that he paid her enough to harden her heart against what he did here. She'd get the guards.

If she hadn't already.

Bly tensed as another form shifted in the shadows behind Emerson. She opened her mouth to warn him, but it died on her lips as Kerrigan entered the room. His eyes swept over her, zeroing in on every bit of blood on her skin. Pure fury tightened his face when he looked into her eyes, and for a second, she thought it was directed at her. She flinched slightly as he strode into the room and reached for her, but his hands were soft as he cradled her face in his palms and wiped his thumbs across the blood on her cheeks.

Her arms dropped to her side, hands opening so that her weapon dropped to her feet once more. The calmness that flooded through her was jarring against the pure adrenaline she felt only moments ago. The quick shift was too much for her body to handle.

"We came to rescue you," Emerson said, stare shifting from Bly to the vampire sprawled out at her feet. "But it appears you had that covered."

Part of Bly wanted to crack a smile and gloat a little bit about how she didn't need saving, which was true. The proof was at her feet. But she was also unbearably thankful that they had come. She didn't have to consider what terrible fate might have befallen her if her plan had gone wrong because they would've been here.

Emerson.

And Kerrigan.

She knew Emerson would have never left her trapped in here, but Kerrigan kept showing up . . . even now. Every time he said he was done with her, he came back. That had to be an echo of what they'd had—a feeling he hadn't let go of no matter what he claimed.

Kerrigan's focus finally slid away from her, and his stare landed on Callum. His expression didn't change, but Bly felt the way his hands tightened against her cheeks, which he still held.

"Don't . . . ," she said gently.

"I should kill him."

She knew he meant it, and that he was capable. She could see it happening. He'd let go of her and rip Callum's head from his body and then Kerrigan would end up in one of the vampire prisons just like Alexander had for hurting the vampire who'd killed the bleeder he loved.

The last thing she needed was another person she had to rescue.

She locked eyes with Emerson standing behind Kerrigan's shoulder. He took a quiet step forward, sensing the same thing that Bly had. But neither of them would be strong enough to stop Kerrigan if he decided to murder the sleeping Callum.

Bly lifted her hands so that she could wrap them around Kerrigan's forearms. She winced as the slice across her hand split wider and fresh blood soaked out into Kerrigan shirt.

The feeling of her blood seeping through and touching his skin pulled his focus away from the vampire at their feet, and he glanced down at her hand holding him. She let her body go limp, clinging to him as if he were the only thing keeping her upright.

"Get me out of here," she whispered.

Kerrigan shot one more look at Callum before his arms were around her. She didn't protest as he scooped her up against his chest and strode toward the door even though she could walk just fine. It was nice to be held.

Emerson gave her an unusually wry look as they passed, and she smiled faintly in return. He'd known her too long not to see through the act, but he certainly wasn't going to spoil it for her.

Kerrigan carried her out of the darkness and down empty streets soft with morning light. When they'd gone some distance, he stopped and slid into a tight alley that ran between the wider streets. Emerson paused at the mouth of it.

"You know my place isn't far from here," Emerson said.

"Yes," Kerrigan said. "We'll meet you there in a minute. I just need a moment with Bly."

Emerson didn't budge until Bly nodded at him, and then he disappeared.

Kerrigan glanced down at her. She could still see his earlier anger in the set of his lips. "Can you stand?"

She nodded, and he set her on her feet and then scanned her body once more before running his thumb across his fang. He reached for her, cradling the back of her head in one hand as he gently pressed his thumb to each of the wounds under her eyes before reaching for her palm.

He unfolded her fist and prodded the wound with his bleeding finger as she hissed. "This is one of the most painful places for a cut," he said apologetically.

"I imagine that's why he chose it."

He stilled, and even though he didn't look up, she knew he was considering turning around and finishing what she had started.

"It's fine," she said. "It's already healing."

He dropped her hand and glowered down at her. "It's not fine, Bly. What in the bloody hell were you thinking getting blood matched? Why? To get my attention? Well, here I am. It worked, and now you have a powerful vampire who's going to want you dead when he wakes up." He ran a hand through his hair, shaking his head.

"You think I did it . . . for your *attention*?" Her cheeks flamed. Of course he would think that. "I thought Benedict would choose me. I'm trying to get my sister back. None of it was about you!" Her voice turned sharp and loud.

He laughed. "I guess I shouldn't overestimate you giving me the tiniest thought."

"That's not what I meant."

They stared at each other, both of them breathing too hard.

"You came to save me," she said.

He shook his head as if he could deny it, as if he hadn't carried her against his chest and used his blood to heal her. She was going to force him to stop pretending that he felt nothing but hate for her.

If that were true, he wouldn't be standing here with her blood on his hands as evidence. His first instinct had been to come to her and wipe the blood from her face with tender fingers.

"You came for me," she said.

"I came . . ." He floundered, looking away. "I was rash last night. I need your help to get Donovan back. That's why I came. I need you for the moment, and once I've got my brother back, I'll never run to you again."

"That's a lie." She knew it, but her voice sounded as if his words had broken her.

He turned back to her, his face softening faintly.

She tried to reach out a hand to rest on his chest, but he stepped back. "All I was thinking about when I handed over Donovan was . . . you."

He scoffed. "Now who's lying?" He took another step back until he was against the wall, looking as if he'd walk away at any moment.

"I mean . . . what *you* meant to *me*. I knew you'd never have wanted me to take Donovan. That should have been enough to stop me." A tiny sob left her lips. "I just kept imagining getting

Elise back and looking at her and thinking about you. I worried I'd look at my sister one day and wish I hadn't traded your life for hers."

She stared down at her feet. That was the shameful truth of it. She'd taken Donovan because deep down she worried she'd always regret saving her sister if she lost Kerrigan.

Crying raked her body. "I'm a terrible person." She'd thought the words plenty of times since the day Elise had collapsed in the forest, but she'd never spoken them out loud.

Standing there in all her grief and guilt, she wondered how it would be possible to find any semblance of a happy future even if she found her sister and Donovan. There were too many hurts that would haunt whatever dreams she managed to conjure.

The one thing she was certain of was that she didn't want to look at Kerrigan again in this moment. She didn't want to see the same disgust she felt for herself on his face. Not anymore.

It'd be a good thing if he left her alone.

The inklings of hope he kept giving her were too painful.

She'd ripped his world apart in one blow, but he was slowly tearing her to pieces in return.

The alleyway was silent. She was certain he'd gone, but still, she didn't look up. Instead, she drew a deep breath to stop her crying, noticing for the first time how cold it was. The air singed her lungs. The material of her ridiculous gown was thin as gauze.

Her body began to tremble.

And then his hands were at her throat. She jerked in surprise, staring up at him, but there was no violence in his touch even though his eyes held something much different. He seemed to be at war with himself. He wanted her. He hated her. He might even feel love for her, but that love was a knife he wouldn't stop using to lash out at her.

The only thing that mattered was that he didn't let her go. His thumbs stroked the side of her jaw, and then his lips pressed under her eye where he'd healed her only moments before. Featherlight kisses trailed down her cheeks to the side of her mouth before following the same trail on the other side.

He pulled back slightly, his mouth stained with her blood and tears.

Her lips parted, and he took that as a welcome.

Their kiss was blood and salt.

"I'm sorry," she whispered when they separated just long enough to breathe.

His lips crashed back into hers with a force that might have made her stumble if he weren't holding on to her. It felt like an answer to her apology. A rejection. But at least he was showing her exactly what he felt instead of walking away.

She wound her hands between them and wrapped her fingers around his throat, squeezing an answer, meeting his force with her own, their lips locking and releasing, their breathing sharp and hard.

This wasn't affection. It was a battle. And then his fangs grazed her lip and fresh blood bloomed between them. He pulled back just barely, his breath still heavy on her face, and she tightened her hold on his neck, reeling him back in. He pulled her lip between his teeth and ran his tongue across the cut with a groan before sucking lightly.

She whimpered, and he pulled back immediately, but she followed.

"Please don't stop," she begged.

He hesitated, and she desperately didn't want him to end this. She'd open an artery for him if it meant him staying close to her for another moment.

His lips came back to hers, and this time they were softer and slower but still occasionally tugging her bleeding lip, taking the blood she was offering even if he wouldn't take her apology.

They stayed like that forever: taking, giving, biting. Until the sting of her cut faded. Her lips felt numb, but she felt . . . complicated. She'd wanted this, but she knew a kiss and offered blood wasn't going to fix things between them, and when Kerrigan pulled back, his expression said the same.

He looked ashamed.

Her stomach turned heavy. She didn't blame him. Kissing her was like if Bly kissed Benedict and enjoyed it. She'd find it hard to live with herself.

She should have just left Kerrigan alone like he'd asked.

"I'm sorry," he said. "I shouldn't have . . ."

His apology hurt worse than his bite.

"I can't forgive you," he said.

"I understand." Her voice was a breathless whisper.

He reached his thumb to his mouth, cutting it once again on the point of his fang before awkwardly reaching toward her lips, but she took a quick step back from him, and his hand dropped to his side.

She wanted to keep the wound. She wanted to feel it throb back to life when the numbness wore off. She wanted to remember this because something told her that it wouldn't happen again.

"I should go," Bly said. "I'll only have so long before Callum wakes up and then all the guards will be looking for me."

"I doubt it," Kerrigan said. "He'd have to admit that a human girl got the drop on him and escaped his clutches. I don't know him well, but I know enough to guess he'll never do that."

"But *he'll* be looking for me," Bly said.

"Yes." Kerrigan's expression was dark. He was thinking of murder again.

Perhaps Bly shouldn't have stopped him earlier.

"I'm running out of time to find Elise." She turned away, taking a step toward the main street.

"I found her," Kerrigan said. "I found your sister."

EIGHT

She didn't believe him. He was saying it just to see the hope on her face and then rip it away one second later.

"You're lying," she said.

His brow scrunched. "I wouldn't do that to you." There was a hint of sadness in his voice and also . . . condemnation. Despite what he'd claimed before, he wasn't going to hurt her the way she'd hurt him.

"At least . . . ," he added, "I found where Benedict closes himself up when the sun comes out, so it's assuming that my brother didn't lie to you. Benedict *is* his best friend, so it's not unreasonable to think he's playing with you and sending you to Benedict like a gift."

"Donovan told me things about Elise that he'd only know if he'd seen her."

Kerrigan nodded. He wasn't going to dampen her hope.

"Take me to her."

"No," Kerrigan said.

Her racing heart stuttered. He *did* want to hurt her.

"Please."

"I need something from you first," he said.

"Anything."

"Help me get Halfryta."

"I've *been* helping you." She strode toward him until she stood as close as they'd been when they were kissing. "Tell me where Elise is right now."

She clutched the front of his shirt in her fists as if she could shake it out of him. But she saw the set of his mouth and the coolness in his eyes and understood that he'd been planning to hold this over her. She dropped her hands from him.

"So you've known all this time, and you were just enjoying watching me suffer?"

"Of course not," he said. "Are you trying to make me a monster so you don't feel as bad about yourself?"

She took a quick step back from him as if he'd tried to cut her. And he had, if only with words again.

"I've been searching for her all along with Halfryta, and then I started searching for Benedict when you told me she was with him."

As much as his other words had hurt her, these ones were the knife twisting in her heart.

He'd never stopped trying to save Elise for her.

But now he was using her sister as leverage.

"Please just tell me. You know I'll keep helping you."

He laughed and the sound was sharp and sad. "But I don't know that, do I? What's to stop you from taking your sister and disappearing and never thinking about me again?"

"I couldn't do that."

"You forget that I know what you're capable of, Bly."

She swallowed. She couldn't blame him for not trusting her. She hadn't exactly given him any reason to.

"Let's get Elise, and because I trust you, *you* keep her until we find Halfryta. Who knows how long until Benedict snaps her neck?"

"Benedict's a cad, not a killer."

"Is that supposed to make me feel better?"

"I don't really care how you feel," he snapped. "If she's been there all this time, she'll be fine for a little longer."

"It could be days or months before we find Halfryta, if we ever find her!"

"We already have," Kerrigan said.

Bly shook her head, not understanding.

"The last prison. The empty cell. I think they're keeping her invisible—I don't know why I didn't think of it before, but I've never seen that many guards. It has to be for her." There was a trickle of excitement in Kerrigan's voice. "But it would take a small army to get through that number of guards."

The rebels. He needed Bly's connections.

She wanted to beg again for him to just tell her where to find her sister, but his expression was resolved. He'd already decided. She'd kept his brother caged until she had what she wanted, and he'd do the same.

"Fine," she said. "I'll help you, and then you'll help me, and then we'll be even, and we'll never have to see each other again."

He didn't quite meet her eyes when he nodded.

NINE

Every rebel was invisible. In all the prison breaks that Bly had been a part of since she'd joined them, this had never happened. Invisibility spells, Hazel had explained to her once, drained a witch's power so that they couldn't make another spell for two weeks, not to mention the fact that the dragonfly wings to make the spells were rare and usually required hunting parties just to find them. Which was why the spell would cost a human half a year's wages or a body's worth of blood.

Rebel resources were too scarce for unlimited spells.

But tonight, Jade and Benedict had shown up with a collection of those precious wings with Benedict grumbling that he'd never be able to afford fresh blood again with what they had cost him.

It took everything in Bly not to shove her knife into his throat.

Hazel had also seemed annoyed by the sheer number of spells. "We could do this with just half of these and save the rest for another time. A lot of good could come from them," she'd said. But Kerrigan wouldn't hear of it. They weren't going to take any chances.

Hazel had only frowned in response.

It had taken a lot of convincing on Bly's part to even get Hazel to join them. After all, they were planning to free someone who'd done immeasurable harm to their world.

If Halfryta was even here.

Bly didn't share Kerrigan's confidence.

An empty cage could just be an empty cage.

Standing at the edge of the clearing, she craned her neck to try to see through the slivers of space between guards, but their formation was just as tight as before.

An owl hooted deep in the forest.

A few of the guards shifted uneasily on their feet, but the sound was too common to warrant real worry.

Bly crept forward across the open expanse. She'd have twenty seconds to get into position. They'd all been assigned a guard, with the easily identifiable captain being number one. Bly was five, so she counted her way over and reached a woman vampire with blond hair cropped short and steel eyes ringed in deep blue that stared sharply through Bly. Like most vampires, she looked like someone who wouldn't hesitate to lop Bly's head from her shoulders.

Bly steadied her hand as she lifted it toward the vampire's neck as close as she dared without touching her. She held her breath. If any one of them miscalculated and let their skin brush a vampire or struck too soon, this would turn into a bloodbath.

The sharp nasal call of a blue jay pierced through the night, and Bly's vampire reached for her sword, smart enough to know that such a sound shouldn't be heard after dark, but Bly was faster.

"Sleep," Bly said. The word echoed as all the rebels spoke at nearly the same time. The vampire's eyes grew angry just before the spell touched her neck and then she collapsed onto the ground with every other guard in the circle, creating a ring of fallen red uniforms.

Bly let out a heavy breath, but she wasn't interested in celebrating yet.

At first glance, the same prisoners were still there along with the one empty cell. The witch with the dead eyes that had stared at nothing spun around, taking in the dropped guards as a flicker of life crawled back into his expression. Even the man with the beard who'd been curled into the fetal position lifted his head before pushing himself up on an elbow.

The imprisoned vampire laughed maniacally, his eyes wild. "Where are you?" he sing-songed. His voice was unnerving in the otherwise silent night.

Bly ran to the empty cage even though they were supposed to hold the perimeter just in case another guard shift arrived while they were here, but she wanted to watch.

She couldn't see Kerrigan, but she knew he'd already be here, pulling out a revealing spell made from the ground-up dragonfly wings of a cast invisibility spell.

"Reveal," she heard Kerrigan say. The word soft and reverent on his lips.

He believed.

Kerrigan blinked back into existence when the dust of the spell touched his skin as he cast it. His palm was held gently to his lips, and his mouth was still in the soft *o* as he blew the powder into the cage. His copper hair hung damp and dark against his cheeks from the rain that had caught them on the walk here.

It wasn't the right moment for it, but Bly couldn't help but wonder at how beautiful he was. He'd spared no expense in how he'd dressed for the occasion. His boots were the soft brown of dried pine needles and laced to his knees over dark brown britches. His shirt was the soft green of grass dying in the heat, embroidered at the collar with threads of golden sunrise. His signature scarf was a deep green embroidered with minuscule leaves of gold. The only practical thing about him was the brown cloak that could easily hide among the trunks of trees without an invisibility spell.

He looked like a prince.

If this was to be their last day in each other's lives, then she wanted to remember him like this.

But then his face fell, and Bly turned from him to the still empty cell.

"That's not possible," Kerrigan whispered.

The caged vampire laughed again.

Kerrigan fumbled into the pocket of his cloak and pulled out a small tin, pouring a heaping mound of dust into his hand once more before blowing it again.

This time the magical dust hit Bly, and she popped back into existence next to Hazel, who Bly hadn't realized was standing so near. Benedict reappeared on Kerrigan's right.

And Halfryta appeared in the cage with the vampire.

The vampire wrapped a hulking arm around her chest, holding her off the ground. Halfryta seemed only mildly annoyed at her predicament as she glared out at them.

"They told me to kill her if this happened. They wanted her alive, but they'd rather have her dead than freed. Do you know how hard it was to not kill her before? I've been longing for you to come." His laughter was sharp and deranged.

"Wait," Kerrigan said. "We can pay you—"

The vampire ripped into Halfryta's throat. He could have killed her in an instant by snapping her neck, but his bloodlust won, and Kerrigan was already breaking the lock on the cage.

A knife seemed to appear from nowhere, implanting itself in the vampire's neck, which was just enough to make him break away from Halfryta. Kerrigan jumped into the cage, leaping onto the vampire's back and wrapping his arms around his thick neck. The vampire slammed his back—and Kerrigan—into the bars again and again until Kerrigan slipped to the ground, landing in the blood pooling around Halfryta. The vampire glanced between Kerrigan and Halfryta. Bly was running toward the cage with a binding spell in her hand when the vampire suddenly dropped into a heap.

Jade reappeared, standing over the giant vampire with her lips pulled back into a snarl. She plucked her knife from the vampire's throat before wiping it across his ragged shirt and putting it back into her belt. She met Bly's stare and smiled.

Kerrigan was on his knees, staring at Halfryta lying in her own blood with his hands reaching slightly toward her as if he'd frozen. His distant expression made Bly want to get down on her knees and wrap her arms around him . . . shield him from his past as it tried to overwhelm him.

Like she'd done for him before. But they weren't those people to each other anymore.

He was looking at something that he'd surely dreamt about—the witch who had killed his parents dying in her own blood while he watched. The perfect symmetrical revenge for what Halfryta had inflicted upon him. And now his dream had become a nightmare. The witch's life was tied to his brother's. He couldn't have both the revenge he'd spent years longing for *and* Donovan back. His face said exactly how that ripped him in two.

Kerrigan couldn't be the one to save the witch's life. Jade was too busy hauling the downed vampire from the cage to notice Kerrigan's dilemma.

Dropping to Halfryta's side, Bly pressed her hands into the witch's gushing neck, staunching the bleeding before looking up for someone to heal her. Hazel watched with the coldest expression Bly had ever seen on her face. It had taken some convincing to get Hazel to bring the rebels once Bly had told her their plans to free Halfryta. Bly had only won her over by reminding her of the other prisoners they could save.

"Please," Bly said as Hazel met her eyes. "I need her."

She could see the battle on her face, but after a moment, she nodded, waving at Marianna to come with her. They brushed Bly aside as they worked to save Halfryta's life.

Bly stood, her hands held loosely in front of her, covered in the witch's blood. She may have fantasized about the head witch's blood on her hands once or twice, but she'd never imagined it would be from stopping the blood flow instead of causing it.

Kerrigan watched Hazel and Marianna work on the witch.

His expression had slackened.

Bly wanted to reach for him and at least lay a hand on his

shoulder, but she didn't want to bloody him and didn't think he'd welcome her touch now besides.

"We did it," Bly said.

Kerrigan didn't look up.

"You'll get Donovan back."

"He'll hate me for this," he whispered without looking at her. "He'll hate me for freeing her."

"To save him," Bly reminded him.

Kerrigan swallowed. "You know he won't see it that way." He laughed, and several of the rebels glanced warily in their direction at the harsh sound. "That's why he convinced you to work against me." He shook his head. "You've both been working against me this whole time."

"He'll forgive you. It was the only way."

Kerrigan gave her a sharp look. It hadn't been the only way. They could've had everything if she'd been quicker to release Donovan during the last prison break.

She glanced away, looking out through the bars of the cage.

"Donovan doesn't *do* forgiveness," Kerrigan reminded her. "But you'll have everything, won't you?"

"Not everything," she reminded him softly. She looked back at him, and they held each other's stares as they held each other's betrayals in their hearts: her sending Donovan to die in Kerrigan's place and him keeping Elise just out of her reach to ensure that she would help him.

Bly looked away first. It seemed fair since she'd caused the first tear between them.

"Time to go," Hazel said.

Bly hadn't even noticed that they had already loaded Halfryta onto a cloth stretcher and carried her from the cell. Only Kerrigan and Bly remained in the cage. He stood, squared his shoulders, and pushed past her. "Jade. Benedict," Kerrigan ordered. "Grab the witch."

"Wait." Hazel stepped in front of the unconscious Halfryta with her hands spread out in front of her in a gesture of peace that Bly knew would end in bloodshed if she tried to stop them from taking the witch.

"I wouldn't." Kerrigan guessed what she was about to do as well.

"Hazel . . . ," Bly said. The witch belonged to them.

"She's done immeasurable harm. There's a reason we don't free everyone," Hazel said. Bly may have convinced her to save the witch's life a moment ago, but Hazel's expression said she regretted that decision.

Alexander moved to hover behind Hazel like a hulking bear waiting for her order to rip Kerrigan to shreds. It was a fight Bly didn't want to see.

"She's mine." Kerrigan took a step closer.

"We should kill her." Everyone turned to look at the rebel who had spoken. A young man with dark brown hair that hung straight to his shoulders and the hard expression of someone who'd seen too much.

His statement was met with a murmur that traveled through some of the other rebels standing nearby. Plenty of them wanted to see the witch dead. It was her rules, if not her own hand, that had probably led many of them to this group.

Kerrigan tensed. Benedict and Jade now stood on either side of him. Emerson was at Bly's shoulder.

Kerrigan's icy glare slid over everyone gathered around them. "This witch will pay for her crimes, but not until I trade her for my brother."

The murmuring stopped. The restrained violence in Kerrigan's voice and body made Bly sure that if one day he wanted to see Halfryta bleeding out in front of him again, he would make it happen.

The promise was enough for Hazel. She lowered her hands and backed away, nodding at her people, who handed over the stretcher to Jade and Benedict. Once the witch was secure, Kerrigan turned to Hazel one last time. "Thank you," he said. "I owe you."

Hazel gave him a brisk nod. Bly had no doubt that she'd call in that favor one day.

Kerrigan strode into the woods, and Jade and Benedict followed. Bly turned to Emerson and wrapped her hand over his, squeezing. The person they both loved most in the world was waiting for them.

TEN

BLY KEPT HER FINGERS WRAPPED AROUND Emerson's wrist the entire way back to Vagaris. She could feel the barely contained energy in him now that they were so close. His eyes were trained on Benedict's back as they walked. Bly didn't know what Kerrigan's plan was for bringing them to Benedict's home, but it wouldn't do for Emerson to lose control now and try to rip Benedict to pieces. Bly wasn't going to let him risk his life again right after she'd worked so hard to save it and when they were so close to getting Elise back.

So she anchored him—the way he had done for her so many times before.

When they reached the walls of Vagaris, Kerrigan paused.

"We can't march through the city with the witch," Jade said. "We should skirt the perimeter and head straight for Havenwhile."

"I'm fairly certain you lot can handle yourselves, right?"

Benedict asked. "I'll hold down the fort here and, you know, make sure no one decides to come after you."

Everyone ignored him.

Kerrigan looked back at Jade. "We don't have any supplies. No blood to drink. We'll be weak by the time we reach the witches. That would be a mistake."

Jade jerked her chin toward Bly. "We have a blood bag. We can feed her berries and then we feed on her. Simple."

"No," Emerson and Kerrigan both said together.

Jade rolled her eyes. "Like I said, I'm not walking through the town with a stolen witch. Do we have any invisibility spells left?"

Everyone was silent.

Kerrigan strode over and pulled his cloak to the side. He reached for the sleeping witch, whom they had spelled earlier just in case she regained consciousness. Hesitating for only a second, he roughly grabbed her and tossed her over one shoulder. He pulled his cloak back over her body.

Benedict groaned. "Well, that's not suspicious."

"Do you have a better idea?" Kerrigan asked.

"I believe my lovely sister did." Benedict winked at Bly with his stare zeroed in on her neck.

Jade smirked.

Bly wondered if she could get away with killing Benedict once she got Elise back.

Kerrigan led them through a gap in the wall hidden by climbing brush and onto the streets where they turned down alleyway after alleyway. A few vampires stopped to glance at them but none of them said a thing. Bly supposed if a group of vampire royals wanted to march along the street with a body clearly hidden under one of their cloaks that not a lot of people would question them.

None of them spoke to each other until they stepped onto a wider street, and Benedict stopped in his tracks. "Where did you say we were going again?"

Kerrigan stilled. He shifted so his back wasn't to Benedict anymore before he answered. "Your place."

"My . . . How did you . . . ?" Benedict turned slightly and met Bly's eyes.

Any doubt she'd had about him having her sister faded. The truth was on his face: He knew who she was. She dropped her hold on Emerson and lunged. She didn't know what she was going to do, but she wanted to hurt him, to make him feel the barest echo of what she'd felt without her sister.

Benedict's eyes widened, and his hand fumbled at his waist, probably for a dagger that he'd undoubtedly plunge into her heart before she could do enough damage to his pretty face to die happy, but Emerson's arm locked around her waist as Benedict blinked out of existence. The liar had another spell.

"What the hell?" Jade's stare flicked between them all.

"Your brother has Bly's sister," Kerrigan explained.

Jade's face scrunched as she inspected Bly as if she'd never really seen her before, and then her eyes widened slightly. "Elise?" She laughed, and Bly wanted to lunge at *her* now, but she didn't have time for that. She turned to Kerrigan. "He's going to take her somewhere else."

For a second, she thought Kerrigan would delay them on purpose the same way that she had delayed freeing Donovan. More payback. But Kerrigan turned and ran, Halfryta jerking as he did. Emerson let go of Bly and bolted after him, and she followed, wishing she had the same speed. They turned down another street, and Bly was certain they'd lose her in this maze of chaos that was the city, but Kerrigan stopped in front of the black door at the front of a stone house that was four times as large as everything else on the street with three small towers that rose up against the night sky. Kerrigan grabbed the brass knocker on the door and pounded.

Nothing.

"Benedict!" he hollered. "Don't make me break this down."

"Brother," Jade called. "He's right. We need to get the witch off the street. Let the girl see her sister."

Bly glanced over her shoulder at Jade's sour expression. She clearly didn't want to be on Bly's side, but for the moment, she was. Bly thought she saw a flicker of sympathy in her eyes. She knew what it was to miss a sibling.

The door cracked open. And then paused, revealing nothing but a sliver of black that started to disappear again as if he'd changed his mind.

"Benedict," Kerrigan warned.

The door flung the rest of the way open, and Benedict, visible once more, flashed a ridiculous grin at them. "Welcome to my humble abode." He stepped back and waved a welcoming arm. "You'll have to excuse my sudden departure. I only wanted to freshen the place up for you."

"If you did anything to her . . . ," Emerson growled, stepping forward in unison with Bly.

A hand grasped the back of Bly's cloak, stopping her. "Don't do anything rash," Jade said behind her back, and Bly turned slightly. The vampire held Emerson in a matching grip on the back of his shirt. "You are guests in my brother's house, and if you do anything unsavory, I will end you."

"I'm not making any promises," Emerson said.

"Me neither." Bly attempted to jerk out of Jade's grip.

"Your funeral." She released them.

In an instant, Emerson crossed the threshold and shoved Benedict against the door. "Where is she?" he snarled.

"Upstairs."

Emerson released him, darting away, and Benedict ran a hand over the crumpled silk of his vest as he shouted after him, "First door at the top."

Bly followed, taking the stairs three at a time, fumbling in her cloak to dig out a spell to break the lock. Emerson stood with his hand on the doorknob, waiting for her. His face held more than Bly had ever seen on it before: hope, relief, fear. What kind of state would Elise be in after so much time?

Benedict's house reminded her of Callum's. Had Elise been kept in a cold stone prison all these months?

Bly reached her spell toward the door as Emerson turned the handle, but it wasn't locked, which meant Elise would be chained inside. She braced herself for the sight as the door swung open. Bly expected the door to groan and screech and add a wounded sound to the moment, but it was whisper soft.

Gentle humming drifted out.

Elise sat at a table, bent over with her hands full of sapphire-blue silk. She ran her fingers over the material before grabbing a needle she held in her lips. The golden thread attached to it glimmered in the well-lit room. Orbs of multicolored glass dangled from the ceiling, each one casting the room in a soft rainbow glow. The windows that had burgundy shutters outside were covered with rose-pink tulle drapes.

The whole room held racks with waterfalls of material in both rich and pastel colors.

"You know I don't like to be disturbed when I'm concentrating," Elise said. Her voice was light and teasing and not meant for Bly or Emerson. She still looked only at her hands, stitching golden sunbeams around the buttons on the vest in front of her.

The sound of her sister's voice built an odd feeling in Bly's chest. It was exactly how she remembered, the gentle quietness that sometimes held a joke. But Bly had imagined their reunion so many times: the way Elise would sob with relief when she saw that Bly had come for her. The way they'd hold each other without being able to speak for a long time. The way, when they did finally speak, they'd both sound a little bit broken, but also happy, because they'd be together.

But Elise just sounded . . . *fine*.

It wasn't the nightmare Bly had imagined every day since she realized her sister was being held in Vagaris.

The scene in front of her was lovely.

That didn't mean there wasn't horror underneath it.

"Elise," Bly said. Her sister's name on her lips had been weighted with pain for over a year, but when Bly spoke it now, it was a careful whisper, the way you'd speak to a fawn in the woods when you didn't want it to disappear into the brush.

Elise's nimble, working fingers stilled. Her face pinched in confusion, and for one long moment she didn't look up.

When she did, she spoke Bly's name in return. Her name held shock and disbelief, and Bly searched for the relief in it that

Elise had to be feeling. Elise blinked her golden-brown eyes. "Bly," she said again, and this time there was excitement. Her cheeks dimpled.

Bly felt the curse she'd been under for months and months dissipate. Until Kerrigan brushed by her and plopped Halfryta into a pile of scraps of fabric. He'd be a chasm in her chest for a long time to come, but now she had Elise. Kerrigan had what he needed to get his brother back. Bly had righted her wrongs the best she could, and that had to be enough for her to heal, even if it wasn't enough for her to dream again without thinking of copper hair and gray eyes rimmed in green. That image would probably always bring an ache of unmet longing, but she could learn to live with that.

Bly glanced behind her and smiled at Emerson. He returned it. Part of her was waiting for *him* to rush to Elise. Bly wanted to give them the space to bloom without her choking off what they might grow into. But Emerson didn't move. He was waiting for Bly.

She turned to Benedict, standing just to the other side of the door. He wore the blue he always favored that matched the material clutched in her sister's hands. "She's coming with us. Don't try to stop me."

"I won't . . . if that's what she wants." His smile held an edge—a joke that hadn't been played yet.

Elise had stood when Bly turned back to her, but she hadn't moved an inch, as if she were cursed to stay here forever.

She was going into shock. She'd thought she'd never be saved. Her eyes were no longer on Bly. They were fixed on Benedict.

Elise was scared.

Bly rushed to her, putting her hand on Elise's cheek, hesitating only briefly as if she'd be able to feel the death curse under her touch.

Bly'd done this to her.

Her thumbs rubbed one of the black webs under Elise's eyes as if she could smear the curse away. How much longer did her sister have? The Games were months away, and the curse looked as if it'd consume her before then.

Bly turned back to Emerson to see if he'd already realized the same. He'd have to turn her. They'd have to run away and live together in the woods after all. Bly's original plan would be the thing to save them.

But Emerson's face held something odd. Why wasn't he pulling Elise into his arms? Bly had imagined that moment so many times, not with envy but with joy.

Something wasn't right.

It was Benedict, not Emerson, who strode toward them.

"My dear," Benedict said. "Endless apologies for the delay."

Bly shifted her body between her sister and Benedict as he approached, but he moved past them to a quaint wooden hatch at the back of the room and scanned the shelves full of tiny trinkets. He came back with the white porcelain teacup painted with yellow roses and a bottle of wine that he sat on the table where Elise had been working. Pulling the small dagger from his belt, he said, "I fear it's been far too long."

Elise's hand reached out toward the teacup, but Bly grabbed her arm and shoved it back down to her side.

"You'll not take another drop from her," Bly snarled.

"We really don't have time for this." Benedict slid the dagger across his own wrist, his blood splattering into the teacup, turning the pretty thing garish. Then he poured a bit of wine in with his blood.

Elise pulled free of Bly's grip and then reached once more, lifting the cup with steady fingers and pressing it to her lips before drinking it down with her eyes pinched closed.

Bly stared in horror and then in awe as some of the black lines on Elise's face receded until they only reached her jaw.

"Wh-what . . . ," Bly stuttered. "You're curing her?"

Benedict sighed. "Unfortunately, no. I don't believe very many humans know this—we don't want you running around trying to get blood from us instead of the other way around—but drinking vampire blood can stave off a death curse. Alas, becoming a vampire is the only thing that cures it."

Bly should have felt some type of gratitude. Clearly, her sister was only standing here because of Benedict's blood, but all she could think of was one pounding question in her head. "Why?" she asked. Surely he could find a human to sew his silly little shirts without the need to keep them alive.

"Love makes you do wild things," he said. "I believe you of all people would understand that." His eyes shifted between her and Kerrigan.

Bly laughed. "That's ridiculous." *She* might have fallen in love with a vampire, but calm, practical *Elise*? There was no way.

It had to be something else. Her sister must have tricked the vampire into loving her just to keep the curse at bay until Bly could rescue her, but Bly was here now, and she didn't have to pretend for one second longer. She grabbed Elise's shoulders and shook her, trying to wake her from what had surely been a nightmare to live. "You're free now, Elise. Emerson's a vampire. He will save you."

Elise's eyes widened, her stare breaking away from Benedict at the news that Emerson was a vampire. She turned to look at him. Bly did too. She still didn't understand why Emerson hadn't approached. Or why he looked ill when they finally had what they'd fought for. What they'd killed for. She just needed to break whatever odd spell had descended upon them. Bly grabbed Elise's hand and stepped toward the door. "Let's go."

Jade stood by the door with a grin on her face. She'd be a problem if Benedict gave the word. Kerrigan stood next to Halfryta's unconscious body. Bly couldn't read his expression, but she was certain that he would help them get out of here if only to uphold their deal. Jade and Benedict wouldn't be able to stop them.

"It's okay, Elise. We can go."

Elise hadn't budged. They were going to have to carry her out. Bly turned pleading eyes to Emerson. He still seemed frozen. Everyone's expression seemed full of something that Bly hadn't grasped.

"Elise." Benedict's voice was soft and sweet with none of his usual smarminess.

Bly's chest tightened. Elise turned back and lifted a hand toward Benedict, and he took it in his own. When she looked back at Bly, her eyes had cleared as if the shock had worn off. Her mouth twisted the way it always did when she was about to say something she knew Bly wouldn't like. The familiar quirk warmed her before her stomach sunk.

Elise cleared her throat. "Benedict is not my captor," she said. Her lips pursed, and she looked back at Benedict once more. "I love him."

Now Bly was the one who felt frozen by a curse, but then she broke it and tugged her sister's hand. "He's brainwashed you. He trapped you here and made you dependent on his blood."

Elise's laugh, light and tinkling, was a knife in Bly's chest, not because she didn't love the sound of it, but because it reminded her of everything she'd been missing over the past year.

"Trapped me? Benedict saved me," Elise said. "He's the one who found me in a witch prison and brought me here."

"That doesn't mean you owe him anything. You're confused. You're indebted. That's not love."

Elise swallowed. "Bly," she said softly. "I was in love with him *before* I was ever cursed."

Bly stared at her sister, at her hands, one in Bly's and one in Benedict's, as if torn between them. It made no sense.

"But . . . You and Emerson . . . ?"

Elise's face pinched. "You . . . know about that?"

"He told me." She turned around to find that Emerson had disappeared.

"Told her about what?" Benedict's voice was overly cheerful.

"Emerson and I . . . ," Elise started. Bly watched the way Elise's hand clamped tighter on Benedict's. "I always thought he was in love with you until that day he kissed me."

"Pardon me?" Benedict said.

"I guessed how you felt about him even before you told me. I'd never go after him behind your back. Besides . . . by then I was already in love with someone else." She squeezed Bly's hand, but then she dropped it and stepped away. Toward the vampire.

Bly had wanted Benedict dead before, but now the urge was overpowering.

Kerrigan had told her he was a cad. He wasn't someone to be trusted. Whatever Elise thought she felt for him had to be based on a lie.

"But I'm glad you found me," Elise added.

Bly wanted to soak in her sister's warm smile and soft eyes, but there was too much that needed answering.

"If he's not holding you prisoner, then why didn't you come home? You let me believe you were dead. I entered the Games for you. I . . ." Bly couldn't even give voice to all she had done. Emerson had been death cursed and forced to become a vampire. Donovan was now in the hands of the witches. Vincent was dead. She'd wounded Kerrigan beyond repair all to raise a sister from the dead who was alive, if not well.

But well enough to come home.

"You *what*?" Elise's voice was sharp.

Bly looked at her sister's wide eyes.

"You shouldn't have done that." Elise wore a familiar expression—horror at something reckless that Bly had done.

But it wasn't reckless. It was the only choice she'd had. Surely, Elise understood that. Bly shook her head. "What else did you expect from me?"

Elise shook her head. "I didn't think you'd enter the Games if you believed I was just . . . dead. I thought if I came home death cursed and you had to watch as I got closer and closer to leaving you that you'd do something reckless." She paused and then whispered, "Like enter the Games. I told myself that if I stayed gone, you would get past it eventually. You and Emerson would fall in love and live your happily ever after and forget about me. You were supposed to *forget about me*. You were leaving me behind anyway, weren't you? You planned to get that dress and then run away with Emerson and leave me behind."

"I didn't think you'd want to come," Bly whispered.

"You never asked."

Bly winced. She hadn't. She'd assumed she'd known exactly what Elise would choose. "But you really thought I wouldn't fight to bring you back from the dead?"

Elise shook her head.

"Then you didn't know me at all." Her words were harsh, and it was Elise's turn to wince.

Good. She wanted Elise to feel at least a flicker of the guilt that pulsed through Bly's veins with all the poison of a curse. Every horrible choice she'd made had been to save Elise because Bly had believed Elise was dead. She could live with all those choices when they were weighed against the life of her sister, but Elise, not just alive, but comfortable and free, took that counterweight away, leaving Bly crushed by the burden of what she'd done.

Her chest ached with the realization that she now had no justification for her actions.

Actions Elise could have stopped if she'd just come home.

But Bly's anger wasn't just for Elise, it was for herself. Because even though Elise had underestimated how far Bly would go to save her, that she would try to thwart death itself, Bly had underestimated Elise as well. She didn't know her sister was capable of falling in love with a vampire or wanting a life for herself beyond the Gap, where she'd always seemed so content. Bly had thought those desires were hers alone. Elise had never mentioned wanting *anything* beyond what they had, but Elise was right. Bly had also never really asked.

They weren't as close as she'd thought.

Bly had fought through hell to get back to Elise, and Elise hadn't tried to get back to her.

"If I'd known you were in the Games . . ." Elise didn't finish.

"*He* knew." Bly shot an accusing stare at Benedict. "You guessed who I was, didn't you?"

"I . . ." Benedict paused, and the hesitation was enough for Elise to pull her hand from his grasp.

"You didn't," Elise said.

"My dear," Benedict started.

"No. Tell me the truth," she said.

Benedict actually looked sheepish. "I suspected," he said with a shrug. "I didn't actually *confirm* anything."

"You didn't want to," Bly said.

"Of course not," Benedict snapped. His expression softened again as he looked at Elise. "I didn't want to lose you. You talked about your sister so much that when I saw her for the first time, I thought it might be her. I even asked her name, but I didn't ask anything beyond that because I didn't want to know. If I'd known for sure, I would've had to tell you. I made myself live in the doubt because I couldn't live without you." He reached out and tried to brush the back of his fingers against Elise's cheek, but she turned away from him.

Good. This would be the end of it, then. "Elise, let's go." Bly had a feeling Emerson wasn't gone. He couldn't have given up that easily. He'd be waiting for them.

Emerson reappeared at the doorway as if he'd sensed their need of him, and Bly felt a rush of relief. They'd get through this together. He was hurting. Bly knew exactly what that felt like, and yet she and Emerson had remained friends. He'd be able to fight back to that place with Elise. None of them would have exactly what they'd hoped for, but they'd be together.

She started to wave him forward. They'd drag Elise out of here if they had to, but her hand froze in the air.

A blade glinted in the hollow of Emerson's throat. And then a hand resting on his shoulder shoved him forward. He stumbled into the room with a vampire guard dressed in blood red at his back.

ELEVEN

Kerrigan drew his sword, and Jade freed two daggers from her waist as she crouched. Elise's hand was ripped from Bly's as Benedict grabbed her and pushed her behind his back, his own sword swinging free. Surprisingly, he gripped it like he knew how to use it.

None of them moved to strike as more guards poured into the room. Too many. Kerrigan's knuckles went white against the hilt of his sword, and Bly understood what would happen. He would not give up the key to saving his brother any more than Bly would've given up the key to saving Elise. His focus was singular. Even if he knew the fight wasn't fair, that some or all of them would surely die, he would take the gamble.

Bly drew her own dagger and backed up until she was shoulder to shoulder with Benedict. She shared a look with him, an understanding that surprised her. They would both die to protect her sister.

Kerrigan lunged, blade swinging down in a deadly arc aimed at the nearest guard.

"Stop," spoke a woman's voice from the shadow beyond the door. Kerrigan's attack stalled, blade hanging in the air just shy of decapitating the vampire in front of him. The blade trembled. Kerrigan trembled.

Bly's stomach sunk.

Melvina strode through the door. The vampire queen was petite in every way, and her curly blond hair bounced with airy lightness. She wore a pure white gown that bit into her small frame, highlighting her slight curves.

And yet her voice had stopped Kerrigan in his tracks. He was used to obeying her orders, and there was a sharpness in the way she'd spoken that could stop a blade, and a shrewdness in her eyes as she scanned the room that made Bly certain she was not one to double-cross.

But they already had.

Queen Allena entered the room behind Melvina, a whole head taller than her lover and dressed in a wispy black gown that made you wonder if there was anything at all underneath or if she was nothing but Melvina's dark shadow. Her expression was bored.

"You continue to be my naughtiest child, Kerrigan," Melvina said. "Now you've dragged your siblings into it as well." She made a soft tsking sound that sent a chill down Bly's neck.

Melvina's eyes landed on Halfryta in a heap behind Kerrigan's legs. "And all to secure the witch." She cocked her head. "I'd be impressed if I thought you simply wanted to kill her, given your history, but that's not what this is about, is it?" She raised one single condemning brow. "The witches have someone you want, and you'd go against this whole kingdom just to save your blood." She nodded as if Kerrigan had answered her, but his face was stone. "Not that I don't understand. I risked it all once for someone I loved, and it paid off." Allena placed a hand on Melvina's shoulder, and Melvina's expression softened for a fraction of a second before hardening again. "But even though it's noble, it doesn't always mean it's going to work out. And in your case, I'm afraid you failed."

Kerrigan withdrew his sword from the vampire guard's neck, but instead of sheathing it, he gripped it in both hands. "You'll have to kill me if you want her back."

"Speak for yourself, you bloody fool," Benedict said, but his grip on his own sword didn't slacken. He'd fight if it came to it. If not for Kerrigan, then for Elise.

Melvina smiled. "Well, that's perfect then, since the punishment for a treason as grave as this is death."

Tension choked the room. Soft fingers wrapped around Bly's, and she started before glancing back at Elise. Her sister's eyes seemed to be trying to say too much. There was sorrow there. Regret. Guilt. All things Bly knew well and all things she thought she'd be free of after she found her sister. Elise was supposed to heal her, not make things more complicated. And now there was no time to repair that. To understand.

Bly squeezed Elise's fingers in return, hoping it said enough.

"However . . ." Melvina let the word dangle.

It sparked hope in Bly's chest, but also dread. Surely what came next would not be a pardon.

"*However*," Melvina repeated, "we got what we needed from

the witch already. We were just keeping her alive for fun." She shrugged. "So your crime isn't completely unforgivable. A penance besides your blood could be found." Melvina looked behind her at Allena. Something unspoken passed between them in a way that could only happen with someone you'd known for an eternity. Allena nodded her head.

"Then it's settled," Melvina said. "The witches have created a spell with the roots of a flowering plant that only grew around the Hallow Pool where we were created. The spell is an abomination. It steals the magic from any vampire or witch it is cast upon and releases it back into the earth, leaving them nothing but a shallow husk." She shuddered. "A *human*. We heard rumors of such a spell, but we didn't know where the source of power came from until you brought us the witch." Melvina smiled. "We broke her eventually with truth spells."

Bly had thought truth spells were nothing but bits of legend said to be made from a mixture of herbs. They certainly weren't sold on the market—not that they would be of any interest to humans anyway.

"Luckily for us, the witches only have a limited supply of the root that some of their leaders had kept and carried through generations. They don't know where the original pool is." Melvina leaned forward as if about to tell a secret. "But we vampires love maps. Now we find ourselves in need of a merry band of fools to find that pool before the witches do. If you agree, you'll live. If not . . ." She shrugged.

"No way," Benedict said.

Melvina leveled a glare at Benedict. "You have the skills. We had planned to ask you and your sister regardless."

"I like hunting gold so I can buy pretty things."

"You're buying your life," Queen Allena said.

"And," Melvina said, "you may take the witch and trade her for Donovan, as is obviously your intention. Witches need royal blood for a spell of this magnitude. No doubt they've already been collecting from him, but it's in our best interest not to leave them with an endless supply if they ever do get their hands on some of these roots." She eyed each of them in turn and then frowned as her gaze slid behind Bly and Benedict. "My dear boy, I don't know why you're arguing with me when it seems you need my mercy more than anyone else. Is that a cursed pet human that you're keeping alive with your blood?"

Benedict's sword lowered.

Jade grumbled and shoved her daggers back into the waist of her pants.

"We'll do it," Kerrigan said, lowering his sword.

"Excellent choice," Melvina said.

✦ ✦ ✦

Instead of sneaking out of Vagaris like they had intended, they had a royal escort of guards with their hands on their weapons. A threat, but Bly was almost glad for it. As they'd been led out, she'd seen Callum's sharp face in the crowd, watching her like a hawk in search of a meal. He didn't try anything.

The queens insisted that two of the guards accompany them for the entire journey as well, making it less likely for their group to betray them.

Not that Bly had plans to. She didn't want to spend her life running from vindictive queens. How long of their eternity would the queens spend hunting them before they grew bored? Probably longer than Bly's short human lifespan offered.

They'd find the roots. Bly wasn't about to let one more obstacle stand between her and a peaceful life with Elise and Emerson on the other side of this, even though she wasn't sure how to imagine that life anymore.

The one thing she was certain of was that she wasn't painting Benedict into that picture.

She'd already driven a wedge between him and Elise.

Their entire group was more than a little fractured.

Kerrigan and Jade led the way with Halfryta strung between them on a stretcher, and behind them trailed Emerson and then Bly and Elise, walking side by side even though they weren't close enough to touch. Benedict followed at their backs, grumbling under his breath every so often. The guards brought up the rear. They hadn't introduced themselves or spoken at all. One had black hair and the other blond. Both had translucent skin from likely working nights in the city. Their veins were glaringly blue along their thick necks. They followed them with their broad shoulders almost touching like a wall of threat pushing them forward whether they wanted to go or not. They looked like the kind of men who could have removed your head from your shoulders even when they hadn't been vampires.

Bly decided to ignore them. She had no intention of betraying the queens, so the threat of their presence didn't matter.

She focused on her sister, watching as Elise removed a glove to pluck one of the plump red berries that lined the path. Bly opened her mouth to warn her of the thorns, but she'd already moved her hand back, unscathed, and popped the berry into her mouth.

The act seemed too easy for someone caught between two worlds. Bly had seen Elise staring at Emerson's back, but she'd also seen her turning around to glance at Benedict behind them. Whatever they had wasn't severed yet.

Bly needed to understand how this had happened.

She needed to understand *Elise*. A flood of guilt washed over her once more. She'd thought that she'd be done with guilt when she had her own sibling back and had helped Kerrigan get back his, but that guilt had only shifted and somehow deepened.

Bly had given up her heart and soul for something that her sister had never even wanted.

But why hadn't Elise just told her about Benedict? It seemed a simple thing to share when Bly was spinning all her own wild fantasies.

Elise's blond hair, the color of summer-dried grass, was pulled back in a familiar loose bun at the nape of her neck. Bly could imagine her just like that sitting in the glow of the fire at their parents' house, positioning an apple tart over the flames. Her face was the same, her expression soft and contented even as they marched forward on a dangerous mission. Perhaps that was why Bly had misread her happiness before. Her sister was just the type of person to find contentment no matter what situation she was in. Even if she'd wanted something different in her heart, she'd never had Bly's restless spirit.

Elise's clothes told a different story—they were the clothes of a dreamer. Her cloak was tan wool stitched on the edges with vines of climbing daisies. Her gray skirt underneath might have been practical if not for the ruffles sewn every few inches from the knees down. She wore a vest of the same material with matching miniature ruffles sewn where the buttons closed. They were the details of someone who cared about such things.

They were the clothes of someone who'd spent the past year living a dream while Bly had lived a nightmare.

Her need to understand turned to acid in her stomach. She reached out to the ribbon still tied tight enough for discomfort around her wrist. The edges had frayed to nothing but strings, and the sapphire blue had faded and become tarnished with splatters of mud and rusty brown stains Bly didn't want to think about— enough blood had been spilled that she wasn't even sure who it belonged to. She thought she'd be able to take it off when she saved Elise, that it would be a moment of redemption and forgiveness for all she had done, but Elise hadn't needed saving, and so Bly's crimes stayed heavy on her heart. She didn't deserve to take it off.

She twisted the ribbon tighter, turning her skin white and then blue as the pain numbed to nothing.

When she finally let go and looked up, Elise was watching her with her eyebrows drawn together and worry on her face. She opened her mouth to speak, but Bly didn't want to hear it. She didn't want to try to understand after all. Not yet.

Bly made her way up to Emerson. Before, they had shared the hurt of Elise's loss. Now they shared the complicated joy of finding her in a way they never expected.

Emerson didn't glance at her as she settled in beside him. Perhaps he'd realized that it was Bly at the heart of every problem. She'd gotten Elise cursed, and then Emerson too, and even before that, she'd been a barrier between the two of them being together.

"I'm sorry," she said. The apology sounded weak even to her ears.

"You told me to do it for Elise." Emerson's voice came out low, with an ache in it that mirrored the pain in Bly's chest. "I became a vampire because I thought she'd need me. Clearly, she doesn't."

Bly sucked in a breath. That hadn't been what she was apologizing for. She was sorry that she'd been a wedge between the two of them without realizing it. She'd never be sorry that Emerson was a vampire.

"You'd rather be dead? I thought you liked it—you have the forge. You have more power."

You have me. She didn't say it, but she thought their friendship had gotten stronger and truer, built on what they could each give each other instead of what they wished the other would be.

Emerson finally looked at her, his face drawn. "I'm sorry. I don't mean it." He shook his head, drawing a ragged breath. "Well, part of me means it. It's . . ."

Complicated. He didn't need to say it. Her own emotions were a roiling mess of contradiction inside her.

"I get it," she said. "I'm sorry."

He reached out and grabbed her wrist, fingers closing over the ribbon.

"However I feel isn't your fault. I needed someone to blame . . . besides her." His grip tightened. "You're so full of guilt that you're looking for more of it to bury yourself in because that's what has kept you going for the past year. You don't need it anymore. We got her. That hasn't changed. Everything else . . . doesn't matter now."

His words suffocated her, making her keenly aware of the guilt he'd spoken of pressing in on her. She *was* buried alive in it, and Emerson was trying to shovel some of it off her. He thought she wanted to stay buried, but in truth, she just didn't know how to claw her way out. Finding Elise was supposed to make it easier, not harder.

Emerson let go of her wrist. "You know, I never would've met Elise if it weren't for you following me around incessantly when we were kids." He gave her a gentle smile. She could see the hurt lingering in his eyes, but he was trying to mask it for her. "You gave me a best friend and someone I love. The rest is on me and Elise. Our paths will come back together if they are meant to. The future is up to us." He spoke the last sentence with a hint of steel in his voice.

"Then you need to talk to her." She bumped her shoulder against his.

He huffed. "Stop being so practical."

"You're rubbing off on me," she said with a grin.

They fell into an easy silence that only existed between best friends who had been through the worst and still clung to each other. Bly still felt the guilt contracting her chest, but Emerson had made it just a little lighter. With all that had happened between them, neither of them was going to hold their missteps over the other. The past was a thing to be forgiven, but it took two forgiving people to lift the weight of it.

TWELVE

THE REST OF THE TRIP TO HAVENWHILE didn't get any better. They were traveling more in pairs than a group, Kerrigan and Jade with the captive and the singular focus of getting Donovan back, Elise and Benedict, who had drifted back together, and then Emerson and Bly.

She'd been worried before that Emerson and Elise would become an item, and she'd be the one on the outskirts. Now she longed for that dynamic.

They all just needed time.

Preferably time when they weren't trekking through the woods with a series of dangerous tasks in front of them.

The hedges of Havenwhile were in full bloom with their purple morning glories open to the sunrise. Flakes of snow dotted the petals, making them appear even more magical. Elise let out a soft gasp. "Beautiful," she said, and she moved toward them, running her fingers across the petals as her hair glistened in the brightness of the new day. A soft smile touched her lips.

For a moment, everyone in the group stared at her. There she was, someone who had gone through something horrible at the hands of the witches, and yet she could still find something that belonged to them wonderous.

Bly imagined the petals were soft and silky to the touch, but she'd never felt them. The first time she'd stood here, she hadn't even thought of reaching for them.

Elise had kept the part of her that could find joy in little things while Bly hadn't.

Bly blinked, staring at the wall of green with bursts of purple with tiny yellow centers. For a moment, she let herself imagine plucking a flower and tucking it into her hair while she smiled.

She ached from the vividness of it, and yet she didn't join her sister. Elise turned around, her smile dropping at whatever she saw on Bly's face. But Bly couldn't force herself to pretend to be okay for Elise the way Emerson had for her.

Jade broke the trance first, shaking her head as she stepped past Elise to yank on one of the doors of twined manzanita that peppered the hedge. It didn't budge.

"I have a key," Bly said. She'd gotten it for winning the witch's prize in the Games, but it came with the warning from Demelza not to use it. She'd only tried that one time and almost had Nova's ax in her back as the result.

"I don't believe we'll need it," Benedict said.

As soon as he spoke, a small guard of witches stepped out of the woods, forming a loose semicircle around them. Their eyes flitted nervously from the vampires to their captive leader on the stretcher between them.

An older witch with dark brown skin and thick graying hair stepped up, slinging his unstrung bow across his back. His stare flicked from Halfryta to Kerrigan. "Is she alive?"

"Yes. Spelled asleep. Demelza . . . or rather . . . Una," he said, switching to Demelza's given name that the witches knew her by when she wasn't glamoured, "is expecting us."

The man's face was stoic. As Bly took in all the witches' faces, she saw no excitement at their leader's safe return. They were clearly not doing the witches any favor.

Bly had a horrible thought that they might slaughter them all where they stood, bury them all in the woods, and pretend they'd never returned.

But the older witch nodded. "We have instructions on where to take you." He sighed, his only hint at what he really felt. "We've been watching these woods for your arrival for weeks now. Come."

He turned and swung open the door, then waved them through.

Kerrigan entered first, and Jade followed behind with the other end of the stretcher. Bly didn't hesitate to go after them even though she wanted to.

She drew a deep breath at the familiar sight, waiting for panic to rise in her chest as they began to walk through town. It looked the same as before: the quaint little village that blended with the forest, the happy bustle of the witches going about their business.

All the things she'd hated when she'd thought Elise was dead at their hands.

Now it reminded her of hauling Donovan through the town, her heart half full of terror at what she was doing and half full

of hope at seeing her sister again, and then leaving with the realization that she'd destroyed the growing future she'd had with
Kerrigan only to not get her sister back.

A hand clenched around the pulse in her wrist.

She turned and met Emerson's steady gaze.

He'd always been the constant in her life even when he'd dis-
approved, and he still knew exactly what she needed.

She let her breath go. The coil of pain in her chest unwound.

"Elise," she said softly, and Emerson nodded, letting go of her
as they both looked for her sister.

Elise would have memories of this place, even if being outside
hadn't fazed her, but Elise had stopped on the side of the road,
smiling down at a little girl, who couldn't be more than four,
holding up a handful of wildflowers that Elise complimented. The
girl's tiny fingers plucked a daisy free of the cluster, offering it to
Elise, who didn't hesitate to put it in her hair.

She touched the child's cheek and moved on.

Bly couldn't breathe again, and she wasn't sure why it hurt
her that Elise wasn't traumatized by lake-blue eyes and clothes
the color of the trees. Bly had worked so hard to disassociate
the witches that had taken Elise from the whole of them. She'd
thought Elise would at least share that struggle with her.

She slid up beside her sister even though tension was still taut
between them.

"How are you okay here?" Bly asked. "I thought the memories…"

Elise blinked, her wide fawn-brown eyes confused for a
moment. "Oh, I was held in the woods. I was mostly unconscious,
so I don't remember it well." She glanced around. "This is lovely. It
reminds me of what you used to describe … Remember? A home

built into the branches of the oldest oak, trimmings painted the color of sunset, a stream running at its base."

Bly's face heated as the memory grew molten inside her.

Elise didn't notice. She was looking up at Benedict. "I never even saw this place. Benedict got me out quickly."

Benedict's and Elise's hands wound together.

So she had forgiven him for not telling her about Bly.

Bly couldn't look away from their intertwined fingers.

Elise finally noticed Bly's fixation and winced apologetically, letting go of Benedict. "Bly . . . ," she started.

"Good," Bly said. "Good. I was worried you had . . . memories." She moved away before Elise could speak again.

She shouldn't be disappointed that her sister didn't appear as haunted as she was. But Bly knew how a shared pain could bond; she'd felt it with Kerrigan. She'd thought that Elise and she would at least share the same pain of their year apart, but they didn't.

Bly had been guilt-ridden, weak from starving herself and giving blood to the point of fainting, desperate to enter the Games, unable to think of anything but the soft thud of her sister's body. Elise had been in a room cascading with bright fabrics, sewing the beautiful things Bly had once dreamed of wearing, happy and in love and not thinking of Bly at all.

Bitterness lanced her heart, splitting it in two—the part that was only relieved that Elise was alive and well and the side that felt angry that Elise had chosen to stay away and live a dream she hadn't bothered to share.

But then she looked back at Elise. Her sister watched her with a worried expression that Bly knew well. Elise had spent her life worrying about Bly climbing too high in a tree, or forgetting her lunch, or wandering a little too far in the woods. Like Emerson, her sister's worry had been an anchor that let her feel free to be a little wild.

Maybe their year apart had been Bly's turn for worry.

Elise had been safe and happy, which was something Bly hadn't dared to hope for. Bly would take on all the pain in the world in her sister's place if given the choice.

Elise smiled at Bly. The corners of her mouth trembled a little, perhaps with the strain of the tension between them, but even though she wanted to, Bly couldn't smile back. She could hold all the guilt and pain instead of Elise, but it was too much to smile under the weight of it.

She turned away.

Havenwhile had been crawling with life when they arrived, but it had turned eerily silent. Witches gathered along the edges of the road. Few smiled. This was not the raucous crowd that cheered when she'd handed over Donovan in the Games.

Halfryta was not loved.

She *was* feared. Even bound and unconscious, nobody made a move against them.

They took a trail that wound against the side of the lake, passing the trees with hammocks that stretched out over the water. Bly's chest ached at the sight of them. She stared at Kerrigan's back in front of her, but he didn't so much as glance up at the place where they'd clung together, suspended for the moment above the chaos, their lips finding each other.

She really was dead to him now if the memory didn't even turn his head.

They turned from the lake down a narrow path that took them deeper into the brush until it abruptly widened into a huge open field sprinkled with wildflowers and dotted with trees laden with lemons, apples, and oranges. On the far side rose the largest structure Bly had seen here, a mansion built with logs that rose regally against the backdrop of the forest beyond it.

They marched across the field, the smell of flowers and fruit a sweet distraction.

This could go badly. Demelza held the upper hand.

Bly had no reason to believe the witch would keep her word. She'd tried to betray them once before.

After climbing redwood steps to a round white oak door, the witch leading them opened it and waved them forward into a grand hall that rivaled the vampires' in size. Where the vampires' fortress was cold stone, the walls of the witches' hall were all the décor it needed. The trunks of trees lined the edges, but unlike the outside, these seemed to grow from the floor, their trunks curving around each other and their branches weaving together in arms that peaked toward the center of the room, creating a canopy above them. From the branches hung an impossible number of golden lanterns, each one shaped like a butterfly or a bird with a spell glowing softly within.

At the end of the room, Demelza rose from a throne of manzanita and ivy that twined together into a high back the shape of a rose petal. Her red hair was twisted with matching ivy into a mass that crowned her head.

Nova stood on her right, and a line of guards dressed in an array of browns and grays stood in front of them.

"Come," she beckoned.

Kerrigan led them forward, but only halfway across the room. The witch guards who'd walked them here fanned out at their back.

Demelza's fingers tapped in waves across the arms of the throne as she looked at the limp figure of her mother. "Didn't I specify alive?"

Kerrigan nodded at Jade, and they dropped the stretcher roughly to the ground. Removing a spell from his pocket, Kerrigan bent over the witch, waking her before jerking her to her feet. She sagged for only a moment before she straightened, chin rising and shoulders pulling back as if she weren't still bound.

She coolly took in the scene around her and said nothing.

Demelza's face pinched. Bly thought it might have been disappointment, but she wasn't sure if it was because they'd brought her mother back or because of Halfryta's reaction.

Demelza nodded at Nova, and the girl disappeared for a moment before returning with Donovan led in front of her, arms bound behind his back, a deep frown on his face.

His eyes went first to Kerrigan. He sighed. "Brother." He looked at Jade next. "I didn't think you'd participate in this. I thought you'd know me better."

Jade looked sheepish for a split second before she glared back at him. "You should know me better than to think I'm going to leave you here."

Donovan's frown lifted for the briefest moment before he turned to Bly. "And you . . . ," he said. His eyes shifted pointedly over Bly's shoulder where she knew Elise stood with Benedict and Emerson on either side. Donovan didn't need to say anything else.

They both knew that he'd upheld his end of their bargain and Bly had not.

Once again, she was the reason everyone was in this situation.

"Unbind her and release her," Demelza ordered.

"Kerrigan," Donovan said. "Snap the witch's neck."

"I'll kill every last one of you," Demelza said.

"And I'd die happy knowing that your mother died first." Donovan looked over his shoulder at Demelza. "You know I'd be doing *you* a favor with a mother like that."

Demelza pursed her lips, her pale face reddening, but she ignored Donovan, speaking only to Kerrigan. "We had a deal. Release her."

Kerrigan hesitated. He wanted his brother's approval. He wanted to make up for the things he'd failed to protect Donovan from in the past, but Bly knew that he wasn't going to let Donovan die even if it made his brother hate him all the more. Kerrigan's fingers slowly peeled back from Halfryta's arm.

Donovan sighed. "I should've known you didn't have the guts. Years ago, you would have, but not now." His voice was thick with disdain.

"Just come," Kerrigan barked.

A flicker of concern passed over Donovan's face as he looked at Halfryta, already halfway across the room.

Donovan bolted.

"Seize him." Halfryta spoke for the first time.

The witch guards didn't hesitate. Whatever brief hold Demelza had had over them was nothing in comparison to years of living under Halfryta's reign of terror.

Jade had been right. Walking in here had been a mistake.

The witches had clearly used speed and strength spells before they'd entered the room. They overtook Donovan easily with his hands still bound behind him, and even though Kerrigan and Benedict and Jade had launched into immediate action, the witches were too fast and too many. The whole room erupted and then stilled within seconds.

Bly hadn't even had time to draw her dagger.

Demelza had risen from the throne. "I gave my word," she said. "We must honor it."

Halfryta, arms still bound, climbed the steps to stand beside her daughter. Demelza was half a head taller, but she seemed to shrink beside her mother.

"You were foolish to make that bargain in the first place, and now I must clean up your mistakes," Halfryta said. "Unbind me, child." The word *child* on Halfryta's lips sounded like a curse, not an endearment.

Demelza glanced around the room at the guards who had obeyed her mother in an instant. Her face slackened with resignation as she pulled an unbinding spell from her pocket, hesitating only a moment before freeing her mother's arms.

"Good," Halfryta said. "Now stop playing pretend and get down from here." Her attention slid to Nova. "Take your human pet with you. Where's Samuel?"

Demelza raised her chin, clearly trying to hang on to any dignity she had left as she stepped down. Nova followed her, eyes darting warily between everyone.

Donovan had been dragged back below the throne.

"I will start a war." Kerrigan took a step forward despite a witch's blade holding him at bay. "Your daughter and I made an agreement while she ruled in your stead. You must honor it."

"Must I?" Halfryta's smile was sharp. "Captives handed over in the Games are supposed to receive a clean death, not be held and given truth spells." Donovan cleared his throat pointedly, but Halfryta ignored him. "War has already begun, and there's only one weapon that matters." She stared at each one of them intently. "Which of you has the map?"

Kerrigan and Jade shared a look.

"Surprised?" Halfryta grinned at Kerrigan. "You were not as diligent with your sleeping spells as you should have been, vampire. I heard every word. Those roots are the witches' heritage. *My* heritage. My parents were at the Hallow Pool after the last drop had been drunk. They were there when the witches first realized they could put magic back into objects, and when everyone began to leave to find a place to settle, they were smart enough to gather some of the plants that they'd only seen grow around that pool. They wondered what spell they might hold, but they forgot about them as they struggled to keep their new world from the brink of collapse. They told me about them years later, but they never saw a reason to try to create a new spell. Once they were gone, I did. I knew roots that drank from the magic had to be powerful, and I spent years experimenting before I realized that they did the opposite of the pool. The water gave, the roots take. But my supply is limited. I wasted too much, and I need more, and I *won't* let you have them. I'll take the map in exchange for your brother."

None of them moved. If they gave it up, they'd have the vampire queens hunting them, and that was *if* Halfryta let them walk out of here, which seemed increasingly unlikely.

"Or I'll hack you all to pieces and dig through the carnage for it."

"I have the map," Benedict said.

Bly turned around in time to see Elise grab Benedict's arm. He patted her hand. "I'm fine, my dear," he whispered, giving Emerson a quick look. Emerson grabbed Elise's hand as Benedict pinched the witch's blade at his throat with two fingers. "Pardon," he said, pulling it back, lip curled disdainfully. He stepped forward.

"Hand it over," Halfryta said.

"Oh, I cannot."

"Kill him." Halfryta waved a hand.

Elise cried out, and Bly knew Emerson had to be holding her back.

"Let me rephrase." Benedict spoke too calmly for someone with swords swinging for him. "I am the map."

"Stop," Halfryta ordered.

Benedict tapped his head. "It's in here. Nowhere else."

"You're lying," Halfryta said.

"Feel free to strip me. I'm not shy."

Halfryta stared at him, her expression calculating. When she finally spoke, she smiled, which couldn't be good. Her smiles held the same edge as a blade about to break skin. "Then your group will continue on, but you will return the roots to *me*, not my bloodsucking counterparts, if you want this thing back so badly." She jerked her chin at Donovan.

Donovan groaned.

"We're not leaving without him," Kerrigan said. "We'll bring you the roots, but he comes too."

"I'm not naïve enough to think you'll come back of your own free will."

Bly looked at Kerrigan. His face was drawn. They didn't have anything to barter with for his release. The only way forward was leaving him behind and coming back with the roots.

Bly turned back to Halfryta. "I'll stay in his place. I'll be your leverage."

THIRTEEN

"No," Elise whispered behind her.

The pain in the word pierced Bly's heart. She didn't dare look back at her sister. She'd lose her nerve. She knew the hurt she'd be causing Elise, and despite her anger at Elise for letting her think she was dead, Bly didn't wish the same on her.

Instead, she caught Benedict's eye as he returned to the group. He nodded, understanding what she asked without words. Keep Elise from interfering.

She could feel Kerrigan's stare on her. Technically, their bargain was done. She'd helped free Halfryta, and he'd taken her to Elise. But she'd sworn to herself that she would get his brother back. She needed to do this.

Halfryta laughed. "A human girl for a vampire prince?"

"Make the trade," Demelza said.

Halfryta scowled at her. "Don't be daft."

"She's the one that bound you in the battle in the woods,"

Demelza said. "She's the reason the vampires got you in the first place."

Halfryta's face drained of all expression. For a second, she wasn't a fearsome and powerful witch; she was small and tired. Bly wondered what the vampire queens had done to her beyond just the truth spells.

"Let her come," Halfryta said.

The sword that hovered near Bly's throat dropped away.

"What are you doing?" Desperation wobbled in Elise's voice, and Bly couldn't stop herself from turning. Her sister struggled to step forward even with the blades threatening to pierce her if she moved. Only Benedict's grip on her kept her in place. Bly wished she could hug her and reassure her or explain exactly why she was doing this. She had a feeling Elise would understand.

"Bly," Kerrigan said.

She turned to the vampire she'd betrayed. He looked . . . confused.

Bly wasn't. She knew exactly what she was doing. "I told you I'd get him back for you."

She strode forward. The guards released Donovan at Halfryta's command. For a second, he just stood there before taking slow, wary steps toward Bly. He stopped in front of her as they met in the middle.

Donovan raised his eyebrows. "You know he's going to hate you for taking my place."

"He'll be glad to be rid of me."

Donovan looked beyond her shoulder, probably at Kerrigan, and then he laughed. "You've underestimated his feelings for you."

Bly shook her head.

"Or *he's* underestimated his feelings for you," Donovan mused.

Bly's throat squeezed. "I doubt that."

"I know my brother better than you, believe it or not." Donovan smirked. "Here we go. Any second now . . ."

"Come," Halfryta barked. "Before I change my mind."

"Wait," Kerrigan said. "I'll take his place instead."

Donovan rolled his eyes. "There you go."

"No," Halfryta said.

Bly refused to look back at Kerrigan.

"Tell him I said I'm sorry," Bly said. "If I don't get out of here alive."

Donovan's face grew deathly serious. "I will."

Bly walked past him into the hands of the witches.

Nova was the first to reach her, grabbing her by the arm so fiercely that Bly was sure she was trying to snap her bone with her bare strength. She laid her ax on Bly's shoulder, nestling the tip of the blade against her throat.

"You have no deal unless she comes," Kerrigan shouted. "It makes no sense to keep her. Wouldn't you rather have a prince? More blood to harvest for your precious spells?"

"I believe your brother was right. I'd rather have you dying in the woods." Halfryta turned to Bly. "A fair number of you seem to love this one for some reason. Perfect leverage." She turned and whispered something to a witch with burgundy hair who had appeared at her side a few moments before. He looked around Demelza's age, and Bly vaguely remembered him questioning her authority at the end of the Games. It had to be Demelza's cousin, Samuel. He disappeared again as soon as Halfryta finished speaking to him.

Donovan had reached the group, and Jade, in an uncharacteristic display of an emotion that wasn't violent, pressed herself into his side. He put an arm around her, but his focus was on Kerrigan.

"You didn't hear me," Kerrigan said. "We will *not* leave without her."

The room grew restless. The witches' blades snuck closer and closer toward the draw of blood.

"Brother," Donovan said. "We can get her back after we get this silly little root everyone is so worked up about."

"No," Kerrigan said. "You have no reason to keep her alive once we're gone to do your bidding." He nodded at both Demelza and Nova. "Those two have already tried to kill her once."

Halfryta looked appreciatively at her daughter, and Demelza stood a little straighter. "Good girl." There was praise in the words but also condescension. "Although I can't help but notice she's still alive."

Samuel reappeared with a flat redwood box in his hand.

Kerrigan's eyes narrowed in on it. He shifted forward slightly, forcing the blade at his throat to draw a line of blood. "What is that?"

Nothing good, Bly thought.

"Compromise," Halfryta said. "I'm a reasonable woman." She beckoned, and Nova shoved Bly up the stairs where two more guards held each of her arms. Halfryta reached out and opened the box.

Inside on a bed of fiery orange and red leaves was an odd-looking rope of snaking brown vines studded with thorns and braided with threads of black metal that gleamed with hints of shimmering rainbow in the light. Bly had never seen anything quite like it.

Halfryta reached in and lifted the rope, holding it lovingly in her hands. "One of my greatest creations," she said as she stepped in front of Bly, eyeing her. "Hopefully it's not a waste on you." She plucked her finger against one of the thorns before winding the rope around Bly's neck, holding the two ends in front. Bly started to jerk her head away, but the scratch of thorns stilled her.

Kerrigan shouted something. He was being foolish trying to save her.

Halfryta's eyes flooded with blue. "Fuse," she spoke. The two ends of the rope bonded together until Bly couldn't see a seam. Halfryta reached into the box and pulled out a tiny vial of flaky dust. She took out a single speck and pressed it to the rope around Bly's neck. "Constrict," she said.

Bly's eyes widened. She struggled to pull her hands free from the guards who held her, expecting the rope to squeeze around her neck until it strangled her, but nothing happened.

"Let her go," Halfryta said.

As soon as the guards released her, her hands flew to her throat. Her fingers bled as she grazed the thorns, but she tried to lift it over her head anyway. It wasn't tight, but it was small enough that she couldn't remove it.

"Bly!" Elise called.

Bly took a tentative step back toward her group and then another, half expecting the vines around her neck to squeeze tighter at any moment and take her life right in front of them. Kerrigan stepped through the witches' blades blocking his path, ignoring the edges that drew blood on him.

The guards started toward him, but Halfryta must have called them off because Kerrigan reached Bly. His hands went to her throat, wrapping around the strange necklace without hesitation. His brow furrowed as he tried to snap it.

The thorns sliced at her neck, but she didn't stop him.

Kerrigan grunted. All his vampire strength didn't so much as bend it. When he let go, his hands were bloody from where he'd ignored the thorns biting his skin. He turned to Halfryta. "What is this?"

"A guarantee."

"What's it spelled with?"

"None of your concern. What *is* your concern is that it cannot be broken by force or spell—aside from the one I've made to remove it. It will constrict slowly over time until those thorns puncture that pretty neck. I'm sure they'll be less forgiving than your fangs."

Kerrigan growled, and Bly put a hand on his arm just in case he decided to do something.

Halfryta just smiled. "Bring me back the roots, and I'll free her. Succeed or she dies. Take the roots to your queens and she dies. I'm giving you exactly what you demanded: She may go with you, but you must bring her back if you want her to live. Demelza and Samuel will accompany you as well. Along with these three guards." She pointed to the nearest three—a woman with a sharp, narrow face that reminded Bly of a hawk and gave away no emotion; a man who grinned and brushed back wavy, soft blond hair as he puffed his chest at being selected; and a petite girl with short brown hair and a nervous face full of freckles.

"I won't risk more," Halfryta added.

"Mother," Demelza said.

"Don't you need me here?" Samuel asked.

Halfryta cocked her head at him. "To do what exactly? Demelza held the people's respect enough to take power in my absence. You did not." Her stare shifted from Samuel to her daughter. "Let's hope the forest chooses an heir for me since it seems I cannot decide."

"And if we both die?" Samuel asked.

Halfryta shrugged. "I will choose another. Blood is nothing if your family is weak." Halfryta waved a hand. "Pack your things. You'll leave in an hour."

FOURTEEN

THE GUARDS DUMPED THEM IN THE WOODS behind Havenwhile. Thick mushrooms glistened with the remnants of snowfall that had hardened to ice. Bly cringed at the soft breaking as she stepped on one.

She couldn't help but glance back at Elise. Her sister stood unmoving, her face as pale as the ground at her feet. Bly wasn't the only one who'd had nightmares of white ground laced with curses.

Only this time would be different. No matter what bitterness still poisoned her heart, Bly wouldn't leave Elise's side.

Bly stepped back, reaching a hand for her sister just as Benedict stepped up behind Elise, scooping her up into his arms.

Elise gave a startled laugh that jarred against the tension and made everyone glance her way.

"I've got you, my dear." Benedict pressed his lips against Elise's temple.

Elise's pale face regained a flush of color.

Bly saw it then—the way Elise must have fallen in love: Benedict was danger in fine clothes, fangs behind disarming smiles. He was a fantasy—the tales that young girls in the Gap told themselves about vampires who fell madly in love with humans and whisked them away to live in castles of stone in Vagaris.

Bly had never bought into that particular fantasy, especially after Emerson's sister had died. She didn't realize that Elise had soaked in those stories and dreamed in them, but then Bly remembered something from the day she'd thought Elise had died: On their way to pick mushrooms, Elise had turned toward Vagaris, an odd look on her face that Bly hadn't taken the time to decipher but which might have been longing, and her promising Bly that not all vampires were horrible.

Bly should have asked more questions then. Elise might have told her about her own plans if Bly had just been a little less consumed with her own escape.

Too late now. Bly turned, catching Emerson's pained expression. He'd been stepping toward Elise too. They'd both been moving to save her, but Benedict had reached her first again.

Another wave of bitterness coursed through Bly.

Benedict had saved Elise.

"Great. The humans are already tired." Samuel had begun marching away through the woods, taking the lead with the witch guards flanking him, but he turned around to glare back at them.

"Watch you don't lose that tongue," Benedict said with a smile.

"Try me, vamp." Samuel pulled open his vest, showing off the array of spells sewed into the lining.

"Scary." Benedict yawned dramatically. "But I don't need silly little spells to relieve your shoulders of your head." He sat Elise down, safely past the mushrooms.

Samuel took a step toward him, and the witch guards placed their hands on the swords.

"Boys," Donovan said. "Now hardly seems like the time."

"Agreed." Samuel nodded sagely as if he hadn't been the one advancing toward a fight a moment ago. He spun around and started walking again.

"Wrong way," Benedict called gleefully. "I'm the precious map, remember?"

Samuel turned around, folding his arms over his chest as Benedict strode northwest. Jade followed close behind him. "Let the real muscle lead the way," she said as she passed the group of scowling witches. "Donovan," she called, glancing behind her for the man she'd fought so hard to retrieve.

Donovan gestured for her to go on without him, and she scowled in response, but there was lightness in her eyes that took the edge off her expression. Bly suspected their relationship wasn't one of soft touches and longing glances.

Donovan seemed to be waiting for Demelza and Nova to follow next. Bly could feel Nova tracking her every movement. She'd probably only come in hopes of watching the collar choke the life out of her.

"Witch, there's no way I'm having you at my back," Donovan said, waving them forward.

"Afraid?" Demelza smiled.

"Absolutely traumatized." Donovan gave her a wolfish grin.

Demelza shook her head at him. "I'm the one who shouldn't

want *you* at *my* back. You did regale me with some inventive ways you were going to kill me right after we imprisoned you."

Donovan gave her a wistful look. "And I've lulled myself to sleep every night since picturing them." He waved a hand again for her to go first.

She laughed and moved past him without looking over her shoulder, which Bly thought was rather brave of her.

Emerson trailed after them, and the vampire guards followed him. Their silence made Bly uneasy. They were there to make sure the roots made their way back to the queens, but the mission had been commandeered by Halfryta. The only reason they weren't objecting was because they probably planned to make a play for the roots later.

The choker at her neck meant nothing to them, but she didn't want to dwell on that future problem when the present had plenty. She turned, looking behind her. "Where's—"

"In the woods. Probably counting the reasons not to forgive you." Donovan's eyes narrowed. "Clever of you to trade yourself for me, offering your life for someone he loves even though you're the one that put me there. It worked. He wouldn't leave without you." Donovan eyed the tree line. "And now he's off sulking because you forced him to reveal his feelings. Knowing him, he feels guilty about showing he still cares for you in front of me."

Bly understood guilt. She hadn't meant to give him more of it. "I didn't do it for him to forgive me."

"No?"

"I wanted him to stop hurting. I thought getting you back would fix him."

Donovan laughed. "Kerrigan hoards guilt like most vampires

hoard blood. I'm not sure he knows how to live without it."

"Whose fault is that?"

His expression darkened. "I forgave him. I was dying, but I took the time to tell him."

"Exactly. That was under duress. Tell him again. He thinks you'll hate him more now for freeing the witch."

Donovan sighed. "I knew he would. That's why I bargained with you. Despite your tedious human weaknesses, I knew you had the dead heart of a vampire underneath and would get in his way if it meant getting your sister back."

Bly winced.

"That's a compliment," he added.

"Just . . . forgive him again," she said. "He's been acting more and more like . . . you. You can save him. I can't." She was tired of the whiplash—every time she was in danger, Kerrigan was there, helping her only to turn around and leave her cold and aching from his absence.

Donovan raised an eyebrow. "You want me to save him from being like me?"

"Do you *want* him to be like you?"

His expression hardened and then softened. "I think I'd like to see what he's like with you . . . when he's not trying to die."

"It's a little late for that."

Donovan had started to walk away when he turned back around. "Don't underestimate yourself. You have the heart of a vampire, and vampires get what they want no matter who has to bleed."

He said it like that quality was a gift when it was nothing but a curse. She'd made too many people bleed for what she'd wanted already.

And she doubted they'd get through this journey without more people bleeding.

With that in mind, she sought out Elise, who had drifted to the rear of the group since Benedict had taken the lead.

A smile tugged at Elise's lips before dropping as Bly slid up beside her.

Bly desperately wanted to know what her sister was thinking, and if she resented Bly or if she felt some guilt too for staying away and letting Bly believe that she had died.

Both their choices had put the other in danger.

Maybe the real reason that Elise didn't come back home was because Bly had let the witches take her when she hadn't even been dead.

Part of her wanted to let the hurt win and widen the chasm between them until they both grew numb from the distance, but she needed to keep fighting past her anger and guilt.

She thought of Elise's pained cry when she'd offered to stay in Donovan's place.

Her sister loved her. Bly needed to fight for their relationship. She'd spend every day building a bridge between them if she had to. She had to be the one to do it. Elise had never been the fighter. Bly had. That was still true.

Bly cleared her throat. "Did you make that dress you're wearing?" A simple question.

"Yes." Elise fingered the stitching on the edge of her cloak. "Do you like it?"

There was an earnestness in her question that made Bly smile. "I *love* it. Will you make me something? When we're back?"

"Of course." Elise beamed at her.

"Unless you hate sewing or something," Bly rushed out. Benedict could have made her do it.

Elise's face fell. "I've always loved it." A trace of anger hugged her words. "Why do you think he gave me a whole room for it?"

Elise had always sewn lovely patches into all her clothes at home, but Bly always thought that was because of practicality, not because she liked to do it. Benedict had given her a room overflowing with fabric and thread, and it wasn't because he loved her work. It was because Elise loved sewing. Benedict had understood something about her sister that Bly had not and had helped her achieve that dream.

Bly swallowed, and it felt like bark scraping down her throat.

She couldn't undo the past like she thought she could. She'd played the Games so that she could raise Elise from the dead and completely erase what had happened, but without a spell to wipe the memory, there never would have been a clean slate. She'd wanted to ignore that truth, but now the reality was in front of her, and Elise was staring ahead at Benedict's back with her lips set into a grim line.

Not only was the past still with them, but there was an entire year of it that Bly hadn't been a part of. She might not have known her sister as well as she thought before, but she knew her even less now.

That was Elise's fault. It hadn't been the witches who'd stolen that year from them—Elise had.

Bly again fought back that surge of bitterness.

"Tell me about him," Bly said.

Elise turned back to her. "You don't like him."

Bly gritted her teeth. "I don't know him."

"You think he's evil just because he's a vampire," Elise said, but then she frowned. "But no . . . that can't be true. You just traded yourself for Donovan back there. Why?"

Bly shrugged. "I owed him from the Games." She didn't elaborate or bring up Kerrigan. Instead, she looked over her shoulder at Emerson. "You know I don't believe vampires are evil. Not anymore."

"Right," Elise said, as if she'd forgotten. "How did it happen?"

"Helping me save you."

A tiny cry left Elise's lips. "No," she muttered. "No," she said again, like the word could change something. "He must hate me then."

"He doesn't," Bly said, and then added, "I don't think he could."

Emerson and Elise hadn't spoken to each other since they'd left Vagaris. Bly could feel the hurt rolling off Emerson. He'd lost a dream that had kept him going. She understood.

Bly wasn't sure if it'd help or hurt more for Elise to talk to him.

Elise didn't seem to know either. She looked nervous every time she glanced in their friend's direction.

There'd clearly been something between them. If Elise hadn't been worried about Bly's own interest in Emerson, then something might have grown between them earlier, and none of them would be marching through the forest on an impossible mission.

Bly barely stopped herself from spiraling into an endless series of what-ifs.

All she could do was focus on the present. She could heal something between Elise and Emerson. She could start by telling Elise the truth about what he'd done for the both of them. "Emerson stole a binding spell that I'd still needed to enter the Games. He knew he'd get punished, but he didn't care. I think he wanted to be death cursed so that he could play the Games instead of me, but I refused unless we played for the vampire prize too. I needed to save both of you."

"And it worked," Elise breathed. The admiration in her voice made Bly's chest squeeze.

"I won both prizes." Bly looked away, thinking of Nova and Vincent. That terrible cost. "We saved you eventually, just not the way I expected."

"I didn't need saving," Elise said gently.

"I didn't know that, did I?"

Elise said nothing. No apology. Bly might have been trying to build a bridge, but it felt like Elise wasn't helping at all. Bly had thought she could do it herself, but maybe she didn't want to.

Bly cleared her throat. "Do you have any weapons?" She wasn't about to let her sister march through the woods without at least arming herself. Elise may have spent the last year in the safety of Benedict's home, but Bly had learned that the woods were *always* dangerous, and not just because of cursed mushrooms.

Elise's eyes widened slightly. "No. I—"

"Here," Bly said, cutting her off. "You need something to defend yourself with if the worst happens." She pulled two of her arrows from her quiver and pointed to the spelled twigs of birch bound to the tip. "These are binding spells. The spells have already been cast, so don't accidentally prick yourself with them. Even if you use the spell, don't let go of the arrows in a fight. Keep your grip toward the top of the shaft so they don't break and swing them in your fist like this." Bly gripped one and swung as if aiming for somebody's neck before handing them over to her sister.

Elise looked down at them then back up at Bly. "Where'd you learn to do that?" she asked.

Bly shrugged. "I wanted a way to cast a spell without getting as close to my opponent. I haven't actually mastered a bow yet, which would be even better, but the length of the arrow still gives me more range in a fight. In case something happens, and I can't get to you in time. Fight."

Elise glanced down at the weapons in her hands. "I was starting to think you hated me."

Bly bit the inside of her cheek. "Of course I don't." The words sounded strained. "And I don't want you dead," she added fiercely, because there was no lie in those words.

Elise's sharp eyes analyzed Bly's face, unpacking everything the way only a sister could. She gave a slow, heavy nod. "I know you never wanted me dead, but you thought I was, and it would've been easier on you if I had been—if you'd raised me from the dead. You said you've done things . . ."

Bly swallowed the lump in her throat. "I was glad you were fine. I just wish I'd known," she bit out.

"I told you why . . . ," Elise started.

"Why doesn't erase what I did." She couldn't help but glance back at Emerson again.

"You blame yourself for Emerson . . . And it all comes back to me . . ."

"No." Bly's heart burned. "It comes back to *me*—that day in the woods. I let them take you without a fight, and I've been fighting every day since." Her chest heaved. Her body held so much guilt that she felt like she needed to fight something because she'd been fighting for so long now to escape the guilt that it was all she knew how to do.

And now she was fighting Elise . . . the person she'd been fighting *for*.

She didn't know how to make any of this right. She stopped walking. Elise turned back to her, but Bly took a step back and another, and then she turned and sprinted into the woods. If she couldn't fight her guilt, then maybe she could just run from it.

She moved through the woods at a full sprint. She didn't go far, not far enough that she wouldn't be able to find her way back, just enough to feel the burn and ache in her legs, enough for her to fight for each breath, which was easier than fighting her guilt. She leaned an arm against the rough moss coating the thick trunk of an oak tree and focused only on her breath.

But she needed to go back, so she could find a way forward.

"I thought this would be a lot harder."

Bly spun at the sound of a deep voice behind her that she didn't recognize, but before she could even turn, something pricked against her wrist as the voice spoke the binding spell, and rough hands pulled her wrists around her back so that the spell would lock them there.

Turning, she kicked her leg out without waiting to see who'd caught her. The hulking blond vampire guard smiled at her as he dodged her attack easily. His hand darted out for her throat as she tried to run, but he hissed, jerking back after his fingers hit her collar.

She yelped as the thorns sank into her neck like fangs, sending a stream of blood pooling to her collarbone.

The vampire grabbed her arm with his other hand as he wiped the wounded one against his red pants. He eyed the blood at her throat and then the collar. His eyes went black. "You know, I was worried Prince Callum would be angry that I didn't grab you before the witch put this thing around your neck, but I actually think he'll quite enjoy it. Maybe he'll even give me a bonus."

"Callum . . . ," Bly said. Bile rose in her throat.

"He tried to get the queens to just give you to him, but they didn't want to stir up a fuss with your merry little group, so he offered me a very large sum of money to bring you back." He sighed as he stared at her throat. "Unfortunately, he told me not to taste you. I've been known to get carried away."

Bly opened her mouth to scream. His hand was already coming down in anticipation of her cries for help, but then he froze. His eyes went wide, the black in them fading away to gray in a single moment as his hand dropped to his side.

She heard a thump she knew all too well, followed by another, before she noticed the arrowheads protruding from the vampire's heart. Blood deepened the red of his uniform as he collapsed to the ground.

FIFTEEN

HER EYES SCANNED THE TREE LINES, looking for *him*. Maybe she'd run into the woods on purpose in hopes that he would find her. But it was Donovan who stepped out and strode toward her as he slung his bow across his shoulders. "Glad that's out of the way," he said as he stopped in front of her, pulling an unbinding spell from his vest and freeing her hands.

"What? Saving me?" she asked.

"Owing you after that little stunt you pulled with the witches, taking my place and all. Although let's not act like that was for me."

"Well, we're free of each other now. No need to run around saving me."

"I doubt that."

Her eyes narrowed. "How did you even know I was in trouble?"

"I saw you run off, and I saw that guard sneak away a second later. I'm suspicious by nature, so I decided to follow. Good thing

I did." He kicked the dead guard in the shoulder with the tip of his boot. "You sure have a way of pissing off vampires. What did you do to this one?"

Bly shuddered. Her fingers went to the blood at her collarbone. Donovan's eyes tracked her movement, but they stayed gray rimmed in green without a trace of hunger in them.

"Callum sent him," she said.

Donovan's eyes darkened at the name even though she hadn't given any details yet.

"It's a long story, but I got blood matched with him while I was trying to get to Benedict, and things didn't go well."

"Did he hurt you?" Donovan's voice was a low growl, and Bly eyed his unreadable face. It actually sounded like he cared.

"Not as much as I hurt him."

Donovan remained stoic for a moment more before he barked out a laugh and clapped Bly on the shoulder. She winced as he jostled her wound. "Good for you. Although when we get back, he'll have to be dealt with."

"I can handle it myself."

Donovan stared pointedly at the vampire at their feet.

"He got the drop on me. I wasn't thinking."

"Right," he said, laughing again.

He bit his thumb and then reached for her bleeding neck.

She started to pull away.

"Don't worry, you won't owe me for this."

Sighing, she let him heal her as she scanned the woods behind him.

"Looking for someone?" he asked. "Am I not the redheaded vampire you wanted to come to your rescue?"

She flushed.

His voice lowered. "He came. I just beat him to you."

She looked at the trees again and saw nothing. She wasn't sure she believed him, but he seemed done with the conversation. Spinning, he walked away, and she had to run to keep up with him.

They walked for a moment in silence before Donovan glanced down at her. "Are you okay?"

"Of course. It's not the first time someone's tried to kill me," she grumbled.

"Yes. I would know. I tried more than once." He raised an eyebrow. "You're surprisingly lucky for human."

"*Lucky?*" she scoffed.

He laughed.

She glared at him, and he raised his hands in defense. "You and I are the luckiest people I know," he said. "We should probably both be dead at least three times over."

"Maybe avoiding death isn't lucky."

"Dark," he said appreciatively before his expression turned solemn. "I wasn't asking whether you were okay after that incompetent animal grabbed you. You and your sister . . . I would've thought you'd be arm in arm, giggling and skipping through the forest. I mean, you did turn me over to be killed just to get her back. I'm a little offended that you don't seem happier."

"It's complicated."

"Then uncomplicate it."

"You're one to talk."

"Exactly. I'm an expert on holding on to anger. I would've thought that you didn't want to be like me."

"Maybe you're not that bad."

"I. Am. Terrible." He flashed a grin. "You just like that about me."

Maybe she did like that he was horrible, and Kerrigan still loved him unconditionally. Perhaps it gave her hope.

He turned serious. "I mean it, though. Don't be like me."

She frowned at him. "You're sure giving me a lot of advice. It's like you think we're friends now just because we saved each other's necks."

He scoffed. "Friends? We'd have to save each other at least three times to reach automatic friendship."

She didn't get a chance to respond. Shouting drifted toward them, and they both bolted toward the sound.

Bly took in the scene as she burst through the trees. Kerrigan had the remaining vampire guard by his throat against a tree. His dagger was poised against the vampire's chest. "How much is he paying you?" Kerrigan shouted, jostling the vampire in his grip so that his head hit the trunk.

"I don't know what you're talking about." His hands were splayed out to his side.

"Callum," Kerrigan hissed.

So he *had* come for her right behind Donovan. He'd heard her tell him that Callum had sent the guard.

She turned and found Donovan giving her a smug smile.

"Aren't one of you going to do something about this?" Demelza asked, sliding between them. She turned to Donovan. "*You're* supposed to be the loose cannon."

"Love makes all of us a little reckless," Donovan said.

Bly shook her head as his grin widened.

Demelza gave them both an exasperated look. "Get him under control. We're wasting time." She glanced around. "Where's the other vampire guard?"

"I shot him three times in the heart," Donovan said as Kerrigan shook the other guard again. Benedict and Jade stood nearby, watching, but neither seemed interested in intervening.

Demelza stared at him, her mouth agape before she snapped it closed again. "Something tells me I should have kept you in that cage."

The look Donovan gave her was full of wicked promises. "You're probably right."

Demelza's pale face turned a startling shade of red, but she didn't get a chance to retort before Donovan was jogging over to Kerrigan without another word, talking to both him and the vampire in his clutches. It must have been decided that he wasn't working for Callum too, because Kerrigan let go of him and Donovan dusted the front of his guard uniform before slapping him on the back. The guard wobbled toward Bly.

It took everything in her not to step back as he stopped in front of her. He really was huge, with shoulders like boulders and a neck like a tree trunk, but the worried look in his eyes and the way his black hair stood on end made him look almost vulnerable.

Almost.

"I had nothing to do with that," he told her. "He didn't even tell me his plan."

She swallowed. "I believe you."

"Joseph." He supplied his name even though she really hadn't asked.

She nodded and started to walk away but stopped as he

followed her a little too close. She turned on him.

His cheeks flushed a pretty pink. "Sorry. Kerrigan said if anything happened to you, it would be on me, so I need to stick close." It seemed like he genuinely feared for his life.

Bly turned to look at Kerrigan, but he was disappearing into the tree line without so much as a glance in Bly's direction.

"Fine," she said, turning back to Joseph. There was no point in arguing with him. She wasn't going to strike fear in him the way Kerrigan had.

She began to walk with her new hulking shadow.

"New friend?" Donovan said as he came up beside her once more.

She scowled at him.

He gave her one barking laugh before he grew serious. "Fix things with your sister," he said. "I'm guessing you believe that everything that you did was for nothing because she was never even in danger, but if you have her back, that should make it all worth it . . . even if my foolish brother doesn't come around, but something tells me he will."

+ ✦ +

Kerrigan didn't reappear until they made camp the next evening. Still, he avoided Bly, his stare scanned through her as if she wore an invisibility spell, which was for the best. Eventually, he disappeared into the night again without saying a word to anyone.

Donovan was wrong in thinking he'd come around—being angry that Callum had interfered with their task didn't mean that he wanted her again. She had to let him go. If she'd been willing to sacrifice herself for his brother to undo her mistakes and he still couldn't forgive her, then the capacity for it didn't exist in him.

Repairing something you'd broken did not mean you were owed forgiveness for the breaking.

Even when they'd both weakened and given in to an attraction that hadn't faded, he'd warned her that forgiveness wasn't possible. Which meant she'd always carry around that regret.

She'd focus on her sister now, the heaviest regret on her heart. Bly didn't know why she was listening to Donovan, but the damn vampire's advice had been needling her. She'd fought like a ruthless wolf to get to Elise. Maybe it was on *Bly* for that not to be in vain. If she kept running from their wounds, it'd make everything worse, not better.

Bly sat cross-legged on a blanket magicked to repel the damp ground beneath her and stared across the fire toward the edge of the woods where Elise leaned against a tree, talking to Benedict.

The rest of the vampires huddled together on one side of the clearing. Joseph occasionally cast a look in her direction to make sure she was still alive, and it made her angry that Kerrigan couldn't bother to look at her, but he'd threatened someone else into constantly watching her.

The witches congregated on the other side, with Nova the odd human among them.

Only Emerson sat by the fire with Bly.

"I can't see this ending well," he said.

Bly thought he was talking about Elise and Benedict, but he was looking between the clearly divided groups.

"We have three ruthless leaders waiting for us to deliver roots that could tip the power of our world in either direction, and all their favorite henchmen with us," he said.

"They'll probably fight it out in the end, but we can stand back and watch," Bly said.

Emerson stared pointedly at her neck until she became painfully conscious of the weight around it. "You can't afford to sit back and watch. We have to side with the witches."

He was right, of course.

Who would Kerrigan side with when the moment came?

She shouldn't be thinking of that.

She should focus on someone else's love story instead.

"Did you talk to Elise yet?" She knew he hadn't.

Emerson stared into the flames.

"You won't make her fall in love with you again by being all silent and brooding. Actually, never mind—you've always been silent and brooding, so stick with what worked for you before." She grinned at him.

"She wasn't in love with me, Bly. At least not when I finally told her how I felt."

"Sorry about that."

"It's not your fault. You are my best friend. I could have talked to you, and you would have given me your blessing. That's on me."

"You're giving me a lot of credit," Bly said. It would have broken her heart to learn he loved Elise if she had still been imagining a future with him . . . if Kerrigan hadn't already shown her what true and hungry passion looked like.

"Don't make the mistake of taking too long again," she said.

"It's already too late." Emerson looked back over his shoulder. Elise and Benedict had become silhouettes against the setting sun. "She's happy, and I won't add any turmoil into it. She's been through enough."

He plucked a twig from the ground and snapped it in two before tossing it into the flames, keeping the turmoil inside himself.

They both stared at the fire like it had all the answers until two figures sat down with them.

Bly jerked as she took in Demelza's hair flickering in the glow of the fire as if it were burning too. Nova's hard eyes gleamed in the light.

They both wanted Bly dead. Both had already tried and failed; perhaps that meant that Bly should want the same of them. Surely her life would be easier if they simply disappeared. But she couldn't muster the hate.

She used to be so full of it after Elise was taken: for the witches, for their entire world, for herself.

Now she wanted forgiveness, which meant she had to give it. It could be a mistake to forgive people who still wanted to kill you, but it somehow seemed easier than forgiving those you loved.

Demelza had tried to kill her because she was desperate to prove herself to her mother and Bly was standing in the way. Nova blamed her for her brother's death. Their actions weren't justified, but Bly understood them.

So she said nothing. The silence was a type of peace, even if it was temporary.

Emerson broke the quiet first. "You're not staying with the other witches?"

The witches had begun setting up their bedrolls and tents against the edge of the woods.

Demelza gave a bitter chuckle. "I believe Samuel wants me dead more than anyone else here. I spent the last month looking over my shoulder. Only the threat of my mother possibly return-ing kept him from doing it out in the woods . . ." She shrugged.

"You don't think Donovan wants you dead too?" Bly asked. She wasn't trying to be cruel, but she genuinely wondered if Demelza would find herself on the wrong side of Donovan's sword before they returned.

"He can get in line. I'm sure you'd both love to stick a knife in me."

"I wouldn't," Emerson said after a long moment.

"I was planning to betray you and hand you over to my mother." Demelza sounded annoyed that he *didn't* want to kill her.

"You tried to erase the good you did for me before, but you can't." Emerson's eyes had shifted away from the witch to watch Elise once more. "You tried to help me save her," he said softly. He looked back at her. "Do you still want me dead to prove yourself?"

"I never really did."

"And Bly? Do you want her dead?"

Demelza glanced in Bly's direction, but her focus shifted back to Emerson. She'd clearly always liked him. "I thought it would impress my mother."

"And now?"

"I don't like her."

"Me or your mother?" Bly asked.

"Both."

Demelza smirked at her. She had been attempting and failing to be like her mother, but the one thing they had in common were smiles they wielded like blades. Bly couldn't help but notice that she said nothing about whether or not she still wanted to kill her.

It'd be less unnerving if Nova weren't staring relentlessly at Bly.

"I still want you dead." Nova's voice was the barest whisper.

"But not her." Bly nodded to Demelza. "She's the one that killed you. Vincent never would have fought me if you weren't dead."

"Oh, she tried to kill me," Demelza said. "I spared her, and then I gave her family a plot of land in Havenwhile if she'd protect me instead."

"You're the reason I died," Nova said to Bly. "You convinced us to help you get your vampire back."

"You had a choice," Bly said.

Nova's eye twitched, and then her expression went blank.

Demelza waved a hand in front of her face. "She does this a lot."

"Nova," Bly said gently.

She didn't respond. Her stare was fixed on an empty spot over Bly's shoulder. What did she see? Vincent's ghost? Her own?

Bly'd seen this expression before in the Gap with Mabel, who'd been resurrected by her brother Ackley. The difference was that she'd had Ackley to pull her back.

Nova had no one here who loved her.

"Is she okay?" Elise had joined them. She stood looking down at Nova, and then she walked around the flames and put a hand on the other girl's arm.

Nova jerked at the touch. Her eyes rolled wildly and then narrowed on Elise's hand before she blinked up at her face.

Bly didn't like the way Nova's expression shifted, turning calculating.

"Don't," Bly said sharply.

Elise looked confused. She pulled her hand back slowly as Nova turned her half-dead stare on Bly. "I wouldn't. I am not that cruel." She pushed herself to her feet and marched back to her tent.

Demelza stood as well and followed her without a word, and Bly wondered if the witch actually cared about Nova.

"What was that about?" Elise asked as she sat down in Nova's place.

Bly and Emerson shared a look and an understanding. Neither of them wanted Elise to know the full cost of their failed attempt to resurrect her. They'd carry that burden themselves, hopefully forever, because they loved her.

Elise cleared her throat at their silence. "You went through a lot to . . . to get to me."

Bly noted her carefully chosen words. They hadn't saved her or rescued her. They'd merely found her.

It was exactly why Bly was still struggling. . . . Heroic rescues were worth terrible costs, but Elise hadn't needed saving, and she wouldn't stop reminding them of it.

And now Bly faced the consequences of her actions without the ability to justify them.

Though perhaps nothing would have justified them, and she'd still have been carrying the weight even if Elise *had* needed rescuing.

Neither Emerson nor Bly had spoken.

Elise cleared her throat again. "I'm sorry you're a vampire."

"I'm not," Emerson said. There was fierceness in his voice that made Bly look up at him through the flames. She knew it was a lie, that some part of him did regret it, but he spoke the words he knew Elise needed to hear.

Elise was looking at her feet when Emerson reached across and took her hand. Her head jerked up and her eyes widened, but she didn't pull away.

"I'm not sorry," Emerson said. His voice had calmed, but there was still a hardness in it. "Being a vampire means I can save you. I can turn you. I don't give a damn about keeping my station in their bloody city. I care about you." He looked across the fire at Bly. "*Both* of you. Bly was right all along. We should have stopped playing by their rules a long time ago. I can turn you . . . and then maybe with the roots . . ."

He trailed off. There was an unusual amount of hope in his voice. Bly hadn't even considered the possibility that the spell that made witches and vampires human again might mean that Emerson could be human again, and Elise could be turned into a vampire to end her death curse and then turned back, but they didn't know how the spell worked. There was no guarantee that they ever would, no matter who ended up with the roots. The queens and Halfryta weren't known for sharing.

"Emerson . . . ," Bly said. She didn't need to say the rest.

His face pinched. "I know." He took a deep breath. "I know that's a long shot, but I can turn you, Elise. You don't have to be death cursed."

Elise's mouth was open. "I . . ." She pulled her hand back. "I'm not dying."

Emerson's hand hung in the air, empty.

"But you're not free," he said. "I'm not asking you to be with me . . . romantically. I know you never felt that way about me. I just want to help you as a friend."

Elise's head snapped up from where she'd been staring into

the flames. "That's not true."

"Of course it is," Emerson said. "I'd help you without expecting anything."

"No," she said, giving a small, broken laugh. "The part about me never loving you like . . . that. I did for so long, but I always felt like I was the odd one out, that it was you and Bly. I thought I was a little sister to you, and that the way I felt was just a childish infatuation. But I loved the way you were deadly serious until you laughed, the way you seemed content and happy doing little things that others might think were tedious—I thought we were the same like that, like we were made for each other in a way, but . . ." She glanced at Bly. "I didn't think you *saw* me until that day in the woods when you kissed me."

"But you ran," he said.

"I'd already moved on. I'd met Benedict, and he was so *different* and offered me a life completely unlike the one I'd imagined with you, and I thought only something drastic would make me get over you."

"And did it work?" he asked softly.

Elise stared back into the flames as if they could burn away the truth on her face. She might love Benedict, but at least part of her still loved Emerson as well.

"Look at me." He reached out, fingers lightly touching her arm. "Elise," he said as he got up and kneeled beside her as she turned to him. "I'm not going to make the same mistake again. It doesn't matter if we ever get the roots and become human. A simple, human life would be everything I've ever wanted, but forever would be a blessing with you."

Elise leaned toward him, her eyes blinking as if she wasn't sure what she was doing, but then she pulled away abruptly, beginning to stand.

Emerson tightened his grip on her arm. "I'll love you no matter what you choose . . . or who."

He let go of her, and she rose, her expression torn and confused.

Her hands trembled as she smoothed her skirts, and then she stepped away before pausing and turning back. "Thank you," she said to Emerson before turning to Bly. "Both of you." And then she went looking for the vampire she loved.

Bly glanced at Emerson. She wanted to tell him it would be okay, that Elise would choose him in the end, but she didn't know what would happen in the future. She scanned the clearing, looking for Kerrigan, who'd seemed to have disappeared again.

She was no longer the person to offer words of hope.

◆

Bly woke with her heart racing and her limbs liquid with a fear she couldn't place yet. She scrambled out of her tent, disoriented.

Emerson emerged from his tent beside her.

"Elise!" Bly called as she moved in toward the dark shadows clustered near the witches' tents. Bly blinked as someone lit the night with spells.

Donovan, Jade, Benedict, and Joseph lay on the ground, arrows protruding from bound arms and legs. The witches stood over them, swords drawn.

Elise kneeled next to Benedict, yanking an arrow from his arm as he yelped.

"What's going on?" Bly moved toward Demelza, who was staring placidly at the scene. Taking her dagger from her waist,

Bly pressed it against Demelza's throat.

Nova's ax was against Bly's neck a second later.

"Nova," Demelza said calmly. "Do not kill her." Demelza reached up and grabbed Bly's wrist, shoving it and the knife away. "I've got nothing to do with this."

Bly eyed the arrows. They had binding spells tied to the tips, just like hers. She wasn't the only one who'd recognized the value in that. She turned to Samuel and the guards. "You're breaking the agreement."

"They broke it first." Samuel kicked Donovan in the arm.

Donovan growled in response, denying nothing.

Bly blinked, taking in the scene more thoroughly.

Each of the vampires had fallen next to one of the witch's small tents. All their swords were lying near them, which meant they had been out when the witches had fired.

All the witches' tents had been sliced cleanly down the center.

The vampires had clearly tried to murder them in their sleep. At least most of them. Emerson stood silently by Bly's shoulder.

Kerrigan was nowhere to be seen.

Bly scanned the woods, hoping for a glimpse of him.

"You being vampires," Samuel said, "we had a feeling that you would try to double-cross us, but because *we* have honor—"

Jade scoffed. "Your grand speech is growing tiresome."

Samuel pulled his sword out, pointing the tip down so that it hovered near Jade's ear. "I should relieve you of your ears then."

"I will rip your limbs from your body and hang them in the trees for the crows." Donovan's calm tone sent a chill down Bly's spine even though the threat wasn't for her.

Samuel smiled, but he moved his sword back. "As I was saying, because we have honor . . ." He paused as if giving them another chance to interrupt. He reminded Bly of Halfryta more than Demelza ever had. ". . . we decided not to strike first and see what would happen. We climbed into our tents, used invisibility spells, and then crept out to the forest without you being any the wiser. Then we waited, and sure enough, you did not disappoint."

"You wasted that many invisibility spells?" Demelza asked. "We might've needed those later. You knew our supply was limited. We could've just talked to them."

"It seems you already have some type of agreement, cousin," Samuel said. "Why weren't any of them dropping a sword through your tent? Or your little puppet?" He jerked his chin toward Nova. Nova took a step toward Samuel, but Demelza's hand on her arm stopped her.

"I owed her one," Donovan said. "Plus, she fed me really well when I was her prisoner. You witches aren't good for much, but your honey mead is to die for."

Samuel smiled at Demelza. "Too soft, just like your mother said."

Donovan laughed. "I wouldn't say she was *soft*. I was in a cage."

Samuel's stare flicked between Demelza and Donovan. "You treated a prisoner like a pet, and now he cares for you. I can't wait to tell your mother."

"Leave Demelza out of this," Donovan growled.

Samuel grinned in response. "Maybe you're not just soft, maybe you're a traitor. That's why they didn't try to kill you. You're one of them."

Donovan strained against the spell that held him.

"Stop," Demelza said, directing the command at Donovan

before turning a cold stare to Samuel. "*You* are too reckless. My mother agreed to send all of us for a reason, you fool. Because that one"—she pointed at Benedict—"has the map in his pretty little head, and the rest are expendable muscles. And it's not lost on me that you thought they'd try something and left me asleep in my tent. My mother won't care about that, but she will care about you not following orders."

A tiny flash of fear crossed Samuel's face.

"Release them," Demelza said.

"Too late for that," Samuel said.

"It's never too late," Benedict said. "I, for one, do not like holding grudges. I believe it causes wrinkles. I don't want immortal wrinkles."

"Right," Donovan added. "I can promise you a clean death instead of scattering your limbs into the trees."

Benedict groaned.

Samuel stood in a glaring match with Demelza. When he finally broke, he nodded at two of the guards. "We release the one without royal blood and the one with the map to continue the journey." He eyed the witch guards standing with him then nodded toward the hawkish woman. "This one and I . . . ," he said, clearly not knowing his own guard's name, "will escort the others with royal blood back to Halfryta. Once I explain that they broke the truce first, she'll be pleased to have the royals as payment." He gave Demelza a haughty stare as if daring her to disagree.

"You don't know my mother as well as you think," Demelza said.

"The people want someone new to follow," Samuel said. "Your mother doesn't matter as much as she thinks. I wonder how loudly our people will cheer when I march these vampires through the streets."

"When my mother was gone, who did the people back?" Demelza taunted.

Samuel screamed, the sound full of pent-up rage, as he raised his sword and lunged toward Demelza.

Bly wondered if this was the result that Halfryta wanted, to pit these two against each other until one finally snapped and made sure that they would be the chosen one. They'd begin their rule with blood on their hands—like Halfryta.

Donovan roared a threat that did nothing. The guards' eyes widened even though they'd been following orders from Samuel. One of them took a step toward Demelza as if he might intervene, but nobody landed a blow.

Kerrigan darted from the darkness in a blur of shadow with a hint of copper that flashed in the moonlight. His hands wrapped around two of the witches' heads, slamming them together with a thwack that was loud enough to turn Bly's stomach. The third witch spun toward Kerrigan, sword raising, but Kerrigan grabbed his wrist, twisting it until the sword fell, and then he tossed the witch into the darkness. The sound of him hitting a tree and crashing to the ground was followed by silence.

Samuel had already spun, changing the direction of his attack toward Kerrigan, but he never reached him. Emerson's thick arm closed around Samuel's neck while his hand grabbed Samuel's sword arm, squeezing until Samuel's fingers went limp and the sword dropped to his feet.

Kerrigan assessed Samuel and then his brother. "It seems we've all made some mistakes tonight," he said.

"Agreed." Demelza's voice matched Kerrigan's with its careful calmness, and she strode forward, palms out, until she stood over the fallen and bound vampires. She pulled open her vest, a cascade of green fabric that reached her knees, and dug into one of the many pockets sewn inside, taking out a handful of unbinding spells. She knelt by each vampire in turn and freed them.

Elise was wrapping her arms around Benedict as if they'd been separated for a year.

The kind of reunion Bly had imagined for herself.

Kerrigan reached down, offering his brother his hand.

"Thanks, brother," Donovan said.

Kerrigan hauled him to his feet, and then his smile dropped. He pushed Donovan backward until his brother's back hit a tree and Kerrigan's forearm pressed against his throat.

"What were you thinking?" Kerrigan stood over his brother, glowering down at him.

"That I don't want to spend the next two weeks worrying about those witches pricking me with a nasty little spell while I'm sleeping. Seemed better to eliminate the problem from the start."

"You could've gotten others killed in the process," Kerrigan hissed.

"What *others* were you worried about, brother?" Donovan stare slid past Kerrigan's shoulder to Bly. He winked.

"We need the numbers we have," Kerrigan said. "Besides, it looked like you cared quite a bit for some of the *others* too."

Donovan's eyes flicked to Demelza.

She scowled back at him. "I can take care of myself, for the record."

"Yes. I would know," Donovan snapped back.

Jade was staring daggers at Demelza. Donovan might have come to Jade's defense, but she clearly didn't like that he'd defended Demelza as if they were friends.

"No more." Kerrigan let go of Donovan, stepping away. He pointed a finger at Samuel. "No retaliation or I'll rip your head off myself."

Samuel nodded. "You have my word until I have the roots."

They all knew that didn't include the journey home.

SIXTEEN

THEY NO LONGER WALKED IN A LINE because nobody wanted anyone else to be behind them. The vampires walked far to the left, except for Bly's new shadow, and the witches walked to the right with Nova and Demelza trailing their group. Elise stayed with the vampires.

Bly and Emerson walked together between the two groups, and Bly wondered if he was as painfully aware of Elise's absence as she was. How could she feel more distant now that she was back?

Kerrigan was once again nothing but an invisible predator just out of sight. Every once in a while, the hair on the back of her neck rose, and she wondered if it was his eyes on her, but whenever she scanned the tree line, she found nothing but the empty space between the trunks and branches.

Perhaps this was his way of keeping good on their promise to leave each other alone. If that were the case, he should have left her with Halfryta.

Her fingers drifted to touch the cord of vines and metal around her neck for the hundredth time this morning. It rested against the pulled-up collar of her shirt, keeping it from constantly cutting her, but it still needled her like a rock in her boot. It felt tighter already, but maybe she was imagining it.

"I could try again to break it," Emerson said.

She shook her head. She had no doubt that if Halfryta said it was unbreakable, then it was. Besides, Kerrigan had already tried.

"I have an idea."

Emerson and Bly both jerked at the sound of Elise's voice, not realizing she'd drifted so close. She gave them a soft, nervous smile, and then she reached out, hesitating only a moment before tugging Bly to a stop as Emerson walked on. Stepping in front of Bly, Elise swept a critical eye over the choker before unwinding her beige scarf from her neck and threading it between the vines and the back of Bly's neck. Then she continued to wrap the whole thing in soft wool.

It reminded her of Elise calling her back every time Bly left the house in the winter, and she'd have something in her hands that Bly had forgotten—a coat, a pair of gloves, a scarf that she'd wrap a little too tight around Bly's neck. Elise had been the younger one, but she'd been the one to remember such things.

Bly's carelessness had forced Elise to act older and wiser.

Part of her wanted to pull away, keep the distance and hurt between them because she'd needed Elise's soft touch over the past year, and it had been so close, but this was Elise trying, with her quiet love of small gestures. Bly had proven that she'd fight for Elise, and this was *Elise* was fighting for *her*.

"There," Elise said as she finished. "Now it'll at least be a little more comfortable until we get it off."

Bly's cheeks were warm with tears when Elise finally looked her in the eye.

Elise's face fell. "Bly?"

Donovan's words rang in her ears. If she didn't fix this, then her actions really would be for nothing at all.

"I've missed you," Bly choked out.

Elise's arms folded around her, and they squeezed each other like their hug could erase the year they'd lost.

It wasn't that easy, but it felt like it could be.

"I did come home," Elise said.

Bly pulled herself from Elise's grip. "What?"

Her sister looked at her feet. "Of course I did. I had to make sure the witches hadn't gotten you, too. I saw you and Emerson sitting at the edge of the forest. His arms were around you, and I thought . . . I thought I was out of the way, and you would get what you wanted, and I couldn't bear the thought of a lifetime watching the two of you in love." She looked back up but she didn't meet Bly's eyes. "I was surprised at how much it actually hurt to see the two of you together, even if I already loved Benedict." She finally faced Bly. "We *both* had plans to leave each other, so it seemed . . . better. I was death cursed, but Benedict would keep me alive. I thought it was better."

"Emerson hated me," Bly said.

"But I saw . . ."

"Not at first, but I wouldn't tell him why you and I had been in the woods that day. I didn't have him. I didn't have anyone . . . and Mom and Dad . . ." The way they'd looked at her was too hard to describe. "I didn't have anyone."

The pain on Elise's face crushed her. They were breaking each other a little more with every truth, but sometimes you had to rebreak a bone to heal it properly. They'd seen their mother do it.

This was what they needed.

To break all at once and then let themselves mend together.

"You said you had plans to leave too?" Bly asked.

Elise nodded. "I knew when you asked me to gather in the woods with you that you were finally leaving. You'd been talking about it for so long." She gave Bly a little smile. "Knowing you were going . . . it made me want my own life. I had planned to run away with Benedict that night when we got back. I knew I was the only thing holding you in the Gap, besides Emerson. I decided to leave first so that you could leave free of guilt."

"But why didn't you just tell me?"

"I didn't think you'd understand me loving a vampire. I knew Emerson wouldn't, and I didn't want to hurt him more than I already had. I didn't want to hurt myself." She paused, giving Bly an inquisitive look. "But it seems like you understand it just fine."

Bly's cheeks heated. Elise had watched the exchange between her and Kerrigan—the way he'd ripped his own hands apart to try to take the deadly vines from her neck, the way he'd attacked Joseph when he thought he might have been hired by Callum too.

"I understand the appeal of a vampire. I don't understand the appeal of Benedict."

"I'm an acquired taste."

Elise scowled at the sound of Benedict's voice, but her eyes lit up with a mirth Bly longed to see more of. "I thought I told you to give me some space," she said.

"I would, but the two of you have stopped walking, and I

cannot in good conscience leave you behind." His eyes drifted beyond them to the woods.

"I have a guard," Bly said.

Joseph nodded at her from where he'd patiently stopped a few feet away.

"Actually, it seems you already have *two* at the moment. One is just hiding." He smirked at Bly.

Bly turned, hoping for a glimpse of copper, but if Kerrigan had been there, he'd already disappeared again.

Elise smirked at her too. Elise never smirked, and Bly didn't like it.

Bly huffed and started walking again. Her sister came along beside her, and Benedict kept pace as well.

Bly had been envisioning Emerson and Elise together, but she owed it to her sister to support her regardless. Emerson was selfless enough to understand that.

Bly gave them a small smile. It might have been fake, but she was going to try. "How did you two meet?"

"Ahh, well," Benedict said, then stopped and laid a hand on Elise's arm. "You don't mind if I tell it, do you, my dear?"

Elise sighed. "Go ahead."

Their dynamic was odd. She'd imagined that Elise had been tricked, that she didn't know the real Benedict at all, but they interacted with an easiness that put Bly on edge. It seemed comfortable. *Real.*

"Well, I usually don't bother with tedious little tasks before I lead an expedition for gold, but one of my men who was supposed to handle such things was missing, drunk on blood and wine, lying in a sunny alley, but that's beside the point. I couldn't even punish him because it forced me to go to the tanner to secure new furs for our bedding, and there she was, sitting outside the shop on this little stool, her golden hair glimmering in the sun. I used to love the sun when I was human. I'd lie in the fields until it turned me golden and left my vision spotty, but I'd forgotten about those days. The sun had become nothing but a nuisance that weakened me without enough blood, but . . . when I saw your sister and how the rays of light loved her, I remembered how I loved basking in warmth." Benedict spoke to Bly, but he beamed at Elise like she *was* the sun.

"She was stitching patches of fur together into a cloak, and I asked her if I could buy it. She didn't even bother to look up at me when she told me that it wasn't finished, but I came back the next day and asked again, and then the next, and finally she looked up at me on the third day. I think I'd annoyed her into acknowledging me. I believe it was love at first sight for you, my dear?"

"Hardly," Elise said, but her dimples deepened.

"Well, she agreed to sell me the cloak, and I insisted on coming to check the progress regularly, and eventually, she saw past these." He flashed his fangs. "Did I mention that I don't even like wearing furs?" He shuddered. "Luckily I buy her other materials to work with now." He stroked a hand down his silk vest.

All this time Bly had been so close to her sister without knowing it. She'd been next to something her fingers had made. The one thing she wasn't sure she could forgive was Benedict keeping Elise from her once he suspected who she was.

Elise seemed to read the souring of Bly's mood.

"He's sorry he didn't tell you about me."

Bly met her sister's eyes. They were pleading.

"It was cowardly of me," Benedict added. "I was so afraid that she would leave me to return to you."

His voice held a painful sincerity that startled her.

She didn't offer forgiveness, but she swallowed her pain. "How did you save her from the witches?"

Benedict gave her a grateful look. "Elise had promised to meet me on the edge of the Gap to leave for Vagaris that night. I knew she had plans with you to forage. I encouraged her to forage for berries where it'd be safer and I could keep an eye on you. I wandered the forest near Vagaris all day but hadn't seen you two. When she didn't show, I assumed the worst. I assumed that she'd decided she couldn't love me—that she couldn't live a short happiness with an immortal. I went home, but I kept visiting the tanners, and I finally saw your father. One look at him, and I knew it was worse than I'd imagined, that the two of you had gone toward Havenwhile and something had gone wrong.

"So I did something terribly reckless. I went after her. Jade came with me, even though she scolded me the entire way for falling in love with a sack of blood. No offense," he added, giving them each apologetic looks. "I stood at the gates of Havenwhile until they let me in, and I got an audience with Halfryta herself. I'd brought heaps of gold to barter with, but she wanted blood. Jade and I gave blood every day for a week to get Elise back. I thought they might keep us prisoner since we'd walked into their hands, but two missing royals might have caused a stir, so at the end of the week, they brought us Elise and let us go. She was being held in one of their prisons."

It was worse than Bly had thought. Benedict *and Jade* had saved her sister.

"I really did think you were dead," Bly said softly. She tried not to count how many days Elise had been held in that prison, waking up hanging in a cage from a tree with no idea what had happened to Bly.

Elise's fingers were wrapped around hers. "I touched a sleeping curse and a death curse at the same time," she said. "You couldn't have known I wasn't dead. Anyone would have assumed I was gone."

"I could have—"

"Stop. You couldn't have done anything but end up taken as well," Elise said. Her voice was firm and so familiar that Bly couldn't help but feel a bit better. "Whatever happened, happened, and now we are together."

There was no erasing a horrible past, only building on top of it.

She knew that, but hearing Elise say it too helped.

She wished Emerson could hear this too. Though she didn't know if it would help him or hurt him more.

"You know Emerson broke into Havenwhile too. For your body. He thought you were dead, but he risked his life so the witches couldn't keep you." She couldn't stop herself from saying it. She wanted Elise to understand that Benedict might have been the one to save her, but that Emerson had tried too. They'd both loved her enough to risk their lives.

Benedict looked straight ahead, but his jaw was clenched. Elise just looked . . . sad. Maybe for something that never had a fair chance.

That was partly Bly's fault, so she shouldn't be the one to keep dredging it up, but she pushed the guilt away. When everyone was a little bit to blame for where they were now, it did no good to hold on to it. It forced them all to live in it, and she didn't want Elise to carry guilt.

Guilt consumed more greedily than the worst vampire.

They had to kill it or be killed.

"Sorry," Bly said. "The past is the past."

"No. I should thank him."

Bly jerked in surprise. It wasn't Elise who had spoken but Benedict.

Elise smiled at him with soft wonder on her face, and he smiled back.

"He's your friend. Don't avoid him for my sake." Benedict's voice was tight but earnest.

He might be a selfish bastard, but he seemed to care for her sister. One thing still bothered her, though.

"He tried to bite me, you know," Bly blurted.

"Emerson?" Elise's eyebrows shot up.

"No. Emerson has never bitten anyone. He'll only drink what he has to in order to survive, and only from a glass." Bly stared pointedly across her sister to Benedict.

Benedict coughed. "I was really hungry. She offered me her bleeding neck! I didn't want to leave the party, but all the bleeders there were too flirty for my taste. I knew Bly wasn't looking for anything more since she was so clearly in love with that redheaded fool. So I was going to take a little blood." He shrugged.

Elise glared at him. "From my sister?"

"I was quite hungry."

"You know he's always drinking from people at those parties," Bly added.

"Oh." Elise laughed. "Well, I don't mind that. I don't like being bitten." She shot Benedict another look out of the corner of her eye. "I don't know about biting my sister, though."

"Apologies," he grumbled, then added, "It's just food. Fresh blood is like eating berries from the vine, warm in the afternoon sun." His voice grew wistful.

Bly ignored his poetics. "So you're okay with him biting other people?" She really didn't understand it . . . or how Elise didn't like the feeling, not when half of Bly's fantasies involved Kerrigan's fangs.

"I really don't care," Elise said.

"Okay, then." Bly didn't add that it was another reason Emerson would be the better choice. He didn't even like biting people. But if Elise was fine with it, then she needed to be too.

There was one more thing she needed to confront him about, though. "Can we talk alone for a moment?"

"Of course," Elise said, turning back to her.

"I meant Benedict."

Elise frowned.

Bly forced her smile to widen as she shrugged. "I just want to get to know him better. Interrogate him a little more—my sisterly duty."

Elise's eyes were suspicious, but a soft smile pulled at her lips.

Benedict stared at her, a sharp look in his eyes. "Anything for the sister of the love of my life."

Bly tried not to gag.

She slowed, dropping back, and Benedict followed.

When they were far enough behind Elise, Bly let the pleasant smile she'd held for Elise's sake drop as she stared critically at

Benedict. "I believe that you think you love my sister."

"I don't *think* anything. I do love her. Did you miss the part where I waxed poetically about how she is the sunlight in my life?"

"So you love that she warms your cold, dead heart. That's not the same as loving *her*."

Benedict's eyes narrowed. He looked at Bly with an intensity that made her want to step back. "I love the way that she hums joyful little tunes whenever she's sewing, and when I ask her what she's humming, she hasn't even realized that she's doing it. I love the way her eyes always smile first before her lips catch up. I love that she's always worried about everyone else, and that when the housekeeper comes, she's already baked an apple tart for the woman's breakfast. And yes, I love that she makes me feel . . . human again, but that is only the result of all the other things that I love about her."

For a moment, Bly just stared at him. Utter devotion clung to each of his words.

His gaze was intense as if daring her to call him a liar.

She couldn't.

But that didn't mean he loved her the way she deserved.

"Your blood will hold off the death curse forever?" she asked.

"Yes."

"So she's tied to you forever unless she finds another vampire to do the same."

"She doesn't seem to have a problem with that."

"If you truly cared about her, you'd turn her."

He scoffed. "If anyone found out, the queens would have my head despite how much money I bring in for them. There's a census every year, and everyone is accounted for and all the houses searched. It's not something you can just get away with."

"Convenient," Bly said.

"No. Just the facts."

"The fact is," Bly said, "you don't want her cured, do you? But you entered the Games. Why?"

"For Elise. She asked me to."

"But. You. Didn't. Try."

His face pinched, and he turned away from her. When he looked back, he said, "I did."

Bly gave a harsh laugh. "I was there. You had a chance to steal Halfryta from us, and you didn't even try. You made it sound like it was a joke to you. And that's how I know that despite all your pretty words, you don't actually love her."

"It wasn't a joke . . . I . . . Your sister loathes the taste of blood. I hate watching her face scrunch up every time she has to drink it. For some vampires, it tastes different, sweet like honey. But there are others that never get used to the taste. She has to drink a tiny amount now to live out her human life, but as a vampire? Blood *would* be her life. Forever. She'll crave it relentlessly, even if she hates it. Do you really think she wants that?"

Bly didn't have an answer for that. She thought of Emerson— who clearly would choose to be human again if he could. He and Elise were so similar.

Benedict sighed. "So you're correct. I didn't try. It would've been foolish of me to fight your group for Halfryta anyway. I would've lost, and did you really want me to try to steal the immortality that your friend obviously needed?"

"That's not the point. You told her you'd try, and you didn't."

"I thought she'd resent me for turning her one day."

"Is that the only reason? Those cursed lines that cover her skin are a cage that you're keeping her in," Bly said. "She's dependent on you. You can't tell me that's not a factor."

"What part about 'I can't just turn her' do you not understand?" Benedict growled, but she saw on his face that she'd hit a nerve. It wasn't just about what he thought Elise needed.

"Emerson offered to turn her last night."

"*What?*" Benedict's head snapped back toward her, his eyes wide.

"He'd turn her and give up the life he knows and live with her in the woods just so she could be free of the curse. *That's* love."

Benedict turned away from her.

"You're keeping someone tied to you because you don't love them enough to let them go," she said.

He was quiet for so long that she thought she'd won, and she started to pull away from him, but then he spoke once more. "Did you think that you loved Kerrigan when you handed over his brother instead of him? I bet he didn't interpret that as love either."

She winced, but she didn't look back at him.

✦ ✦ ✦

Spotting Kerrigan was like trying to spot a cougar. He only appeared at night . . . if you caught a glimpse at all.

Bly had given up on seeing him until the fifth day of walking when he stumbled out of the trees, his face grim. He'd probably spotted something coming for them, but his mouth didn't part in warning. Bly noticed the odd angle of his arms held behind his back just as the dark shadows behind him stepped out. A sword glinted, held carefully behind Kerrigan's head, ready to take it at a moment's notice.

Witches, Bly thought at first as she noted their clothes, the colors of moss on oak bark. Then she took in the dark gray eyes.

Banished.

Vampires that were so ruthless, they couldn't even find a place in the city fueled on blood and violence.

One of the shadowy figures stepped up beside Kerrigan. The banished vampire casually brushed his greasy dark brown hair behind his ear as his scanned them. His lips moved slightly as if he were mumbling something.

Or counting.

"What a nice haul," he said, but he wasn't even speaking to them. He spoke to a vampire just behind his left shoulder—a woman with a wild smile on her face and eyes that flitted too fast from one thing to another. The way she kept spinning the hilt of her sword in her hand made Bly's instincts to run flare like confronting a wolf with a foaming mouth. You didn't fight something like that.

"What do you want?" Samuel asked. "You can keep the bloody vampire."

"Shut up!" Donovan barked at him. When he turned back to the vampire, his voice was calmer, dangerously reasonable. "Let's sort this out, shall we?"

"Let's," said the banished vampire. "I appreciate a little civility. My name's Borden. Now drop your weapons."

"Don't do it," Kerrigan finally spoke. His stare shifted from Donovan to Bly, then back again. "Don't."

Donovan groaned dramatically. "I can't believe you let these assholes get the drop on you. I told you your sulking would be the death of us, and that you needed to let it go or at least get a little of the girl's sweet blood in your system to tide you over until you came to your damn senses." Donovan scowled at Bly, and her cheeks flushed. Obviously, he meant *her* blood. When she looked back at Kerrigan, he wouldn't meet her eyes, but he had a scowl that matched Donovan's on his face.

"I don't care about whatever petty squabbles you have." Borden pulled a dagger from his belt and casually held it above Kerrigan's heart. "Make one single move, and I'll fill him with more holes than a vampire can heal."

Donovan raised a hand, slowly reaching for his undrawn sword with the other. Freeing it, he dropped it onto the forest floor.

"I think not," Samuel said. He gave a clipped nod to the witches with him as his fist closed around an arrow in his quiver.

"Don't." Donovan took a step toward Samuel as the air filled with a soft swishing sound followed by tiny thuds.

Borden lifted his hand to his shoulder and gripped the shaft of the arrow that impaled him there. Several vampires around him did the same, plucking out numerous arrows. A few had dropped to the ground, looking like pincushions, including the one who'd had the sword raised behind Kerrigan's neck.

Borden ripped the arrow from his shoulder, turning to Samuel, but Samuel and his guards hadn't even notched arrows onto their bows yet.

"A coven," he roared.

The banished vampires around Kerrigan shifted, pulling crude wooden shields from their backs to their forearms and raising them over their head as they bounded into the woods after the archers.

Within seconds, everything became songs of singing arrows,

clangs of metal, yelps of pain, and cries of deeper death notes.

Bly whipped around as Joseph cried out behind her. Arrows protruded from his arm and shoulders. "Turn around," she yelled, pushing him. He listened, putting his back to her so she could yank the arrows from him just in time for him to meet a banished vampire barreling toward them.

She spun again as Donovan grunted, a series of arrows piercing his leg. As he bent to yank them free, a banished vampire sped toward him, sword poised to steal his head.

Darting forward, Bly plunged her dagger in the vampire's arm. He hissed, changing the arc of his swing to come for her head instead. She ducked, and Donovan righted himself, planting his sword in the vampire's chest before shoving him to the ground. Donovan's sword sliced through the vampire's neck a moment later.

He turned, raising an eyebrow at her despite the battle raging around them. "You know, if you keep saving me, I'm going to start thinking you're in love with me instead of my brother."

"Don't flatter yourself. But that's two saves now. One more and you'll have to start calling me your friend."

He shook his head, laughing as she spun away, searching for Elise.

She'd only taken a dozen steps when a hand snatched the back of her shirt and yanked her toward the ground. She spun, dagger ready to bite whoever had caught her, but arrows pierced the tree where her chest had been only moments before.

She took in the broad form that bent over her.

Donovan hissed, teeth clenching, and Bly had no doubt that his back had just taken an arrow for her as well.

She opened her mouth.

"We're even again," he ground out, grimacing around his flashing grin before he grew serious. "Kerrigan."

It was the only word he got out before a banished vampire roared toward them, sword raised. Donovan fought through the pain he had to be in, rising to his feet, charging the vampire head-on and taking them out at the waist.

Kerrigan. Elise.

Donovan didn't want her help again, and she didn't have time to give it.

Kerrigan's arms were bound. Not helpless, but close to it. She needed to free him. He was their best fighter.

But Elise. She fumbled in her vest for an unbinding spell as she scanned the forest for her sister.

Samuel fought in the open. A Havenwhile guard lay wounded and groaning at his feet, but so did two bodies that were either rogue witches or banished vampires. Each side wore the same dark colors.

Demelza and Nova fought someone together, dancing around their opponent's sword, Nova swinging her ax with practiced arcs as Demelza tried to stick a long dagger into their opponent's side. Both moved with speed and probably strength spells.

Bly should have spelled herself too, but the desire to keep moving, to find Elise, made her refuse to pause. She crawled around the trunk of the tree. The forest grew denser. It made it impossible to fight but easy to hide.

She finally caught sight of her sister's golden hair. Both Emerson and Benedict stood in front of her, swords drawn. Emerson had an arrow in his thigh, but he didn't seem to notice as his sword sliced through the neck of a vampire that Benedict had impaled through the gut. They didn't even look at each other as the body fell at their feet, just shifted their stance and waited for the next attack.

Elise held the arrows Bly had given her in her hands. She stayed behind the men, but as two more vampires attacked, Elise's arm darted between Benedict and Emerson, sticking the arrow with her spell into the leg of a vampire about to jam a dagger through Emerson's heart.

She may not have been a fighter, but she was smart.

Still, Bly wanted to go to her. She remembered what it was like, the first night of the Games, the first time she understood that the sound of a death scream was different from the scream of someone wounded.

She shuddered.

There was no time for comfort, and Elise was as safe as she could be. Bly rose to a crouch and then darted from her oak to a pine, where she clung to the branches as she leaned out from behind the trunk to find Kerrigan.

An arrow nicked the branch she held before flying by her. She dropped back and down, drawing a deep breath, and then peeked out again. Kerrigan leaned against a black oak, arms still behind him. He was watching her, shaking his head.

Pretending not to notice, she bolted. More than one arrow pierced the ground around her, and she almost stumbled when she thought about how easily one could pierce her neck.

She dove for him, forgetting that his arms were bound, and he wouldn't be able to catch her. Crashing into his chest, she grabbed his vest, popping the buttons loose and ripping it open as she caught herself.

"Bly," he said, raising an eyebrow. "This is not the time to try for a reconciliation."

It was his flirty mask, but at least he was speaking to her.

She panted against his chest for a moment before wrapping her arms around him and pricking his wrist with the spell. "Unbind," she said, even though she kind of liked him like this.

She shook herself. He was right. Now wasn't the time for such thoughts.

The second his arms were free, he grabbed her, spinning them both so her back was against the tree and his body pressed flush against hers.

She liked this even more.

The threat of death was making her lose control of her thoughts. She wasn't being rational at all.

Kerrigan wasn't looking at her, though. He peered around the trunk.

"We're in trouble," he said.

"I got that."

"No, look." He moved slightly so she had the space to turn around while still keeping his body pressed to hers like a shield.

She looked around the trunk with him.

The leader of the banished vampires stood in the center of all the chaos talking to a witch with a heap of brown hair on her head that bobbed as she nodded and held out a hand.

They shook.

Then they both turned, shouting instructions to their people: to stop fighting and capture anyone from the cities.

Kerrigan spun around, his sword already in his hand, but he'd barely raised it before it clashed with the blade in the hands of another vampire. Two witches appeared on either side of them. Kerrigan grunted as he held his blade firm with one hand against the other vampire's two. He snatched his dagger from his waist and thrust it at the witch on one side of him, who jumped back.

Bly slashed at the witch on the other side, but Kerrigan's back trapped her too firmly against the tree. The witch caught her hand in his, tossing her dagger to the ground before reaching out and stabbing Kerrigan in the arm with a binding spell.

The magic forced his hands together in front of him, yet he held his grip on his sword, swinging it in an arc at everyone's legs.

Bly hit the witch that had disarmed her with her own binding spell, but then her arms were being wrenched behind her back by brute force as someone yanked her away.

Kerrigan's legs got kicked out from under him, and he hit the ground.

She screamed his name, and he twisted toward her, struggling to his feet again before he dropped like a stone, sleep spelled.

They hauled him after her, dragging his legs carelessly over rocks and branches until they tossed them into a pile with the banished on one side and the witch coven on the other.

"You have first choice," the witches' leader said as if Bly's group were simply a plate of shared food at a meal. "You found them, after all."

"Fair," said Borden. He grabbed an unconscious Kerrigan by the neck, yanking him up and tossing him into a heap behind him.

The witch raised her eyebrows. "Not to question your choice, but a vampire?" A vampire's blood was worth more to the witches, who'd use it in spells.

"I recognize him. A favorite of the whore queens. They'll pay for him."

"Ahh," the witch said. Her eyes landed on Demelza, unconscious and without the glamour she still usually wore. "I may do the same." She nodded toward her, and two witches pulled her from the pile.

The vampires selected the rest of the witches, and the witches selected the rest of the vampires, including an unconscious Benedict and Emerson and a bound and squirming Jade and Donovan. Joseph was awake and bound too, with a nasty cut across his neck as if someone had tried and failed to slice through it. When they pulled him away, he gave Bly an apologetic look as if he could have prevented this.

The witch leader sighed, eyeing Nova, who had one eye closed and purpling. "Her."

Borden yanked Bly up by the collar, dropping her at his feet so she practically kissed his boots. "The delicate one is yours then. I hate when they're already broken." He chuckled.

Elise's cheeks were streaked with tears and a long red scratch from the side of her mouth to her ear. She'd fought. Bly had no doubt Benedict and Emerson had gone down before anyone managed to lay a finger on her, but she'd fought too.

Her terrified eyes met Bly's.

"Until next time," the coven leader said.

"I look forward to it," Borden said. "Everyone grab someone. Spell them if they're not unconscious."

Elise's hands were bound in front of her already. A witch had her under the armpits, tugging her away.

Borden gripped Bly's arm, yanking her to her feet. He wrapped an arm around her throat.

Someone laughed.

The sound roared in Bly's ears.

She wouldn't watch this again: laughing witches taking her sister away from her.

"Elise!" she screamed, tugging against the vampire's grip on her.

Her sister's hair had come undone in the struggle, her blond waves draping over her face.

Bly couldn't lose her again. Not when they'd just begun to mend the hurt between them.

All Bly wanted was to sit behind her sister and brush her hair in front of the fireplace in her parents' house before helping her wind it into the high bun that she preferred. And then Elise would insist on doing the same for Bly, despite the fact that Bly's hair was curlier than hers and often held sticks and brambles and remnants of sap from a tree Bly was too old to be climbing. Elise would capture her strands into a braid that would make her look respectable for a few days before a stray branch would catch it and turn it unmanageable once more.

She refused to never have that again.

Elise managed to shake her hair from her face as a witch hauled her roughly from her knees to her feet.

Elise's lips moved. Bly thought she was mouthing *I love you* or *I'm sorry*.

Bly didn't want any of that. She didn't want a hurried moment of love because there was a good chance they would never see each other again, that one or both of them would surely die once they'd disappeared into the forest in opposite directions.

She wanted to continue the slow and painful stitching of their wounds. The type of healing that would leave faint scars to remind you that you survived and were stronger for it. They'd end up closer than they were before.

But that couldn't happen if they were ripped apart again right now.

The wound would tear open once more and fester if these vampires didn't murder her first. She knew that firsthand.

She'd make sure this time that they killed her before she lost Elise.

Shifting her chin down, she sank her teeth into the arm that wrapped around her throat, biting until she tasted the sharp tang of blood. She wanted to retch but bit harder instead.

Borden let go of her with a hiss, and Bly lunged forward, running toward Elise. She didn't have a plan or even a spell in her hand. She only had one thought—the same one that had propelled her for months.

She had to get her sister back.

Elise's eyes were wide. Bly got close enough to see the fear in them before her legs were swept out from under her. She hit the ground hard, and a boot kicked her shoulder, shoving her onto her back and she stared up into the face of the vampire who'd held her. Blood still dripped down his arm.

Bly didn't care. She flipped back over and crawled toward Elise, hand reaching out. Elise had managed to drop to the ground again, but her hands were still bound behind her back. If not, she could have reached out too. They could have held hands one more time.

But Bly didn't get a chance to touch her before a blow to her temple crashed her into darkness.

SEVENTEEN

"BLY."

Her name was distant in the dark.

"Bly."

Pain lanced through her shoulders and wrists, but she didn't want to wake up.

Worry threaded through the way he said her name.

She didn't want to open her eyes if it meant that he'd keep sounding like he cared. It'd be the sweetest dream if it didn't feel like her arms were ripping out of their sockets.

"Bly! Wake up!" The fear in his voice shattered the illusion.

Bly blinked. The snow under the harsh glare of the sunlight blinded her eyes, and she squinted until a sickening smell rolled her stomach.

Someone groaned beside her, and she tried to spin before finding herself trapped.

Her wrists were bound with ropes hung from the lowest

branch of an oak tree. Her toes just barely brushed the ground, unable to support any of her weight. She tried to adjust and find purchase with her feet to ease the pull in her shoulders and the biting of rope on her wrists, but there was none to be had. Across a small clearing filled with vampires sitting on packs, their black eyes all focused in her direction, she spotted Samuel, dangling from the branches of a pine. The petite witch guard was strung up beside him, her eyes wide with terror. On his other side was the hawkish guard, her lips set in a grim line, but Samuel's face was expressionless as he returned Bly's stare.

"Bly." Her name was a frantic whisper to her right, and she turned to find Kerrigan. He was on the same branch nearer to the trunk, and his wrists bound with heavy chains that held his hands above his head. His feet actually touched the ground, but his bindings wouldn't let him reach her.

"Elise . . ." Her mouth tasted like cotton.

"Not here."

"Donovan?"

Kerrigan shook his head.

"We have to . . ." Bly trailed off.

They'd both been fighting for so long to reach their siblings, and now Donovan and Elise were lost and in danger.

At least she had Kerrigan. For the first time, there wasn't the flicker of hate in his eyes when she said his brother's name. Just fear, and she knew by the way his eyes roved over her body, zeroing in on her aching wrists and shoulders, that some of that fear was for her.

She knew he'd never really stopped caring about whether she lived or died, but in the past month, he'd always looked like he hated himself for caring. She found none of that on his face now.

Just fear and desperation.

His expression should've woken terror in her, but for the briefest moment, she felt the crush of relief.

He was worried about her.

Which probably meant she was about to die.

She really shouldn't be so happy about it.

Another groan to her left forced her to rip her attention away from Kerrigan. She gagged at the horror. The witch guard with the soft blond hair was strung up beside her. Only one of his arms was still tied to the branch, and his other was held out to the side by Borden. A long gash ran from the witch's wrist halfway to his elbow, and blood dripped from the wound into a bucket below. Like Bly, only his toes touched the ground, but there was no more tension in his legs, and the single arm holding him up strained in its socket. His head had slumped to his chest, but he was still alive. Another horrible groan bubbled from his lips, though it was fainter than the last one.

"I don't see why I can't have a taste." The voice came from the vampire with the wild smile and dancing eyes. Her tongue flicked over her fangs as she stared at the dying witch.

"Because this blood is worth more in gold than it is in our stomachs."

"But one nibble would be nothing."

"Then everyone would want a taste, Katrina."

She pouted. "I'm not everyone."

"I'm not playing favorites, and that's the end of it."

Katrina huffed, but she also took a step back.

The blood from the witch's arm had slowed to nothing more

than sad little drips when Borden dropped it and fisted his hand into the witch's hair, pulling up his chin and peeling his eye apart. "Cut him down and then string him up by his feet and open his throat so we can get the rest," he commanded.

Two vampires strode forward and hauled him away to another tree.

"Things would go a lot faster if you would just slit their throats from the start," Katrina grumbled.

"Wait," Kerrigan said. "Why are you killing him? Why not drain him and heal him and drain him again?"

"We do keep some, but those slots are filled. You can't haul around too many prisoners through the woods. It's a hassle," Katrina said. "Plus, we like the hunt *and* the kill." She turned back to Borden. "Right, my love?"

Borden didn't look at her. Instead, his eyes roamed over Bly. "There are many things in life that call for speed, and sometimes death must be one of them, but not when we have a choice." His lips curled into a smile. "Death begs to be savored if we can oblige it."

"You're sick," Katrina said before laughing. "And that's why I love you."

Borden stepped closer to Bly, so close that he had to look down his nose at her. Her toes scratched the dirt as she tried to move her body away from him but all she accomplished was swinging.

His hands reached out and clamped around her waist, stopping her movement.

"Don't touch her," Kerrigan growled. Borden's grin widened at Kerrigan's words even though he didn't bother glancing in his direction.

"A human who fights like a vampire certainly deserves the honor of a slow death," Borden said.

"I'll kill you." The branch shook as Kerrigan tried in vain to break free, and Bly winced as her arms yanked with the movement.

"Will you?" Borden raised his eyebrows as he finally gave Kerrigan his attention.

Kerrigan stilled. "You know who I am. You can ransom me to the queens, and I can give you ten more humans in exchange for that one."

"Don't . . . ," she started. He didn't really mean that. He was only saying whatever he needed to in order to get them out of this horrible situation. Kerrigan would never barter human life so carelessly. She wasn't worth that. But Kerrigan's face was hard, and his mouth was set in a grim line, and she knew deep in her gut that he meant every word. The ruthless beast she'd awakened again when she'd stolen his brother was still close to the surface. He'd do exactly what he said.

Borden ran his fingers across his torn sleeve where she'd bitten him. "This human's blood is worth more to me than another ten."

He turned to Kerrigan. "But you already know that, don't you? Describe what she tastes like to me, and I'll entertain your bargain."

Kerrigan hissed through clenched teeth as he strained against his bondage.

Borden's eyes brightened. "You know you're making things so much worse for her, don't you?"

Kerrigan stilled. His focus shifted to Bly, and his expression almost broke her. She was going to die and watching it happen was going to kill him, too.

"Bucket," Borden snapped.

A bucket was placed by Bly's feet as Borden reached into his belt and extracted a dagger that he used to cut through the ropes binding one of her wrists. She found a moment of relief as the new position allowed her feet to find more purchase on the ground but then the dagger was at her sleeve, cutting it away with rough strokes before he pushed the remaining fabric up to her elbow. One hand gripped her wrist, and the other placed the tip of the knife against her skin. She didn't get a chance to beg before he parted her flesh and she gasped at the bright pain of it. Blood trickled fast and warm down her fingers, and the soft smack of it hitting the bottom of the bucket made her stomach lurch.

"Fight, Bly," Kerrigan begged.

She didn't know what good it would do, but she'd do anything if it made this less painful for him. Swinging out, she aimed for Borden's shin, but he kicked away her attempt with a laugh. She didn't have enough purchase with her feet to do any damage, not that a kick to the shins was going to save her.

Borden chuckled.

"I'll do anything you want," Kerrigan said. "Anything."

"You really should have shut up. Now I want you to watch her die." He turned to Katrina. "Hold her wrist over the bucket."

Bly's head grew lighter and distant as if it were floating away from her. She thought dying would make you feel small and alone, but her mind was drifting and boundless as if it were rising above this moment.

Borden moved behind her.

"Don't you dare." The fury in Kerrigan's voice should have frightened her, but she could barely latch onto any one feeling anymore.

Elise's scarf pulled around her neck. Thorns bit her as he unwrapped the choker.

"Interesting accessory," he murmured, and then he tilted her head to the side without any fight from her.

Fangs tore into her neck. There was no gentle pricking that was replaced by soft lips. This was like getting eaten by an animal.

A high keening sound left her lips.

She knew the sound. It sounded like death.

Kerrigan roared.

Bly jerked as the branch that held them trembled. Borden's teeth tore from her neck, leaving behind mangled flesh. She screamed with more strength than she'd thought she had left, her blood coming hot and fast. Her vision blurred, and she fought it. Her hand that Katrina had held over the bucket was limp at her side.

All the while, she braced for the killing blow that would end her.

But Borden wasn't behind her anymore.

She turned her head slowly, the movement making a fresh rush of blood stream down her neck.

Borden stood in front of Kerrigan, shaking his head. "A pity you're worth too much to kill."

Kerrigan lunged at him, teeth snapping. The branch holding them groaned. It might break eventually, just not soon enough. Borden pulled his sword from its sheath. "Although, I could maim you a bit." His black eyes flicked to Bly. "She can watch you bleed a little too in the few moments she has left." He lifted the sword, shifting it around Kerrigan's body as if deciding where to cut first.

She couldn't watch. She couldn't look away. Kerrigan's eyes

met hers, and she wanted to read a million different things in them, but mostly she saw regret.

She pulled weakly at her stuck wrist. Her lips moved as she tried to say something, but she didn't have words, just a faint scream that bubbled in the blood on her lips.

Borden's body jerked before he could make a cut, then lurched again and again as arrows filled his back. His sword dropped to his side, but still he refused to fall . . . until a shadowy figure slid behind him and sliced his head from his neck. His body dropped into the snow in a gush of red. You really couldn't grasp how much blood there was when someone lost their head until you had a white canvas to spray it on.

She might have vomited if she'd had more life left in her.

Katrina rushed the dark-clad figure until a cluster of arrows pierced her heart, dropping her.

The figure that had killed Borden stood in front of Kerrigan for a moment before twisting away and joining the fight again.

Bly's head rolled against her chest.

"Stay with me, Bly." Kerrigan jerked against the tree again. Her arm pulled from the force of it, but the pain was gone. She felt a pleasant numbness.

"Look at me, Bly." The emotion in her name on his lips jerked her chin up. She couldn't see straight anymore, and everything was a blur of white and red as the fighting waged around them, but she managed for a moment to focus on Kerrigan's copper hair. It gleamed like something she could hang on to.

He put his weight into pulling at the branch again and again until it started to splinter with cracks that got louder each time. Blood leaking down from where the chains around his wrists sliced into him with each pull, staining the cuffs of his white shirt a bright and terrible red.

Stop. She tried to speak the word, but she was pretty sure it didn't leave her lips. He didn't need to hurt himself for her. They didn't owe each other anything anymore, and she certainly didn't deserve for him to come to her rescue. But as she tried to tell him again to let her go, the branch shattered, and Kerrigan crashed to his knees as Bly fell to the ground. Her cheek hit the icy snow, but she didn't feel it. Her arm that was still tied to the tree wrenched in an awkward angle behind her back where the branch rested on top of her.

She wanted desperately to close her eyes, but she wanted more to see Kerrigan one more time. She wanted to tell him something even though she couldn't remember what it was.

And then her wrist was cut free. Her body was flipped over and dragged onto a lap.

She stared up into Kerrigan's frantic face as he ripped his own palm open with his fangs, pouring blood onto her neck and then her wrist.

She wished she could feel the warmth of it. The strange thought was enough to pull her back into herself a little. Blood wasn't just about death. It was lifesaving as well.

Kerrigan drew a dagger from his boot, putting a deeper cut in his wrist that he held over her mouth. "Drink. It'll help you heal faster if the blood is inside and out," he explained as if she would refuse, but her mouth was already open and waiting, and he pressed his skin to her lips. The blood trickling into her mouth *was* warm, and her body shuddered awake with it.

She'd given up on ever feeling warm again. His blood running down her throat felt like comfort. She didn't even register the taste, not really. It just tasted like life.

He put more blood against her neck and then her wrist before pulling back. One of his hands still clenched the dagger, and his other hovered above her as if not sure what to do now that he'd given her his blood.

She reached up her hands, one burned raw from the rope and the other dripping with his blood and hers. She gripped his free hand, which was stained with his efforts to save her. They both stared at their red fingers winding together. She wanted to say something with their skin and fears split open and bare, but her throat burned with discomfort.

"Shhh," he said, seeing her struggle. "There's time for that later." He stared at their linked hands and swallowed.

She hoped he wasn't lying.

A shadow blacked out the sun above them, and Kerrigan snarled before shifting and swinging his dagger up toward the looming figure. He froze, and the dagger stopped midswing, even though his grip remained tight.

"Bianca?" His voice was disbelieving.

Bly blinked, trying to focus on the silhouette above them.

All she could make out was a flash of white teeth as Bianca grinned down at them. "I see you're still in the business of saving humans."

EIGHTEEN

Bᴵᴬɴᴄᴀ sʜɪꜰᴛᴇᴅ ᴏᴜᴛ ᴏꜰ ᴛʜᴇ sᴜɴʟɪɢʜᴛ and kneeled next to Bly, who was still lying in Kerrigan's lap, clasping one of his hands. Bly craned her neck, wincing at the stretch of her tender flesh that wasn't even close to done healing, but she needed to see the girl who'd first reignited Kerrigan's humanity, the one who'd led a rebel group with him that had helped so many humans escape the Gap before they were caught and Bianca was tossed out into the wilderness.

Bly admired her. Bly was part of a rebel group, but her motives had never been that selfless.

Bianca reached out a hand, placing two fingers against Bly's neck. "Pulse is still weak. She'll live, though."

"Your eyes . . . ," Kerrigan said.

Bly had been too caught up in the girl's beauty to notice the color of her eyes. Bianca had dainty features, cool brown skin, and sleek black hair that ran in a long braid over her right shoulder. At first glance, she might've seemed too delicate to be the girl from Kerrigan's stories: a girl who refused to stop fighting, even in the face of certain death. But there was a tension in her jaw as if she never truly relaxed, and droplets of blood splattered across her face that were clearly someone else's.

Her eyes were dark gray rimmed in brown. This girl was Bianca, but she wasn't human anymore.

Bianca shot Kerrigan a glare. "You think I survived all these years out here staying human?"

Kerrigan nodded. "But you didn't lose your humanity. You're here, running around saving prisoners."

Bianca's face darkened. "It's hard to be that noble out here. In truth, I saw you. I came for you."

He swallowed. "I tried to come for *you* . . . to reach you before."

Before she became like him. Kerrigan's face was an odd mix of relief and sorrow.

Bianca's expression softened for a moment even though her body stayed tense. "Someone else found me," she said, and she looked over her shoulder at another vampire hovering close by—a girl with light blond hair draped in two braids down her shoulders and a rigid stance that made Bianca look relaxed.

Kerrigan smiled. It was the first real smile Bly had seen on him since she'd stolen Donovan. And even as she relished it, it was like a wound opening back up. She was grateful to even see a look on his face again that she hadn't thought possible, but in her most untethered dreams that she occasionally still let herself slip into, she'd always imagined that look being directed at her once Donovan had been returned.

She knew she had no right to be jealous, but it pierced her anyway.

"I'm excited to meet her," he said.

"Well, her name's Astrid," Bianca said. "She wants to meet you too. She said if she ever got the chance, she'd rip your throat out for letting me get captured."

They held each other's stare for a second before they cracked matching grins.

"I like her already," Kerrigan said.

"I knew you would." Bianca's hand squeezed Kerrigan's forearm before she glanced back down at Bly. "And this is?" Kerrigan focused on Bly, looking slightly startled as if he'd forgotten she was even there. His eyes flicked to her face and then their bound hands.

Whatever emotions seeing his friend again had brought out of him drained away and left behind a cold blankness.

Bly didn't want to hear how he'd describe what she was to him. She was the person he'd asked to spend eternity with him while he held her in his bed. She was also the person who'd ripped his heart out and stole his ability to choose his own fate. She tried to swallow, but her throat burned in refusal.

Clearly the worry for her when her life was in jeopardy had been pure adrenaline. It wasn't forgiveness.

The blood on their hands made it easy for him to pull away from her grip.

She struggled to shift herself off his lap before she had to suffer the pain of him moving her himself, but her head swam. Her wounds were healing, but the blood she'd lost hadn't fully replenished yet.

A hand pinned her down to stop her from rising, but it wasn't Kerrigan. Bianca held her in place. "You're in no shape for that yet."

"Elise . . . Donovan." Kerrigan's eyes pinched at his brother's name on Bly's lips, but she didn't care. Both their siblings were in danger, and it surprised her that she actually cared about Donovan, and not just because he was important to Kerrigan. They'd saved each other's necks twice, after all. They were teetering on the edge of friendship.

"Your prick of a brother is out here?" Bianca asked.

Bly immediately liked her.

"We were attacked on both sides by a band of witches and a band of vampires before they decided to share us. The witches have him and the rest of our group."

Bianca sighed. "I don't suppose you want to just leave him behind?"

Kerrigan glowered at her.

"You always cared too much about him," she said gently.

Kerrigan shook his head. "I didn't care enough once."

"You know you can forgive yourself even if he doesn't."

"I'm going after him. Will you help me?"

"I owe you."

"You know I don't believe that."

"I'm always going to help you." She looked down at Bly. "If you want to leave now, you're going to have to carry her."

Bly tried to push herself up again, but her arms wobbled, and Kerrigan didn't hesitate before cradling her against his chest so he could push himself to his feet.

Her body went limp in his arms and her head rolled back

until he shifted his grip on her to cradle it in the crook of his arm.

She should've thanked him, but his arms were tense, and she couldn't tell if it was because he wanted to protect her or because he really didn't want to touch her. She stayed silent and closed her eyes so she could feel him without seeing his face.

It made it easier to pretend.

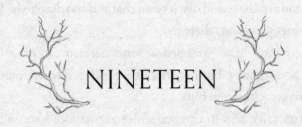

NINETEEN

KERRIGAN'S FULL VAMPIRE SPEED MADE
Bly whimper as her body jerked and throbbed where the wound
on her neck had healed only at the surface level. Kerrigan held her
tighter in response so that all she could feel was his hard chest and
strong arms pressing in on her from all sides. His caging touch
made a rush of calm wash over her before her fuzzy mind cleared
and reminded her of all she had to be afraid of.

They reached the witches faster than she expected. Unless she
had drifted off. She wasn't sure, but Bianca's group lost no time. It
was much different from being with the rebels with their careful
planning and stalking and calculated moves. These banished vampires launched themselves at the witches' caravan before they'd
even register the sound of them upon their approach.

The battle had begun, but Bly was still in Kerrigan's arms.

She squirmed, fighting his grip.

Elise. Her sister's name drummed in her like a heartbeat. She had to get to her. Even if it meant leaving Kerrigan's arms. She'd done it once before.

Kerrigan finally stood her on her feet. At least, Bly thought he had. She still couldn't quite feel her extremities as she tried to take a step toward the sound of a scream that was too deep to be Elise's, but Emerson was out there too.

Kerrigan's hand wrapped around her arm, locking her in place. She strained, but his grip didn't budge. She was much too weak to get away from him.

"You can't help in this state." Kerrigan's face blurred before her, but his voice was firm.

"More blood," she mumbled. She could help if he just gave her more blood to heal faster.

"There's no time. I need to get out there, but I can't have you coming after me. Someone will shoot you down in a second. Stay here."

"Elise." Her voice was slightly stronger.

"I will get Elise."

She tried to pull against his grip once more.

This time Kerrigan jerked her arm back, probably harder than he meant to or she was just too weak, but she stumbled in the other direction, and he had to catch her by the shoulders, steadying her on feet that she still couldn't quite feel. Her head wobbled until his hand reached out and gripped her chin, lifting it and holding her steady until she focused on his face.

His expression was hard and sure even with her blurred vision. "I will get your sister. Wait for me." He let go of her before turning back and pulling a spell from his pocket. He turned her invisible. "Now you're hidden," he said. "Just stay still." Without his touch, her body sagged against the trunk of the oak tree behind her.

She took a couple deep breaths, willing her vision to right itself. There were too many screams. None of them sounded like Elise, but she'd never heard Elise scream. Elise, who was so careful and safe and had never slipped from a tree and fallen like Bly. She didn't know her sister's scream. Bly didn't really know her sister at all, and the thought of Elise dying before she really could had Bly taking a shaky step that ended with her on her hands and knees in the snow. The cold bit her fingers. It brought her back to herself a little more, and she crawled through a cluster of manzanita, gripping the smooth branches and using them to pull herself into the thick of it. Kerrigan was right about one thing—she didn't have the strength to save anyone. She had to trust that he would.

For some reason, she did. Holding Elise over her head before had been born out of desperation to save his own brother. She understood that. He had no reason not to help her now.

Searching the brawling figures, she saw Benedict and Jade fighting side by side with a couple of witches sprawled at their feet. She found Emerson, smashing a witch in the back of the head with the hilt of his sword, choosing not to kill.

It had to be a good sign that they were already free.

And then her eyes finally landed on Kerrigan. Donovan stood beside him. They both had a witch by the throat.

Kerrigan flung his witch to the side, and the witch crashed into a tree before slumping at the base of it. Donovan snapped his witch's neck, letting the body crumble to his feet.

That's when Bly saw her. Elise was on the ground behind the brothers, her hands still bound behind her back, her legs kicking furiously at a witch above her, holding him at bay. Bly started to pull herself out of her hiding spot, but Kerrigan spun around and drove a blade into the witch's side before he dropped on his knees beside her sister, scooping her up into his arms and standing. He said something to Donovan, and Donovan turned around, glancing down at Elise with his cool face splattered with blood. He reached for something in one of his pockets and then stretched out a hand toward her sister, releasing Elise's bound hands.

Kerrigan held her for a second more before Benedict and Emerson both stood in front of him, each of them reaching out their arms for Kerrigan to pass Elise to them.

Bly rose to her knees. She wanted to be there too. She wanted to be the one holding her sister and making sure that she was okay, but her eyes crossed, and it looked like there were two Kerrigans holding two Elises, one for both Benedict and Emerson.

Bly laughed, the sound sudden and out of place. The side of her head was starting to throb from where the vampire had kicked her earlier.

She blinked. There was only one Elise, glancing between the two men standing in front of her. Elise said something to Kerrigan, and he put her on her feet instead of into one of the waiting sets of arms.

Bly pulled herself up just as something snapped behind her. She turned. Two witches tugged a bound and gagged Demelza through the brush just behind where Bly hid.

One of the witches, a younger girl with straggly blond hair and an innocent face that didn't seem to belong in these rough woods, stopped dragging Demelza.

The other witch, a boy who didn't look much older but whose face had a hardness to it like storm-worn bark, spun to the girl.

"Keep going," he hissed, glancing over his shoulder at the battle that was all but over.

"Let's leave her," the girl's voice was pleading. "They'll come after us if we have her."

"Her mother is the reason our parents are dead—the reason we're out here getting attacked by vampires every other day." He shook Demelza's arm. "We can buy a better life with her head." He leaned in closer to Demelza's ear. "Don't for a second think I plan to sell you back to your mother. We're going straight to the vampires."

Demelza didn't so much as flinch at his words, and Bly had to wonder how many times she'd been in this position before as the daughter of a powerful and evil woman.

Bly had been responsible for one of those times.

The way Demelza accepted her fate made Bly feel something for the witch that she never expected: sympathy.

A lot of terrible things had happened to Bly, but she was still fighting back—what had to happen to you that you reached the point that you stopped?

Demelza had tried to betray them to earn her mother's respect, but how much of the evil in Demelza's heart was simply the shadow of her mother? She deserved a chance to step out from it, the way she had once before.

Demelza wouldn't get that chance if these witches got away with her, but the two that held her were glaring at each other.

"I'm scared," said the girl.

Her brother's face softened just a fraction before his jaw clenched. "Fine, but I'm not letting her live. We'll have revenge at least." He drew a crude wooden-handled dagger from his belt.

Still, Demelza didn't flinch away. No muffled screams came from her gagged mouth, and Bly wondered if this was a fate she had accepted a long time ago—to be killed by an enemy of her mother.

Bly acted without much thought. The remnants of the battle hid her steps as she crept, still invisible, behind the girl.

Bly's fingers trembled as she tried to reach for her spells. She was still in no shape to rescue someone, but if she cried for help, then she had no doubt that Demelza would be dead before anyone could reach them.

She finally managed to pinch a sliver of mushroom in her fingers.

"Sleep." Her voice was hoarse as she pressed the spell against the unsuspecting girl's neck. The witch dropped to the ground in an instant.

Her brother had been hardened to the point that he didn't even flinch as his sister hit the ground. He only drew his knife up to Demelza's neck, drawing blood before Bly could even speak.

"Kill her, and I death curse your sister." Bly's voice sounded surer than she meant. She held no death curse, but while she was invisible, he didn't know that. She hoped her spell held. She hoped her voice held a cruelty that she no longer felt. The days of her wanting every witch buried were gone. She didn't want this girl dead. She felt bad for her. These witches knew an unimaginable loss, a loss that Bly had felt once . . . a loss that had driven her to a murderous frenzy.

A loss that had made her willing to trade one life for her sister's just to end her own suffering.

So she understood the girl at her feet, and she understood

the boy with his knife already leaving a trickle of blood against Demelza's throat.

The boy's lips twitched with indecision. He had something he'd probably dreamt of within his grasp. How far did he want to go to keep it?

"Take your sister and run. Either you both live or at least one of you dies." It seemed like an easy choice, but Bly knew that if there was enough rage in his heart, it wouldn't be. She quietly fished something else from her pocket. A blue jay feather that would give him enough speed to run with his sister in his arms.

Reaching out, she placed the feather at his feet. When she pulled back her hand, it blinked into existence.

She wanted to tell him that he didn't really want this. That he'd just become angrier when it didn't stop the hurt. But the bodiless voice of a stranger in the woods would never convince him. Only his own heart was capable of that.

His focus shifted to his sister. He'd been avoiding looking at her because, of course, she was probably the sliver of heart that he had left. Bly could relate.

Finally, the boy tucked the dagger back into his pants and plucked the feather from his feet before pulling his sister into his arms. Spinning, he ran into the woods.

One of Bianca's vampires who was closest swiveled their head like a wolf picking up the scent and bounded in their direction, but Bly shifted, sticking her leg out to catch their ankle and sending them sprawling face-first into the dirt. The vampire rose, snarling in Demelza's direction, but Demelza was too far away to have done it.

The vampire turned and stared into the woods where the

siblings were no longer visible before huffing and marching back to the rest of the group. He didn't bother helping Demelza, who stood there with her arms still bound.

Bly staggered over to Demelza and pulled the gag from her mouth.

Demelza's eyes narrowed. "So is there another knife to my throat?" She sounded bored. "I recognize your voice, Bly. I can't remove the collar around your neck, if that's what you're hoping in helping me, and if you give my mother her precious roots, then I doubt she'll really care if you come back without me. She'll honor her agreement. So go ahead." She laughed. "I bet she doesn't even ask you what happened to me."

Bly thought of her own parents. The way their disappointment in her had pushed her into the forest before Elise's death and then had pushed her into the Games after. If they had loved her uncondi- tionally, then perhaps she would've been able to mourn Elise's death, to cope with the guilt without throwing her own life to the wolves. Sure, she'd survived. She'd won, but they hadn't expected that.

They still didn't know. She'd never gone home.

She hadn't expected to have something in common with Demelza, but there it was again... the barest hint of understanding.

Bly fumbled into her pockets for an extra vial of revealing dust left over from the raid. Sprinkling it into her own palm, she spoke the spell.

Demelza seemed genuinely surprised that Bly didn't even have her dagger out. "Why?" she asked bluntly.

Bly shrugged.

But Demelza wouldn't let it go. "You could have just let them kill me."

"Can't say I didn't think about it." Although the truth was, she *hadn't*.

"No. Tell me why." There was a note of desperation in her voice. Bly looked at the other girl, noticing for the first time that her calm had faded and there was a slight tremble in her arms and lips. Demelza was familiar enough with danger to not flinch with a knife at her throat, but she didn't know anything about being saved without an ulterior motive.

Bly struggled to put her reasons into words. She understood one thing: Demelza would not want Bly to feel sorry for her.

"Nobody deserves to die for their parent's crimes," Bly said.

"I've done horrible things all by myself."

"Yes." Bly thought of Vincent's bleeding body, but Bly was partially responsible for his death too. She couldn't hand out punishment for a crime that was hers as well. She swallowed. "You kept Donovan alive." Demelza could've left that knife in after the resurrection spell succeeded. She could've let Donovan die, and that blood would've been on Bly's hands just as much as hers, and there would've been no redemption for that. Bly hadn't known what would happen to Vincent, but she had known Donovan might die when she let the witches have him.

Donovan's survival had left open the door for redemption when Bly hadn't even been thinking about how much she'd hate herself after, only about keeping Kerrigan alive and saving her sister.

Demelza's moment of kindness had saved her.

Demelza scoffed. "I realized I could use him for leverage. That's it."

"Ouch," said a deep voice behind them. "Here I thought it was because you saw something you liked about me."

MARGIE FUSTON

Both girls turned to face Donovan, who'd crept up beside them. His face was splattered in blood, but he wore a jovial expression that didn't fit someone who'd just been in battle. His eyes roamed over Demelza and then Bly.

Demelza flushed pink before scowling. "I saw the blood of a prince."

"But you didn't take any of my blood, did you?" he said softly. "I imagine your mother will not be pleased when she realizes that."

Demelza's scowl deepened. "I was getting around to it. I was busy."

"Busy sharing your fears and hopes with a caged vampire?"

She shrugged. "I talked to you because I didn't care what you thought of me, and I couldn't trust any of my people. It's easy to trust someone behind bars."

Bly glanced between them then shook her head at Donovan. "I thought it was weird that *we're* practically friends, but now you're friends with a witch, too?"

"Wait one second." Donovan waved a hand between him and Bly. "We're not friends yet. We've only saved each other twice. It takes three times for automatic friendship." Then he waved a hand between him and Demelza. "And we're definitely not friends. I just pay my debts, and like I said, she didn't drain me dry, so I figured I'd come after her when I saw those witches leading her away. I just had to dispatch a few people along the way." His eyes narrowed at Demelza. "You didn't even fight them. Why?"

"I think we're done here." Demelza tried to push past them both, but Donovan grabbed her arm.

"Why?" he pressed.

Demelza looked like she wanted to stab him, but she glared into

· 260 ·

the brush behind him and answered. "I recognized them. The boy had no talent for spells, and my mother banished him once he was old enough. The parents fought her, and the entire family got cast out. Clearly the woods haven't been kind if the parents are gone."

"So that's a good reason to let them kill you?" Donovan growled.

Demelza tried to pull away from him. "I didn't try to help them."

"I've had enough of guilt-ridden people with death wishes in my life," he said.

"Then let me go," she hissed at him.

He didn't.

"You're not your mother," Bly said.

Demelza's pale face pinched with annoyance, and Bly realized her mistake. She'd probably been told that all her life, but it had only ever been a negative thing—that she hadn't measured up. Demelza's voice was cold when she finally spoke. "I'm not. I've always been . . . weaker than her. Did you know I tried to stop her once from banishing witches who couldn't create spells? I presented a whole plan to the council when I was fourteen. I thought she'd be proud of my initiative. Instead, she left me in the woods for a week with nothing but my clothes. One day . . . I can be different, but I have to play by her rules to survive."

A lot of evil could be done by playing by the rules. Bly had participated in it herself by entering the Games. And she regretted it.

"You helped Emerson," Bly said.

There'd been no ulterior motive for that. Clearly Demelza hadn't totally turned her back on that fourteen-year-old who wanted a different world.

"You know that I tried to correct that mistake."

Bly hadn't forgotten. Demelza had planned to hand Emerson over to her mother, the very human boy she once tried to help, just to show that she had a ruthless heart because she'd been shamed for having a kind one.

"If you're saving me because you think you see something good in me, then don't. You should take your knife and shove it into my heart right now because you'll only be disappointed."

Bly shook her head. "That's not who I am anymore." Her words hung between them like an invitation. If Bly could change then so could she.

Bly reached into her pocket, took out an unbinding spell, and released Demelza's hands, which were still bound.

Donovan didn't let her go, though, until he ran a finger across his fang and wiped his blood over a scratch that ran down Demelza's cheek. Her eyes widened at his touch.

He turned and strode away without another word.

A moment later, Demelza spun on her heels and started to leave before she stopped, looking back over her shoulder. "Thank you," she said curtly.

Bly nodded. The movement reminded her that her head still ached. She swayed slightly on her feet, and she thought she might hit the ground once more, but a slender hand gripped her elbow.

Demelza's hand.

"Thanks," Bly muttered.

"I owed you," Demelza said simply. Bly wanted to point out that steadying her while she found her footing wasn't exactly the same as saving someone from certain death, but Demelza had already let go of her and walked away again, and this time she didn't turn back.

TWENTY

BLY'S BODY REMINDED HER OF HOW SHE
felt before the Games when she'd been skipping meals and giving
blood—that hollowness in her limbs—but her neck no longer
ached, and there wasn't even a scar on her wrist.

She should be okay.

The vampire blood had done its job. What the blood couldn't
heal was the memory of the taking.

She shuddered, trying not to think of it even as her body
refused to obey. Fangs ripping, flesh tearing. Her fingers drifted
to her neck as if to stop the flow of blood. Dry flakes broke away
from her smooth skin. You couldn't staunch the flow of a memory.
She knew that all too well.

Her fingers brushed the tangle of vines and metal at her neck.
She lifted it gently, trying to get a feel for how much closer it was
to her skin than when they had started. The scrape of the thorns
told her it had tightened. They'd lost time being taken and then

more time searching the dead to replenish the weapons they'd lost in the fight. She couldn't afford to dwell on the way that vampire had torn into her when she wore something around her neck that would do the same soon if she didn't focus.

She was alive for now. That was more than could be said for everyone. One witch guard had died at Borden's hands.

A hand closed over her wrist, and for a moment, she thought it was Emerson, but she met Elise's worried eyes.

"How's your head?"

Bly gingerly touched her temple. "I'll live." That was all that mattered.

Elise stared at the collar of death around her neck. "You lost the scarf."

"Sorry."

"That's not what I'm worried about." Elise's eyes drifted down to Bly's clothes, and Bly glanced down at her chest as well. Her gray vest was covered in the horrible reddish-brown color of half-dried blood. The blue ribbon at her wrist was unrecognizable without a trace of blue on it. Bly reached down and pulled at it.

Elise tracked the movement before grabbing Bly's wrist and pulling it up to her. "You're always touching this, but I don't remember it. Is it special to you? I think I can clean it." Her fingers began to loosen the knot on the ribbon.

"No." Bly jerked her hand away.

Elise frowned. "What is it?"

Bly swallowed, her throat thick with the past. "After you got taken, I traded the mushrooms I'd gathered that day. I didn't buy the dress, but I bought the ribbon that matched it to remind myself of what I'd traded your life for."

"But I'm here now."

"Yes." Bly glanced at the stained whisp of fabric. Even though Elise was here, it still somehow felt like she didn't deserve to take it off.

But she didn't have to. Elise grabbed her wrist once more, working her fingers into the knot until the ribbon fell away with an easiness that felt wrong. It drifted to their feet, and Bly couldn't stop herself from looking over her shoulder as they left it behind. Elise's hand wrapped around where the ribbon had been as if she knew Bly would feel the loss of it.

Elise eyed Bly's bloody clothes again. "Too bad we can't get rid of the rest of your clothes."

Bly reached a hand up, hovering over her chest. Her fingers trembled.

"Bly," Elise said. She wasn't asking the question even if it hung in the air with her name.

"I'm fine." Bly swallowed, and the movement hurt like there were still fangs in her neck, but the pain was a phantom.

Phantoms couldn't hurt you.

"Let me," said Demelza.

Bly hadn't realized the witch had been following close behind, listening, but she stepped up alongside them, fumbling in her vest. She pulled out something white and paper-thin. "The petal of a lily," she explained. "It will clean anything." She reached out slowly toward Bly as if she were approaching a wild animal. Part of Bly was grateful for the tenderness, but she also hated it. She clearly looked weak if Demelza was treating her softly.

She didn't stop the witch. She wanted the blood erased.

Demelza muttered a spell as she broke the petal against Bly's vest.

It wasn't the first time that Demelza had magicked away the stains on her. The first time was after the witches' trial, when she'd clearly done it to win Bly's favor. But Bly couldn't fathom why she'd bother now. To the witches, Bly was nothing more than the leverage that would ensure the roots would be taken to them. It shouldn't matter if Bly was bloody or not.

Perhaps it was merely payback for what Bly had done for her earlier.

"Thank you," Bly said.

Demelza nodded and drifted away again.

Elise smiled. "That's better. Do you feel better?"

"I'm perfect." She almost believed it herself. It felt good to have her sister with her, hovering over her with worry, like she always had before.

"You looked like you went through hell," said Donovan, replacing Demelza at Bly's side.

She turned to him, watching as he scrutinized her from head to toe.

"The witch cleaned you up nicely, but she didn't fix your eyes. The memory of your own blood is clearly in them still."

Bly held his stare. He could see through her, but she wasn't going to let him see any weakness.

He looked away first. "I remember the first time I bled so much I thought I might die. Kerrigan and I were pitted in the arena together where vampires train human children to become them. Did he tell you about that?"

He waited until she'd nodded before continuing. "He sliced me across the leg, and the blood rushed out of me so fast and so hot that it felt like everything inside me had become untethered and was leaking out of that one wound. The vampires rushed in and saved me. We were only supposed to wound each other enough to break the spirit, not remove the soul from the body." He laughed. "Kerrigan stood over me as the vampires saved me, and I thought he was there to gloat, but his expression was . . . haunted. I'd seen him look that way only once before, when our parents died. I never wanted to see him look that way again."

"Did he take it easy on you after that?" Bly asked.

"The opposite. At the time, I thought he was trying to kill me. Or trying to kill the last piece of his heart that he had left so that he could be a true vampire. Now I think he wanted to make sure he never saw me that close to death again. He wanted to make sure I never let someone else land a blow like that. He did me a favor."

"He doesn't see it that way," Bly said. It wasn't her place to try to mend things between the brothers. All she'd promised was to get Donovan back. This was none of her business, but she couldn't stop herself. "He thinks he made you too hard."

"He made me what I needed to be."

"Then why does he think that you hate him?"

Donovan scowled. "Because I did for a while . . . for a lot of reasons. We all hate the things that make us. Bleeding out with the knife stuck in your throat makes you put things into perspective."

"You should tell him," Bly said.

"That's not why I'm telling you this. I'm not looking for sage advice."

"Then why?"

"My brother has been looking at you with that same haunted expression on his face. You almost died when those banished had you."

Bly said nothing.

"I can see it in your eyes, and I can see it in his."

She'd seen it too. He was still drifting along the outskirts of the group, but he was no longer invisible. His eyes were on her every time she glanced his way.

"I'm not sure what you want me to do about it."

"I told you I don't like seeing him look like that. Fix it."

She opened her mouth to protest, to tell him that it wasn't her problem.

Donovan grabbed her arm, pulling her to a stop. "I'm putting an end to this now."

"By killing me?" she asked.

"Tried that. Shot my damn brother instead. I've switched sides."

"Hey." Elise had spun back around and marched over, getting in Donovan's face. "Let go of her."

"I'm doing your sister a favor, princess. Run along."

"I told you not to call me that." Her cheeks flushed. There was an antagonistic glint in her eyes that Bly hadn't really seen before.

"Go find your little prince," Donovan said, "while I go snare one for your sister. Won't that be lovely? Two human sisters with vampire princes obsessed with them—don't humans write songs about such things?"

Elise just glared, shaking her head.

Bly couldn't look away from their interaction. Donovan didn't just know *of* Elise; he actually knew her enough to joke with her and bicker . . . like a sibling. Bly and Elise had never really had that type of relationship. They'd never fought. If they'd both been more honest with each other, they would have. Her chest pinched to think of Donovan and Elise together this past year ... bonding.

"I'm fine," Bly said softly to her sister.

Her sister gave her a half-smile. There was a twinkle in her eye before she turned way. Elise actually trusted Donovan.

The rest of the group had moved on, following Benedict, who had stayed in the lead.

Except for Joseph, who looked quite worried at the prospect of intervening. Bly couldn't imagine having to make a choice between which redheaded brother to anger.

"Run along now." Donovan gave him a dismissive wave.

Joseph hesitated until Bly nodded, reassuring him. He turned around, following the others without looking the least bit reassured.

She thought about going back to the rest of the group too. Donovan's grip was loose. Bly could pull away from him easily, but if he were offering to help her, offering *his* forgiveness, then how could Kerrigan refuse? "Okay," she said. "Help me."

He hauled her quickly into the woods. Scanning the trees around them, he called, "Show yourself, brother."

Nothing but the repetitive thump of a woodpecker high in a pine answered.

"Maybe he's gone ahead ...," Bly said.

"He's here. He'd never trust me alone with you after what you did to me."

An icicle of fear pierced her chest. She reminded herself that he'd saved her twice already.

Or he could have saved her only so he could be the one to see the life flee from her eyes. She thought of stepping away from him, but he still had her arm in his grasp, and no matter how gently he held her, if he decided she wasn't going to get away, then she wouldn't, so she didn't try.

"I guess you don't care then," Donovan spoke to the watching trees. "In that case, I have no reason to care about her either." He turned a sharp smile down on Bly. "I'll figure out why her blood turned you into such a fool in the first place."

The small prick of fear expanded in Bly's chest until it felt like her lungs had grown too big for her body. Her throat tightened. Each breath became a struggle.

"Bly." Donovan's sinister grin faded. He dropped his grip on her arm. "You're safe," he said, his voice less than a whisper. Then his eyes shifted from her to over her shoulder. He held his hands up in surrender one second before he was flying backward, landing hard on his back.

Kerrigan stood next to Bly, glowering down at his brother. "What are you doing?"

"Proving a point." Donovan climbed to his feet, dramatically brushing leaves from his cloak. Kerrigan's fists clenched at his sides. He still didn't turn to Bly.

Donovan searched her expression though. "I really didn't mean to frighten her. I thought you'd understand what I was doing," he said to her.

Her breath still rasped in and out. Too shallow. Her vision darkened at the edges.

Kerrigan finally looked at her. His furious expression softened. "Bly," he said her name gently. When she didn't respond, he stepped in front of her, blocking her view of his brother, lifting his hands ever so slowly to cup her cheeks. He tilted her head up to meet his storm-gray eyes ringed in bright spring green. "I've got you," he said.

He repeated the words again and then again. Each time, she drew a slightly deeper breath until her chest rose and fell without a fight.

His hands pulled away from her face, and her throat tightened again with the sheer pain of losing his gentle touch. She wanted to beg him to hold her. All she needed was his fingers on her skin to keep her together.

She could survive all of this if only he'd stay with her.

He moved back.

Donovan stepped up from behind them, placing a hand on Kerrigan's shoulder. He didn't touch Bly again. "You're not running away and hiding in the woods again."

Kerrigan scowled. "I'm not hiding."

Donovan raised a brow. "Stalking, then? What word would you prefer to describe sulking in the trees with all that self-hatred, because that's what this is, right? You've always been good at hating yourself, and I know that you don't hate her."

"She handed you over to die," Kerrigan ground out.

"I'm over it."

"Since when do you get over things?"

Bly shot Donovan a pointed look. She'd been right. Donovan's words as he lay dying hadn't eased any of Kerrigan's burden over the past.

Donovan sighed. "Since she handed me over and the damn witches put a knife in my throat. Life is long until it isn't. We both should've understood that a long time ago."

"I've always understood it." Kerrigan's face fell. "It's why I wanted us to become . . . what we are."

He wanted them to become immortal. Not just immortal; the kind of ruthless immortality that made you willing to kill and squash others just to hang on to it.

But then Kerrigan had changed. He thought Donovan never had, but he'd been wrong.

Kerrigan started to leave again.

Bly couldn't do it anymore. She was done feeling like a curse he had to fight.

She took a step back too. He wasn't the only one who could increase the distance between them.

"Wait," Donovan said.

Kerrigan paused.

Bly did too.

"I forgive you," Donovan said, his focus still on Bly, but then it slid to Kerrigan. He might've spoken the words to her first, because it was easier, but they were mostly for his brother. "You did what you needed to for us to live. There's no shame in that. And our parents . . . we were both kids. If you'd fought back, you would've died, and I'd never have had someone care enough to make me stronger. You're the reason I survived at all. Hard choices don't need forgiveness, but I'll tell you what you need to hear."

Kerrigan's face was blank as if he didn't dare allow himself any feeling.

"What I *don't* forgive," Donovan said, "is trying to hand yourself over in the Games and thinking it wouldn't break me to lose you." He looked away into the trees. "I'm glad Bly took me instead of you. It was an easier role to play."

"I didn't think you'd care," Kerrigan whispered.

"I chased you through the woods to try to stop you."

"I thought you wanted me alive just to watch me suffer."

Donovan shrugged. "A little. But I thought I was repaying the favor you once did for me in the arena. You went soft and joined the rebels. You went human. Humans die. I tried to be cruel to you to turn you hard again, to make sure you didn't do anything foolish that would make the queens take your head. I never once wanted you dead."

Kerrigan's chest heaved. He moved toward his brother until they stood face-to-face.

Donovan put his hand on Kerrigan's shoulder and then Kerrigan reached out, bringing him into a hug.

Donovan looked at Bly over his brother's shoulder and winked. His eyes were wet even if he didn't let a single tear fall. Donovan broke the hug first, pushing Kerrigan away from him gruffly. "I appreciate the gesture, but I'm really not the one who's literally dying to be in your arms." He spun Kerrigan around and shoved him toward Bly. "Her turn," he said.

Kerrigan stumbled toward her and then stilled as he regained his footing. Bly took another step back, putting space between them before he could do the same. She started to turn away.

"Wait," Kerrigan said.

She hesitated. His throat bobbed with movement, yet he didn't open his mouth.

The waiting grew painful. But she stayed. Her heart wanted to give him this one final chance to heal it or break it forever.

"Come on," Donovan said. "The girl tried to take my place with the witches. She saved my head from getting lopped off my shoulders in that banished squabble. Her actions are apology after apology, and frankly, I'm worried she'll keep saving me until I owe her my life ten times over. It's embarrassing."

Kerrigan took a slow step toward her before stopping again.

"This is painful," Donovan grumbled. "She's ruthless. I personally love that in a woman."

She cringed a little at the comparison to Jade, but they *did* share that in common. Jade had fought and betrayed the queens to get Donovan back. Bly had risked her life to save Donovan as well, if only for Kerrigan.

"I'm sorry," Bly said to both of them, and to the trees that watched her silently, and to her past and the mistakes she'd made.

She said the words to herself as well.

And in that moment, she realized that she'd been fighting all this time to get Kerrigan to forgive her, but whether Kerrigan did or not, Bly was the only one who could heal her heart.

More than anything, she needed to forgive herself.

So she did. Every choice that she had made had been selfish, but those choices had also been born out of love. She'd wanted to run away and live in the woods with Emerson because she'd thought she loved him. She'd wanted Elise to go with her to scavenge for mushrooms because she loved her and wanted to have one more precious memory with her sister before she left. She'd entered the Games because her love for her sister didn't die when the witches stole her. She'd taken Donovan and handed him over in place of his brother because she loved Kerrigan and would have rather faced his hatred than a world without him in it.

She'd made horrible and careless choices, but the roots of those choices had come from the reckless pool of love inside her.

Donovan was right. She was ruthless . . . when she loved, and that had been her curse.

She didn't realize she was crying until her cheeks grew wet and hot.

She blinked, trying to clear her hazy vision, and then Kerrigan stood in front of her, his hands on her face, his fingers in her tears, wiping at them like he had so many times before—that first time in his room after she tried to capture him and he'd felt her tears with surprise; then again after she'd escaped Callum, he'd wiped away the blood and tears with restrained concern. Now his touch was soft, each brush of his fingers a forgiving whisper that wiped away a little bit more of her sorrow. And then he pulled her into him, crushing her against his chest with the force of someone who'd never release her, and she didn't want him to.

"I'm sorry," he said, his words a delayed echo of hers moments before. "I should have taken you to your sister the moment I knew where she was. I know you would have still helped me. I wanted to pretend there was no goodness in you. I didn't want to risk forgiving you only to have you hurt me again. I was scared."

She wrapped her arms around him, squeezing in return, and some of the tension in his hold relaxed. They'd both carried their own guilt, and they needed each other's arms to ease it.

Cold bit her cheeks, and for a second, she thought her tears had turned to ice, but then Kerrigan chuckled, the sound soft and real—something she'd heard so few times, yet somehow felt deeply familiar.

"It's snowing," he said. He pulled back from her, and for a moment she wanted to clutch at him in case he ran away again, but he kept her hand in his, tethering them together even as he turned back to Donovan, who was watching them with a satisfied expression.

"Do you remember . . ." Kerrigan trailed off before starting again. "Do you remember when we were kids, how Father would take us out to the edge of the woods where the snow would stick and roll giant balls that he used like bricks to build us tiny houses?"

Donovan blinked as flakes of snow dusted his hair, turning it almost white by the time he answered. "I remember." His face held a pained expression for a moment.

Kerrigan's grip tightened on her hand. She had a feeling that the brothers never talked about their lives as humans, but then the corner of Donovan's mouth lifted. It was the softest expression Bly had ever seen on him.

A gust of wind slanted the snow, turning it into a cold assault.

Donovan cleared his throat. "We'd better get back before her sister thinks I murdered her in the woods and comes after me. I have a feeling she'd be just as ruthless as this one."

Bly smiled. She could picture Elise coming to her rescue now, even if she couldn't picture the sister she knew before doing something so reckless.

Kerrigan reached out, lifting the hood of her cloak over her head, nudging the damp strands of her undone hair beneath the shelter of it before he tucked her under his arm, wrapping his cloak over her against the snow.

It would have been faster to walk back separately, letting go of each other if only for a moment. Instead, they stumbled through the forest with Donovan leading the way and occasionally glancing back at them. He never once complained about their speed.

Most of the group had hunkered down against the storm when they arrived. An inch of snow covered the tops of their tents, creating a tiny winter village in the woods. Bly might have appreciated the beauty of it if she weren't shaking from the cold—even with Kerrigan's arms around her doing everything he could to shelter her from it.

A hunched-over figure stood outside one of the tents, so much snow covering him that it created a puff of white when he straightened, shaking it off.

"Thank curses you're back," Joseph grumbled. He eyed Kerrigan warily.

Bly elbowed Kerrigan in the side. "Fix that," she mumbled. She didn't need a vampire guard following her around. She could take care of herself.

Kerrigan strode forward, holding out a hand to Joseph, who took it as if it might be a trap. "Thank you," Kerrigan said as he shook his hand. "I've got it from here."

Bly groaned quietly, biting back her protest that she didn't need a changing of the guards, but even the strongest vampire sometimes needed saving, so she appreciated knowing that someone else was looking out for her.

Joseph gave her a slight smile before hurrying into his own tent. As he left, another tent flap opened to greet them, and Elise poked her head out. She took in Bly and Kerrigan together and grinned at them before nodding at Donovan.

"My dear, close the flap, even I'm getting cold," Benedict called from behind her.

Elise didn't listen. "We set up your tents for you," she said, and then she held out a couple lumps of coal. "Demelza shared her spells, but we only got one apiece."

"Thanks." Bly reached out to take them, and as she did, her sister's other hand closed over top of hers, giving it a squeeze.

"I'm happy for you," Elise said.

A knot tightened in Bly's throat. Elise had found love too, but Bly had never actually said those words to her. Elise didn't know anything about Kerrigan—only that he meant something to Bly, and somehow that was enough.

"You too," Bly choked out—a weak response, but it was the best she could do.

Benedict grumbled something from the tent, and then Elise rolled her eyes and dropped the flap.

Bly searched the scattering of tents for her own. She needed to get out of this cold.

"Stay with me." Kerrigan's fingers brushed against hers. An invitation.

She turned to him. Donovan had already disappeared. They were alone in a world that had turned pure white, as if their forgiveness had created an unblemished canvas and they were two dots of vivid paint that could create whatever new picture they chose.

So she chose. She reached for him. He hadn't bothered with the hood on his cloak, and his hair was damp with ice clinging to it, nipping her fingers as she spread them into his hair to guide his mouth down toward hers. The meeting of their lips was as soft as the kiss of the first snowflake on her cheek, but like the storm, they broke open and their kisses became hurried and fierce as if the strength of them could erase everything that had come before.

She believed it. Kisses were like spells. They could curse and heal in equal measure. The last time they had kissed had been a curse. Their bodies had been warm, but their hearts had been cold. This time their bodies were cold and their hearts were warm and ready.

Kerrigan's hands wound into her hair, and her hood slipped from her head. The flurries of snow clung to her curls until they dampened. A violent shiver raked her body, and her fingers curled in Kerrigan's hair, trying to hold on to him as he pulled back. He grabbed her hand. "Come," he said, the word almost lost in the wind, but she would've followed him even if he'd said nothing.

They trudged to her tent, and Kerrigan opened the flap. She crawled inside where it was dry, the ground carefully spread with a spelled blanket that kept the damp at bay.

Kerrigan hesitated, crouched down halfway in with her and halfway out. She reached up and grabbed his sleeve, tugging him inside.

The flap closed behind him, and he sat cross-legged on the ground, matching Bly, because there wasn't much room for anything else. They stared at each other, their cheeks and lips flushed from the cold and the kissing, neither seeming to know what to say or do.

They'd gone from so much distance between them to a tiny cocoon with the swirl of the storm around them.

Bly shivered.

Kerrigan unclasped his cloak, holding it out to her with a cringe. "This won't do you much good. It's soaked."

Bly opened her fists, revealing the spells Elise had handed her. "Warmth," she whispered, and a red vein of pulsing light threaded through the coal. Heat radiated from them so quickly that her fingers ached as they unthawed, but the spells were small, meant only to be held as you walked or slept. They were already losing the battle against the chill leaking through the seams of the tent.

She held one out to Kerrigan.

"I'm fine," he said. "I'm worried about you. You're soaking wet."

Reaching behind her, Bly brought her wool blanket into her lap. Her fingers trembled as she started to unroll it.

"Bly," Kerrigan said. "You can't put that over your wet clothes. It'll just soak through."

She paused, not quite looking at him.

"I can go back to my tent. You should take off the wet clothes and wrap yourself in the blanket with the spells."

"No," she said, finally meeting his eyes again.

"You can't stay in those clothes."

"No, I mean I don't want you to leave." She sat the blanket to the side, and then unclasped her cloak from her neck, shoving it awkwardly away from her. The sleeves and collar of her shirt were still soaked from their careless kissing in the snowfall. She took her vest off first and then hesitated. Her fingers shook, and it wasn't from the chill.

Kerrigan cleared his throat. She was afraid he'd offer to leave again, so she moved quickly, unbuttoning her shirt and shrugging it off her shoulders. She left on the thin white chemise that ended just above her belly button.

She moved to her trousers, slipping them from her hips, leaving behind drawers that ended at her knees in little frills.

A shiver ran through her. Part of her was afraid to meet Kerrigan's eyes, but she wasn't sure why.

He scooted closer to her, and then he took the blanket and shifted it around her back, covering her.

"You don't like looking at me?" She didn't mean to ask it, to show him that fear. She finally met his eyes.

Hungry black pulsed in and out of them.

Bly's stomach tightened, and her mouth went dry.

His voice was restrained when he spoke. "I don't like seeing you cold." His eyes drifted from between her lips and her breasts, which were very visible through the worn cotton.

Tilting her chin up, she reached for him, gripping his collar, but instead of bringing him to her, her fingers trailed down, undoing the buttons of his vest and then his shirt. All the while, she held his stare, watching the way his jaw clenched and released in time with the blackening of his eyes.

Finally her hands slipped under the wet material and ran along the smooth expanse of his chest. Shrugging his shirt off behind him, he reached for her in return, his fingertips brushing her hips as he gripped her there, pulling her onto his lap to straddle him.

He still wore his half-damp trousers, but she didn't care.

The blanket fell from her shoulders, but she didn't care.

All she cared about was every place their bodies touched— her legs squeezing his hips, his hands sliding from her hips to her lower back and then rising, fanning out as if he wanted to touch as much of her as possible. Her breasts pressed against his chest as his embrace tightened. Their cheeks brushed, each of them breathing heavily into each other's ear.

She kissed him first on the sharp angle of his jaw.

It was his turn to tremble beneath her as her kisses trailed upward, and her teeth grazed his ear.

A tiny groan escaped his lips, and his hands moved up to her neck, jostling the spelled necklace there, making a thorn bite her skin.

She jerked back in surprise. His touch, the snow, the warmth of forgiveness for herself and from him had made her forget. A trickle of blood ran down her throat to her collarbone. Kerrigan brushed a finger across it, catching the drop.

He met her eyes and then brought his finger to his lips, tasting her.

The reminder of death at her throat should have cooled her blood, but it did the opposite. She only had so long. Not only was she human, she wore a curse that would steal her life if they couldn't find what they were looking for.

Kerrigan let go of her, and she had to cling to him to keep from slipping off his lap, and for a second, she worried the reminder of her mortality had given him pause, but his hands reached for the silk scarf he still wore around his neck. He loosened the knot with one hand, sliding it from his neck, then reached behind hers to thread it along the back of the choker. He began winding the silk around the twine of vines and metal. The material whispered against her neck, sending tiny shivers down her spine each time.

She watched the firm press of his mouth while he concentrated. It was torture to hold still.

When he was done, he healed the prick from the thorn before running his fingers up and down the column of her throat.

"Kiss me," she begged.

He smiled. One hand pressed against her lower back while the other one wandered over her body with gentle wonderment. Everywhere he touched, the cold burned away, until finally his fingers gripped her chin, holding her as his lips met hers. Her mouth parted for him, hungry to deepen everything between them.

He broke the kiss only to tug her closer to him, their chests flush again. Fangs grazed her ear and then his lips traveled up and down her throat before settling against her pulse that beat rapidly in answer. His fangs brushed the sensitive skin there.

Her melting body froze.

He felt the shift in her in an instant and pulled back, letting cold air between them so he could see her face.

Understanding and regret flooded his expression. "I'm sorry. I should never have . . . I didn't think."

Bly's chest was too tight to answer. She'd been craving his fangs in her neck again, but the last memory of such a thing wasn't Kerrigan, and the act had been meant to kill, not bring pleasure.

"I want you to do it." Her teeth chattered. Some of the heat had left her body.

His fingers pressed softly into her neck, finding her pulse. He kept them there like a bandage staunching an invisible blood flow.

The memory of violent fangs faded away, and her pulse slowed.

"I want you to," she repeated.

"I know." His fingers drifted away, and his lips took their place, but not to bite. He left tender kisses in time with each throbbing beat of her heart.

"Do it," she said.

"Another time," he whispered against her skin, and then he shifted, stretching out on the ground with her on top of him. He grabbed the blanket, covering them, and she nestled into his chest, her heart beating for both of them.

TWENTY-ONE

EMERSON LAUGHED, AND BLY LIFTED HER
chin, searching the group for him. The only time she'd heard him
laugh since Elise had gone missing was during the Games when
they'd been talking about her. And now she found Elise at his side
once more. Her hand rested on his arm, and Emerson beamed at
her.

Bly's chest squeezed with happiness. At least the friendship
they once had was growing between them again. Bly knew the
pain of being friends with someone who you wanted so much
more from, but Emerson was the type to accept what it was and
not constantly long for something it wasn't.

He'd be okay no matter what happened.

"If only Benedict would disappear," she muttered to herself.

Kerrigan chuckled beside her.

"Sorry," she said.

Her fingers reached out for his hand, and he took them.

It had been five days of walking since they had begun to stitch themselves back together again. Five nights of keeping each other warm.

Somehow it felt blissful, and in those moments when it was only his touch and his lips, she forgot where they were and what loomed ahead of them.

"You know," Kerrigan said, "it was Benedict who found me and told me you had gone with Callum."

"What? I thought . . . Emerson . . ."

"Emerson found me too, but I was already on my way. Benedict located me first. He told me the suspicions about Callum's . . . tastes."

Bly said nothing, but she eyed the blond vampire who led the group and occasionally turned around to glance worriedly at Elise and Emerson. To his credit, Benedict had done nothing to stop the two from being together.

"Why are you telling me now?" she asked.

"I thought you should know. I said he was careless, but people change. I would know."

She squeezed his fingers as Bianca slid up beside them, grinning at their linked hands. She'd been spending time with them when she wasn't taking her group of banished to fan out in the woods, looking for threats. She'd told Bly stories of the band of rebels that Kerrigan and she had led and the people they had saved.

"You two look pleased. Good night?" she asked with a wink.

Kerrigan sighed and elbowed her. She stumbled dramatically before righting herself.

Bianca's smile dropped. She had the uncanny ability to go from joking to serious at a moment's notice, and Bly wondered if she'd always been like that or if that was the result of living in the forest where you'd have to fight for your life without warning.

Her tone was solemn when she spoke again. "The snow stops ahead abruptly," she said. "Clearly magic."

"So we're close," Kerrigan said.

"To something. Groups rarely venture this far from the cities. We may be banished, but we still trade there, and people who go too far away tend to disappear. Half my group wants to turn around. The vampires—their loyalty to me only goes so far."

"I understand," Kerrigan said.

"But my loyalty to you is boundless." She grinned as if she were joking again, but there was a glint in her eyes that said she was not.

"You know you owe me nothing," Kerrigan said.

"I owe you enough."

"*He* is the one who owes *you*," said a deeper, harder voice.

Bly glanced to her left at the girl who'd approached. Astrid. She remembered her vaguely from the battle when Bianca had saved them from Borden.

"Look who decided to come out of the woods." Bianca's voice was once again sharp and light at the same time, half joke and half blade.

Astrid said nothing to Bianca, looking instead at Kerrigan. "*I'm* the one who saved her," she said. "You went on living your pampered life under your mothers' thumbs while *I* found her in the woods, starving, a long gash down the side of her neck from where a banished vampire had already tried to kill her, but she'd managed to kill him instead." Her eyes gleamed with respect. "You put her there, and I found her. I won't let you put her in harm's way again."

"I looked for her," Kerrigan said. He looked at Bianca as he spoke.

"Not hard enough."

"I made my own choices that put me there," Bianca said. "I make my own choices now."

"Clearly," Astrid huffed out.

Bianca sighed. Some of the fight seemed to leave her. "I've missed you," she said to Astrid. "You've been avoiding me."

Astrid seemed on the verge of melting too, but she ground her teeth together. She looked at Kerrigan. "Tell her to leave you to your foolish task. She won't listen to me."

"I have," Kerrigan said. "I tried to get her to stop saving people before as well. If you love her as much as I think you do, then you know that nobody can tell her what to do."

"I know," Astrid said darkly. She looked at Bianca with resignation. "I'll send those who want to leave back."

"You should take them," Bianca said.

"If you stay, I stay. Don't order me to do something foolish again." She turned and faded into the woods without another word.

"She loves you," Kerrigan said.

"A bit too much." Bianca's face split into a grin again, but she couldn't quite erase the worry in her eyes. Bly understood that it wasn't for herself but for Astrid.

Being reckless with your own life was much easier than endangering someone you loved.

Bianca turned serious again. "I'm going to pull my people back. You won't see me, but I'll be near." Her tone lightened again, just as quickly. "By the way, I think you lost one of your group to ours."

"Who?" Bly glanced around.

"Big vampire with black hair in a Vagaris guard uniform?" Bianca raised her eyebrows.

"Joseph?" Bly had noticed his absence, but she'd figured he was only avoiding the possibility of Kerrigan reenlisting him as Bly's personal guard.

Bianca shrugged. "He's been walking with us for the past few days. Seems a bit smitten with one of my best fighters." She laughed, glancing between them. "Nothing I love more than danger *and* love in the air."

◆

They walked for another three hours before the snow abruptly ended just as Bianca had promised. The landscape went from soft white over barren gray to vibrant greens as if a line had been drawn between winter and spring.

They came to a stop, staring at each other. A field opened up ahead of them—sprawling grass dotted with yellow and purple wildflowers, and on the other side of it, the forest thickened once more. The sight of an open field of flowers should've made Bly's heart lighter. She should've wanted to run her fingers through the soft grass and gather a vibrant bouquet, but she could feel the cold of the snow at her back and the warm spring air at her front. Fear spiked through her at the sensation even though she could see no threat.

Benedict's golden compass gleamed in his hand. "We should be almost on top of it. Just beyond those trees."

"Let's get on with it," Samuel said.

Bly glanced at Demelza. "Doesn't Havenwhile use spells like this?"

Demelza's expression was tight with unease. "Yes, but weather spells are incredibly hard to make and maintaining it like this . . ." She eyed the flowers. This wasn't a temporary melting of winter. This was spring that had been allowed to flourish and grow.

Demelza eyes shifted to Samuel already halfway across the clearing. She moved after him, keeping her hands tucked inside the vest that held her spells.

They didn't have a choice. The choker was heavy on Bly's neck, and they all needed the roots unless they wanted the wrath of the vampire queens and Halfryta.

Bly drifted over to Elise and took her hand. It felt right and easy. If there was an unknown to face, she wanted her sister close to her, and Kerrigan at her back, and Emerson at her side. Benedict was at Elise's other side. His eyes sharpened as he scanned their surroundings.

"I don't particularly like this," he said as he snapped his compass shut and tucked it back into the pocket of his vest.

Donovan and Jade walked ahead of them, and Donovan turned back around. His brow was furrowed.

She could practically feel the tension in Kerrigan at her back.

The vampires' unease made her skin prickle too. It was like being in the woods when the birds suddenly fell silent.

She tightened her grip on Elise.

Emerson pulled his sword first, twisting suddenly to the right.

A girl stood in the field where no one had been a moment before. A faint breeze jostled the sky blue of her skirts. Her hands were tucked into a red vest that covered a purple shirt. Her curly black hair bobbed in two pigtails tied in yellow ribbons as she swayed back and forth with the wind. She pulled a hand from her pocket and waved.

Elise let go of Bly's hand and took a step toward her. "Are you lost, honey?"

Emerson had lowered his sword only slightly.

Benedict reached for Elise's arm, holding her with them.

The hum of Donovan's sword being released and Jade's daggers being drawn pulled Bly's eyes away from the girl.

A woman stood up ahead of them, blocking their path to the trees. She wore the colors of sunset—orange, pink, and creamy blue. Her teeth flashed in a bright smile.

Samuel stalked toward her, his sword drawn.

But a man appeared beside her, blinking into existence.

The field exploded with people dressed in the bright colors of the wildflowers of spring. Many were children with dimpling smiles.

Bly spun back the way they had come, but there were others who blocked the path back.

The amount of invisibility spells they'd have to use to pull off this trick was astounding.

They didn't have a chance in a fight.

"We punch a hole back the way we came," Benedict said.

Bly reached a hand to the choker on her neck. It was noticeably tighter now. Even with Kerrigan's scarf around it, the thorns scratched at her skin with any quick movement. She didn't have time to go back.

"The roots are ahead." Kerrigan stared at Bly's neck.

"Yes, so are more of these creepy rainbow people." Benedict turned to Donovan. "We go back and regroup. We'll tell the queens we need an army."

Donovan glanced at Benedict, then Kerrigan, then at Bly's choker. "We don't retreat."

Bianca, her banished, and Joseph were nowhere to be seen. They were outnumbered, but hopefully Bianca's group was fanned out somewhere beyond in the trees.

Kerrigan straightened from the defensive crouch he'd sunk into. "Hello," he said to no one in particular.

"Welcome," a disembodied voice answered before a man blinked into existence only a foot away from Bly. She jumped, stumbling back into Kerrigan.

The man smiled, his eyes twinkling as he assessed them.

Bly couldn't decide if the expression on his face was warm or gleeful at having surprised them. The ambiguity made her skin crawl.

The man's smile broadened as he stroked a full white beard that fell to his chest. "How may I be of assistance?" he asked.

"Who are you?" Kerrigan asked.

"Cornelius." He patted his purple vest—not the dark purple one shade away from blood that the vampires favored, but a glowing vibrant color that matched the swaying wildflowers surrounding them.

Kerrigan eyed him coolly.

Cornelius's eyes creased at the corners with something that looked like mirth. He knew a name was not the answer they were searching for. "How may I assist you?" he asked.

"You're speaking like you own the field we're standing in," Donovan stated bluntly.

"We don't believe anyone owns the natural world. We are merely humble servants, and I wish to serve you."

"Who's we?" Kerrigan asked. He and Donovan had both

shifted positions, each one at an angle where they could easily overtake the man together at any moment.

"The people with me." Cornelius waved a hand, and even more people sprang to life in the field like wildflowers opening in early spring.

None of them held weapons, but Kerrigan's and Donovan's swords whistled from their sheaths in response.

Cornelius held out his palms in a slow surrender. "That hardly seems necessary." His smile lingered, but there was a hardness in his stance that made Bly believe they did not want this to turn bad.

"We're just travelers," she said as Donovan spoke over top of her, "Then tell us who you people are."

Cornelius's eyes flitted between her and Donovan. "We are stewards of the lake." His eyes narrowed. "And we don't get groups traveling through these woods. Especially not ones made of humans, witches, and vampires."

"Did you say lake?" Benedict asked. "You don't happen to mean a dried-up little pool, do you? That's what we're looking for, and I'm sure it's just through that line of trees." Benedict nodded his head in the direction they'd been heading.

Every single one of their group glared at Benedict.

He shrugged under their scrutiny. "What? We're obviously in the right place. These people are here for a reason." He turned back to Cornelius. "So what exactly is this, a group of humans worshiping the dried-up ground, praying for a chance to dip yourselves in some magic and be something else?"

Cornelius laughed. "What makes you think we are all humans?"

Bly took in the people closest to them, noticing for the first time an amount of blue-and-gray eyes that wouldn't be present if this were merely a human population.

"Let us speak to whoever's in charge," Benedict said.

"I am." Cornelius's tone lost its jovial nature. "No one here is above anyone else, but I am the one who works to keep us organized."

Benedict scoffed.

Bly eyed the man in front of her. In a group of vampires and witches and humans, how had a human managed to become a leader? How had a witch not just cursed him or a vampire snapped his neck to take his place? It should have given her comfort, but the idea was so unusual that she shifted on her feet as if the idea itself were a threat to her.

"Now," Cornelius said, stroking his beard again. "What do you want with the pool? Why travel all the way for something that's nothing more than a dried-up ruined hole in the ground that humans might worship?" He raised his eyebrows as he repeated Benedict's words.

"Roots," Bly said. "All we want are the roots of a plant that used to grow here." It was her turn for everyone to glare at her, but Benedict had already said that they were searching for the pool, and she didn't see much point in lying. If these people really were guarding the remnants of the magic that created their world, for whatever reason, then they wouldn't be able to walk in and take what they needed without some form of honesty. Not when they possessed enough magic to turn winter into spring.

Despite the fact that nobody had brandished a weapon at them yet, they were grossly outnumbered.

"To what purpose?" Cornelius asked.

"Creating a spell that releases the magic in any vampire or witch back into the earth and turns them human again." It was a risk saying so much.

Cornelius's eyebrows rose. "To what purpose?" he asked again as he eyed their group. "I may live outside your wicked world, but you've come from the direction of Vagaris and Havenwhile, and I know enough to be certain that no vampire or witch is willingly going to give up their power in that place."

The choker weighed heavily on Bly's neck. Neither the witches nor the vampires wanted to release their power—they would both use the spell to make themselves *more* powerful. Cornelius knew that.

Bly swallowed, glad for Kerrigan's scarf wound so tightly around the curse that made her a servant to Halfryta.

"We come from a group of rebels made of vampires, witches, and humans, much like you." Bly waved a hand at the field of quiet, waiting people. "We heard rumors that such a spell was possible from the witches, and we stole a map from the vampire queens to get here. We need the spell to even the playing field, to give us the power for a fair fight against rulers that aren't interested in any semblance of fairness." Her voice sounded strong and passionate even as she lied. Her heart burned with longing for her words to be true. The roots *could* change things for the rebels, but putting them into rebel hands would only be a death sentence, not just for Bly, but for all of them.

Cornelius scrutinized her and then the rest of them as if he could read every lie they'd ever told. Bly struggled not to fidget and give herself away.

Cornelius nodded slowly. "Power corrupts eventually no

matter where it grows from." He spoke the words as if in a trance, and she wasn't sure if the warning was for them or for himself.

"Lovely," Benedict said. "Can you show us where the pool is, or do we have to find it ourselves?" The implied threat of the second half of his question fell heavily among them.

Cornelius merely smiled in response, his eyes clear and bright again as if he'd cast off whatever worry momentarily plagued him.

"Follow me," he said with a wave of his hand as he headed toward the thick trees up ahead.

They shared a wary glance before falling in line behind him.

All the smiling, bright people flanked them as they walked.

Donovan and Kerrigan kept their swords out while the rest of them left their hands hovering near the hilts.

They moved through a layer of oak and pine before the trees began to change, and leaves the color of sunset dotted the sea of green, and then trees with boughs heavy with flowers turned the air cloying and sweet.

Eventually the trees thinned as a grassy knoll rose in front of them. They paused as Cornelius climbed it first, turning around at the top, beaming down at them with the pure blue sky behind him.

His people smiled back at him. He might have claimed they were all equal here, but they looked up at him as if he were a ruler . . . or a god.

But he was human.

Uneasiness pulled at her again.

"Welcome to the lake," Cornelius said, waving them up.

"More like the hole in the ground," Benedict muttered before bounding up the hill. He stopped at the top, standing and looking at whatever was below. When he turned back around, his eyes were wide. "I stand corrected."

Bly climbed after him with Kerrigan at her side. She froze at the top, certain her expression mirrored Benedict's.

The knoll they stood on dropped off into a deeper slope leading to a valley below that was peppered with an array of giant oak with low, sprawling branches and fruit trees bursting with ripe color. Among it all were small circular houses with thatched roofs built against the trees and sometimes in the thick oaks themselves with ladders that dangled to the ground.

Beyond all that, a deep blue lake shimmered and sparkled with an array of colors as if it held rainbows captive beneath the surface.

Bly's eyes watered at the beauty of it.

Magic existed in her world, but it was hardly visible, especially to those who couldn't pay. This was altogether different.

Something inside her pulled toward the water. She took a step, practically tumbling down the steep hill.

It was Cornelius's hand that steadied her. "This place has that effect on people."

"This isn't supposed to be here," Benedict said.

"No. It's not. We all did our best to strip this world of its magic, but after the war when the vampires and witches and humans moved away to other lakes full of water without magic that they could suck dry, some stayed behind with a truce to live together in harmony. We shared our skills to survive off the land, and eventually we were blessed. The pool refilled a little more with each rain. The magic was still there in the broken dirt. It just needed time to heal."

"You speak like you've been here from the beginning," Kerrigan said, his eyes sharp and calculating. "Yet you are human. How?"

Cornelius's chest puffed out. "I was the first person to go into the pool and come out human." He chuckled darkly. "Everyone mocked me then, saying I had broken the magic, but I'm still here. I stayed until the magic came back, and now there are plenty of life-lengthening spells for those who want to partake."

"An immortal human?" Donovan scoffed. "Why not have a vampire turn you?"

Cornelius's expression went cold. "Power isn't about physical strength. To think otherwise is the sign of a weak mind."

Donovan looked ready to prove him wrong by ripping his head off when Demelza put a staying hand on his arm.

"But how has nobody found this?" Samuel asked. "Raw magic." He shook his head, his eyes gleaming with lust. "That news would've made its way back to the cities."

"Very few people stumble here," Cornelius said. "Most who do, choose to stay. Those who don't, they have their memories of our home taken before they go. Shall I show you to the roots you seek? What do they look like?"

"You're just going to show us?" Donovan's voice was skeptical.

Cornelius shrugged. "There will be rules, of course, but our community is built on sharing, and that includes those who stumble on us . . . or find us, in your case. The old world ended thanks to our greed. We will not make the same mistake now."

"But then you'll wipe our memory before we go," Bly said. Memory spells were precarious things. They could be created to wipe a day or a week or a year or more from your mind depending on how much blood went into the spell. She glanced at Kerrigan. What if they didn't remember they'd forgiven each other? What if they only remembered the hurt?"

"Our witches are very good," Cornelius said. "You'll wake up in the woods with your roots and no memory of this place only. Do you have the root that you seek?"

"Yes." Demelza slowly opened her vest, pulling out a white root that shimmered blue in the sun.

"Ahh yes. The root of the winding flowers. You'll be pleased to know they run rampant. You'll be doing us a favor by taking a few." He laughed. "Follow me."

They shared another glance between them, some of their wariness clearly fading to excitement. Bly had half expected them to get here and find nothing.

She was the first one to step after Cornelius, walking down the steep hill at an awkward angle that left her one wrong step away from tumbling, but the thought made her giddy. If she'd been a kid, she'd have climbed to the top of this hill every day just to roll down it, letting the grass nip at her bare limbs. Her heart ached for a childhood she didn't have. Nobody rolled anywhere in the Gap, where you'd just end up coated head to toe in chilly mud.

They reached the edge of the town. People moved languidly through the trees and wooden hutches. They looked at their group with curious eyes and tentative smiles. In some ways, it reminded Bly of Havenwhile when they'd first entered it for the trials, but the witches had bustled with overly bright smiles.

Nothing here seemed forced.

They passed a tree with branches laden with apples, and she

reached out a hand, brushing the smooth matte skin of one.

"Help yourself," Cornelius said, glancing over his shoulder as if he could sense her longing.

She pulled her hand back for a moment. Her instincts told her to distrust anything offered so freely, but there was no guile in his voice. She found herself wanting to believe in the apple, this place, these people.

Plucking it in her hand, she held it as they walked, rolling it in her palms.

"How does this place work?" Kerrigan asked. "With witches, vampires, and humans living together . . ."

"How are all the humans not dead from bloodlust, you mean?" Cornelius laughed. "The water." He waved a hand.

They had reached the edge of the lake. Up close it was even more stunning. An array of color shimmered in the water, but what grew around it was just as beautiful. Willows bent over the lake. Everywhere they kissed the water, the tips had soaked up a different color, creating a rainbow of leaves swaying in the breeze. Trees blooming in pastel blossoms grew in clusters around the willows. And around the roots of the trees, flowers wove together, creating another layer of vividness that left Bly blinking as if trying to rouse herself from the remnants of a dream.

"Explain," Donovan said.

Cornelius raised his eyebrows at the command, but he kept a pleasant smile on his face. "The water has all the power of the original magic. The witches can use it to create the spells without blood, and the vampires drink it to sustain themselves. We thrive from the lake, not from blood."

"And everyone's fine with that?" Benedict asked. "I personally love a sip of hot, silky blood. I can't imagine water being quite as satisfying."

"It's what's fair," Cornelius said. "Why take when you don't have to?"

"Because it's fun." Jade smiled sharply.

Donovan barked a laugh.

For the first time, Cornelius's expression darkened. "If you stay, you'll follow our rules. There is no blood sharing. Bloodlust is too easy for your kind to fall into." He stared pointedly at Jade, then Benedict. "We share other things: our labor. You'll be expected to work as if you live here and gather roots in your free time, but I think you'll agree to our terms." He strode over, carefully picking his way through the flowers to do the least harm, and then he plucked a vine from the array that was peppered with tiny white petals gathered around dark blue pistils. He followed the vine to the edge of the softly lapping water where he dug deep into the mud with his bare hands until he unearthed the root. It glistened white and blue.

Bly took in the flowers again. The white vines ran through everything—there had to be more than they could even harvest in the time they had.

"We will follow your rules," Kerrigan said. "You have my word." He glanced at Bly, his eyes dropping to the hidden choker on her neck.

They'd saved her. As long as they made it back alive.

"Then you may start harvesting tomorrow. We ask that you stay only on this side of the lake. We try to keep the far side pure from our touch. You understand."

Kerrigan nodded.

"Then come." Cornelius led them through the town to a circle of oak trees with overlapping branches. Each tree held a little house just off the ground in the lowest branches and one beneath as well. In the center of all the trees and houses was a long wooden table laden with bowls of fruit. "We keep this lodging available for guests. I imagine you're tired and hungry. Feel free to eat and call this place home for as long as you like." He winked. "Forever is an option. I doubt anyone back home would fault you for staying if they saw this place. Let me know if you need anything. Just ask anyone where I am, and someone can always find me." He turned and walked away.

Elise moved to the table first, reaching for a peach. Bly had the sudden urge to run forward and smack it away from her as if the soft flesh held another death curse. Elise bit into it, and Bly cringed, but her sister only smiled as a ribbon of juice ran down her chin.

"It's wonderful," Elise said. Her eyes shone.

Bly still held the apple in her hand. Her stomach had soured, and she couldn't put her finger on why. She sat the apple on the table in a bowl with all the others.

TWENTY-TWO

CORNELIUS HAD BEEN QUITE SERIOUS about making them work while they stayed at the Hallow Pool. Each morning as the sun appeared, so would he with a list of tasks for the day. Kerrigan and Donovan hauled supplies to build a new home, Nova split wood for fires that everyone gathered around at night, Benedict and Jade patrolled the borders with the towns-people. By nightfall, they would drag their tired bodies to the pool and dig through the mud, pulling out roots that glistened under the moonlight. Sometimes Bly would forget herself and stare at the pool in wonder, a glimmering black rainbow in the dark. She'd never had so much magic right in front of her, even if they were forbidden from touching the pool directly. The water's use was strictly controlled, even for those who lived here, to guard against the draining that happened before.

Though magic itself was far from forbidden. Spells were given freely instead of hoarded and kept for only those who could pay

in blood or money. Bly had even used spider's silk to spell herself a
new shirt without sleeves and breeches that ended above her knees
so she could kneel in the dirt as she dug.

Even with their aching muscles, it might have been a dream,
but each day, the choker scratched at her throat a little more. She
worried that by the time they made it back, she'd be dripping a
constant stream of blood. Or maybe she'd be dead.

But it was slow work to dig the roots from the ground. They
needed enough roots to make whoever they decided to give them
to grateful enough to protect them from whoever they did not.

She had to wonder if Cornelius was filling their days with
more work than usual to keep them from collecting as much as
they possibly could. Perhaps he had regrets about giving something so valuable away freely.

But part of her loved the simple but hard work of living in a
community.

On the third day there, she was assigned to harvest in the
orchard with Donovan and Demelza and a couple of townspeople as their guides. On their way there, with wicker baskets in
hand, she spotted Elise, sitting in a circle with some of the other
townspeople as she laughed, her nimble fingers stitching away at
something in her lap. She looked at peace.

Emerson sat beside her, looking a little bit helpless with a
needle and thread in his hand.

Bly couldn't help but laugh at the sight. "I think you got
assigned to the wrong detail!" she hollered to him.

He shrugged, but he looked happy.

Elise looked up with a wide grin on her face. She rose to her
feet and made her way to Bly, and Bly paused, waving for Donovan

and the others to go on without her.

Elise held a whisp of sapphire-blue fabric in her hands. Along the edges, she'd been stitching a pattern of trees with bare branches reaching inward like claws. It was beautiful and a little eerie.

She held it out. "Do you like it? I'm making it for you."

Sapphire blue. The color Bly's ribbon had been. "The color . . ."

She didn't really need to explain. Elise's understanding was on her face when she shook her head. "The color suits you."

"Thank you." Bly's throat was tight, but she didn't mind the feeling. "You're happy here."

Elise nodded, but her smile slipped.

Bly looked behind her to Emerson, who sat watching them. "You and Emerson seem . . . close."

A slight blush colored Elise's cheeks. "Things between us feel so easy, like there used to be this block between us before and now we can really look at each other."

Bly laughed. "Yes, there was a block, but I got out of your way."

Elise shook her head. "I didn't mean—"

"I know."

Elise returned Bly's smile before it faded again. "I asked Benedict if he'd ever turn human . . . if he'd ask the queens for some of the roots when we got back. He laughed. He thought it was a joke."

Bly could picture his reaction. She couldn't picture Benedict as human.

"It's a lot to ask," Bly said hesitantly. Her sister deserved it though. Elise deserved someone who wouldn't just fight for her, he'd live for her.

"Emerson turned into a vampire for me, but Benedict won't turn human."

Bly nodded.

"I know Emerson loves me more," Elise whispered, and she didn't seem to be talking to Bly anymore. Her expression had gone distant.

"But who do *you* love most?" Bly asked, because even though she held a dream in her heart for Elise and Emerson together, it wasn't her life. Elise needed to follow her own dreams, and dreams weren't always practical.

Elise pursed her lips but didn't answer.

✦ ✦ ✦

When she caught up with Demelza and Donovan, one of the townspeople was scolding him for picking the apples wrong.

"Like this," said the man, who'd introduced himself as Jonothan. He had a wide, easy smile that left behind lines on his face whenever it dropped. He reached out and wound his fingers around the apple before twisting it free from the branch. "Softly or you'll bruise them."

"You're asking the wrong person to be soft," Demelza said.

Donovan nodded at her. "Exactly. I don't need to be *soft*. Isn't there something I can lift or cut around here?"

"Everyone can be soft," said Mary, the other townsperson who'd come with them. She had long brown hair that reached her hips and looked like it hadn't been combed in a year. Like Jonothan, her smiles were easy, and her face bore the signs of a life under the sun. "Watch," she said as she reached her hand toward the apple. "Let your fingers caress it, barely putting any pressure, like you'd touch a lover." She twisted the apple off the branch and grinned. "I assume you've caressed a lover before?"

"I wouldn't bet on it," Demelza muttered.

Jonothan laughed, glancing between them. "I bet nothing is soft when the two of you make love."

Demelza blanched. "What?"

"I— We're not . . ." Donovan's face turned red. "I do caress someone, and it's not her."

Jonothan raised his hands. "Just reading the energy."

"Just pick the damn apple," Demelza snapped.

Donovan reached out and plucked one as he glared at Demelza.

"You know," Bly said, "I do think that was a little sensual."

Donovan turned and pointed a finger at her, apple still in hand. "See if I save you a third time." He grabbed his basket and dropped in the apple in a way that probably bruised it before stalking off.

Demelza grabbed her basket and headed in the direction opposite of Donovan's.

Jonothan and Mary shared a look before turning to Bly.

"Well, then," Mary said. "I guess you've got the gist of it."

Bly didn't know if she was a soft person, but the sweet smell of the apples mixing with the rich, damp dirt beneath her feet made her feel like she'd be softer and softer the longer she stayed here.

Glancing between Mary and Jonothan, taking in their relaxed stances and easy expressions, she felt like this place had softened them. They were both humans, but there was no trace in their eyes of hunger or fear.

They had begun to turn away when Bly stopped them. "How long have you been here?" she asked.

They both grinned like that was a question they'd been waiting for.

"Two years," they answered in unison.

She looked between them. "The two of you came together?"

"With a group of humans that fled the Gap," Jonothan answered.

"And you all stayed?" Bly asked.

"Oh no," Mary said. For the first time, her face was empty of any trace of a smile.

A slight frown pulled at Jonothan's face.

"Why'd the others leave?" Bly asked.

Mary shrugged, already turning away. "Who knows? They disappeared without a goodbye. But it was their mistake." She waved a hand at their surroundings. "Clearly."

✦ ✦ ✦

In the evening as they ate their meal before bed, Cornelius stopped by and invited them to stay and become a part of their community, as he'd done every night.

Bly watched the longing on her sister's face.

The choker on her neck felt a little bit tighter.

TWENTY-THREE

THEY SAT AROUND THE TABLE, THE IRIDES-
cent white roots glimmering in piles like snow catching the sun.

"This is plenty," said Kerrigan.

"I agree," said Jade. "We can always come back. I'm tired of it here." She shuddered. "There's too much smiling. People are way too . . ."

"Happy?" Elise supplied, her voice holding the sarcasm she reserved for Jade and Donovan alone.

"Exactly." Jade gave her a sharp grin. "I knew you'd get it. There's only room for one excessively smiling person around me, and you've already filled that spot."

Elise turned to Bly. "How does the choker feel? Is there time to gather more? Should we stay a little bit longer?" Elise couldn't quite hide the yearning in her voice.

Bly touched the choker at her neck. Already the thorns pricked her skin through the scarf almost to the point of drawing blood.

They needed to leave soon. She was pretty sure she'd be bleeding on the walk back, but it shouldn't be enough to kill her. Yet.

"We could stay another day or two," she said. She met Emerson's worried yet resigned eyes. He knew they needed to leave. He knew she'd bleed to make Elise happy for as long as possible.

"Bly," Kerrigan warned. He gave Elise a pointed look.

Elise's focus drifted down to the choker, and she shook her head. "We leave tonight then."

Knuckles rasped softly on the entrance to their compound, and then Cornelius came inside. He moved to the head of the table, making Donovan scowl as he stepped back to make room for the older man. "I've come once more to implore you to stay," he said as his eyes roamed over the table. "It seems like you're almost ready to go, but why?" His focus slid to each one of them slowly as if he could read their deepest thoughts. "Why go back and try to fix a broken world when we're offering you one that doesn't need fixing?"

"That's a matter of opinion," Jade said.

Cornelius turned to her. "You feel that way because you've always been at the top, haven't you? Fairness seems like punishment when you've always had more than your share. In fact," he said slowly, "some of you do not strike me as rebels with your fine clothes and jewel-crusted weapons."

Hands shifted imperceptibly to those weapons.

"I *am* a rebel," Bly said, her voice firm. In all her time working with them, she'd never truly felt at one with their cause. Her goal had always been to save Elise, and she hadn't dared to fight for anything else, but the words rang truer to her now.

She'd need something else to fight for when she got back. Her adrenaline from the past months would never fully fade away and let her melt into the life she'd once longed for. She'd never get over her urge to move and to save and to change the unchangeable.

The rebels would need all the help they could get once they'd handed over these roots. Whether they gave them to the witches or the vampires, the power in their world would shift, leaving the most vulnerable caught in the crossfire.

She wanted to be there to fight against the damage they were causing.

Because once again it would be her fault. It'd be better if she let herself die here, but there was no way to convince everyone with them that the roots were better off left alone.

Holding Cornelius's eye, she reached up, untying the scarf that hid the spelled choker at her neck. "I am a rebel, but this is why we cannot stay. A witch put this spell around my neck, which will kill me in another ten days if we don't return with the roots. The vampires also want our heads if we don't give them the roots. We don't have any choice but to go."

Cornelius's expression darkened. "So you're not taking these to heal but to start a war."

"Unless . . . ," Elise said. "Would anyone here know how to remove the spell?"

Cornelius walked around the table to take a closer look at Bly's neck. "I've never seen a metal like that," he said, "but I will ask around. Usually a spell and a counterspell are developed at the same time using the same material. So you'll stay if we get it off her?"

"Yes," Elise answered. "But we only have two more days before we must leave."

Nobody else agreed with her, but Cornelius nodded at them before striding away.

"If the counterspell needs the same substance, that won't be simple," Benedict said. "I know that metal. It's not easily found."

He gave Elise an apologetic look, but he didn't sound sorry at all.

Like his sister, he had a better life back home.

Most of them did.

"We can try, though," Emerson said. "Trying doesn't hurt."

Benedict cast a sour look at Emerson, but he didn't notice. His words were for Elise.

"We *aren't* staying." Samuel rose from the table where he'd been seated next to Bly.

"We have two days to try," Elise said. "And then if Bly is free, anyone who wants to stay can. You can take your roots and go."

"And face all those cast-out witches and vampires who are crawling in the woods by ourselves?" Samuel asked. "We had a deal. You're supposed to be the ones returning with the roots, and I'm just along to make sure you do it."

Samuel moved with the speed of someone spelled. His arm wrapped around Bly's chest, and his dagger rested across her throat as he yanked her back from the table and out of her chair, just out of Kerrigan's reach.

Kerrigan was on his feet in an instant, stepping toward them, his face blank and deadly.

"I wouldn't," Samuel said. The blade cut her throat.

Bly's vision darkened at the edges. Her throat tightened.

Kerrigan looked murderous, but he didn't move closer.

"We're leaving now," Samuel said. "All of us. And you damn

vampires will make certain we make it back."

Elise raised her hands in surrender. "We'll go." Her eyes were calm and sincere, and Bly had a new respect for her. She may not be great in a fight, but in a tense situation, Elise could make everyone feel like it'd be okay. Her sister held out a hand toward Samuel as if offering him something. "Come back to the table, and we'll make our plans to leave."

Samuel snorted. "I trust humans less than I trust vampires. Vampires are nothing but animals that want to eat. Humans want too much to be trusted." He backed Bly up another step with the pressure of the blade. "Luckily Halfryta prepared me for this."

Emerson rose, taking almost imperceptible steps toward her and Samuel.

Demelza's eyebrows drew together. She whispered something to Nova, and they both stood.

The witches had a plan.

Bly opened her mouth to shout a warning as Samuel whispered a word into her ear. "Constrict."

The same spell Halfryta had used when she attached the choker.

The knife left her throat, and Kerrigan pulled her away from the witch in an instant. "What did you do?" His hands hovered over Bly, looking for something wrong besides her bleeding neck.

"I made sure you'd leave immediately." He held up a small glass vile in his hand. "A rare snakeskin spelled to constrict anything it touches. The speed it works at depends on how much is used." He shrugged. "I sped it up."

"How long?" Panic bled at the edges of Elise's voice.

"I only used a little. I think it'll speed it up by a few days." He clapped his hands. "So let's hustle."

"You *think*?" Kerrigan snarled. He moved toward Samuel, and the hawkish witch guard stepped up to Samuel's side as Donovan came around the table, caging in Samuel at his back.

"I wouldn't," Samuel said. "Do you think Halfryta will really take that off her if you come back without me?"

"We'll still have her daughter," Donovan said, nodding toward Demelza. "Good enough."

"Except I'm her favorite."

Demelza didn't notice the dig. She was frowning at Bly, and then she started crawling over the table across the roots to get to her.

Benedict reached around from the other side of Elise and grabbed Demelza's ankle. "Not so fast, witch."

Nova took her ax out, holding it over Benedict's wrist. She didn't need to speak a threat. It only took Jade a moment to bring a dagger to Nova's throat, completing a chain of threats.

And then Bly felt it. A prick of pain. A trickle of blood down her throat that wasn't from Samuel's blade.

Bly's hand flew to the choker. She couldn't fit a finger between it and her neck.

"Kerrigan." Bly's voice trembled around his name. The choker was closing in much too fast. She didn't have days. She had moments.

He spun toward her, taking in her hand at her throat, and then reached out, grabbing Samuel by the neck and hauling him toward her. "Undo it."

The hawkish witch guard drew her sword, raising it toward Kerrigan.

Donovan's sword erupted through the witch's chest from behind.

Samuel turned as the guard slowly sunk to her knees. Donovan placed a boot against the dying witch's back, extracting the sword as he toppled the witch face-first onto the ground. The petite guard with freckles stepped back, trembling and holding her hands out without drawing a weapon.

Donovan pointed the blade, slick and dripping with blood, at Samuel. "I'd focus if I were you."

"Do it." Kerrigan shook Samuel by the neck, practically lifting him off his toes.

"I can't," Samuel choked out. "I ... I must have used too much. I don't have the counterspell. Halfryta only gave me the spell to speed it up, not undo."

Kerrigan tossed Samuel onto the ground and reached for Bly. He tried to fit his fingers under the choker and couldn't. Elise had run around the table too, her hands hovering around Bly's throat. Emerson looked on with horror on his face, his sword drawn uselessly at his side. The choker could not be fought.

"I have the spell to release it." Demelza's voice was calm, but it took on an edge as she turned back to glare at Benedict still holding her despite Nova's blade threatening to remove his hand. "If you let me go."

Samuel scoffed. "You can't possibly."

Demelza reached into her vest, and then black metal glinted in her hand—a tiny blade no longer than her pinkie. It appeared to be made from the exact same metal that was entwined with the vines that made the choker.

Samuel's eyes widened at the sight of it.

"Let her," Bly said.

"Doesn't she want you . . . dead?" Benedict didn't release his grip.

"Let her go!" Elise yelled.

He dropped Demelza's ankle, pulling his hand back slowly as he eyed Nova's ax.

Demelza scrambled across the table, crushing some of the roots under her knees and filling the air with a bitter and tangy scent, and then she stood in front of Bly. Her blue eyes were like unsettled water.

Another thorn bit Bly's neck, and she gasped.

Demelza lifted the knife. For a moment, Bly thought the witch might just stab her with it instead of releasing her, but then she focused on Bly's neck, sliding the knife so snuggly between the choker and her skin that more blood poured from her cuts.

"She'll destroy you for this." Samuel's voice was a shocked hiss as if he truly couldn't understand Demelza's betrayal, despite the way both he and her mother treated her.

Demelza's slight pause was her only acknowledgment of his words before she spoke the spell. "Sever."

The metal grew painfully hot against Bly's skin, and then the knife sliced through the vines and cords. Demelza carefully peeled the contraption away.

Samuel shook his head, casting one more glare at Demelza before slipping away with the remaining witch guard hovering behind him. Nobody bothered to stop them.

Kerrigan began tenderly rubbing his own blood into every wound.

Bly stared at Demelza as he worked. The witch's face was

pinched with worry. Her eyes were distant as if lost in a bleak future.

"Your mother gave you the spell to release me?" Bly asked.

Demelza shook her head. "Of course not. I stole it before we left." She hesitated, as if deliberating how much to tell them. "I've known for a while that she wasn't sharing everything with me anymore, so I started using invisibility spells to spy on her. I knew about her precious choker and the spell she hid away to release it. Lucky for you, she underestimated me." Her expression turned worried.

"Your mother won't like this." Donovan spoke Demelza's worry out loud.

"My cousin lost our leverage when he messed with the spell." She shrugged.

"But she'd surely have rather seen me dead, leverage or no," Bly said.

"Yes." Demelza guessed her next question. "But I owed you, and I keep my word. You're right about one thing—I'm not my mother."

"Thank you," Bly said as Kerrigan healed the last cut on her throat.

Demelza nodded and turned away, beckoning Nova to follow her down one of the small paths that led to their hutch.

Bly caught Nova's hard eyes as she turned away. She'd almost gotten to witness exactly what she wanted.

Kerrigan's hands were still on her, his thumb gently stroking where her pulse had just begun to slow.

She was tired of her neck being on the line. She wanted to use her neck for other things.

A body crashed against her chest, and Elise knocked her out of Kerrigan's grip. Her sister's hands wrapped around her arms, squeezing too hard as she pulled back. "We can stay," she said.

Letting go of Bly, she spun around to the rest of them. Emerson smiled softly at her.

"We can stay." There was a lightness in her voice that should have lifted Bly with it, but Bly's chest tightened in response. She'd never really let herself look at the possibility of staying when it meant having the life choked out of her.

This place was so similar to what she'd longed for once—living in the woods in harmony with those around her—but in her dreams, they'd all been human. She looked away from Elise and met Kerrigan's vampire-gray eyes. That didn't fit anymore.

The last time she'd allowed herself to dream, she'd been wrapped in Kerrigan's arms in Vagaris, imagining a life there, with him. Even if they returned with the roots, she wondered if the queens would let them stay.

Now this whimsical place beckoned her. She didn't have to imagine it. She was here.

So why did she feel like running?

Elise's smile had drooped at the edges. Bly grabbed her and pulled her into another hug as if that was her answer, and after a moment, Elise squeezed her in return.

Until Benedict cleared his throat, and Elise pulled back, turning to face him.

"My dear," Benedict said. "We have a life elsewhere. A good one, I might add."

"*You* have a life," Elise said. Her voice was sharp. "I have a room."

Benedict looked as if he'd been slapped. He swallowed, and for some reason he looked at Bly. This was the moment she'd told him he'd need to face. What was he willing to do for her sister?

Elise held up her hands, staring at the black webbed across them. "I can turn. Vampires don't even have to drink blood here. I can live here forever and be part of something . . . peaceful."

"I . . ." Benedict's mouth opened and closed. "I thought you loved being with me. At home."

"It's *your* home," she said. "I'm just a fixture. What happens when you get tired of me and throw me out? Then what? The death curse will finally take me, and you'll move on with the next phase of your immortal life. Love should be limitless, but I have a ticking clock, and you like that."

"I do not." Benedict's voice was solemn. "But I do like the life that I have. This"—he waved a hand around—"this isn't me." He chuckled as if trying to throw his charm up like a shield. "Can you honestly imagine me here?"

"Yes," Elise said. The word was soft and heartbroken. "I've *been* imagining it." She spun and ran.

Emerson took a step after her and then stopped, turning to Benedict—the vampire who should have been the one to chase her.

Benedict moved as if he would follow but then he paused, hanging his head for a moment before looking up at his sister.

"Let her go," Jade said.

He looked at Bly.

"Go after her," she said. Not because she thought Benedict was the right choice for Elise, but because Elise clearly wanted him to choose her, and Bly would help her sister's dreams come true if she could.

Benedict stared down at his feet for a long moment, and then he left. Bly didn't know if he went after her or not.

TWENTY-FOUR

Bly sat cross-legged on the rocks that jutted out over the water. She wondered what it would feel like to be submerged, to have the magic ripple through your body and decide for you: witch or vampire? Or human. She was a human girl full of human mistakes. The magic would deem her unworthy. She'd crawl out with nothing.

Picking up a pebble, she tossed it in the water, making it ripple with color.

She needed to stop thinking like that. There was power in human blood, but the vampires and witches had used their physical and magical strength to push the humans into poverty long ago. Never having enough made it impossible to remember the power that existed within them.

But she felt it when Kerrigan fed from her. He wasn't taking with his power, she was giving with hers. She had what he needed, not the other way around. Humans had power.

They had been told they didn't for so long that they'd forgotten how to wield it. Things were different here where everyone acknowledged their equal parts in existing fully.

This place felt like a dream. That was why she couldn't shake her desire to run—she'd grown too wary of such fantasies.

Everything she'd dreamed had turned bad.

She'd always planned to run away, though, so why was she looking back?

A twig snapped behind her. She jumped. It wasn't Kerrigan. His steps were too light. She looked over her shoulder, expecting Samuel to be there. Nobody had seen him or the other witch guard since he'd almost killed her, and she'd been wondering if he might try to finish the job. She probably should not have come out here alone.

But it was Nova's shadow that fell over her. "So you're free."

Bly's hand pressed to the tender part of her neck. "Am I?" In some ways, she was. The looming threat of death around her neck was gone. She had Elise. A best friend. A road toward healing with Kerrigan.

She still had her guilt, though. It wasn't as easily erased as she'd thought.

Nova was the embodiment of it. Bly's guilt holding an ax, coming to collect its due. For some reason, her heart did not pulse with fear. Maybe it was the beauty of this place, tricking her into thinking nothing bad would happen. Or it was resignation. She'd been running for too long, fighting too hard.

Nova would never stop chasing.

The only option was to accept her fate or keep running.

Her body was tired. She had everything except peace. She had to have this confrontation if she ever wanted to find it. She just had to hope she came out of it alive, even if it seemed unlikely. She would not kill Nova if it came to a fight. She would not have more blood on her hands.

Nova stepped closer but looked past Bly at the water. Bly followed her stare. A school of pink minnows shimmered just underneath the surface.

"You have your sister, your lover, his brother. Somehow you got everyone back while I lost the one person I had."

Bly turned back around, shifting her body so she faced the other girl. "You have more than Vincent." Nova had surely given her winnings to her family back home, but she was here, obsessed with Bly. "You lost him, but your family lost both of you, didn't they?"

"Don't talk about my family." Nova pulled her ax free of her belt.

"They're probably grieving you as much as him. You could stop that."

Nova screamed, the sound wounded and feral, as she lunged, bringing the ax down so quickly that all Bly had time to do was lift her arms.

But the blade didn't bite her. It clanged into the stone beside her, cutting a deep gouge in the smooth surface.

Nova panted. She'd fallen to her knees, her eyes wide and wild until they turned vacant for a moment.

"Nova," Bly said.

Nova didn't answer. She needed her family. She needed Vincent's voice calling her back to herself, but Bly couldn't give her that.

"I'll help you get home," Bly said.

Nova blinked. Tears trailed down her face. "Why would you do that? Everything you love is here," she said bitterly.

"I owe you," Bly said.

Nova gave her a hard look. "Then enter the Games with me. Bring my brother back."

Bly blanched. Neither of them had known what resurrection would cost. Two lives for one. The magic was not fair. Even when Bly had been willing to hand over a vampire, it hadn't been right. She'd justified it by telling herself she was playing by their rules.

"You can't mean that," Bly finally said. For a second, the memory burned bright and vivid: the blood that erupted from Vincent's throat; the witch who didn't fight the blade that stole her life because she'd been taught her life wasn't one worth living; Kerrigan falling to his knees as a blade was buried in his brother's neck. All that pain because Bly had thought it was okay, *righteous,* even, to play a game that dealt in death if it won the life she'd wanted.

She'd regretted it instantly.

"I yelled for it to stop," Bly said. "Once I understood what was happening, I tried to stop it. I didn't trade your brother for my sister."

Nova seemed to deflate in front of her.

Bly was watching another dream ruined. They both knew the cost of resurrection wasn't worth it.

"You should've left me dead," Nova whispered.

"Vincent wouldn't have wanted that. He fought for you."

"It's my fault he died. He didn't want both prizes. If I'd walked away like he'd wanted to, then I never would've died. He never would've fought you and lost. I have to live with that now. You should've left me dead," she sobbed.

"He fought so you could get home. Nova, you *need* to go *home*."

Nova said nothing. Bly thought she might've drifted off again, and she said her name, but Nova just stood without looking at her and walked away. Bly knew the guilt she was feeling. She'd been carrying it in her bones for so long it was a familiar enemy. She couldn't tell Nova how to defeat it, though. Bly suspected there was no easy way, only battles that would be fought again and again.

◆　◆　◆

Bly lingered at the water for the afternoon, trying to let her heart melt into this place the way her sister so clearly had. She'd let herself turn to ice after the Games when her hope of finding Elise had become a tiny flicker compared to the flame that had propelled her before. Finding her sister hadn't ignited her again the way she'd hoped. It was hard to restart a fire when most of your branches were already charred.

Now she was a block of winter in this eternal spring. Even though Kerrigan's lips on her in that snowstorm had begun to thaw her, and each time he touched her, a little more ice melted away under his fingers, she still wasn't who she'd been before. She wanted to be that girl again, the one who wanted a simple life, gathering the food she ate and watching the sunset in the evenings with the person she loved.

She feared even Kerrigan's touch couldn't get her back to that place.

Elise wanted to stay though. Her sister fit so perfectly into the dream Bly once had, a dream that she'd thought she had to leave Elise to achieve. Yet Bly had a sinking feeling that it was *she* who didn't fit anymore.

She wanted to run back to her broken world because she had become a broken girl.

She sensed Kerrigan behind her before she heard him.

"You found me," she said.

"Were you hiding?" His voice held a joking lilt, but he couldn't mask his worry.

"Not from you." She'd never hide from him.

"Walk with me?" He held a hand down toward her. She didn't hesitate. Despite his cool touch, slipping her hand into his warmed her, thawing her just a little bit more as he pulled her to her feet.

She let her vision blur as they walked, focusing entirely on the way his hand enclosed hers. She may have felt at odds with the beauty of this place, but she felt at home with him. He knew the darkest parts of her, the lines she was capable of crossing, and she knew the same of him. Home was a place where your faults were known and forgiven, and you didn't have to hide.

She'd always feel like she was hiding here.

"I thought you'd be happy to stay, but you're not." Kerrigan said.

"I don't belong here." She wore no shoes, and a pebble occasionally dug into the soft pads of her feet, but she welcomed it. The discomfort felt real.

"This place is vibrant and full of life and kindness—if anyone belongs here, it's you."

Bly laughed, the sound harsh and pained. "Maybe before."

"You're still that person. You still deserve this."

She gave him a skeptical look. "You didn't even know me then." He'd only seen a glimpse of the hope-filled, dreaming girl she'd been. Now she was the girl who'd handed over his brother to die, who'd gotten Vincent killed. She was a girl made of fangs and blood even if she was still human.

He chuckled, the sound light and free as if *he* belonged here. "I'm not saying that you're not also ruthless and hard and wounded." He squeezed her hand. "We both are, but we're also still who we were. Those parts of us got buried, not erased. You're the one who showed me that that night in the hammock under the stars."

She blew out a soft breath. "Do you want to stay?"

"I want to be with you, and I think you could be happy here. We both could if we let ourselves."

Bly stopped walking, finally taking in their surroundings—the flower-laden trees, the lily pads floating in the glistening water, the soft chirps of birds in chorus with the throaty frogs.

"I'm afraid of waking up."

She blinked slowly, giving everything a chance to disappear, for the dream to fade against the harshness of reality, and then she blinked again before staring up into Kerrigan's eyes, giving him a chance to disappear as well.

That was her truest fear—that Kerrigan would grow tired of this place and her and the simple life . . . or she would.

She closed her eyes for a longer moment, and he let go of her. Startled at the loss, she opened her eyes again, but he was only moving his hand up to brush her face.

"I'm still here," he said, laying his other hand against her chest as if he could read the fear throbbing in her heart.

One thumb gently traced the arch of her cheekbone while the other traced her collarbone.

"What if we stayed?" His stare was so intense it seemed like another question: Would she stay *with him*? Had they done it—found a world where the past would remain behind them and they could wake up each day in a peaceful present?

They were standing with magic pooled at their feet and flowers blooming around them that ice never touched. If it were possible anywhere, then it was here where magic and hearts were free.

What if the place wasn't the problem, though? What if it was her? She'd find a way to want too much and make the wrong choice, and it'd be even harder to keep going if the world that crashed down around her was the one she'd always imagined: one with her sister happy and alive, with magic she could touch, with a person who loved her. Having everything meant the inevitability of losing it.

Kerrigan gripped her chin, as if he could sense her thoughts and wanted to steady her. "Dream with me, Bly," he whispered. "Nothing can come between us here. There are no hard choices."

He leaned down, his lips hovering above hers.

He was wrong, though. Hard choices could hide in lovely things. Kerrigan was a walking reminder of that.

But she desperately wanted him to be right. She wanted to be that girl again who dreamed without consequences, and someone was finally telling her to do it instead of telling her it was impossible.

She pushed her lips into his and felt him smile against her before melting into the kiss.

Her fingers dug into his waist as she parted her mouth for him, and he for her. Her tongue flicked past his lips, and she ran it across his fangs, drawing blood. He groaned as the taste bloomed in their mouths and walked her backward into the trunk of one of the flowering trees that lined the lake. Soft pink petals rained upon them, and they pulled back just long enough to smile at each other, their lips a harsh red against the pastel wonderland around them.

Did they look like villains in someone else's soft and whimsical story with blood on their lips and pasts that were far from beautiful?

When he kissed her again, she didn't care. The blood didn't taste of violence and horror. It was as sweet as the blossoms that hung around them.

Kerrigan's body pinned her against the tree, and she welcomed the weight of it. She wanted to be held down. She wanted him to trap her here in this world and demand that she stay with him. She was tired of making choices when she constantly made the wrong one.

His fingers left her waist to stroke down both sides of her neck, trailing over her shoulders and down her arms where he closed them around each of her wrists just tight enough so that she could feel her pulse raging against his fingers. He lifted one of her hands up between them. His nose nuzzled the soft skin of her wrist, and then he planted a kiss there and another one, letting his lips wander to her elbow and back again.

She quivered against him, waiting.

"May I?" His lips brushed against her wrist once more as he asked the question her body was already giving an answer to as she arched against him.

"Yes." The word was hardly more than a gasp.

His fangs were always gentle and swift, but his tongue that followed was always teasing and languid. He kept his eyes open, meeting hers, as he drank with her wrist held between them, their bodies still pressed tight, her mouth open and hungry as she watched. His other hand wandered until she became nothing but a pulse of sensations.

He was usually the one to stop first. She was pretty sure that she would let him drain her dry in a haze of lust if he didn't, but this time she broke the spell.

"Wait." The word sounded strangled as if it resented being spoken.

He pulled back from her wrist, and his hand left her body. He tried to step back, but she reached out to hold him to her.

His expression was strained. "I'm sorry," he said. "It's too much—after the way I treated you." He swallowed. "I'm going too fast." He tried to leave her again. Refusing to let him run, she shook her head.

"It's not that." She let out a soft laugh, watching some of the tension melt from his body, even though his worried eyes still darted over her as if trying to read the first sign that she didn't want him.

"I want you to take my neck." Her cheeks heated as if she were embarrassed by her own desires. She was trying not to be. She was no longer the girl who cringed at the thought of a needle puncturing her arm. Bloodletting had become something she craved—something that made her pulse pound faster from desire instead of fear.

Kerrigan's eyes had turned a solid black at her words. He'd

bitten her wrist plenty of times since the snowstorm, but never her neck. She wondered if the memory of Borden's fangs ripping through her flesh haunted him as much as her, and now the memory of the choker drawing blood. She wanted to leave as much of her past behind her as she could, not walk around wearing those memories around her throat like another cursed choker she'd never be free from.

"Please," she said. Her voice broke on the word.

His free hand reached out again and settled against her chest, his fingers gently cupping the base of her neck.

"I want to give you everything you want. Are you sure?"

In answer, she let go of his hand, leaving it to rest against the bark above her head. She reached out and cupped his face, bringing it down to her as she tilted her chin to the side. His lips brushed her throat, resting softly against her skin for a moment before they moved, tenderly kissing her until her chest and neck were flushed from wanting. She held his face tightly in her hands to keep him from running and partly to remind herself that it was him.

His fangs just barely grazed her skin, and her thumbs trailed across the sharp angle of his cheekbones in response.

When his fangs broke the skin, he pulled back so that only his breath touched her neck, waiting for her response. She threaded her fingers into his hair and pulled him closer. The act was a culmination of what she'd been trying to do all this time—bring him back to her, and she had. His tongue traced the trickle of blood back up the column of her throat to the source.

His lips clung to her neck as one hand braced himself on the tree trunk above her head and his other hand gripped her hip.

She had no past, no thoughts, there was only a giving and

taking that went both ways. Kerrigan craved blood, and she craved the rush of power that came from sustaining him.

Her heart beat wildly. Freely.

When he pulled back, she tried to cling to him, and he chuckled, the sound rumbling against her and sending hungry wanting through her body that made her wonder who the vampire between them really was.

"If I take much more, you're going to faint," he said.

"Happily," she murmured against his chest.

"I really prefer you conscious."

"Fine." She pouted.

He stared down at her, his expression so vibrant and alive that it reminded her of the pool of magic at her back.

"So you'll stay?" he asked.

"As long as we can still do this in secret. Don't start drinking too much of that water."

He gave her a wolfish grin. "I can promise that."

"Then yes . . ." She held the words on her tongue, afraid to release them, as if speaking her hopes for any future out loud would surely bring a curse, but this wasn't a place for curses. "I'll stay," she said.

"Forever?" Kerrigan raised his brows.

"Do you mean . . . ?" He'd asked her once to become like him. Before it had been an impossible request, a foolish hope in both their hearts, but now it almost felt . . . earned.

And here there were no consequences, no queens demanding sacrifices to prove your worth. No Games.

Just asking and receiving.

She nodded. She wanted him, but she also wanted to be like

him: fast and strong. Being a vampire would amplify her human strengths.

He gave her a kiss of soft lips and grazing fangs. "We should wait until we're a little more settled," he said as he pulled back.

She remembered how ill Emerson had been when he transitioned. She wasn't looking forward to that particular part.

She had one other concern too. "Do vampires . . . drink each other's blood?"

Kerrigan cocked an eyebrow, a wicked grin spreading across his face. "They do. Not for nourishment, but for . . . fun."

"Good," she mumbled, cheeks heating as she looked at her feet.

He reached out and ran a thumb over her chin as he lifted her face to look at him. "You don't ever need to be embarrassed about telling me what you want, Bly."

She didn't even try to stop the grin that spread across her face.

Grabbing her hand, he tugged her after him. "Should we go tell your sister? I don't know if she'll convince Benedict or not, but if anyone can, I gather it'd be her. I've never seen him quite so enamored." He looked both directions. They were about halfway around the backside of the lake where they didn't belong. "Should we go back the way we came or continue around?"

"I like exploring," Bly said. She wove her fingers in between his, linking their hands together in a way that felt more permanent even though she knew that was silly.

As they wound their way around the edge of the water, she let herself feel the beauty for the first time. She'd been holding it at arm's length, but now her fingers brushed petals dripping from the trees as she passed, the silky softness a featherlight kiss against her skin. Grass tickled her ankles. A mixture of heady florals overwhelmed each breath of air, and she loved it.

She let it all wrap around her like a bandage, as if it could heal her if she let it.

And then something bit into her palms and scratched across her cheek. She pulled back.

"What happened?" Kerrigan lifted her arm to inspect the long, thin scratches, looking around them for a threat and finding nothing.

"I don't know," Bly said, but then she lifted her hand again toward the empty air in front of her and was bit once more. She pulled back and lifted her finger. A tiny drop of blood pooled at the tip of it. "Do you still have the spell to end invisibility?" she asked.

Kerrigan pulled open his vest without question and removed the tiny vial of fine white powder. All of them had decided when they arrived to keep their spells and weapons on them anytime they left their compound.

She sprinkled it into her hand and blew it into the air as she cast the spell. A tangle of blackberry bushes appeared before them.

"Why would you hide these?" Bly found a gap in the bramble and stepped inside as she continued to cast the spell, revealing more brush and a sliver of trail winding between the branches.

Her steps slowed, and she came to a stop. "We should go back the other way." She'd just begun to let herself sink into this place. She knew somehow that if she kept walking into these thorns, they'd rip the dream apart.

"We have to see," Kerrigan said, his voice as bleak as her thoughts.

Eventually they reached a tiny patch of bare dirt next to the water that was half hidden behind another tangle of brush and berries. Bly stepped into the clearing, her foot landing on something hard and invisible. Her stomach churned with unease. Her fingers trembled as she emptied the last of the spell into her palm and blew the dust into the clearing.

She gagged. Her foot was on an arm, bent at an odd angle and attached to a dead girl who lay face down in the dirt. She wore the solid black clothing of Bianca's group. "Is this . . ."

"Bly," Kerrigan said.

She looked up.

The spell had revealed a thick coat of white scattered across the ground, and at first, that familiar discomfort at the sight of mushrooms tightened Bly's throat before her mind registered what she was actually seeing. Not mushrooms—*bones*. Broken and strewn, some tangled in the branches. A skull had risen off the ground, caught in the vines, red berries dangling in the eye sockets.

Across the small patch of dirt, two more people lay sprawled next to the water's edge. The last witch guard stared straight up at the perfect clear sky, her lake blue eyes open and murky. Blood splattered her face, mixing with her freckles. The other person was face down, but Samuel's green vest was unmistakable.

Kerrigan moved to him, kneeling on a crushed rib cage before pulling his head up by the hair. "His throat's been cut." He let go. Samuel's head dropped, jerking the body in a way that made bile rise into Bly's throat.

Kerrigan turned toward the water. He called for her to come.

Her ears buzzed. She couldn't hear the frogs and the birds and imagined them dead too, bellies up and wings shattered. Death crept in, turning her world into a nightmare once more.

"Bly." Her attention snapped back to Kerrigan. She may have been in a nightmare, but he was here too.

He was a dream that wouldn't fade no matter how dark the world got around them. The thought was enough to let her breathe again. His expression was worried, and he started to rise to his feet to get to her, but she went to him first, trying desperately not to step on the bones with her bare feet.

He pointed. Blood no longer dripped from Samuel's neck, but a trail of it remained on the slanted rock under his chest that led to the water below. His blood was still bright against the rock, but there were other trails that had darkened to burgundy or a sickening brown.

Many had bled here.

Kerrigan stepped onto the rock, scooting down toward the water. Pulling a dagger from his belt, he sliced his palm and held it out. The water bubbled and shimmered with each drop of his blood. "They're feeding it," he said.

His face was grim as he climbed back up. He took Bly's hand, ignoring the fact that his was still bleeding. The warmth of his blood jolted her.

She blinked.

The reality was worse than she'd feared.

They stole blood the same as everyone else.

She stumbled back, losing her grip on Kerrigan's hand and falling. Bones crushed beneath her, and she rolled, scrambling on her hands and knees until she was out of the brambles, panting in the soft grass.

Kerrigan crouched beside her, pulling her to her knees as he took her bloodied hands in his. She'd cut them on the bones of the dead.

He pulled her to her feet. "Can you walk?"

She nodded even though she didn't move for a moment.

"I started to believe," she said.

Kerrigan's eyes held an infinite sorrow, the same one that welled in her now. They were both always believing that something could be better, only to find that nothing had changed no matter how hard you fought or how far you ran. Someone was always being sacrificed for others to thrive.

Even though her hope had waned to almost nothing before, this was the first time it had truly abandoned her. Her body grew heavy with despair. She was free. The witches had no hold on her. The queens didn't either, but there was no lovely place to find refuge.

"We have to go," Kerrigan said.

That was enough to get her to move. Whatever she felt, however much she wanted to give up, she had to get Elise out of here.

✦ ✦ ✦

Not running at top speed through the town was one of the hardest things Bly had ever done. In some ways, the place had always reminded her of Havenwhile, but the first time Bly had been in the witches' city, she'd already known the rotten heart of it and so did the witches who called it home. This place was different. While the perfectness of the lake had always made her wary, she'd only ever seen the surface—the shiny colorful veneer of fruit dangling on lush green branches, but now she'd found the wormhole.

The pinprick of truth gave way to the spoiled insides.

Each time a townsperson turned a smile in their direction, she searched the sharp corners of it for a bite. Did they know? Did they really live a peaceful life that they thought was bloodless, or did they only care about what was on the surface and not the lives that paid for it? This was just like her world. Worse—her world made no secret of the blood that fueled it. At least it was honest.

She couldn't stop herself from running the last few feet to the entrance of the compound. "We have to go." Her words were rushed and breathless. Nobody was there except for Demelza and Nova. Demelza gave Bly a grim nod, pulling herself to her feet without hesitation or asking for an explanation.

"Go?" Elise's voice was barely more than a whisper.

Bly turned to her, surprised to see Emerson at her side, his hand gently cupping Elise's elbow. A sheen of sweat glistened on Elise's brow. Bly hurried toward her, taking her hand in hers. "What happened?" she asked. "Did they try to kill you?"

Elise's brow furrowed. "Kill me? He saved me."

Bly shook her head, confused, and then she saw it. The pulse of gray around her sister's pupils, slowly eating away at her fawn-brown eyes. The hand Bly held was cold and clammy, but without a trace of the crawling black lines of the death curse.

"He did it," Bly breathed. "Benedict actually turned you." The person whom Elise had given her heart to truly loved her back. Bly had underestimated him. She had a brief moment of relief before her chest tightened. That meant Benedict had agreed to stay because there was no returning to Vagaris with a newly made vampire who had not been sanctioned by the queens. Not when they'd already pushed past the limits of their goodwill.

Yet they couldn't stay.

"I still can't believe he did it," Bly said. She couldn't quite bear the thought of telling Elise the horrible position that put her in now.

"I didn't," Benedict said.

Bly turned. The others had joined them, probably hearing the sound of their voices.

"I didn't," Benedict said again. His voice held no hint of his usual charm or sarcasm.

Jade scowled from her position at Benedict's right shoulder. Donovan's expression was grim.

Tears trickled down Elise's face.

Benedict wasn't looking at her. His stare was fixed on Emerson's steady hand on her elbow.

"You?" Bly asked. She turned to her best friend, the one she knew would always come through and be that steady hand that held you through the worst; the one who'd let himself get death cursed to save a girl he'd quietly loved for years. It didn't surprise Bly one bit. It felt right.

Emerson nodded. "She asked, and I said yes." His voice was firm, but it softened as he added, "Of course I said yes."

"I wanted to stay," Elise said, her voice barely a whisper. She looked at Benedict even if she didn't quite meet his eyes.

Benedict finally tore his focus away from where Emerson supported Elise.

"I was going to," he said. "I was always going to say yes to you." He swallowed. "I just needed a moment."

Bly never thought that she would feel sorry for the vampire, but his face had twisted into something wretched—a vampire who'd thought he was beyond the reach of human pain realizing that he was not.

Elise let out tiny, hiccupping sobs.

Emerson stood steadily at her side. Bly ached for him, too. He was still there, giving Elise exactly what she needed no matter who she decided to love, just as he'd promised.

Bly's heart had started to feel as torn as her sister's clearly was. But Elise's choice would have to wait.

"We have to go," Bly said.

"What?" Elise's hiccupping stopped. She pulled her hand away from Bly's as if afraid Bly would drag her out of there.

Bly would if she had to.

"Samuel's dead," Bly said, glancing at Demelza for a moment. Demelza's expression barely flickered. "So are others. They're bleeding people into the water. Kerrigan and I found their killing ground hidden across the lake where they told us not to go. They're lying about not needing blood here."

Elise shook her head like she refused to believe it.

"Well, well," Jade said. "I like these annoying people a little bit better now that I know they have some bite to them."

"I guess this means we should leave." Donovan sighed. "Seems newcomers are first up for sacrifice." An odd expression crossed his face as he glanced at Jade.

She met his look, and her snarky attitude from a moment before faded. When she looked away from him, her face was drawn.

Bly could never have pictured Donovan here, using his vampire strength to help humans build their houses or haul firewood, but his expression had turned to regret, as if he'd let himself imagine a life here too.

Elise stepped back. "And go where?" She looked at all of them before settling her gaze on Benedict. "The queens will kill me and Emerson if we go back. We'd have to live in the woods . . . How long before a coven or a band of banished finds us?"

Elise was right. Their options were already bleak, made worse by the fact that she had been turned illegally.

Benedict looked between the girl he loved and the vampire who loved her enough to turn her without hesitation, who'd made the offer even before this place had appeared to be a safe haven. "I'll say I turned you," he said. "I bring the queens more money to the city than any other royal. I've never had a transgression that put me on their bad side before you dragged me into this." He shot Kerrigan a glare. "They'll show me leniency. Especially if I offer to come back here and retrieve more of their precious roots."

"You'd do that?" Elise whispered.

"Only for you," he said.

"Bianca would take us in with her group," Kerrigan said. "We still don't have to go back. We can forget about the roots."

"I wonder what the turnover rate is for vampires living in the woods," Benedict said dryly. "You saw how ruthlessly they fought, how easily they overtook us. I won't have her living like that." His hands clenched into fists.

Bly turned to Elise. "What do *you* want?"

Her sister's eyes still watered. Bly understood it was an impossible question to answer when you were standing on the remnants of a dream that had felt too real.

"Vagaris," Elise whispered, falling back on the life she'd had before. She'd clearly always liked the vampire city. She'd planned to run away to it once. But it had become her gilded cage when she'd been death cursed.

Bly nodded. "Then we go back. We give the roots to the queens."

"My mother won't like that," Demelza said. "Even though I set you free of the spell around your neck, she'll hunt you for not fulfilling your deal."

"She won't reach us in Vagaris," Donovan said, but his face held concern. Bly suspected it was for Demelza.

Demelza would have to deal with her mother. She'd survive, at least. The vampires would be safe. The queens would be so happy with the roots that they'd probably be forgiving, even with the transgression of turning Elise.

But Bly was still human.

Humans didn't live freely in Vagaris. They worked there.

She'd have to be a bleeder again, and even though Kerrigan would hire her, she'd never feel like his partner in that position, no matter how much he affirmed her, and Kerrigan would never be able to turn her without the queens' permission. Unlike Benedict, he'd betrayed them too many times.

The rebels were an option, but they relied on their ability to still slink through their world unnoticed and frequently still entered the cities. Bly and Kerrigan would only put a larger target on the group's back if they betrayed the rulers on both sides.

Their life together would be short and sad.

She didn't want to look at him, but she could feel his stare on her back. She turned, glancing over her shoulder. He knew it as much as her. The bleak expression on his face almost brought her to her knees, but they would both do what was best for their siblings. She gave him a tiny nod, and he returned it. A doomed understanding.

"We leave as soon as it's dark," Kerrigan said, his voice strong without a trace of sadness or weakness. He'd fallen back into his role as commander.

Bly took Elise from Emerson's hold, pulling her sister away from the two vampires who loved her. She needed to gather her strength, not spend it fretting about the two of them.

And Bly needed to make sure Elise lived long enough to make as many bad choices as she wanted to in the future.

TWENTY-FIVE

THEY ALL MET AT THE LAKE AT SUNDOWN, each of them leaving at a different time during the day, taking as little as possible with them to not draw suspicion. They'd been carrying rucksacks to and fro and working into the dark gathering roots for some time now. It wouldn't appear unusual.

Elise was the final one to arrive, with Emerson at her side. Bly wondered if she'd taken her time because the place had a hold on her. Even though Bly had experienced her dreams being broken, she'd never really felt like she'd found a home in one.

Except yesterday when Kerrigan had asked her to stay, but she'd only gotten to dip her toe into what that life might look like before it evaporated beneath her feet.

Elise wobbled, almost slipping on a rock. Emerson caught her, but Benedict lunged for her too, pausing with his arm out-stretched. He pulled it back slowly. "Shall we go?" he said coolly. "I could use a warm drink right about now. I'm sick of this magic water and stale blood from flasks."

Elise managed to muster a glare for him.

He shrugged, but he gave her a smile and a wink too as if he just couldn't help himself.

"I think we'll move faster if I carry you," Emerson said to Elise.

"I want to walk." There was a grim set to her lips.

Emerson shot Benedict a pleading look, and the other vampire moved instantly to Elise's side, supporting her other arm.

She glanced between the two of them.

Bly's heart hurt for her. Bly'd never really been in love with two people before, even though she'd thought she loved Emerson while she was truly falling for Kerrigan. What Elise had with both of them seemed real.

"Let's go," Kerrigan said. He led the way around the side of the lake where the houses stopped, and they skirted around the edge of the village and up the steep hill that Emerson and Benedict practically had to drag Elise up.

The trees that waited for them were a momentary refuge before they reached the wide-open field.

"We could go around," Donovan said.

Kerrigan looked back at Elise, barely standing already. "Straight is faster. I'll go first, and you follow if it's fine."

Kerrigan stepped into the field, taking steady and unhurried steps, baiting an ambush if there was one. Bly tried to follow him, but Donovan grabbed her arm. "You're with me."

She tried to pull away from him, but he glared down at her. "Don't make me bind you." She stilled, knowing he meant it.

"Here." Demelza's voice startled her. The witch pressed something that felt marble-hard and sharp into her hand.

Bly opened her palm and stared at a gleaming white vampire fang.

"In case things go bad," Demelza said. The tone of her voice said she thought they would.

"I'm beginning to think you like me," Bly said.

Demelza gave her a long look. "I might. You fight relentlessly for everyone around you. I've only ever fought for my mother's attention. I think that's going to change."

"You want to be more like me?"

Demelza grimaced. "I wouldn't go that far."

Kerrigan had turned back to them. He stood halfway across the field and waved a hand. If they had sentries out, then surely they would have stopped him already.

Donovan stepped out of the tree line first, followed by Bly and the rest of them.

"Almost there," Kerrigan said as they reached him. He turned around again. This time, Bly hugged his side.

"Leaving without saying goodbye shows a lack of gratefulness," spoke a voice in the dark. "I guess we shouldn't have been so hospitable."

"You said we were free to take the roots and go." Kerrigan spoke to the dark that wasn't as empty as they'd hoped.

"Did I?" Cornelius appeared in front of them, cocking his head slowly. The warm twinkle in his eye had gone. "I believe I said you could gather the roots and that we all share magic *here*." He nodded to the forest beyond them. "We don't share with the greedy parasites out there who almost erased the pool in the first place."

"You're just as bad as they are." Bly couldn't temper the fury in her voice. "You're murdering people for your vials of magic."

"Ahh," Cornelius said. "You found the sacrifices. Most unfortunate . . ."

"You lied," Bly said.

"I didn't. I did what any good leader does, kept the unsavory bits hidden beneath the comforts that people desire. Once people have everything they need, they don't go looking for how it came to be. The pool was drained, like I said, and with each rain, we prayed that the magic would refill it, but the rain just sunk into the cracks of earth, and it never grew. But we already knew that the magic we had inside us needed blood to flourish, so it made sense that the magic still in the pool would need it as well. We sacrificed a witch, a vampire, and a human one night out of sheer desperation because our little truce was fraying around the edges. We shared blood amongst each other, but it was never enough. We made a sacrifice. A noble sacrifice, and the next day that small puddle of water had tripled in size, and we knew the answer."

Bly's stomach twisted. She wondered if there was any part of this world that wasn't built on blood and the sacrifice of a few for what people called the greater good. "Those first three people— did they volunteer?"

Perhaps the answer didn't matter. Clearly Samuel hadn't volunteered, but if their world had started with something selfless, then maybe it could be saved.

"To die?" Cornelius laughed. "Of course not—what a fanciful notion. Nobody sacrifices themself for the greater good. Only fools, and there's not enough people like that to keep the world running."

"So your people are okay with you killing them every once in a while."

"We don't kill our own. There are plenty of outcasts from your cities in the forest to meet our needs. The magic calls people here for us. But those who find us always have a chance to join, and we wouldn't have killed you had you decided to stay, but here you are. Leaving." The last word was a condemnation.

"You killed my cousin," Demelza said. "And the other witch."

"We caught them trying to sneak away with a bag full of roots." Cornelius raised his eyebrows. "I guess you didn't know about that. We did wonder if you were in on it, which is why we started watching you."

None of them were surprised that Samuel had tried to leave without them.

"I believe that's enough talking," Cornelius said. "The magic is always hungry."

Spells lit the night around them as tiny orbs of soft yellow light dotted the sky above the meadow. For the briefest moment, a sense of wonder filled her, but the light made visible the horror in the field. Just like before, the townspeople stood in bright colors that had become garish against the night. The curling smiles they'd once welcomed them with were gone, and in their hands, they held scythes on long poles, the blades sinister frowns flashing in the light.

Even the older children were there, standing in the back. They held no blades, though; in their hands were buckets.

For any blood spilled. They didn't want to waste that precious commodity.

Bile rose in the back of Bly's throat.

They were grossly outnumbered.

"Bianca," Bly whispered. Their only hope was that the banished were in the woods, watching, but they could have grown tired of waiting and left.

Kerrigan looked down at her. "I love you," he said.

She'd never imagined those words on his lips sounding so bleak. She tried to say them back, but her throat constricted with sorrow at the thought of it being the first and last time she said them.

His fingertips brushed hers like a kiss. Or a goodbye.

He understood what she couldn't bring herself to say.

She turned back to her sister. Elise's eyes were wide with fear, but there were no tears in them. The set of her mouth was hard, and she looked at Bly with more determination and hope than Bly allowed herself to feel.

Something surged in her at the sight of Elise. They wouldn't go down without a fight.

After spelling herself with the fang, Bly pulled her dagger, widening her stance just the way Kerrigan had taught her. Her limbs were light and strong. Her blood raced with magic as if she could fight her way through an army with ease. Donovan came up on the other side of her, his sword ready.

"Feed it," Cornelius said.

The townspeople swarmed like wasps on a carcass. All of them moved with a vampire's speed. If they were sacrificing the banished that they found in the woods, then why wouldn't they take the teeth and spell them with their precious water? Bly's spell gave her no real advantage.

Kerrigan immediately swung his sword in a killing arc aimed

at Cornelius's neck. Four different scythes came down, making *X*s in front of their leader. One of his defenders went down as Donovan sliced him at the waist.

The clang of metal against metal made Bly lift her hands to her ears as it reverberated through her skull. The spell had given her vampire hearing, and it felt impossible to get used to. The swoosh of incoming arrows became a roar, and the impact of three of them embedding themselves in Donovan's sword arm thudded with a sickening volume.

Kerrigan roared, cutting down several people as Donovan stumbled back, ripping the arrows from his flesh as he switched his sword to his left hand, swinging wildly in an aimless arc that kept the incoming horde at bay. A woman dressed in glaring yellow darted closer in the wake of one of Donovan's swings, scythe aiming for his torso.

Bly threw her dagger with pure instinct. It sunk into the woman's neck, and red poured down her yellow clothes. Her eyes were wide and staring as she sunk to the ground, and a small cry left Bly's lips as she recognized her. Mary with her easy smiles. Bly retreated as two children no older than twelve appeared at Mary's side, each one gripping an arm and pulling her away with empty buckets dangling from their elbows.

Cornelius didn't let *any* blood go to waste.

He wanted this carnage, and it wasn't just to secure the blood of outsiders.

A placid smile sat on Cornelius's face. He reached for no weapon, and Bly imagined that was part of the image that he projected to his people. Inside, he was a man roiling with violence, but on the outside, he was the smooth surface of the pool that they worshiped. An image that they could aspire to.

A lie.

With her dagger gone, Bly pulled two binding spells from the pocket of her vest.

Another witch charged them. Kerrigan blocked the scythe's swing with his sword, and Bly started to jump forward, binding spell raised, but the curve of the scythe made it slide easily away from Kerrigan's blade.

Metal glided toward her throat.

Kerrigan lurched her back by the collar of her shirt, and the blade glanced by.

And then an arrow found purchase in the witch's neck and then another. He stumbled, slouching to his side as an array of black feathers on the ends of the shafts glimmered with deep purple in the light.

The townspeople's arrows had blue feathers.

"The trees," Cornelius bellowed.

Half the townspeople turned, darting to the edges of the meadow. Arrows pierced them, but with their vampire spells healing them, it took too many perfect shots to bring one down.

A sharp scream sent Bly spinning with no regard for protecting her back. Elise. Her sister had been plucked from between Benedict and Emerson, both of them with arrows in their arms and swords flying.

Elise flailed against a man and a woman who dragged her away into the swarm of color, but her fighting did nothing, especially in her weakened state.

Bly moved toward her mindlessly. She could hear Kerrigan shout her name as metal clanged close to her head. He'd probably just blocked a killing shot.

Emerson had tried to disengage and go after Elise, but three people had pinned him down, and his frantic movements barely kept their blows at bay.

A blade swung at Bly's face, and she ducked, stabbing a spell into someone's leg just as a head hit the ground in front of her. The body she'd spelled, headless now, dropped in a heap beside her. She froze, staring at open dead eyes and a slack mouth.

Another scream from Elise, and Bly ripped herself away from the death in front of her. Her sister had been pulled deeper into the clutches of the townspeople. Emerson was still trapped in a flurry of blades he couldn't seem to free himself from.

Benedict broke from the mass around him, heads rolling at his feet. He sliced through two of the men attacking Emerson as he raced by on his way to Elise. He twisted, dodging and blocking too many blades to count before he reached her.

Emerson followed several paces behind him.

Benedict's sword sailed cleanly through the neck of the woman gripping Elise's arm. Elise had stopped screaming, her face gone slack with horror. Benedict spun around the back of her, sword swinging, cutting through the neck of the man who still held Elise's other arm. His perfect control just stopped his blade from decapitating Elise as well.

Bly still struggled to reach them, Kerrigan and Donovan cutting people down on either side of her, with Jade, Demelza, and Nova somewhere at their backs.

Elise turned on wobbling legs to Benedict.

He reached for her, a comforting smile on his lips even though his face was splattered with the blood he'd spilled to reach her.

He lowered his sword slightly as he stepped toward her, saying something.

"Benedict!" The shout came from Emerson, fighting toward the girl he loved and the other vampire who loved her. "Behind you!"

Benedict had started to turn when the sword burst through the center of his chest. His eyes widened. His hand still reached for Elise, and her fingers found his just as the sword pulled free of him.

Their hands were clasped when the blade stole his head.

A horrible scream ripped through the night, but it wasn't Elise's. It came from Jade.

Benedict's body toppled forward. Elise's hands went out as if trying to catch him, but his body only knocked her backward into Emerson's waiting arms. He dragged her, stumbling, as Bly, Kerrigan, and Donovan finally reached him, forming a defense around his retreat.

Elise had gone limp in Emerson's arms. Her head lolled, and Bly wasn't sure if she was conscious or not.

"Hurry," Bianca called. Bly shifted to look behind them.

Cornelius had disappeared. A pile of townspeople lay scattered in the grass, black arrows rising from their bodies. A bloody path to escape lay before them.

"No!"

Bly's head whipped back around. The yell had come from Donovan.

Jade had burst away from their group, entering the thick of the townspeople in a flurry of blond hair and steel. Standing over Benedict, she took down a slew of them before a long scythe removed her head from her shoulders.

Her body fell next to her brother's.

Donovan roared. He tried to go after her, but Kerrigan threw his arms around him. "Don't leave me!" He yelled the words again and again until Donovan went slack, letting Kerrigan pull him away into the dark and waiting mouth of the forest, leaving the idyllic little town drenched in the blood it craved.

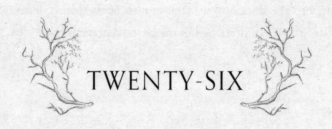

TWENTY-SIX

THEY RAN THROUGH THE NIGHT WITH full vampire speed. Their feet trampling the leaves became a steady sound punctuated with branches snapping as they broke through them without hesitation. Over top of that was the chorus of Elise's wails. Each cry tightened Bly's chest just a little more. If not for the vampire spell she had used, she was certain her sister's grief would've brought Bly to her own knees. Those cries were familiar enemies. Even now, with Elise safe in Emerson's arms, they took her back to the moment when she'd thought Elise had died.

She fought the memory. She couldn't let her phantom grief get in the way of their escape. She pumped her legs harder, savoring their weightlessness despite her heavy chest.

Shadows blurred to her right and left, and she jerked, veering off course so a branch clawed her cheek, leaving behind a stinging scratch. She opened her mouth to give a warning, but the shadows didn't wear deceptively bright colors. They wore black.

Bianca's people.

She had paid Kerrigan back and then some.

Bly let the rhythm of her stride swallow her focus until the spell propelling her broke. Her legs went from featherlight to lead in an instant, and she fell, knees and hands grinding into the dirt as she barely kept herself from face-planting. Her lungs burned as if she'd been drowning.

"Bly?" Kerrigan's hands ran over her back and across her chest, checking for arrows as she gulped for air.

"Her vampire spell wore off," Demelza said. She winced and braced herself against the tree she stood next to, scrunching her face as if her spell had worn off as well. "It can be quite jarring," she ground out.

Even Nova grimaced as the magic left her.

But it wasn't just the rapid change to her body that kept Bly on her knees. She loved how it felt to be a vampire—that strength in her bones that made her feel rooted to the ground even as her legs moved beneath her with the speed that felt like flying. She would've liked a life where everyone she loved was immortal and she could run through the woods with the carefree speed of someone without fear.

Kerrigan hauled her to her feet. "I need to carry you," he said gently, as if he somehow knew that the taste of strength had left her weak in a way she hadn't been before. "They could still be chasing us."

"Let them come," Donovan growled.

Bly reached out a hand and rested it on Donovan's arm. He looked down at it and up at her in surprise.

"I'm sorry," she said. He may not have been crying like Elise, but he was in the same pain. His life had just taught him to no longer be the boy who cried when he lost his parents in the woods but a vampire who buried hurt.

His face caved, a glimmer of what was underneath his hard shell showing for just a moment. He pulled his arm gently away from her. "You're right," he said to Kerrigan. "We need to keep moving."

"I doubt they'll come." Bianca materialized beside them like a shadow coming to life. "They don't know how many of us there are. It'd be reckless to risk it. A place like that doesn't survive in the woods for years without caution."

"You always were the better strategist." Kerrigan pulled Bianca into a tight hug, and she pushed him off her with a laugh that died as Elise wailed again. Her face became solemn. "We should move just to be safe, though. Carry the other human and the witch and get as far as we can before dawn. Then rest."

Kerrigan scooped Bly up against his chest, and her exhausted, quivering limbs melted against the hardness of his muscles. Donovan moved to Demelza, who stood closest to him. "May I?" he asked. To Bly's surprise, the witch didn't hesitate or argue as Donovan lifted her to his chest.

"No," Nova barked as Bianca moved toward her. "I'd rather risk them catching up to me."

"Nova," Bly said. "You need to get home as badly as the rest of us." She thought of the sketch she'd seen once before—that slip of paper filled with beaming faces of children who were happy . . . probably thanks to Nova's and Vincent's efforts to keep them from knowing just how cruel the bite of hunger could be. "You need to get home *more* than the rest of us."

Nova looked as if she wanted to snarl at her, but then her face slackened before her jaw clenched and her eyes hardened. "Fine," she bit out.

They traveled until the sun began to show itself. The soft morning light held no gentleness. All it brought was the ability to see the pain etched on each other's faces.

The moment Kerrigan set Bly on her feet, she staggered toward her sister. Elise had already left Emerson's arms and moved toward Bly, crashing into her with a force that made Bly's still-tired legs buckle. Elise clung to her even as they sunk into the bitter snow.

Emerson stepped toward them, and Bly gently shook her head. Elise may have let him carry her out of there, the fresh cocoon of grief keeping her from wandering even deeper down the dark paths that grief had to offer, but when she calmed, she would take those paths the same way that Bly had when she thought Elise had died. She'd retrace every moment and fill each memory with regret that she hadn't done things differently, and even if it wasn't fair, one of those paths would lead to the moment Emerson turned her. She wouldn't have been weak and unable to fight back if he hadn't. The townspeople may not have been able to grab her and yank her away, and then Benedict would still be there.

Each time she retraced her steps and thought of what might've been, the guilt would eat her a little bit more.

It already had its claws in her, and Bly had no idea how to save her sister from a beast that still hunted Bly even now.

"He died for me," Elise sobbed into Bly's shoulder. "I . . . chose to stay with or without him, and he died for me."

Bly held the back of her sister's head, stroking her hair. "You know he wouldn't take it back," she said. "He died for a love that I don't think he ever expected to feel."

She thought of all the gambles she'd taken to win Kerrigan back. She knew even if the collar had choked the life out of her, she wouldn't have traded Kerrigan's forgiveness, nor the feeling of his hands on her body and his lips on hers, nor the way their souls seemed to thrum as one when they were together. She understood what Benedict had died for. She'd come close to doing the same.

"I know he didn't once regret it," Bly said.

Elise sobbed harder.

Bly held her tighter as if the strength of her arms could reach her sister's heart and pull the pieces back together, but there were no easy fixes for that type of damage. Bly understood that.

TWENTY-SEVEN

THE ONLY THING THAT ATTACKED them was their grief. Even though most of the grief did not belong to her, she could feel it like a familiar enemy, tightening its hold on the people she cared for.

On the fourth night of their journey home, she found Donovan sitting with his back against a tree, his knees pulled up and his arms draped over them. His eyes that were always sharp and calculating were dim and distant.

She hesitated as she watched him. She'd already seen Kerrigan talking to him more than once, his arm across Donovan's shoulders, but Bly felt drawn to him in his pain. She didn't look at him and see the villainous brother of the man she loved anymore; she looked at him and saw a hurting friend. She didn't want to stab him; she wanted to take away that pain. And even though she knew she couldn't, she had to try.

He didn't look up as she approached him and slid down to

her knees beside him.

"You know that makes three," she said.

He blinked, his eyes barely focusing on her. "What?"

"When we were escaping, I saved you. That's three times now, so that means *you* have to refer to *me* as your friend. You still owe me a save, though, before I can return the sentiment." She smiled, her voice light.

He blinked at her again, and for a second, she wondered if she'd made a mistake, joking when part of his heart was broken, but he didn't seem the type who'd want condolences.

Finally, he cracked a sharp laugh. "Well, *friend*. We're not home yet."

The brief light in his eyes faded again. She had a feeling he was imagining what home would look like without Benedict and Jade.

"You know," he said softly, "I had decided to stay." He looked up at her. "I knew you and Kerrigan would stay, so I told Jade I wouldn't go back with her. I didn't ask her to stay with me, and she didn't offer. Now she's there forever, and I'm gone." He turned away to stare at nothing again.

She didn't know whether to reach out and touch him or not, but another slender white hand touched his shoulder. Somehow, Bly wasn't surprised to find Demelza there. She gave Bly a little nod. "I think your sister needs you," she said.

Bly rose. She couldn't find any more words to say to Donovan, but she didn't need to. When she turned back to glance over her shoulder, his eyes were focused on Demelza, listening to whatever she was saying, nodding at her words.

She slipped away, scanning the area for her sister. She didn't see her or Emerson. Elise had been mostly silent the last few days with Emerson a shadow that lingered a few steps behind.

She knew her sister needed to talk, but that had to happen on her time. Perhaps it was now.

The faintest whimper drew Bly into the woods.

Elise sat on a fallen tree trunk. She had her hands fisted in Emerson's shirt, but she was pushing him away even as she held him. He looked up and gave Bly a desperate look. What can you do with someone who needs you even though you're a reminder of their trauma?

Bly walked over and took Elise's hands, gently pulling them away from Emerson.

"I've got this," she whispered to him.

He didn't try to stay, but he cast worried glances over his shoulder as he left them.

For a moment, Elise just folded in on herself while Bly waited.

Finally, Elise straightened and spoke as she stared blankly into the woods. "I thought he was too selfish, that he loved his lifestyle more than he loved me, but he *died* for me. He proved me wrong. I should have given him more time to decide. He said he would have chosen me if I'd given him time."

Bly drew a deep breath. "Look at me."

Elise stared at her, blinking back the tears in her eyes.

"He did love you enough to die for you. He didn't love you enough to change for you. Those can both be true. Maybe he really would have changed eventually, but how long were you supposed to wait for him?"

A sob broke from Elise's lips. Bly didn't know if this was helping or not. She'd be eternally grateful for Benedict's sacrifice, but she couldn't let it overshadow his other choices. She couldn't let it become a moment that loomed over Elise for the rest of her life, that made her place him on a pedestal that nobody else could ever come close to.

"The choices you made before he died did not kill him. You loved him, and he loved you, and he knew that the two of you weren't meant to be when he risked his life, Elise. He knew, and yet he chose to come for you anyway. You'll always love him for that, but don't let that love erase everything else."

"You mean Emerson," Elise said, tears streaming down her face.

"I mean the whole rest of your life. Benedict wouldn't want you to let his death become your only focus."

"He probably would, though." She hiccupped as a small smile touched her lips.

Bly smiled in return. "Well, you might be right."

Elise went back to crying, but there was a calmness to it now, a grief that would linger but would still be conquered eventually.

+ ✦ +

The rest of their journey home was a quiet one. The silence was dense with sorrows—both old and new—for people, places, and dreams.

Bianca led them. The banished needed no maps—the entire woods were their home, every tree a shelter against whatever onslaughts the day would bring.

Bly had already spoken privately to Bianca about the possibility of Kerrigan and her joining her group of banished. Bianca had been blunt. Immortality didn't last in the woods where rogue covens were eager for your blood to make their spells and banished vampires were eager to sell you or trade you for human blood.

Bly wasn't eager to live a life where death lurked in every darkened corner of the woods.

A new kind of hurt settled into her chest—the knowledge that the dream she'd once had of finding a safe haven in the woods or a town of people living off the land in harmony had never even been possible. She'd risked everything for a dress to start a life that would've only turned to horror. She'd lost her sister for over a year. And yes, she'd found Kerrigan, and anytime he touched her and their bodies melted together, he became the embodiment of a new dream, but that feeling could not be sustained in their world.

Yet somehow, she stayed on her feet and kept taking one more step. That's what she'd been doing for months now and maybe that would be the sum of her life, and she'd have to learn to face a reality with the only source of happiness being the refuge of Kerrigan's arms.

She was so focused on taking just one more step that for a moment she didn't notice that Bianca had stopped. Bly plowed several feet in front of the group before she turned back around.

"This is where I leave you," Bianca said. "We're just half a day's walk to the Gap, and both Vagaris and Havenwhile guards wander this far out when they're not being lazy." She reached her hand out to Kerrigan, and he clasped her elbow while she clasped his. His expression looked worn, and his mouth parted to speak before Bianca shook her head.

"Don't," she said. "You know I can't come with you, and you shouldn't stay with me." She looked beyond Kerrigan's shoulder at Bly. "Just survive the best way you can, and if you have the chance to cause some chaos along the way, do that too." She winked, breaking away from him.

Astrid came up beside Bianca. "Whatever debt Bianca thought she owed you is paid."

"I owe her. I always have," Kerrigan said.

Bianca shook her head. "We'll always owe each other. We're friends."

Astrid scowled.

Kerrigan nodded as Bianca pulled away from him and shoved Astrid in her shoulder, pushing her into the woods. They didn't look back.

Another vampire approached—Joseph, wearing the tattered remains of his guard uniform.

"Will you tell the queens I'm dead?" he asked, eyes flitting between Kerrigan and Donovan.

Kerrigan nodded. Donovan sighed.

Joseph grinned, giving Bly a small nod before turning and jogging into the woods where one of Bianca's people stood waiting for him, a matching smile on his face.

Kerrigan turned to the rest of them. "We take the roots to the queens then." It wasn't a question, but he waited for them to object.

They all looked to Nova and Demelza. Nova blinked as if she'd just come out of one of her trances, and she looked at each of them, eyes falling on Bly last and holding her stare. "I'm going home," she said, and she walked off into the woods without another word.

Bly wanted to shout something after her, to wish her luck or just to say sorry one more time, but it would be for her, not Nova. The only peace Nova would find was where she was headed.

Demelza's expression was bleak and resigned. "I'm obviously outnumbered."

"Your mother . . . ," Donovan said.

She shrugged. "She might kill me, but probably not right away. Not having an heir makes her look vulnerable, and now that Samuel's gone, she'll forgive me until she doesn't have to anymore." She started to turn away.

"Wait," Bly said. "Why don't we divide the roots? Some for the vampires, some for the witches . . . and some . . . for the rebels."

Demelza had turned back, her eyebrows drawn together in thought.

"It won't work." Kerrigan reached out and squeezed her hand. "All it would do is buy us time until both sides realize the other has them too, and then when they find we gave them to the rebels . . . there will be no safe place for us." His grip on her tightened. She understood his fear, his desire to keep her safe.

He was right about one thing, though: Dividing the roots would accomplish nothing.

If she was going to be reckless, then she wanted to do it with a purpose that went beyond herself. All her life, she'd been dreaming and fighting, but it had always been for what *she* wanted, not what their world needed. She'd longed for a place outside her world where she could live a peaceful, happy life, and the lake had promised that for a moment, only to show her that such a place didn't exist.

If she wanted it, she had to make it.

To make a world like she imagined, she had to change the one she lived in—there was no other perfect place waiting for her.

"We give all the roots to the rebels." Her words were breathless. A wild kind of hope filled her, making her cheeks flush and her heart skitter. She'd lied and told Cornelius that they were giving the roots to the rebels because that had always been the right thing. The noble thing. But what if it wasn't a lie?

"No," Donovan said.

Kerrigan was shaking his head too, but Bly kept going. "If the rebels have the roots, then it could give humans real power."

"Bly," Emerson spoke for the first time. "None of us will be safe. They'll come after the rebels with everything they have. We'll be dead in a week." He glanced at Elise, a pale ghost beside him.

"Elise can't go to Vagaris," Bly reminded him.

Emerson frowned. Benedict had been the one with a plan to bargain for Elise's immortality.

"I'll talk to the queens on her behalf," Kerrigan said. "I'll tell them Benedict turned her."

"No," Bly said. "It's too risky."

"And your plan isn't?" Kerrigan shook his head.

"My plan is the right risk. The one with the highest possibility of changing things."

"Like all of us losing our heads," Donovan growled.

Bly ignored him. She turned to Kerrigan instead.

"Dream with me." She threw his own words at the lake back at him.

He shook his head, and she understood why. When he'd asked her to stay at the lake, she'd hesitated. She'd tried to fly too high and had fallen too far to want to try again, but he'd convinced her it would be okay.

Only for their happiness to last a moment.

But that moment had been glorious, and what happened after hadn't stolen it from her. She could still close her eyes and feel Kerrigan's hands on her face, the earnestness in his expression as he told her it would be all right and that this time would be different. It hadn't been. There was always a time limit.

That's what dreams were supposed to be. Dreams were not things to be lived in. You chased them, savored them when you caught them, mourned them when they slipped away, and then found another to search for.

The thing Bly had done wrong was to dream only for herself.

A revolution was something that every human had imagined at some point, but very few had tried for. But if enough of them dreamed together, if they had a weapon to give them an ounce of power, then they could make it a reality and hang on to it for a little while until they had to try again.

Kerrigan's face was bleak. She was asking him to dream something he'd already tried. He'd led a rebel group before, and it had cost him friends and driven a larger wedge between him and his brother.

"We can do this," she whispered.

He swallowed. Everyone was watching them, but his focus was on her alone. "The risk . . ."

She knew what he meant better than most. After all, she'd chased a dream and lost a sister, but she'd been doing that for herself.

This was different. It had to be.

"We'll be together though," she said. "And we're not alone."

He finally looked away from her, and his eyes landed on Donovan. "Brother," he said.

Donovan groaned. "I know what you're going to say. Haven't you already made this mistake once before?"

"My only mistake was not asking you to join me."

"I never would have. Not then."

"And now?"

His expression darkened. "I prefer to be on the winning side." He hesitated. "But if you're determined to die, I know I can't talk you out of it." He laughed bitterly. "So my only choice is to go down with you."

"I want you to have a choice," Kerrigan said. "I'm not asking you to die with me . . . just fight."

Donovan shook his head. "You're too much of an optimist."

Bly couldn't stop the smile that spread onto her face.

Donovan shot her a glare. "You two were made for each other. Reckless little assholes. I'm coming with you if only to bring an ounce of common sense. Where are these pesky rebels at?"

"Wait," Emerson said. "What good are the roots if you don't know how to spell them? They'll be worthless until one of the rebel witches figures it out, and the queens and Halfryta will both know that. They'll do everything in their power to wipe us out before we even have an advantage."

"I know the spell," Demelza said.

They all turned to her.

"She never taught me, but I learned a lot while I was spying— way more than my mother could ever guess."

"I don't trust you," Kerrigan said.

"Hear her out," Donovan said.

Bly wanted to believe her. She'd been born into power with advantages that few in their world had, and yet she had not found happiness. All she'd done was struggle to keep that power. She'd been willing to change herself from the girl who would help a grieving boy find the body of the girl he loved to a witch willing to betray that same boy to win back her mother's favor.

Her ruthlessness hadn't helped her.

"Why?" Bly asked. Maybe Demelza had found her way back to being the girl who had helped Emerson, but she also wasn't foolish enough to trust her without question.

Demelza lifted her chin. "My mother is a tyrant. She plans to use these roots to gain an upper hand against the vampires to get more power that she does not need, but she also plans to use the spell against witches that question her rule and those she deems too weak for Havenwhile. She hates that there are rogue covens of witches she cast out in the woods who thrive and still use their magic. She'd rather send them out defenseless to die. As humans." She glanced at Bly. "No offense."

"But the daughter of the legendary Halfryta has a bleeding heart?" Donovan said. There wasn't a hint of snideness in the words, only a begrudging respect.

"I have a heart for my people. I've begged my mother to stop banishing witches. I thought if I became ruthless enough to take her place, that I could change things eventually, but all that's happened is that I stopped recognizing myself. I almost became my mother while trying to beat her."

"Yet you traded my brother for her," Kerrigan said.

Demelza grimaced. "I panicked. I thought I still needed her. I worried Samuel would put a knife in my back or simply gather enough support to overthrow me if she had never formally declared me her heir." Her voice went soft. "And she's my mother. She was never gentle, but . . ." Her expression went distant and pained as if a few good memories were a knife in her heart.

"I believe her," Emerson said.

Bly met his eyes and nodded, then turned to Demelza. "How fast can you make the spells?"

She sighed. "Probably not fast enough to save us."

TWENTY-EIGHT

IT TOOK THEM HALF A DAY TO FIND
Hazel and the rebels. Bly and Emerson had been gone too long
to know their new pattern of locations, but they found members
who still lived in the Gap to help them even though they were
rightfully skeptical of the new recruits.

Even Hazel, who believed in working together, had raised her
eyebrows at Bly and Emerson's companions. "You're going to get us
killed," she said, stare moving from the two vampire princes to the
heir of the witches. "Right now, we are only a nuisance that would
be a pain to squash out, but you're making us a bigger problem."

"But what if we became more than a nuisance? What if we
became a snake they didn't dare step on because they might get
bit, and our bite was poison?"

Hazel's eyebrows drew together. "I'm listening."

They explained their plan, but when they were done, Hazel
still shook her head. "We need more numbers," she said. "If we're

going to have a shot at them even pausing long enough to hear us out, then we need the entirety of the Gap to stand with us. We need someone who can convince the humans join us." Hazel's eyes narrowed in on Bly as if waiting for her to give an answer.

Bly looked at Elise. Her sister was strong and brave in a quiet way, and people knew her from working with their mother. Even if she had gray eyes now, people would listen to her.

"Elise . . . ," Bly began. Because when it came to the human world, Elise had always been the one people chose. Their mother had. Their father had. The people would follow her as well.

Hazel shook her head. "Not your sister, Bly. You. The people need a fighter. They need to feel the spark of rebellion that's been repressed for years. They need to see a heart on fire. Someone who believes in impossible odds. That's *you*."

Bly opened her mouth to protest that she wasn't right for the job, that she'd never been the first choice and being back in the Gap only reminded her of that.

But she didn't get a chance to say a single word before Elise took her hand and squeezed it. "I know just where to start."

❖ ◆ ❖

They stood in front of their parents' house. Bly wondered if it felt like a home to Elise still, but Elise's fingers gripped Bly's just as tightly as Bly gripped her back. After all, it wasn't just Bly who Elise had allowed to think that she was dead. She'd left their parents, too.

Bly had never asked her why she'd done that to parents who clearly loved her best.

Turning to Elise, Bly noticed her eyes for the first time—they were fawn brown instead of the oak gray of a vampire. "Your eyes . . ."

Elise looked away. "A glamour. I didn't want to startle them. I'm not planning to stay a vampire."

That news didn't surprise her, though it stung a little, since Bly was hoping to become one eventually, but that was a conversation for a different day. Elise looked more nervous about seeing their parents than Bly.

"They miss you," Bly said.

Elise gave her a sharp look. "Did they miss me or just my skills?"

Bly noted the trace of bitterness in her sister's voice. Bly wasn't the only one who'd been hurt by her parents constantly wanting Elise to work with them. She'd felt undervalued, but perhaps Elise had felt valued only for her usefulness.

"No," Bly said. "They missed *you*. I saw."

Elise's eyes had already gone wet. Elise had practically pulled Bly here, but now it was Bly's turn to be strong. She stepped toward the door and opened it. It was dinnertime, and at first glance, nothing had changed. Her parents sat at opposite sides of the small table in their respective chairs, but the third chair was back—the one they'd gotten rid of when Elise had died since Bly almost never sat at the table for meals.

A tear escaped down Bly's cheek at the sight of it.

It didn't matter if the chair was brought back in hopes that *she'd* come home or that she'd bring *Elise* back home.

It meant that some small part of them had believed in her.

Her mother finally looked up.

"Bly?" Her name came out a choked question, as if her mother didn't believe what she was seeing.

Her father stood up so quickly that his chair clattered behind him. A sob tore through his lips, and it was for Bly. Elise still stood behind the open door, out of sight.

"We thought you were dead," her father mumbled. "We thought . . ." He shook his head.

Her chest swelled. This reaction was for *her*. She just wished that it hadn't taken them thinking she was dead for them to show that they cared about her. Her heart ached with a pain she was certain would never quite go away, but in this moment, it at least felt like a wound that had been bandaged.

"I won," she said. "I won the Games. I brought Elise back."

Her parents' blank stares didn't register her words at first, and Bly turned to Elise, still behind the door. Her sister's expression was startled. Clearly, Elise had never been dead, but Bly was careful to phrase her words in a way that wasn't a lie but would also allow her parents to draw their own conclusions, false or not. This was a small gift that Bly could give her sister. Their parents never had to know that Elise had left them willingly. Elise gave her a grateful nod before Bly tugged her from behind the door and into the room.

The sight of the two of them together seemed to break their parents. Tears pooled in their eyes, and they made no attempt to stop the flow as they came to them, tugging both sisters into their arms, squeezing them with an equal intensity.

When they finally let them go, they led them to the table. Their mother pulled out the third chair for Bly and their father gave Elise his seat while he went to the stove to put food on for them as they talked.

They kept their story of why they'd taken so long to come home again vague, but they told them that after the Games, they'd gotten wrapped up with a rebel group that now had the means to change their world. And now they needed the humans to stand with them.

"Is that really a good idea?" their father asked. "You beat death," he said, looking at Elise before turning to Bly, "and you survived the Games. What if your luck has run out?"

"It wasn't luck," Bly said.

Her father gave her a sharp look. "No. I suppose it wasn't."

Her mother reached out a hand and gripped her arm. "If anyone can convince people to take a stand, it's you, Bly. How can I help?"

◆ ✦ ◆

Their mother took Bly and Elise door-to-door, since most people in their village knew and respected her. Some people laughed at them with fear in their eyes and told them they'd be dead within the week, but others didn't. They wanted to hear how Bly had won the Games. She was a miracle telling them another miracle was still possible, and each time a spark of hope lit in someone's eyes, it grew the flame burning in her own chest.

Pretty soon, word was spreading through the villages without her at all.

Hazel had been right. Bly had been the spark.

◆ ✦ ◆

On the third day, a small boy from the Gap, who couldn't be more than twelve and spent his days shadowing the rebels, burst through the front door of the house they were staying in, which belonged to one of the humans in their group. The boy's eyes were wild and wide. "They're coming," he said, his voice both breathless and frantic.

"Who?" Hazel asked.

"The witches."

The room buzzed with unease. They'd been meeting, debating different strategies, though they thought they'd have at least a little more time to prepare.

"And what exactly were you doing in the woods scouting by yourself?" Hazel raised an eyebrow at the little boy. Despite imminent death marching toward them, Hazel always made time for the small things like a boy who shouldn't be in the woods by himself with armies heading their direction. It was what made her the perfect leader. She saw the big picture, but she didn't forget about every person who composed it—each individual life mattered more to her than any greater good.

Some of the terror slid from the boy's eyes, and he smirked. "I *was* with one of your scouts." His smirk widened to a grin. "I'm just faster than him."

Bly couldn't help but laugh. The boy reminded her of who she'd once been, and who she was trying to be again.

"Well done, then," Hazel said. "Now go home to your parents."

The boy huffed and didn't argue, but Bly had a feeling he wouldn't be listening.

Hazel turned to Bly. "Go see what we have," she said.

Bly moved to the back of the house and scrambled up a ladder, poking her head into a cramped attic space with a single window that looked out onto the muddy street below.

Donovan looked up from where he sat cross-legged on the floor with his arm outstretched over a bowl. Demelza held his wrist as blood dripped slowly from it.

The two had been sequestered since they returned, working together, only stepping out into the light to eat or bring someone else they needed to their workshop. Demelza hadn't said how it was going.

"The witches are coming," Bly relayed.

Demelza's head snapped in her direction. Her already pale face had taken on an ashy hue, and deep purple had bled under her eyes. Fear flickered in her expression.

Donovan broke free of Demelza's grip on him to grab her wrist instead, not caring that his blood was dripping onto her lap now instead of the bowl. She turned to him, and something unspoken seemed to pass between them. When she looked back at Bly, her expression had shifted to resolve. But Bly thought she was resolving not just to fight but to die. She didn't really think they had a chance against her mother. Of course, they didn't outright, but the roots were undeniable leverage that would keep them alive long enough to negotiate.

"How many do we have?" Bly asked.

"Not enough," Demelza said, then quieter, almost to herself, "It's never going to be enough."

Bly wondered how often she said those words to herself. She'd never been enough for her mother, and now she wasn't enough to make a difference to the rebels.

"How many?"

"I've spelled two roots myself. I found two other witches among the rebels with enough strength to perform the spell, but it drains more than any spell I've seen before. Those witches won't be able to make another one for weeks. It was a miracle that I managed to make two." She lifted her chin a bit. Nobody could deny she had raw power. "I'm about to try for the third, but I can make no promises."

"You should save your strength."

Demelza gave her a hard look, knowing exactly what she meant. They'd need her to face her mother even though she wasn't strong enough to take her down. Her daughter's presence with the rebels could at the very least give Halfryta a moment of shock, make her stay her hand just long enough to negotiate.

"The good news is that it doesn't take the entire root to cast the spell," Demelza said. "The root can be broken up into minuscule pieces. It just has to be enough to break against the skin. We tried it on a witch volunteer from the rebel group, and then we tried it on one more just an hour ago to be sure . . ." She hesitated. "The second one was your sister."

"*What?*" Bly's head spun. Elise would have told her.

"She's fine," Demelza rushed out. "She's human and alive. She didn't want to worry you."

"You should have told me," she said, her glare shifting from Demelza to Donovan.

Donovan held up his hand that wasn't bloody. "I looked for you. I said you'd want to know."

The door to the house banged open hard enough to make the flimsy floorboards beneath their feet tremor. "The vampires are coming too," a man's voice bellowed. This time it was Donovan's face that showed the flicker of fear, and that expression on him was enough to terrify Bly.

"So if we break up the spelled roots as small as possible, how many will we have to use if this becomes a fight?" she asked, expecting the worst.

"Three hundred, give or take."

A rush of relief made her grin.

Donovan's bleak expression shifted, and he winked at her. "Our human with a vampire heart is ready for a fight."

"If it comes to it."

He nodded. Respect glimmered in his eyes.

She was trying to be more like Hazel, careful with her decisions. Someone who didn't fight when they could negotiate.

But her blood was hot with the desire to change things at whatever cost. She was done longing for far-off places. She wanted to watch this world crumble and see something new rise from the ashes, and not a fanciful dream, but something real and raw. Something *better*.

The desire for it thrummed so hard and fast in her chest that she thought she'd burst.

After she went back downstairs and reported their position to Hazel, Kerrigan grabbed her hand and tugged her outside to a small space between houses that barely fit two bodies, which left her pressed against both the house and him.

"Are you okay?" he whispered.

She kissed him in answer, and their mouths moved together steadily with their endless hunger and endless hope that this wasn't their final kiss.

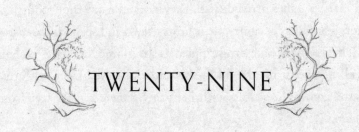

TWENTY-NINE

THEY STOOD FACING THE FIELD BETWEEN
the Gap and woods. Nobody spoke. The only sound was the
crunch of icy mud as they shuffled their feet. A chilling breeze
gusted from the forest, numbing limbs and hearts. Confidence
was difficult when you couldn't feel your nose.

Kerrigan and Donovan stood on either side of Bly. Elise and
Emerson were behind them. Emerson had stayed a vampire for the
battle just to have a better shot at surviving. Bly had tried to get
her sister to stay in the village with their parents, who had set up
an aid station for the wounded at their home, but Elise insisted she
could help even if she wasn't a fighter. Bly glanced at her now, their
mother's healing kit clenched in her hands, her gaze steady. Too
steady. Bly worried she'd gone from feeling too much to nothing
at all, and that left a person reckless.

Bly caught Emerson's glance, and he nodded. He saw it too.
He'd seen it in Bly before—and he'd seen it in himself.

He'd protect Elise with his life if it came to it, just like Benedict, but that would only kill Elise in a different way.

Demelza stood on the other side of Donovan, watching the direction her mother would come.

The witches arrived first. They poured from the woods like ants searching for honey, their bows drawn and spells at the ready. Halfryta's dark blue dress rippled as she moved, her long red hair spilling over it like blood in the water. She eyed them with distaste, coming to a stop with her army a mere twenty feet from them.

When she found her daughter, her cool expression didn't shift beyond the slightest scrunch of her brow. "I'd assumed you had died when you didn't come home."

Demelza didn't answer.

"This is much more disappointing."

Demelza flinched as if her mother had slapped her. Even Bly cringed at the words.

Demelza still didn't speak.

"Nothing worthwhile to say as usual."

"I hate you," Demelza said, her voice as cold as the wind. "How's that?"

"A childish emotion," Halfryta said. She paused for a long moment. "But I can work with it. Hate easily begets a desire for power." She pursed her lips. "I'm changing my mind about being angry over this little slipup. This is the first time I've found you particularly interesting."

Demelza's hands clenched into tight balls at her side.

Halfryta turned her head slightly, addressing her people. "It seems I have finally found a worthy heir. Someone with enough strength of will to stand against me and face death." She looked back at Demelza. "I'm proud of you."

Demelza's hands had unclenched at her side. Bly wanted to reach for her, to hold her with them. Halfryta was offering her everything she been fighting for: position and power, but most of all, her mother's approval. Desires could shift and grow, and clearly Demelza's had, but the roots of them could not be pulled up overnight.

"Come back where you belong," Halfryta said. "At my right hand."

Demelza hesitated for a long, weighted moment. Then she took a step toward the witches.

Bly's heart sunk. "Demelza..."

The witch didn't look back at her as she took another step, then another, each one stiff and slow as if her mother had cast a spell on her and she was no longer in control of her body, but Bly knew it was much deeper than that. Demelza controlled her body. Nobody truly controlled their own heart. Someone else could hold a piece of it whether you wished it or not. Her mother still had a sliver of hers.

None of the rebels made a move to stop her. Demelza finally turned around halfway between the two groups. She seemed to search out Bly, and then Emerson. *I'm sorry,* she mouthed. Her eyes flicked to someone else, and Bly thought it might have been Donovan, before she turned away and strode toward her mother, each step a little bit more confident than the last, until she spun around to face them as an adversary instead of an ally. Demelza wore no glamour, and even though her hair was in a tangled knot pinned back against the nape of her neck and her clothes were in disarray, she was a copy of her mother in the way she held her shoulders straight and lifted her chin. Her face was blank as she looked back at the people she had helped and would now try to destroy.

Bly tried not to let it hurt her. They weren't friends, merely allies, but Demelza had given her hope that if a person like her could change, then their world had a chance of changing too.

Halfryta's smug expression faded as she spotted Bly in the crowd. Her eyes narrowed in on Bly's neck, which was definitely still in one piece, and then she turned slightly to glare at her daughter. Bly had to wonder how long Demelza could stay in her mother's favor.

Halfryta spoke when she looked back at them. "We had a deal, which you need to fulfill," she said.

"The Healers have what you're looking for," Hazel said, drawing Halfryta's focus to her. "You won't get it back."

"You must be the one who's been a thorn in my heel for years." Halfryta took her in with an intensity that would make anyone squirm, but Hazel didn't budge. "And you've been drawn out into the light for something useless to you. It took me years to develop that spell. I only recently got it right. You may have the roots, but it will take you just as long to perfect the magic."

"Your daughter gave us the spell," Hazel said.

Demelza's posture curved in on itself.

Halfryta snarled toward Demelza like a carnivore scenting blood. "Impossible. She's tricked you. I never taught her."

Demelza seemed to force herself to straighten and look her mother square in the eye. "I've been spying on you with invisibility spells for years. You underestimated me."

Halfryta's face twisted briefly into rage before relaxing into a grin. "No matter. You can't have made much. We'll kill you all today to ensure this small infestation won't crop up in the future. Unless you want to end this without too much bloodshed? I will let a few of you live. Not you, of course." Her stare shifted to Bly. "Or her. The princes will make nice blood bags, though."

"And the rest of my people?" Hazel asked.

"They can continue on with their sad little lives."

Hazel seemed to be thinking, but Bly knew she was only waiting. For the vampires. Not because they were more merciful and would give them a better bargain, but because Hazel's group could only afford to put on this show once.

Finally, the vampires leaked from the woods like silent drops of blood in their red uniforms. Melvina led them with her pale skin a slash of white against a red dress that was cut high to her hips at both sides. Allena stood at her side in black, her taller shadow. On her left stood a cruel-looking man with sharp features: Callum. His stare roamed down the line of rebels, moving past Bly before darting back to her. His smile was slow. She took a step back as if he'd pulled his sword and charged.

He clearly intended to see her bleed again before this was over.

Kerrigan let out a low growl as he noticed Callum too. "I'll kill him."

Bly reached out and grabbed his wrist, worried he'd start a brawl before they had to.

As the vampire army reached them, they faced the witches instead of the rebels, who had likely already been written off as nothing to fear. The vampire queens stood only a few paces away from Halfryta.

"I knew I'd regret letting you go." Melvina pursed her lips at Halfryta. "Me and my compassion."

Halfryta gave a cold laugh. "Yes, compassion has always been your weakness."

Melvina shrugged. "A curse, really."

"The roots are mine," Halfryta said.

"I believe *I* sent the party to find them, not you." Melvina finally turned to look at them, her eyes flitting between Donovan and Kerrigan. "Benedict and Jade?" she asked, then answered for herself, "Dead then. They wouldn't betray me like this. You, I expected." She pointed a narrow finger at Kerrigan before shifting it to Donovan. "You, I did not." She curled her finger into a beckoning motion. "Come back where you belong. You did not participate in freeing the witch. You've been nothing but loyal to us. Who took you in when the witches killed your parents? Who raised your station without regard for your brother's foolishness?"

Donovan's jaw tightened.

"Your brother put you in this mess, did he not?" Melvina asked. "Why stay loyal to your human blood ties when your vampire ones have never failed you?"

"This is touching," Halfryta said, "but let's get on with this."

Melvina snarled at her.

Donovan turned slowly to Kerrigan. Old hurts haunted his face, yanked back to the surface by Melvina's careful words. Bly thought they were past this, but just like Demelza had not fully been released from her desire for her mother's approval, Donovan had clearly not fully forgiven Kerrigan.

"Donovan." Kerrigan's voice was broken. Pleading.

Donovan's expression pinched, but he shook his head as he took another step back. "I'll admit I got sucked in by your ridiculous optimism, but this is a fool's game," Donovan said, "and I'm a winner."

Kerrigan's face collapsed. He took a step toward his brother, hand outreached, but Bly was the one who grabbed it, holding him back.

Donovan shot her a grateful look.

She frowned, but his focus had shifted back to his brother. "I do love you, brother. I've never stopped, even when I hated you too. This is no different."

He turned and walked toward the queens, turning to stand beside a smug Melvina, who shouted to Kerrigan, "Last chance. There will be no more crawling back after this."

Bly dropped his hand, just in case he wanted to go too, but he snatched it back again.

"Donovan will be safer on their side," Bly said. A poor consolation. Sometimes you wanted your family to be safe and sometimes you wanted them with you, as if their presence and love were a shield that could save. She knew it didn't work like that, but still, knowing her sister was behind her kept her spine straight and her chin lifted.

Melvina raised her voice again. "I'll take back any vampire who made the mistake of standing against us today—whether you were banished before or not—if you bring me that witch's head." She pointed at Hazel. "Or the head of any human next to you. Let's nip this ridiculousness before it continues."

"I'll make the same offer," called Halfryta.

Nobody moved.

Hazel lifted her chin. "It seems loyalty is not bought by fear," Hazel said.

Melvina shrugged. "No. But submission is." She raised her pale white hand in the air and snapped.

Bows raised and swords whistled free on all sides.

"Wait." Hazel stepped out from the line of rebels. Alexander came with her.

"Coming to your senses?" Halfryta asked.

Hazel lifted her hand in answer. Pinched between her thumb and forefinger was a tiny sliver of white. Alexander held out his hand. Bly knew what was coming, but she was surprised to see him volunteer. From what she knew of him, he seemed to love his vampire's strength.

"Extract," Hazel yelled, despite the fact that a spell needed only a whisper. She crushed the root into his palm.

Alexander bent at the waist, clutching his stomach for a moment. All sides went silent, his heavy breathing somehow loud enough to fill the field, and then grass sprung at his feet from the icy mud where nothing had grown in the all the years Bly could remember. Daisies sprouted too, and purple flowers with blossoms like bells. The land took the magic back and bloomed with it.

He straightened.

The people closest to the front of the vampire and witch lines gasped.

And then Alexander turned back to the rebels, blinking eyes that were an icy blue—no longer the gray of a vampire and too light to be a witch. Human.

He locked eyes with Marianna, who stood a dozen feet down the line from Bly, and beamed. A witch aged the same as a human without spells to ward it off, and a witch could not be turned. He'd chosen to be human for *her*.

"It works, then." Melvina's eyes were wide.

"Of course it does," Halfryta snapped. "I made the spell."

"That's why I had my doubts."

Halfryta looked as if she would leap across the divide and throttle the vampire queen. She gritted her teeth and then turned her focus back on Hazel. "None of this matters. You will still lose the battle, and all we'll lose are a few witches and vampires. We could always use some more human blood." She laughed, but none of her people joined her. A few looked squeamish.

"Exactly," Melvina added, glaring at Halfryta as if annoyed that they agreed.

The vampires shifted on their feet.

Hazel lifted her chin. Her kindness had always been palpable, but it didn't mean that she lacked strength. She held herself like an impenetrable force.

"Killing us will not get you the roots you seek. They've been broken up and hidden, the maps of where you'd find them are only in the heads of a few, some of whom aren't here today. If you strike us down, then more will rise in our place. You'll never be able to catch a human in the forest without wondering if they have the spell on them. We'll steal your people away from you one by one, turning them human, until the scales tip and this world crumbles. Or we can live in peace."

"We already live in peace. Humans have their protections," Melvina said.

"They don't have power."

"They don't need it," Halfryta snapped.

"Leave now, and we will come to new terms tomorrow. Start a new day," Hazel said. "We could build a council that represents all our interests. We can create a world of true equity."

Melvina laughed. "I'd rather take my chances killing you."

Halfryta nodded at the vampire queen.

Hazel sighed. "We thought you might say that." Hazel glanced over her shoulder with a nod, and then the Gap stirred to life behind them. People swarmed from behind and inside the houses at their back, holding kitchen knives, axes, and picks, or anything else they could get their hands on. A few had swords courtesy of Emerson and his father, who had worked night and day for the past three days. But those weren't the most important weapons.

Melvina laughed. "*More* humans? We've been here before, and we've learned our lesson. Perhaps you thought we'd fight each other instead of you, but the vampires and witches will have our battle later with your blood on our hands and your bodies at our feet."

Bly swallowed. Melvina had always unnerved her, but the gleeful joy in the way she spoke about decimating them all chilled her. This would not be without bloodshed as they'd hoped. There would be no easy bargaining.

"And wipe out your entire food source?" Hazel countered skeptically. "You've almost done *that* before too. Did you not learn that particular lesson?"

Melvina's eyes flashed black.

"You're right," Halfryta said, "which means we will simply bind you and share the spoils." She raised her voice. "Anyone standing here today is subject to whatever punishment we see fit. You will never see your family again. You will spend the rest of your lives as the blood bags you are without the illusion of more that we've generously given you."

Bly glanced behind her. A couple of people inched away. But most of them didn't so much as flinch. Their eyes glinted with a hardness that matched the steel in their hands. Humans had been waiting for this moment. They'd lived their lives grinding away in their cold sliver of land that always smelled like smoke and mud, and Bly wasn't the only one with dreams. They all had them. They were all just waiting for the right moment to fight for them.

Bly caught a familiar determined expression. Nova stood not far behind them with her axes already drawn in both hands, the heads of them resting on her shoulders, waiting. She noticed Bly's stare and gave her a single nod that Bly returned.

Hazel's voice, which had been calm and reasonable, took on a razor's edge that Bly had never heard from her before. "I have a better plan for increasing your human blood supply . . . turning you all human."

Halfryta scoffed. "You don't have enough. Even my *daughter*"—she said the word tightly—"could not have spelled more than a single root since your return."

"Actually, she did," Hazel said. "And she taught others."

Halfryta spared another glare for Demelza.

Demelza looked somehow both smug and terrified.

"Did you even know your spell could be broken up into minuscule pieces of magic? It's in our power to free the magic from over three hundred of you today. Not to mention the attacks that we will inflict every day from here on. No vampire or witch will be able to come to the market without the risk of us making them human." Hazel turned her head, addressing the armies. "Do you think your rulers will let you go home again when your heart is beating once more," she asked, turning to the vampires, letting the question linger in the air before turning to the witches. "What about you when you no longer have the power to create spells? Havenwhile is not known for keeping those it deems broken."

Murmurs skittered through the ranks.

Melvina raised her voice above the dissent. "We'll just turn you back."

The vampire queen turned to Halfryta, looking for conformation, and the witch frowned. "The change is permanent. A vampire cannot be remade. I tested it, but it doesn't matter," she added with a shrug. "How many of us do you think you'll actually be able to touch in a battle?"

"Enough," Hazel said. "I wonder who the ones we *do* get will be forced to side with once they're human."

Hazel was smart, reminding the vampires and witches in front of her that *they* were the ones who were risking becoming what they fought against. They were the ones who would lose their power and position with the touch of a single spell—not the rulers who would hide behind their sacrifice.

"Subdue them," Halfryta ordered to her army behind her. "Kill as few as possible," she said begrudgingly.

"Except the traitor vampires and witches," Melvina added, motioning for her people to attack as well. "Take them," she said, but for probably the first time, the witches and vampires hesitated in front of the humans who opposed them.

Callum broke the line first, stalking forward with his cold, dead eyes zeroed in on Bly alone. Kerrigan strode to meet him in the open field between them. Bly followed, pacing behind him so that he wouldn't tell her not to join.

A few other vampires trailed in Callum's wake, their eyes shifting and uneasy with the fear of becoming human.

A witch raised their notched bow, firing a shot into the line of rebels. Someone cried out as it hit their thigh and their legs bound together beneath them so that they fell backward. Someone else bent down and unbound them a second later, but if this became a battle of who ran out of binding and unbinding spells first, then the rebels would lose.

The archer who had fired the shot went down a second later with an arrow in the center of her throat. The rebels had their own archers in the open windows of any home facing the field, and they weren't firing binding spells.

Kerrigan's sword clashed against Callum's.

The lines broke apart. Everyone moving with slow reluctance. Everyone, except for the vampire queens and Halfryta, seemed to understand that too many would lose on all sides, but none of them would stand against their rulers.

Donovan and Demelza hadn't moved. For a moment, they just stared at each other.

Then high-pitched screams froze all the raised swords before they could fall.

THIRTY

THE COMMOTION CAME FROM BOTH
the vampires and witches. Bly turned first to the vampires,
watching as Melvina buckled over, and Allena slid to her knees
beside her.

The muddy ground beneath them exploded with color as the
magic left their bodies and healed the empty land. Melvina slid to
her knees beside Allena, holding her against her chest. Allena was
silent, her eyes wide . . . and green.

Human.

Both queens had been turned human.

Melvina wailed again before it shifted into a roar as she looked
up.

At Donovan. He stood just behind them. He'd never drawn
his sword to move against the rebels. He'd moved against his
queens.

"Kill him!" Melvina shouted.

Kerrigan shoved Callum to the ground, jabbing his sword in and out of his stomach with brutal efficiency before bolting for the vampires. Donovan drew his sword.

"*Kill him!*" Melvina screamed even more shrilly, rising to her feet.

A vampire nearby took a swing at Donovan, who easily blocked the blow, and then Melvina drew one of the daggers strapped to her thigh. She aimed for Donovan's chest as his eyes widened. He didn't lift his sword or his arm to grab her.

Kerrigan's hand stopped the blow as he grabbed Melvina's wrist, shaking her until she dropped the dagger into the flowers still growing at her feet. He shoved her back down to Allena, and the other queen grabbed her hand, keeping her there.

Kerrigan yanked Donovan out of the fray, pushing him back toward the rebels as he kept his eyes and sword trained on the vampires he'd once led. None of them made a move for them.

"What have you done?" Halfryta's voice hissed out, carrying through the battlefield that had gone still.

Bly shifted toward the witches, keeping an eye on Callum, who was still on the ground, hands grasping his bleeding belly as he watched his queens fumble to stand on legs that surely felt hollow after knowing a vampire's strength for so many years.

Halfryta crouched on the ground. Flowers and grass kissed her hands and knees as her magic bled from her. She glared up at her daughter, who'd betrayed her with the very spell Halfryta had not trusted her with. "Kill her," she ordered, looking wildly—and with startling green eyes—at the witches around her. The witches all shifted uneasily, casting glances around the group.

But nobody lifted a hand.

Donovan broke away from Kerrigan still pulling him back to the rebel line and moved instead toward the witches as Kerrigan yelled his name.

Demelza raised her head, her expression cool, her voice lifting to address the witches. "My mother would let you die for her, but I will not."

Halfryta stumbled to her feet. Drawing a knife from her waist, she swung carelessly at her daughter. Demelza stepped away, her hands empty and open as if pleading. She reached for no weapon to defend herself.

The witches stepped back, creating a ring around them.

"Seize her," Demelza ordered.

The witches didn't move.

It was Donovan who broke through the circle, kicking Halfryta in the back of the knees as she lunged for her daughter once more. The witch went down, kneeling in the dirt before her daughter with Donovan at her back, sword already drawing back to take her head.

"No." Demelza spoke so softly that Bly couldn't hear it, but she saw the word rounding on her lips.

Donovan's sword lowered for a moment, as if he'd heard her plea, before he pulled his dagger from his waist. He reached around and slid it across Halfryta's throat—just as she'd done to his parents. Blood poured over her dress, turning the lake-blue into a bruised purple. Halfryta didn't reach for her daughter, and her daughter didn't reach for her. She held her hands to her throat for a moment before collapsing at Demelza's feet.

Demelza stared at her mother with wide eyes and then looked up at Donovan. She blinked, her mouth opening and closing without words.

The witches finally moved, closing in on Demelza, but not to harm her. They made themselves a shield against Donovan, who was already being yanked away again by Kerrigan.

A few witches moved to chase Donovan and Kerrigan before Demelza's voice rose again, ordering the witches to stand down. A few shared uneasy looks, but they obeyed her.

Demelza pushed through the witches who protected her, but she didn't move for Donovan. She faced Hazel. "I assume we can negotiate our new world tomorrow."

Hazel nodded her assent.

Demelza turned, her face pale and stricken, pausing briefly over her mother's body. A few of her people gathered up the fallen witch before heading into the forest. Others began trickling away at Demelza's orders.

Melvina and Allena were on their feet, demanding that the vampires help them home. The vampires exchanged wary glances, but eventually a few took their arms and led them away. Bly wondered if the queens would make it back to Vagaris alive—two humans in an army of vampires.

But all she really cared about was the fact that they were safe for another day, even if the battle for a better world would be far from over. She turned back toward Elise.

As Elise screamed her name.

Emerson barreled toward her.

Bly spun, raising her dagger and free hand to block whatever threat came for her.

She screamed as a blade sliced through her palm.

Callum's black eyes stared down at her, watching her face as he pulled the dagger out of her with excruciating slowness, taking his time despite the violent spread of blood at his abdomen.

She brought the dagger still in her free hand up and planted it in his shoulder.

Instead of flinching, he let out a soft sigh. "Now we can finish what we started." Blood dribbled from the side of his mouth.

Emerson's strong arms closed around her waist, yanking her away, but Callum followed, his movements quick even if his wound made them jerky. He brandished a dagger in one hand and a sword in the other that plunged straight for her heart. If he couldn't play with her, he'd make her bleed all at once.

Donovan kicked the back of Callum's legs, sending him to his knees just before the tip of his sword could plunge into her.

Kerrigan tore Callum's sword from his grip before pulling the sword back like an executioner, a snarl on his lips. Donovan raised his sword as well, as if they intended to leave him in pieces.

"Wait," Bly said, struggling to free herself from Emerson's grip.

The killing blows were already in motion when they stopped, swords hovering.

"Don't go soft on me now," Donovan said to Bly. "Especially since this makes us even." He flashed her a strained smile. "Friend."

"I think she wants to do it herself," Kerrigan gritted out. He was barely containing his own desire to end him.

"I want to do something worse," Bly said with a smile. "Let me go," she said to Emerson.

"Bly," he warned. She knew what he wanted to say. That she wasn't like them. She wasn't ruthless, but he didn't say it. He let her go.

Callum actually laughed until he realized what she meant as

she reached into her pocket and then lifted her hand toward his bare neck.

"No," he said, attempting to stand.

Donovan slammed him back down.

She relished the fear in his eyes. She didn't particularly care if that made her like him . . . a vampire. She touched his neck. "Extract," she whispered.

He shook as his eyes faded from gray to hazel.

"I hope someone bleeds you dry," Bly said.

Donovan yanked him to his feet by the collar of his shirt. "I suggest you try the woods, human." He sneered. "You won't be welcome here, and I doubt you'll be welcome at home." He shoved Callum. The former vampire fell in the mud behind them before scrambling away, and Bly didn't care which direction he went.

She jerked as someone grabbed her hand, but it was only Elise inspecting the wound and then opening her bag of healer's tricks and pulling out a salve. Bly winced as she started prodding it into the cut.

Kerrigan ran his finger over his fang, taking a step toward her to help, but Bly shook her head. He could heal her later. Elise's eyes were clearer than they had been in days.

Emerson stood just beside her, staring at Elise with unabashed love in his eyes. Bly could see his desire to reach for her to pull her in his arms. Elise bent down to her bag again and pulled out a long bandage. She looked back at Emerson. "I need an extra set of hands." He nodded, stepping up to assist her.

The pinch of pain in Bly's hand as they worked was numbed by the sight of them together, helping each other in silence like they had so many times before.

Elise would be okay.

Kerrigan and Donovan both had distant, pained expressions on their faces.

Donovan had gotten revenge for the death of their parents, but the past haunted them still. Now he stared down at the drying blood splatter on his hand. He flexed his fingers. "She's dead." The statement sounded hollow, as if he couldn't find the right emotion for it.

"That wasn't the plan."

Bly jerked at Demelza's voice. She must have doubled back after sending her people home. The witch stared up at Donovan with empty eyes. "We were supposed to turn them human, not kill them."

"She was trying to kill you," Donovan said.

Demelza shook her head. They all knew that wasn't why he'd done it, but there was an earnestness in his voice that said it could have been a small part of why he'd acted.

Bly looked between them. "You planned that?"

"We've spent a lot of time together the last few days. This witch can't get enough of my blood." Donovan's joke landed like a stone. He looked at his feet as if he might actually be feeling a flicker of regret.

Demelza's expression was cold. "It was my idea. He didn't want to go along with it at first. He said he wouldn't be able to bear the hurt on his brother's face, but we needed it to be believable." She huffed, a little bit of light coming back into her eyes. "Vampires aren't as hard as I thought they were."

"Are you calling me soft now?" Donovan growled.

"Most definitely."

The ghost of a smile appeared on both their faces before vanishing as they looked away from each other. Perhaps they'd found a sliver of similarity between them while working together, the beginnings of a friendship even, but that had died with Halfryta—at least for now.

Demelza sighed. "What do we do now?"

Bly's mouth dried. There was work to do, and of course, she wasn't the only one to do it, but the thought of what was to come was daunting. They'd gained an upper hand, but how could they keep it without becoming a version of the thing they had vanquished?

Worry gnawed at her. She needed to leave, to run, to let someone else make the decisions just in case she started making selfish ones again.

She shook herself. That wasn't her anymore. If it were, she would have taken the roots to the vampires.

A hand took hers, and she turned toward Elise.

Her sister's beautiful brown eyes were still clear.

Kerrigan took her other hand, sliding his fingers between hers. "Now, we dream," he said softly, staring down at her.

She squeezed his hand in return, certain of only one thing: that whatever she dreamed with him by her side would come true, and whenever they woke from one dream, they'd fall into another. Together.

THIRTY-ONE

ONE MONTH LATER

They all sat around a table that Emerson had built from oak. Each plank that made the top had been sanded smooth, but the edges had been left wild and rough with bark and moss clinging to them. The chairs were nothing but stumps of wood. The table sat in the middle of the forest like it had grown there.

It had been Bly's idea to make their meeting place among the trees. It put their world into perspective. It reminded her of what they'd fought for—the ability to sit in the woods with a canopy of branches above you, a chilly breeze making your lungs burn with life, the call of birds reminding you that you were not alone, all while not having to worry about someone wanting your blood.

The only trouble was that she lost herself to the sensations of the wilderness sometimes.

She came back to herself as Kerrigan touched her knee. He

gave her a small smirk. He thought it was cute when she drifted off, letting herself daydream.

It was easier now to dream again, even though she rarely had time.

"We have two more houses with farming land ready for humans to move into," Demelza said from her seat on Bly's other side.

"We have three apartments ready," Kerrigan said. "And jobs in Vagaris."

Elise beamed from across the table at both of them. "I know just the right families."

Nova arched an eyebrow from her seat beside Elise. "Families? Is it really safe to move children in there yet? New laws don't make bloodlust disappear. Frankly, I carry my ax to these meetings because I don't even trust this council."

Bly sighed. Sometimes the hostility at their council meetings matched their world, but they were trying. After the rebels won the battle, they knew they needed more than just a change of rulers in Havenwhile and Vagaris. They needed a joint council where they made decisions together. And that's why Bly had suggested this table in the woods, outside everyone's territory, where they could meet and discuss how best to build the world they needed.

Now they sat here every week, four representatives for each city.

They had a long way to go, but they'd already changed a lot. Wages for humans had improved, but people still chose to give blood because they were paid handsomely for it. The new price was slowly shifting the wealth from the vampires and witches to the humans. Their goal was to blend their cities into one larger one that swallowed the Gap in the middle, but that would take years.

They'd started by moving humans into the vampire and witch kingdoms.

"They will be guarded," Donovan said firmly from his place beside Kerrigan. "At least on my end."

"We'll also ensure their safety, obviously," Demelza said, shooting Donovan a glare.

He smiled in return.

"I want to take a group out into the woods to search for witches who were banished," Demelza continued. "My mother banished so many for no other crime than that they couldn't create spells. I want to bring them home."

"Then do it. Why are you telling us about it?" drawled Christopher, one of the new council members. His dark gray eyes were bored.

Just about everyone at the table scowled at him.

Donovan had taken over as king of the vampires. Their law said that anyone who killed the former ruler would take command, and it had been agreed by the vampires that turning the queens human had counted. Nobody knew if they were actually dead or not—they'd fled to the woods with only a handful of vampires who had remained loyal to them.

While those of them who'd led the rebellion originally made up the new council, they'd needed to add more representatives selected by the people in each city. Now they were stuck with Christopher, who was less than friendly, and Serene, a vampire who was always unsettlingly quiet, which was an improvement from Christopher, who constantly wondered aloud why they couldn't just keep things as is.

"The woods are volatile right now," Demelza snapped.

She was right. This change had not come easily. Groups of witches and vampires who hadn't wanted to see humans as equals had chosen to leave, sometimes joining banished groups that already existed. Attacks on the cities and human villages had been frequent enough that both Demelza and Donovan had agreed at the last council meeting to place more guards around the Gap.

"Then let's not go at all." Christopher leaned in his chair, pushing it back on two legs.

Donovan reached out a foot and hooked the leg of Christopher's chair with it, slamming it back onto four legs.

"I'll go with you," Donovan said.

Demelza frowned, but a spark of gratitude flickered in her eyes before they went cold. "You know you need to stay. You don't have the same control over your people that I have over mine."

His eyes narrowed. "I have control." He turned to Christopher. "One more dissenting comment from you, and I'll take your head off."

Christopher appeared only mildly concerned.

"See?" Donovan turned back to Demelza.

She shook her head.

"If you're going, I'm going," he said, his voice low and firm.

Bly glanced between the two. They'd undoubtedly become allies somewhere along their journey, maybe even friends, but there was an iciness between them now. Sometimes it thawed, and there'd be a glimmer of who they might have been if Donovan had spared Halfryta, but the ice always returned.

Donovan's fist was in a tight ball on top of the table.

This wasn't about supporting a fellow ruler. He was worried about her.

"We'll go." Bly waved a hand between her and Kerrigan.

Kerrigan gave her a sharp look but said nothing.

Donovan looked at her gratefully.

"I can come too," Emerson said. His brown, human eyes were steady. He'd never needed to stay a vampire to be fearless.

Elise's worried eyes flicked in his direction. The two of them had been working side by side for the past month, using resources from Havenwhile and Vagaris to improve the Gap. Bly had been watching them, hoping the trauma of what happened during the journey wouldn't pull them apart forever, but they seemed solely focused on work.

Emerson noted Elise's worry, and his hand moved under the table to squeeze hers.

It was a small gesture, but it made Bly's chest bloom with hope.

"I'll take all the help we can get," Demelza said. "The bigger our group, the less likely we'll be attacked."

"The Healers are used to navigating the woods," Hazel added. "I'm sure plenty will be up for the task."

"Thank you," Demelza said, looking at all of them. "I'll set the plans in motion."

Their meeting adjourned, and everyone drifted away.

Elise gave Bly a soft smile before trailing after Emerson.

Donovan and Demelza stared at each other before they headed in opposite directions through the woods.

Pretty soon, it was only Kerrigan and Bly, alone with the trees. She stood up from her seat, and he rose to meet her, his hands drifting to her waist. He leaned against the table before pulling her to him.

She grinned, her pulse speeding. The past month had been hard but being in Kerrigan's arms had been easy.

She was already leaning in for his lips when he spoke.

"I think you should stay behind. I can go with Demelza. Emerson's going. You should stay in case the council needs you."

She started to pull away, but his fingers dug into her hips, drawing her closer instead.

"Don't pretend that's why you want me to stay."

He gave her a guilty grin. "I just want you safe."

"I can handle myself."

"I know." One of his hands trailed up her side, sending pleasant shivers through her body. It stopped its ascent at her neck, gently wrapping around it. His thumb traced her windpipe.

He was trying to distract her and make her more agreeable. He knew she rarely changed her mind.

"But you're still human." His hand at her throat pulled her forward slightly, and his mouth dipped toward her until his fangs brushed her ear.

She struggled to keep her mind focused. He *knew* the effect that had on her.

"I'd rather you were less breakable," he whispered against her neck as his thumb caressed her pulse.

She pressed her body against his, and his hand at her waist slid to her back, trapping her against him as she leaned into his ear.

"Then why don't *you* do the breaking and make me into something new."

His body went rigid against hers as if he hadn't expected her to give in. They'd already talked about this. Kerrigan had offered to turn human for her, but it wasn't what Bly wanted. She wanted speed and strength, and most importantly, she wanted Kerrigan for far longer than what a human life would give her. Her dream was for eternity.

She'd only stayed human this long because after rallying the humans to fight, they'd looked to her to lead them. She couldn't do that as a vampire.

But now, things were more stable, even if they were far from perfect.

"You're ready?" Kerrigan's voice was a hopeful whisper.

Truly, she'd been ready for a while. She'd always dreamed about starting a new life in the forest. It seemed fitting to start eternity here with the trees that had always called to her.

She nodded, leaning away just enough for his lips to crush into hers. When he pulled back, his eyes were black with hunger, but she knew from the way his hands gripped her that it wasn't just a craving for her blood. He hungered for forever with her.

"Now?" he asked.

She arched her neck toward him. His hand slid from the front of her throat around to the back to cup her head as his lips took her offering, trailing kisses and nips that didn't break the skin, until finally he pulled back.

"You know, you'll probably have to let me carry you back after this. You'll have to take a break and let me pamper you." His eyes lit up at the idea.

"We'll see," she said.

He grinned. He'd been trying to get her to rest, to enjoy life again, but she'd been running from one task to another. Clearly, he intended to make the most out of her transition.

Finally, he lifted his wrist to his mouth, using his fangs to tear it open. He gave it to her, and she kissed the bleeding wound even though she didn't drink yet.

She waited until his lips were on her neck again, and then the press of his fangs.

And then he bit.

She felt no fear as he took her blood, and she took his, only a hungry hope for the future.

ACKNOWLEDGMENTS

To my readers, I apologize for the cliffhanger in *The Revenant Games*. Please forgive me! A million thank-yous for picking up this sequel. I hope you loved reading Bly and Kerrigan's ending as much as I loved writing it.

Thank you to Sarah McCabe for your enthusiasm for this book. Undertaking a sequel for the first time was daunting but having your encouragement made all the difference. Thank you, Anum Shafqat, for also being in my corner.

Thank you to the entire team at McElderry Books for believing in my stories and getting them into the hands of readers: Justin Chanda, Karen Wojtyla, Anne Zafian, Bridget Madsen, Elizabeth Blake-Linn, Chrissy Noh, Caitlin Sweeny, Lisa Quach, Bezi Yohannes, Perla Gil, Remi Moon, Amelia Johnson, Ashley Mitchell, Saleena Nival, Trey Glickman, Elizabeth Huang, Emily Ritter, Amy Lavigne, Lisa Moraleda, Nicole Russo, Nicole Valdez, Christina Pecorale and her sales team, and

Michelle Leo and her education/library team.

A special thanks to Debra Sfetsios-Conover and Kate Forrester for the gorgeous cover.

Thank you to my writing group—I always love hanging out with you whether we get anything done or not!

To Bailey Gillespie, Sana Z. Ahmed, Jess Creaden, and Angela Montoya, I'm so lucky to call you all my writing friends. It's such a relief to know I have so many wonderful people I can turn to whether I need to celebrate or commiserate.

To Stephanie Garber, thank you for always being an encouraging light in a difficult industry. You have helped me keep my head above water more times than I can count in the past year.

To my mom and dad: I wouldn't be able to survive on this career path without your constant love and support.

To my nephews, Lucas, Liam, Gabriel: I love you. You're my favorite people in this world.

MARGIE FUSTON

grew up in the woods of California where she made up fantasy worlds that always involved unicorns. In college, she earned undergraduate degrees in business and literature and a master's in creative writing. Now she's back in the woods and spends all her time wrangling a herd of cats and helping her nephews hunt ghosts, pond monsters, and mermaids. You can find her online at MargieFuston.com.